The Diamond PUCK-UP

OTHER TITLES BY LAUREN LANDISH

Stand-Alone Novels

It's Just Business

Maple Creek

I Do With You
The Pucking Proposal

Cold Springs

The Wrong Bridesmaid
The Wrong Guy

Never Say Never

Never Marry Your Brother's Best Friend
Never Give Your Heart to a Hookup
Never Fall for the Fake Boyfriend
Never Kiss the Bad Boy
Never Bargain with the Boss
Never Dance with the Devils

The Truth or Dare Series

The Dare
The Truth

The Big, Fat, Fake Series

My Big, Fat, Fake Wedding
My Big, Fat, Fake Engagement
My Big, Fat, Fake Honeymoon

Bennett Boys Ranch

Buck Wild
Riding Hard
Racing Hearts

Tannen Boys

Rough Love
Rough Edge
Rough Country

The Diamond PUCK-UP

LAUREN
LANDISH

This is a work of fiction. Names, characters, organizations, places, events, and incidents are either products of the author's imagination or are used fictitiously. Otherwise, any resemblance to actual persons, living or dead, is purely coincidental.

Published by Montlake, Seattle
www.apub.com

EU product safety contact:
Amazon Media EU S. à r.l.
38, avenue John F. Kennedy, L-1855 Luxembourg
amazonpublishing-gpsr@amazon.com

ISBN-13: 9781662531996 (paperback)
ISBN-13: 9781662532009 (digital)

Cover design by Hang Le
Cover image: © FTAPE LIMITED; © andreonegin / Shutterstock

Printed in the United States of America

The Diamond PUCK-UP

Chapter 1

Penny

This day could not be more perfect. The sun is high and bright in the blue sky, it's just on the warm side of chilly, there's not a hint of wind in the air, and the hike to the hillside photo spot was easy to the point of being more of a stroll than a workout.

I sit down carefully on a flat rock and take a sip from my favorite water bottle, noting the vinyl stickers from various towns and concerts I've been to, plus my favorite one, an ostrich on ice skates that says, "She is beauty, she is grace, she will not fall on her face." My bestie-slash-roommate, Talia, bought that one for me as a joke when I first made the Ice Hawkettes, our local NHL hockey cheer team, because on the ice is the only place I'm not likely to fall. Slippery, slidey, hazardous? I'm as solid as can be. Flat, smooth, even ground with full focus and attention, and sensible shoes? This girl's going down. It's happened too many times to argue to the contrary.

Thankfully, I stayed vertical today on the way up the hill, though it remains to be seen if my unusually good luck will stick with me for the return trip down.

Trying my best to be discreet, I catch glimpses of the group around me. It's not an organized hike, but this is one of the most popular trails in the area and spring is known to be the best season for scenic outlooks, so there's at least a dozen other people here with me, if you count the mom with the toddler strapped to her in some sort of backpack situation as two people. Damn, lady, your legs must be pumped as fuck, and I say that in full jealousy despite being someone who spends hours dancing and skating every week.

But mostly I'm trying to watch Lance, my client in the navy-blue pullover to my right. He looks a bit sweaty, more than you'd expect with the cool air, and he keeps nervously touching his pocket like he's afraid he might've lost his wallet on the trail.

Actually . . . I pat my fanny pack, making sure I feel the chunkiness of my keys, because it'd be just my luck to have dropped them somewhere over the last two miles.

Lance glances around, and I catch his eye, giving him a supportive smile. *You can do it,* the smile says. But I don't think he understands the message, because he frowns and jerks his gaze back out over the horizon. I watch with bated breath as he lowers himself to kneeling and clears his throat.

Suddenly, everyone realizes exactly what's happening, and there's a chorus of gasps and "aww"s. A kid asks, "What's going on?" A quick look shows that the mom has clapped her hand over her older child's mouth and is telling him "shh" meaningfully while simultaneously bouncing herself to keep the toddler on her back quiet. She's a superwoman, I decide, and then return my attention to Lance so I don't miss the Big Moment.

"Elaina Marie Wilcox, you are the love of my life. You give meaning to the sunrise and the sunset, and every moment in between. You make me see beauty in a world that desperately tries to highlight the ugliness. You bring happiness to my life, and I want to do the same for you with every day that I'm given . . . as your husband, your soulmate, and your best friend. Will you give me that honor and be my wife? Will you marry me?" He holds up a ring, offering it with hope-filled eyes.

You could hear a pin drop. Not even a bird caw breaks the sanctity of the moment.

Which is precisely when I unceremoniously slide off my rocky perch and land on the hard dirt with an unladylike grunt. Another round of gasps sounds out, but these are in horror as a dozen pairs of eyes find me—yes, including the baby, plus Lance and his still-to-answer fiancée.

Shit!

Thankfully, that's an internal thought, not an out-loud one, but even so, my grimace from the impact is enough to make a few people step toward me to offer assistance.

"Sorry! I'm okay! Carry on," I tell Lance, waving a hand to let him and everyone else know I'm fine, though my ass really hurts despite the fair amount of cushion I've got back there. I also suddenly realize that I'm dangerously close to the edge of the sloped hill, and knowing my luck, there's a very real chance the dirt might give way and send me careening down to my death, or at least a broken bone or twelve.

Lance clears his throat again and pulls on Elaina's hand to get her attention once more, and finally . . . *finally* she starts nodding wildly.

"Yes! Yes, I'll marry you!"

I join in the applause that breaks out, holding my water bottle against my chest so I don't lose it and create even more of a distraction than I already have.

It's a special moment like the dozens of others I've been a part of but also *not* a part of. Because Lance isn't proposing to me. I'm not his soulmate. I'm not anyone's *that*. I'm here as the artist who designed the custom engagement ring he's slipped onto Elaina's finger. Usually, I ship out the rings I design and wait hopefully for an email back with the proposal story and a picture of the ring on the betrothed's finger. This time, I was lucky enough to live locally, and Lance invited me to play voyeur because Elaina is a fan of my work.

Carefully, so I don't disturb the newly engaged couple more than I have, I rise to my feet with the aid of an older gentleman who offers me a grip on his walking stick. Yeah, someone who needs assistance with the carefully maintained and graded path up the hill is helping me—a young, strong, healthy athlete who performs at every local NHL hockey game—to her feet.

Why is my life like this?

I don't know. I've learned not to question it anymore, because beyond death and taxes being sure things, with me, it's nearly guaranteed that if there's a way to fall, I will. A way to make a fool of myself, it'll happen. And of course, a way to look like a complete weirdo, that'll be me somehow accidentally volunteering as tribute.

As I tell the older gentleman thank you, Elaina, the soon-to-be bride, starts squealing excitedly. "Oh. Em. Gee!" She actually says the letters as she stares at her finger. "Is this a . . . ?" She lifts wide eyes to Lance, looking so happy I can virtually feel the bliss coming off her like rays of sunshine.

Lance nods. "It is. And even better . . ." He guides his newly bejeweled fiancée my way. "This is Penny Lee."

Eyes locked on me, she whispers out of the side of her mouth toward Lance, "Like *The Penny*? The Ring Girl?"

Lance told me that Elaina is a fan, but I'm still surprised when, after a short second as realization dawns, she throws her arms around me and hugs me tightly. "Thank you, thank you, thank you," she repeats, the exclamation running together as one long word.

When she releases me, I laughingly hold my hand out. "I'm Penny Lee, of PLDesigns. Congratulations."

Elaina doesn't so much shake my hand as she wildly jerks it up and down. "I love your work so much. It's so beautiful." She pulls her hand back, her eyes dropping to her new custom ring, designed and made by *moi*. "It's so beautiful," she repeats.

This is why I love what I do. The look on Elaina's face right now.

Most people think of stores at the mall when they go shopping for jewelry, but there are so many more possibilities. Years ago, I began scouring thrift stores, estate sales, and pawnshops to feed my own desire for pretty, shiny things and quickly realized what I craved wasn't out there. I became determined to create the things I saw in my head, and taught myself how to not only design jewelry but physically make it. What started with copper graduated to silver, and eventually gold, before really taking off. What started out as a hobby making pieces for myself quickly became a passion, and now I have a social media following that snaps up my redesigned heritage pieces, asks for custom designs, and comments on my work.

While I do all sorts of jewelry designs, the majority of my commission work is engagement rings, and they're what bring me the most joy. They're more than a promise to marry. They're an expression of love. They don't have to be expensive or flashy—unless that's what the couple wants. They just need to be from the heart, and that's what I do. Make people's hearts visible as works of art they can wear every day.

"I'm glad you love it. It's my new favorite piece too," I confide, acting like it's a secret confession, when the truth is, each piece is my favorite until I create another, and then that one becomes my favorite. "And when you're ready, we can design the wedding band for it together."

Hearts virtually pop out of Elaina's eyes. And then she turns to Lance, looking at him like he hung not only the sun but the moon, stars, and probably the planets as well. "Did you hear that, babe? We get to design the wedding band with Penny too."

He nods, pushing a lock of hair behind Elaina's ear in an intimate move that only highlights how excruciatingly deep their love is. "We'll make sure it's perfect," he vows.

"Aww, so sweet," someone says.

They are. And I'm happy for them. Truly, and not only because it means another paycheck for me but because everyone deserves love. But what's that saying? Always the bridesmaid, never the bride? How about always the ring designer, never even a bridesmaid? Or hell, a girlfriend.

Because as someone whose bread and butter is engagements, it's rare for me to get a guy to commit to taking me on more than a first date. It's not like my standards are ridiculously high either. The bar's low—like on the floor—but even so, after a few dates, most guys simply quit texting or calling, poofing into thin air like ghosts of dates past.

I don't know why. Best guess? It's probably that weird thing again. Or maybe that most guys hear "ring designer" and think "ready to get hitched," which I'm not. I'm way too busy focusing on my business, and I don't have the time or inclination to be desperately wedding-marching through my days. But once PLDesigns is where I want it to be, I'll put real effort into my dating life, and then hopefully I'll meet someone who sweeps me off my feet intentionally, not trips me like the stupid rock I stumble over as I start back down the hill.

Chapter 2

Griffin

"Fuck yeah!" Brody booms across the locker room, ecstatic. His name's not actually Brody; it's Jordan, which isn't much better, but he's quite the bro type, and in hockey, that's all it takes to get a nickname. Brody flexes and roars out his overhyped excitement before holding up his hands for high fives from everyone around him.

When he gets to me, I reluctantly concede. "I know it's the orgasmic climax of your mind's daily highlight reel, but don'tcha think you're overdoing it for a good practice?"

Because that's all it was—practice. It's not like we won a big game or even nailed an important play.

"*Good?* That was epic, bruh," he argues, sounding more like a caricature of a California surfer than the upper-crust Upstate New Yorker he is. "And you said 'orgasm.'" He guffaws, screwing up his face like he's in pain as he makes a jerking motion near his crotch, which is a visual I do not want.

I'd call him a literal child, but he's twenty-four. He's also a pro athlete, and unfortunately, the stereotype that we all stop maturing around age sixteen exists for a reason—it's true more often than not. Thankfully, at the ripe old age of twenty-eight, I don't fit the stereotype . . . usually. Or I try not to.

I don't answer, not wanting to engage with a young pup who wouldn't know *epic* if it snuck up and kneed him in the balls. Turning to face my locker, I go about the business of shedding my gear. With every movement, I evaluate my body for any tightness or strain that'll need to be addressed before tomorrow's game with a trainer, the massage therapist, or in the cold plunge tub. I'm in the prime of my career, playing better than I ever have, but there's no resting on my laurels when I'm the muscle of the team, so every twinge deserves attention.

Every time I skate onto the ice, I do so knowing it might be my last, because my role, beyond being a defender, is that of an enforcer. If there's a brawl—and there's always a brawl—it'll be me mixing it up, throwing punches and trying to avoid the other team's hothead or, worse, *their* enforcer. The fans love it when enforcers go after each other. The enforcers, not so much. Well, most of them. Me? I don't mind it. The mano a mano physicality of it releases some darker feelings I'd rather handle with violence than something woo-woo like talk therapy.

Out of nowhere, a hand slams onto my shoulder with a meaty thud. I tense, every muscle instantly poised for action and my right hand already curling into a fist despite being among teammates, until I hear the voice that goes along with the hand. "Don't be so rough on Brody. He's just excited he made that shot on Howe."

I frown at my best friend and teammate, Dominic. His nickname is Dom, not because it's short for his actual name but because he dominates on the ice as the Ice Hawks' left defenseman. "By 'excited,'" I deadpan, making sure my voice is loud enough to carry over to Brody; he's completed his victory lap of high fives and is now shedding his gear in some shitty makeshift version of a *Magic Mike* show, as if any of us want to see that, "you mean he's like an ADHD-riddled puppy that's jacked on espresso and booger sugar, right?"

I intend for it to be a cutting insult about the youngster, who can't control his dick, his hockey stick, or his mouth, but Dom snorts out a laugh, which is agreement enough because he knows I'm right.

Half dressed and with his dick hanging out the leg hole of his tighty-whities, Brody holds a palm up to Vernon Howe, our goalie. Maybe Brody took one to the melon? He must've if he thinks Howe is going to congratulate him for slipping one between his legs, and I'm not talking about his dick. Pigs have a greater chance of growing wings and taking flight than Brody does of getting a high five from the gruff goalie.

Fuck, Howe likes me, and though he has raised a hand at me, it sure as shit wasn't for a high five. He once smacked me because I let an opposing forward distract me and sneak a puck through my skates with some fancy footwork. The rebuff was deserved, and I learned a valuable lesson. Hopefully, Brody does the same and chills on the over-celebratory moves that are bordering on rubbing Howe's nose in his slipup.

"Come on, man. You gotta admit that move was slick. Almost as slick as your mom last night," Brody taunts Howe, even sticking his tongue out in what I fear is his approximation of eating pussy. If that's the case, he's never pleased a woman once in his short life, which I swear he wants to end after that comment.

The three closest guys to them take noticeable steps away, getting out of the danger zone. Someone mutters under their breath, sounding exactly like that kid from *The Simpsons*, "I'm in danger!"

Deciding to stay out of their impending and inevitable tussle, I ask Dom, "What's the plan?"

We don't always hang out after practice, but more often than not, we'll at least grab food before going our separate ways. To be honest, he's not only my best (and only) friend, he's more like a brother, and we spend a good chunk of time together. It's been like that since we were rookies on our last team, hoping to make a name for ourselves. We did, as a unified team of two on the right side of the ice, and as friends who no one and nothing could break apart.

There's one thing that could tear your friendship to shreds in the blink of an eye.

I swallow hard, forcing that thought back into the lockbox it's supposed to stay in, safe and secure and far away from Dominic, who would very likely murder me with his bare hands if he had any idea why I don't date beyond the occasional casual fuck. Or not exactly *why* . . . but *who*.

"You wanna grab protein bowls?" It's one of our usual pregame dinner options, so I'm already nodding, which makes it too late to say no when he adds, "I just want to swing by Penny's first."

Fuck. My. Life.

Dominic's sister's place is the last spot I want to go, and seeing Penny is the thing I want to do least in the world. I'd rather go to the proctologist, or have a glass rod shoved up my dick without lube and then broken, or wherever and whatever is worse than that. Hell, I'd rather referee Brody and Howe, because they've moved on from verbal sparring to some slaphappy roughhousing on the other side of the locker room. Yes, with Brody's dick still playing peekaboo, which means Howe is sticking to shots to Brody's northernmost head. So far.

"All right, I'll meet you at Pro-Bowl, then," I suggest, hoping he'll take me up on the offer to secure our preferred table in the back corner of the cafeteria line–style restaurant that lets us load up on protein and healthy veg while giving us a discount, saying it's for the good of the team. "Triple chicken, brown rice, double guac, and veg, yeah?" I confirm, though I know his order as well as my own.

"Nah, come with me. We can give Penny shit and see if she wants to grab food too."

Dom's a thoughtful, protective, caring brother. Did I mention *protective*? Because fuck, is he. He's the only one who can give Penny shit the way he does. Anyone else, he'd destroy without hesitation. But it's done out of love. His whole family dotes on her like she's the golden child of the household, but the truth is, she's not. They take special care of her because she nearly always has some drama happening in her life, and though it's typically not her fault, it doesn't change the fact that Dom often spends his time worrying about her, to the point of wanting to make sure she eats, but is just as likely a ruse to do a wellness check and make sure nothing has imploded in her vicinity today. Literally or figuratively.

The first time I met Penny, Dominic and I were rookies. He dragged me to his parents' house during an off week, promising good food, relaxation, and some parental affection. We'd only known each other for a few weeks, but it was like he'd already homed in on my weak spots. To be fair, food and relaxation are something everyone enjoys, but the family angle? That's always been the special seasoning spice in my fucked-up life.

The team was a brotherhood of sorts, and all the guys would have their families—wives, girlfriends, kids, moms, dads, former coaches—come to cheer them on. Except me. No one ever cheered my name, or came to watch me play, or gave a shit if I was alive or dead. Back then, I wore that hurt like a chip on my shoulder, which is probably how Dom saw it so easily. Now I dodge any questions about family and, if pushed, usually say I haven't talked to my parents since the day I turned eighteen, even though the truth is, I stopped talking to them long before that. I just existed in their house like a ghost, me ignoring them and them ignoring me for years before the quiet noncelebration of my eighteenth trip around the sun set us all free.

So Dominic had pestered me to go with him until I finally relented just to get him to shut up about it. He'd spent the whole flight telling me all about his amazing parents and his annoying sister, but even as he bitched about her, he had this stupid grin on his face, so I knew he cared about her. The picture he'd painted was of a dorky, weird, much younger brat. What walked out of the kitchen that first night had been anything but.

Penny was then—and is still—an absolute stunner, with curves that beg for a man's hands, a mouth that you never know what'll come out of, and a sunny disposition that could make Eeyore smile. Or a grumpy asshole like me.

I'd been smitten before Dominic had even introduced us. Then I'd remembered the first rule of brotherhood—a man's mother and his sister are strictly off-limits. Multiply that rule times a billion, and you've got an approximation of how protective Dominic is about his sister. His mother, too, but I've never had any desire to have her sit on my dick. Penny, though? Yeah, I've thought about that particular fantasy a few thousand times over the last five years.

Which is why it's always been safest to avoid her at all costs. It's doubly hard when I'm forced to be in her vicinity and treat her the way Dominic does, which is to say, like the annoying brat she can sometimes be.

I sigh heavily, resigned to seeing her, talking to her, and later, a night of replaying the whole encounter and punishing myself for being the asshole I always am to her. It's for her own good, but also for mine.

Dominic is the one thing I have in this world. My teammate, friend, and brother. And his family is the only family I have. I won't do anything to fuck that up. Even if it makes me miserable and angry at the unfairness of the world and the hand I've been dealt.

The errant thought is enough to make me want to punch something. But my locker walls are made of steel mesh that'll do real damage to my hand, so I force myself to relax, splaying my fingers to stop me from fighting my own hatred for myself.

"All right. Let's see if Penny-Nickel-Dime has broken any bones today," I grunt, using the childish name her family bestowed upon her and rolling my eyes like I'm annoyed by her accident-prone nature and don't worry about her as much as Dominic does.

Or maybe even more.

"Get dressed, Honey," Dom tells me, using the nickname I got because my last name is Mahoney. Well, the name and the fact that I'm sticky as hell on the ice, never losing my footing or a brawl. I don't mind it. It could definitely be worse. Just ask our center, Jack Off, whose actual last name is Jacofovich.

I could delay things, get dressed so slowly that Dom gives up on me and agrees to just meet me at Pro-Bowl, but I don't. As much as I don't want to see Penny, I also want to see her more than anything. It's been weeks since we've had an actual conversation, though I see her when she's doing her Ice Hawkette duties during the games. I try to ignore her then as much as possible, though. I have a job to do, and if I saw some spectator getting handsy with her in the little crop tops or short skirts the cheerleaders wear, I'd likely end up in jail.

So before Dominic has even pulled his jeans on, I'm fully dressed and telling him to hurry his slow ass up. "I'm hungry, man."

I am. But not for a chicken-rice bowl. I'm hungry for two seconds of Penny's eyes on me, full of fire and fury, as she spouts out ridiculous comebacks to my rude commentary. It's the only way I can keep her at a distance . . . by treating her like a bothersome little sister, just the way Dom does.

Chapter 3

Penny

Bang-bang-bang.

I don't stop the delicate work I'm focused on, because the square-cut emerald in fourteen-karat gold on my worktable deserves my full concentration. Instead, I simply yell toward the apartment door, "Talia, did you forget your key again? I swear I'm gonna put it on a ribbon around your neck like a latchkey kid."

Almost instantly, Mrs. Rosenthal bangs on the wall between our apartment and hers to let me know I'm being too loud.

I freeze, waiting for my roommate to answer me, or for whatever lost soul accidentally made their way to my doorstep to wander off. I don't need a new internet provider or whatever crap they're selling.

Unless . . . what if it's cookies? I love when those adorable little girls come around selling boxes of yummy goodness.

I lift the magnifying lenses of my loupes so I can see. Still, I have to blink a few times for my eyes to adjust before I can stand and make my way across the room. I peek through the door's peephole, crossing my fingers for some Thin Mints, and have to blink again because it's not my roommate standing in the hall, nor is it adorable cookie-laden kids. It's my pain-in-the-ass brother.

I swing the door open, already demanding, "What do you want, Mom's Least Favorite?" It's a long-running joke that I'm the most favorite and he's the least, but truthfully, Mom has always been determined to love us equally, which is why we can make the joke without hurt feelings.

Immediately, I regret opening the door at all, because it's not only Dominic in the hallway. His best friend, and the bane of my existence, Griffin, is standing at his side. To put it mildly, he drives me fucking crazy, and if Dominic didn't swear that he was redeemable to some degree, I'd downright hate him for the way he acts around me.

To him, I'm invisible. As if he deems me worthy of only looking at for a mere moment, like I'm a waste of his time. Like he hates me.

And I have no idea why.

I first met Griffin five years ago when Dom brought him home. I'd been so excited to see my brother, whom I'd missed desperately, and wanted to share basically everything that had happened during the first few months of my sophomore year of college, like that I was dropping out and hadn't told Mom and Dad yet and wanted him to back me up when I did. Instead, he'd come home with a new friend.

Which was fine, and I'd been welcoming . . . at first. After all, a friend of my brother's is a friend of mine.

My first impression of Griffin was that he was smoking hot, all huge and muscly, with a soft smile of appreciation for my parents for letting him "tag along with Dom," as he called it. But my impression changed, quickly and drastically. He stole Dominic's attention the whole week while Mom and Dad treated him like a royal guest, both of which would've been 100 percent A-okay with me, except, almost instantly, he started glaring at me for reasons I didn't know then and still don't know now.

It was like he hated me on first sight, and I have no idea why.

"That's no way to greet your favorite brother," Dom says as he strides in without an invitation. Not that he needs one. He's annoying, but he's my brother, and I love him despite his overbearing nature.

"You mispronounced *only* brother, though I'm still hoping the DNA test comes back with some good news about that." I cross my fingers and close my eyes like I'm making a wish, but don't bother hiding the grin that ruins the image of some hardcore sibling rivalry between us.

We love each other. We've just perfected shit-giving as a form of affection.

I watch him pass, and turn back, locking eyes with Griffin. His lips are curled, and his nose is wrinkled like I have body odor so bad that he can smell me from three feet away. Frowning, I glare back at him. I showered with vanilla-scented body wash after my hike, and I'm 100 percent certain I don't stink. I probably smell delicious, and he's some rare freak who hates vanilla.

Griffin moves to follow Dom but pauses directly in front of me. I crane my neck to look up at him, finding that he's peering down the crooked length of his nose at me. His dark-brown eyes, with their cold depths and unfairly long lashes, scan my face and then lift to my forehead. With a hint of a smirk on his stupidly full lips, he murmurs flatly, "Cute."

As he walks in, I furrow my brow in confusion, then raise a hand, realizing that my dorky loupes with the magnifiers are likely making every pore on my forehead look humongous. "Of course," I utter, ripping the glasses off but folding them carefully. I shut the door, resigned to the next few minutes of interrogation at my brother's behest. *Might as well get this over with,* I tell myself in what's probably the worst cheerleader pep talk ever.

The guys have already made themselves at home on my couch—no easy feat, since the two of them take up the entirety of the three cushions, even with minimal manspreading. Delaying the inevitable, I put my work into the biometric safe, set my loupes in their cushioned case, and turn off my LED desk light.

"Come to dinner with us," Dominic orders. He's always bossy like that, thinking he knows what's best for me. Unfortunately, he's usually right.

Turning around, I shake my head dismissively. "No, thanks. Already ate." I pat my stomach to really sell it.

Dom tilts his head, seeing right through my lie.

"Not hungry?" I try, though it's even more obvious that I'm lying now.

"Get dressed so we can get this over with," Griffin grunts angrily, shoving his hand through his dark-blond hair. Both he and Dom have typical hockey flow hairstyles, but where my brother keeps his trimmed short in the back, Griffin's hair is more flipped along his neck, giving him a rougher, casual appearance, though the man is anything but carefree. He's more care-*less*, in that he doesn't care about anyone or anything. Well, except Dominic. But beyond that, Griffin is more likely to throw hands than speak words, usually seems suspicious of anyone who claims to be a fan, and has never mentioned a single interest other than hockey.

I glance down at myself, making sure that I didn't forget to put on clothes after my shower, but I'm wearing a sweatshirt dress and slouchy socks. The casual vibe coordinates perfectly with my air-dried brunette waves and bare face. I didn't need a full *look* to sit at home and work, but I'm glad they didn't get here earlier when I was doing both a hair and face mask with moisturizing gloves and booties on. They would've teased me mercilessly and probably come up with some nickname like *Loch Ness Monster* because of the green goop.

My eyes return to Griffin to find him scowling at my legs, which are so freshly shaved there's not a single pokey hair on them. And suddenly, I know what to do. "Let me get my boots."

I step into my bedroom, slip my feet into my favorite calf-high boots, and intentionally ignore the mirror over my dresser. Back in the living room, Dominic stands. "Let's go. I'm starving."

"Hi, Starving. I'm Penny."

My brother doesn't even pretend to laugh at my classic dad joke, which is blasphemy as far as I'm concerned. At a minimum, I deserve a fake *har-har*, and I won't forget the omission next time he pops off with a dad-level witticism.

Griffin snorts in derision, but not at my joke. "You are *not* going out in that." He points at my dress, as if there's some confusion about what he's referring to.

I don't bother looking at myself again. "Yes, I am." To my brother, I say, "Suddenly, I'm starving too. You're right, I haven't eaten since this morning."

I slip my arm through Dom's, encouraging him to move and letting him escort me toward the door.

Behind me, Griffin snaps, "Your ass is nearly hanging out. Does nobody care about that?"

At Griffin's assertion, Dominic gives my outfit a quick glance, but he shrugs because my ass is not hanging out. Or even close to it. My sweatshirt dress is almost mid-thigh. Well, within inches of being mid-thigh, but the banded elastic hem keeps everything scooped under my butt, so there's no chance of an accidental Marilyn blow-up peekaboo moment.

"Nope," I throw over my shoulder. "And quit looking at my butt."

Feeling sassy, I shake my ass in a corgi-esque wiggle, making sure he can't help but notice. Not waiting for a reply, I urge Dominic into the hallway by confiding that I had a yogurt parfait hours ago, knowing that'll get him moving. I'm trusting that Griffin will follow us, and a moment later, when he does, I feel a sense of triumph that's probably discordant with the scale of the actual win, but I don't care, because I'm unexpectedly craving a protein bowl of my own. And a bit of sweet victory.

You'd think I'd be used to the stares. I'm not. No matter how many times I walk into some store or restaurant or bar with my brother and Griffin, the stares get me every time.

I get it. They're huge and draw more than their fair share of attention on their own. But together? There are people swooning, ones in awe, others who cower, and occasionally, fans who recognize them and want autographs.

Put the two guys together with lil ol' me sandwiched in the middle like the tiniest of Vienna sausages in their huge hot dog buns? A whole different kind of curiosity overtakes people, and I can see the lewd questions written on their faces. The questions that make me want to yell, *That one's my brother and that one hates me,* but I don't bother. I don't owe strangers an explanation for why two walking, talking, real-life demigods are hanging out with an average plain Jane.

Okay, I'm *not* that humble.

I know I'm cute, if you consider an hourglass shape with a few extra minutes and a face without a single sharp angle to be cute. I'm what's affectionately called *slim thick*, and while once upon a time a skating coach told me I needed to lose weight, my body type is having a *moment.* Not that I care what's in vogue. This is who I am, and I rock what I've got to the best of my abilities, which, on the ice or with choreography, is pretty damn good.

In real life? Not so much.

Still, I hold my head high, swish my hips a bit more, and carry my bowl to the table we always sit at. Per my life and karma, however, I promptly spill a handful of shredded lettuce onto the table's surface. "Shit," I mutter, sweeping up the evidence of my blunder with my hand before grabbing the rest with a napkin.

"Here," a gruff voice says.

I wish it were Dominic. Nope, it's just Griffin, holding out his hand for my lettuce-filled napkin.

"It's fine. I've got it," I argue, balling up the paper and pointedly ignoring the couple of pieces of lettuce that fall to the floor at my feet. I try to step around him, intending on throwing my own trash away like the strong, independent woman I am, but Griffin grabs my wrist in a big, calloused paw of a hand. His touch is gentler than I would've expected, but still insistent. I can't remember the last time he actually touched me. Usually, he keeps a solid three-foot distance, like it's a league rule, and barely looks at me unless it's to see how his barbed comments land.

"Give it here," he demands, plucking the paper from my hand, which has opened unconsciously. Oddly graceful for a monster his size, he strides across the dining area, not bumping into a single table or chair the way I likely would've done, and deposits the napkin in the trash can.

When he turns back, I'm still standing stock-still, staring at him in shock. *He touched me and the world didn't immediately explode.* It seems like a small win for mankind, but an even larger one for me. Like not only did I poke at him with my dress (sc0re) but, surprisingly, by making a mess (another score). I make a mental tally mark in my column—*Penny: 2; Griffin: big fat goose egg.*

I smile triumphantly as I sit. Our usual table is one of those booth-on-one-side, chairs-on-the-other type deals, and Dominic takes his place next to me on the booth, while Griffin sits across from me. I used to wonder why he didn't sit across from Dominic instead of me, since Dom's his friend, and once I asked him. He grumbled about their knees bumping since their legs are so long, which made sense, but something about it seemed like a convenient lie. I decided it was probably another way my protective brother keeps everyone away from me, by bookending my existence with his friend.

Maybe that's why Griffin hates me so much? Because Dom's always forcing him to hang out with me like some sort of de facto second brother to a younger, annoying—I mean, awesome!—little sister. Maybe?

"Ready for the game?" I ask once we've all had a few bites.

Hockey is a safe topic that'll have the guys talking for hours. I don't mind it either. I grew up with hockey and love it almost as much as Dom does. Though maybe not as much as Dad, who could easily be described as a superfan of the sport, which means he's deeply proud of his pro son. And pretty happy about his hockey cheerleader daughter, too, though our uniforms aren't his favorite.

"Yeah," Dominic says. "The Beavers are known for their defense more than their offense, so we're going to be hammering Beavers all night long. Right, Honey?" He ends with a chuckle, as if the bad pun isn't cringeworthy all on its own.

"That's my hope. Nifty wrist shots all night," Griffin deadpans in the worst lie to ever be told. He's a beast on the ice, more violence than finesse, and enjoys every clock-ticking second of it. The attitude carries over off the ice, too, only with slightly less fighting. Very slightly less.

Dom laughs at Griffin's joke, and I listen while the two of them dissect the likely action they'll see tomorrow. After a bit, Dom asks me, "What'd you do today?"

I freeze, a too-big bite of chicken and rice halfway to my open mouth. "Huh?" Lowering the fork, I answer, "Oh, I hiked up Devil's Hill to witness a proposal. The ring was gorg! An heirloom solitaire I reset into a high-profile cathedral setting with tiny hidden birthstones for the bride and groom." I wiggle happily, remembering Elaina's wide, joy-filled eyes as she looked at the ring I'd made with my own two hands.

"You hiked Devil's Hill by yourself?" Griffin barks.

Surprised that's what he got out of my sweet love story for the day, I scoff. "Yeah, and I lived to tell the tale, as evidenced by my being here." I dramatically wave a hand at myself as if to remind him of my presence, alive and well. "I also got myself dressed, made my own breakfast, and drove my car to the trailhead and back, because I'm a full-grown adult who can take care of herself," I add snidely.

"Devil's Hill is a beginner trail, right?" Dominic asks, seeming confused about Griffin's concern over my hike.

"Yeah, easy-peasy lemon squeezy, so don't worry-purry over it. I only slipped off a rock once, but it was no biggie. I'm fine," I confess, laughing at my own misfortune. What else am I gonna do? It happens too often to be embarrassed by it, and despite my ass being a bit sore earlier, after a hot shower, it's fine.

"You fell?" Dom asks, looking me up and down like I've somehow hidden a broken leg or arm. "Are you okay?"

"Yes, *Dad*. Again, I'm fine," I drawl in annoyance. "Did you hear the part about the ring? Another happy couple!" I'm trying to get the focus back on the good stuff, so I add, "They want me to design their wedding bands too." I clap quietly in delight, both for the opportunity and the guaranteed paycheck.

Being a small-business owner isn't easy, but I stay busy with custom commissions and fill any downtime with redesigns of heirloom pieces I find, which tend to sell quickly on my website. I'm doing well—great, to be honest—but that doesn't mean I don't stress over every order and want to pack every blank date on my calendar. I've still got the hustle mentality that helped me get PLDesigns off the ground, and that mindset is what will help me reach the next level of success for my little baby of a business.

"Congratulations," Griffin says, sounding only slightly less pissed off. "But next time you're gonna traipse up Devil's Hill, text me and I'll go with you to save you from yourself." He blinks like he's only now realizing that he's volunteered to spend time with me, and then adds, "Or Dom. Just don't go out into the wilderness alone like that."

I roll my eyes. "It's hardly wild, and I wasn't alone. There were at least a dozen other people up there enjoying the beautiful weather. Even a nice guy who helped me up when I fell and walked back down the hill with me." I purposefully don't mention that he was white-haired and old enough to be my grandfather, and that we walked down with his wife, who took my business card with a promise to call about me redoing some of her jewelry pieces for their children and grandchildren.

"What guy?"

"What's his name?"

I'm not sure who asked what because Dom and Griffin both snarl their questions at the same time.

"Nobody to worry about," I say airily. "I don't know if I'll even see him again." It's the truth; even if his wife calls about her jewelry, it'll probably be me and her working on the designs. But I intentionally make it sound more scandalous because Dominic's and Griffin's reactions are hilariously over the top.

I mean, do they think I don't date? That I don't meet guys at the coffee shop or the grocery store or at games? I don't—or at least, not very often—but there's no reason to rub my nose in my lack of a dating life. Because I'm fine on my own, thank you very much.

"If you do, tell me first," my brother orders.

I laugh. "No way. You'd do some FBI-level background check on him, show up ten minutes before our date, and then scare the shit out of him so badly that he cancels on the spot."

I level him with a look, daring him to disagree, because we both know it's not an educated guess. It's exactly what happened when I naively and excitedly told Dominic about Jacob, a guy I did, in fact, meet at the coffee shop down the street, thinking he'd be thrilled for me too. Instead, he invaded my apartment, greeted Jacob at the door, and then literally asked about his intentions toward me like I was some fifteenth-century princess whose hand in marriage had been requested. I haven't breathed a word about any other dates since then—not that there's been many. Since my last serious boyfriend three years ago, I've been on maybe ten dates? That's less than one per quarter, as Talia likes to remind me. It's not that I'm averse to dating, I'm just busy. In that same amount of time, I've created around 150 pieces of jewelry, a statistic I'm proud of, unlike my dating history.

"If he's scared of me, then he's not the guy for you," Dom argues.

Okay, he kinda has a point there. Except . . .

"You're terrifying and you know it," I counter. "And then you play it up even more when you meet any of my friends. Talia thought you were going to murder her and nearly backed out of being my roommate because of you, ya fucking menace." I give his shoulder a sisterly punch at the memory, but like the jerk he is, he doesn't even drop a single grain of rice from his fork at the impact. "Talia is the best roommate

I've ever had, and if you'd screwed that up for me, I would've never forgiven you."

"But has she ever swiped your food from the fridge or borrowed something without asking?" he asks, looking mighty pleased with himself as he points at me with his now-empty plastic fork. I purse my lips, refusing to answer, because he already knows what I'll say. "I rest my case."

Griffin watches our sibling back-and-forth with a deep scowl on his face that makes me cut my eyes back to him, snapping, "This is your fault, you know? You started it by giving me a hard time for simply going on a hike, which is a nice, normal, perfectly reasonable activity."

Griffin's sharply arched brow says he disagrees with that particular declaration, and fine, he maybe has a point, given my history and the fact that I did slip. No, *half* a point. Maybe even just a quarter.

Begrudgingly, I amend, "Reasonable for most people. It's not like I went skydiving or swimming with sharks. I hiked a professionally plotted trail." I walk my fingers through the air like that's all I did today. "And basically just sat down . . . a teeny-tiny bit hard. And unintentionally." I hold my finger and thumb up, so little space between them you can't see light.

He inhales loudly and deeply, his brown eyes unblinkingly locked on mine like he's searching for the strength to deal with me. "Just be careful," he finally says, the three little words effectively negating his earlier offer to go with me.

I'm glad. I don't want to spend time with him, anyway—with his grunts and growls, frowns and scowls, and cutting remarks—and now, next time he tries to scold me for going out alone, I can remind him that he simply told me to be careful, something I always am anyway.

"Excuse me, I'm going to the restroom before we leave," I clip out, sounding bratty even to my own ears. I stand and see that I'll have to step over Griffin's ridiculously long outstretched leg to get out, so I glare at him for creating the inconvenience despite there not really being room for him to bend his legs beneath the tiny café-style table.

To his credit, he does try to move out of my way as I high-knee it over him, but instead, he manages to catch my back foot, effectively tripping me.

I'm going down.

Twice in one day. I'd love to say it's a record for me, but it's not even close. I should really consider walking around with music playing in an earbud, because if I stay on beat, there's no stopping me. Unfortunately, this time something else stops me.

Griffin.

I land haphazardly against his shoulder, one of his arms wrapped firmly around my waist and the other around my thighs to catch me, and somehow, in my mad scramble to grab for something, anything, and hang on for dear life, I've clutched his head in my hands and pulled him right into my abundant cleavage, forcing him into a motorboat position.

"Shit!" I hiss, pushing him away immediately, even before I've gotten my footing.

But Griffin doesn't let go, his sure grip the only thing holding me steady. I can feel the restaurant's air-conditioning hitting my skin way too high, which means I'm exposed in a not particularly family-friendly sorta way. I also feel the heat of his big hand on my thigh, right beneath the dress's band I thought was going to protect my modesty, making him in dangerously intimate territory, and when he peels his hands from me, instead of going cold, I get even hotter.

"Sorry," I utter, annoyed with myself. Yes, I'm clumsy, but it's usually no big deal, and I'm used to it. Around Griffin, it always feels like a bigger, more embarrassing situation, though. Praying I haven't exposed myself to the whole restaurant, I shove my dress back into place too forcefully to be discreet, and more carefully, I step past Griffin. "Back in a flash."

That is not what I meant to say, but still, I giggle at my own slip of the tongue. So worried that I'd mooned everyone, I basically highlighted the humiliating move. Griffin grumbles in displeasure. Dominic shakes his head, disappointed in me.

Fine, if that's how they want to be, but I choose humor because, in my experience, if you can't laugh at yourself, someone else will do it for you. "Get it? Flash? Because everyone saw my butt? Do you think they saw the tattoo that says 'kiss here' on my cheek?" I turn like I'm going to ask the couple at the table a few feet away, though I'm not really. They seem really into their conversation, like maybe it's a first date. Or a last one.

"Just pee so we can go. I need my beauty sleep before the game," my brother clips out in annoyance.

I can't add a tally mark in my column for that one since the scores are me versus Griffin, but still, irritating my brother always warrants a point in our never-ending battle.

I hurry to the restroom, taking care of business and washing my hands, but I guess I wasn't fast enough, because when I step back into the dining room, there are two new occupants at our table. A blonde sitting in my spot next to Dom and a redhead beside Griffin. The women are obviously on their A game, smiling and batting their lashes while twirling their hair. Might as well have "DTF" written on their foreheads, or maybe on their cleavage.

My first reaction is to march over there and run the women off. After all, Dominic is annoyingly protective of me, so turnabout is fair play. He's due for some cockblocking.

But I don't do that. The women aren't doing anything wrong. They just only see the pretty exteriors of the pro athletes, and either don't know or don't care that they're assholes beneath the hard muscles, chiseled jawlines covered in scruff, and cocky arrogance.

Or hell, maybe they do know and they're into that? Some girls are. Fuck knows I've seen that with my brother over the years. I swear the more he acts like a jerk, the more girls flock to him. I'm sure that's true for Griffin too. I've even had teammates and friends ask me to hook them up with my brother, his bestie, or both—though if they're into that, I don't know or want to know about it.

Luckily, I'm not one of those types of girls. I like guys who care and are soft inside, not filled with acidic barbs and thorny nettles. Which is too bad, because though I hate Griffin, I can admit he's hotter than hot, but only on the outside. Inside, where it matters, he's made of solid permafrost ice.

So I don't intrude. If Dom wants to date Blondie, that's on him. And if Griffin is into redheads, that's fine too. It's not my business or concern.

Instead, I wave to the workers behind the line, pointing back at my brother and Griffin with a knowing smirk that they return, and slip out the door.

Free from the overbearing guys and their barked orders about what I should and shouldn't do, I walk the few blocks back to my apartment. I've already kicked off my boots and turned on the television when my phone dings.

You ditched us?

Dominic's text doesn't have a single emoji, but I can read the hurt anyway.

You looked busy. Didn't want to interrupt, I reply.

Never too busy for you, PND. You home?

I can't help but smile at the initials of my family nickname. As maddening as he is, Dom's a good brother.

Yeah, settled in to binge watch Drag Race. See you tomorrow at the game?

You know it. G'night, sis.

GN, bro.

I don't ask about Blondie. I especially don't ask about the redhead, though I am curious how that ended up. Is Dominic texting me while Blondie waits for him? Is Red already riding Griffin's dick since he didn't have to do the brotherly check-in thing?

Probably so. He's got a reputation for being a good-time guy. And I do mean *good* time. Girls talk, and though Griffin doesn't fuck around with cheerleaders, he can't help but be swarmed by puck bunnies who are all too excited to share on social media about their time with the oversize, tattooed, alphahole hockey player.

Not that I care. Or read the posts and watch the story-time videos. Nope, I've never spent a night scrolling the comments on one of those posts. Not a single night.

A knot twists in my gut, but not wanting to examine that too closely, I decide it must've been the spicy salsa in my protein bowl and turn up the television a bit more. Mrs. Rosenthal bangs on the wall almost immediately.

"It's not even loud," I yell back at her, trusting she'll hear me through the wall. She probably can't even hear the television but is simply banging because she heard me come home. I used to think she was lonely and wanted some sort of connection with her neighbors. One offer of a freshly baked batch of cookies cured me of that idea when she sneeringly informed me that she doesn't eat from "strange and likely filthy kitchens." Instead, I think she wishes she could live alone in the middle of nowhere, with nothing and no one to disturb her peace, but unfortunately, she lives smack in the middle of the city, with neighbors on every side.

I wait for her to bang again, but she stays quiet.

And as RuPaul tells the queens they'd better *work*, I almost forget about the women at Pro-Bowl . . . and the guys they might've gone home with. Well, *the guy*, because I don't care what my brother does, as long as I don't have to hear the TMI details of it. But Griffin? Yeah, I'd like to know. For science, and nosiness. The science of nosiness!

Chapter 4

Griffin

There's a storm cloud over my head shooting out lightning bolts at anyone who gets too close and rumbling with thunder every few seconds. Or fuck, maybe that's me growling and snarling?

As if they can feel the charge in the air around me, everyone in the locker room leaves me alone, assuming I'm psyching myself up for tonight's game. Truth is, I'm tired.

I didn't sleep a wink last night.

Not that I'd admit it.

When Penny didn't return from the restroom, worry crawled up my throat like the cheap tequila I drank too much of in high school. While Dom chatted up some overly eager puck bunny, I'd volunteered to ask one of the workers to check the stalls. She'd grinned as she informed me that Penny had walked out several minutes ago after seeing the "guests" at our table. I'd been pissed off . . . at the bunnies for ruining the few precious minutes I get with Penny, at Penny for leaving without a word, and at Dominic because I can't swing by her place to check on her without him finding out about it. He'd laughed at his sister's wingman behavior, promising to text her to make sure she was good. I'm sure he did, but he had no reason to inform me if Penny was snuggled cozily into her bed at home or dead in a ditch somewhere.

So I tossed and turned, and considered texting her myself about a dozen times. But I couldn't. She wouldn't have answered me anyway. Hell, she would've enjoyed *not* texting me back and gone to sleep dreaming of ways to irritate the fuck out of me. Not that it takes much where she's concerned. Her beautiful, chaotic existence is enough to do that.

This morning, when I was supposed to be doing my trainer-prescribed meditation and silently reciting positive affirmations, all I could picture were her muscular legs sticking out of that too-short dress. I can't believe Dom let her go out in that. I can't believe she ignored my order to put something else on.

I can't believe I felt her soft skin beneath my palms and her full breasts on my cheeks, or smelled the soft, feminine, faintly vanilla scent of the skin between them. Fuck, I'd wanted to nuzzle in closer, but surprisingly, I don't have a death wish. Though I can still imagine the way she felt, and it does seem worth potentially dying over.

"Let's do this!" Brody yells across the locker room, his hands clenched as he flexes, his eyes wild. He starts beating on his chest, the thuds echoing hollowly as he roars out some anxious energy. He's hyped and trying to get the rest of us in the zone with him. A few of the guys do chime in, answering back with chest bumps and shouts of their own.

Bad mood aside, that's not the vibe I prefer before games. No Viking rally cries for me. I'm typically quiet, tuning out everyone and everything, going introspective as I prepare for two and half hours of war, which is probably why no one has noticed my silence. Usually, I prep by visualizing the checks I'm gonna make, the fights I'm gonna have, and the win we'll secure before the night is over.

Tonight, all I can think about is Penny, which is not only stupid but dangerous.

I consider asking Dom if he heard back from her last night, but don't. He's wearing headphones, his head bobbing lightly as he listens to the same playlist he always does before a game. By now, he's probably raging out to "Bodies" by Drowning Pool, and it'd take a solid tap to pull him from his routine.

He's here, though. That's answer enough to reassure me that Penny is fine. She must be, or Dom would be scouring the streets for his beloved little sister, and her parents would be on the news promising every cent they own to get her back.

Fuck, I'm so far gone it's ridiculous.

For a woman who hates me. For a woman I can't have. For a woman I don't deserve.

I grind my teeth on my mouthpiece as I close my eyes, telling myself that the cheerleaders will be out there before the game starts. They'll do their pregame performance, then line up to shake their pom-poms as we skate onto the ice. I'll see Penny and then get my head right before the puck drops.

That's the plan until a glove appears in my peripheral vision. I slowly turn to see who the hell dares to interrupt my mental prep.

Fucking Brody.

I lift a brow in question, and he moves his fist closer. "Come on, man, hit it. For luck."

"You mean the way I hit your mom last night?" calls Howe. He mimes some ass-slapping to go with his hip thrusts as he grins devilishly at Brody. The two of them obviously haven't gotten around to shaking hands and singing "Kumbaya" yet, but they won't let it affect them on the ice. In the locker room, though? All bets are off.

I sigh but tap my fist to Brody's in solidarity. He's annoying, but he's my teammate and I've got his back. He'd just better have mine and not get me into any unnecessary scuffles.

I chuckle to myself at the thought, because if there's anything necessary in hockey, it's fighting.

Finally, it's time.

As we march closer to the rink, my heart thuds dully in my chest and the hallway gets colder. Eventually, I can hear the crowd getting louder and the announcers calling out stats for tonight's game. Then I see the cheerleaders.

I do a quick search, having long ago memorized exactly where Penny stands in the lineup, and when I see her, the knot in my gut finally relaxes. I take a deeper breath than I have in what feels like forever. She looks different today, her hair curled and a full face of makeup. But mostly, the difference is in her smile. She always smiles when she's cheering, like it makes her happy to the depths of her pretty soul, and she rarely smiles at me, only when she thinks she's gotten one over on me.

Even now, as I pass, I see the edges of her lips waver like she doesn't want to give me the gift of her encouragement, even though it's her literal job to do so.

But she's okay.

And now, so am I.

In the words of my teammate, "Let's do this!"

The horn blares for the ending of the second period, and I'm soaked in sweat. We're up one to the Beavers' nothing, but Jack Off had to skate like a demon to get that point. I've already been in three mid-level serious scuffles, but nothing with lasting damage.

We reconvene in the locker room with a round of hoots and hollers, fist taps and chest bumps, celebrating the progress we've made so far and vowing to take the Beavers down, dam and all.

"Those Beavers are uglier than Brody's mom, and I had to close my eyes when she sucked my dick."

"Beav-ah, you make me wanna heav-ah. *Huuurggghuh.*"

There's also some pointed comments about whether they shave their beavers, but before we can get too carried away, Coach motions us over for his version of a pep talk. "Good work out there so far, guys. Keep the pressure on goal. Sneak it in on the left corner. That's Mack's weaker side, and it looks like he's got some groin tightness there tonight."

Coach is an eagle-eyed observer and catches everything on the ice, for the Hawks and the opposing team. I haven't noticed the Beavers' goalie, Mack, looking any worse for wear, but if Coach sees it, it's there. It might be just an inch or a tenth of a second, but it's there.

Having said his piece, Coach goes into his office, where he'll watch plays from the first two periods and make any further notes for the last one.

The rest of us have our own intermission routines to prevent our muscles from cooling down and tightening up. Me? I take off my skates and wiggle my toes, getting blood flow to the extremities, while basically inhaling a bag of sour apple gummy bears, washing down each bite with measured sips of Red Bull. Sugar and caffeine feel like the nectar of the gods mid-game, and the sourness keeps my mouth from going dry. All around me, guys are doing their own things—retaping their sticks, stripping out of their gear or leaving everything on, listening to music or hitting the trainer station, and everyone pees. If you're not peeing mid-game, you're dehydrated.

As the timer over the door ticks down, we simultaneously start getting geared back up. Coach reappears and leads us out without further advice, which means we're doing something right. He's not a yeller, but if we're fucking up, he'll always be the first to let us know.

Skating back onto the ice, my focus stays rink level. I don't even hear the crowd at this point, keeping my mind on the last period and my job. But there's still some intermission bullshit going on at the centerline. Internally, I grunt in annoyance but then realize that it's a fan surrounded by four cheerleaders. Instinctively, I search for Penny and find her to the right side of the face-off circle, on my side of the ice, which means I can warm up in my space and still see her.

I almost smile, but catching the reflex, I quickly bite down on my mouthpiece as I skate over and start my drills. But my eyes are on her. She's wearing the cheerleader uniform I hate the most of the two they rotate between. The less-hated one consists of skintight black yoga pants with the team name emblazoned down the leg and a matching crop top. What she has on tonight exposes even more—the top slightly longer but the skirt barely past her ass. The ass I don't want anybody looking at.

Except me.

As if she can hear me thinking about her, Penny glances my way, and when she meets my cold, dark stare, a shiver visibly works through her. She plays it off as an excited shimmy, but I don't think the shiver had anything to do with the icy temperature of the rink, but rather my own frostiness.

I scowl even harder. I know my reactions hurt her, and that kills me. But if I acted the least bit friendly, the slightest bit warmer, or even vaguely indifferent to her, it'd be the death knell for both of us. Penny is the sort who makes friends in line at the grocery store, talks to people everywhere she goes, and lets people into her heart easily. An asshole like me, if given half a chance, I would shove my way right in there and take up the whole space, not leaving room for anyone else. I don't want that for her. So I'm resigned to letting her think I barely tolerate her, for Dominic's sake.

Praying he hasn't noticed a possibly blatant eye-fuck of his sister, I send a sly glance Dom's way, knowing he's warming up next to me. But he's playing it up for the crowd, doing some fancy footwork and not paying any attention to the cheerleaders and fan. Or me, thankfully.

Overhead, the announcer says, "Drop the puck for him, ladies, and let's see if he can . . . *score*." There's a snicker of laughter at the way the announcer makes it sound like the male fan might have a shot with one of the cheerleaders, not in getting the puck past Howe, who seems unsurprised by the game and has taken his position in front of the net, acting like this schmuck has an actual chance at getting one by him.

One of the other cheerleaders, Layla, drops a puck to the ice in front of the fan, and Penny hands him a hockey stick. He taps the stick to the ice a few times, acting like he's got some game, but anyone who's played a bit can see that he's attempting to mimic whatever hockey movie he's seen and doesn't actually play. He fakes like he's going to slam it, and Howe doesn't react in the slightest other than the brow raise of *really?* he gives the fan. Finally, he slaps the puck toward Howe, who easily deflects it.

"Oh! So close," the announcer calls. It wasn't close at all, but stating the obvious wouldn't have the same energizing effect on the crowd. "Take two!"

Layla drops another puck, and the guy lines up his shot. This one doesn't even make it to Howe, who has to skate forward to retrieve the puck. Instead of picking it up, he sends it back for a redo, skating a looping circle to return to his place in front of the net.

"All right, guys, let's give Josh a little help. In the net . . . in the net . . . in the net," the announcer chants like Josh must be confused about where he's aiming, but it seems to work, because the next shot makes it there. Howe barely feigns reaching for it, and basically has to help it in, but the puck slides past the line. "Goal!"

The charade doesn't fool anyone, and the crowd claps politely for Josh as Howe dribbles the puck back. He expertly flicks the puck into the air, catching it in his glove, and then hands it to the fan, who is obviously excited to be face-to-face with one of the goalie greats. They exchange fist bumps, and Howe skates off to do his prep and stretches.

Josh waves to the crowd like he's the superstar, and Layla says something to him. He nods, then lays an arm over her shoulder. Penny skates up to Josh's other side, and he happily plants an arm over her shoulders, too, smiling at them and the crowd as if he's some big-shot player. With the cheerleaders in skates and Josh in boots, they carefully help him toward the rink's gate, and my heartbeat begins roaring in my ears as they get closer.

I want to break Josh's arm off and beat him with it for daring to touch Penny. I'm not a total monster. I don't give a shit about Layla, so he can keep the other arm. He'd be able to write and wipe his own ass and jack himself off. But the one wrapped around Penny? Fair fucking game.

She's not mine. But I don't want her to be anyone else's either. Or for anyone else to consider that she might be available. As far as I'm concerned, if she's off-limits to me, she's off-limits to the world. And Josh might need a little lesson in that math, especially when he's at a vantage point that lets him look down her cleavage, which he's surreptitiously doing.

Given her tendency for clumsiness, it's funny that on the ice is the one place I don't worry about Penny. She's got skills, equally at home with graceful spins from her figure skating days and hockey drills from her time practicing with Dominic. Still, when Josh finally steps onto the carpet and lets Penny go, I let out a sigh of relief.

In total, the silly game and exit takes less than four minutes, but being this close to Penny, having some guy touch her, and not being able to intervene is an unexpected hit to my mental game. I slap my helmet a few times on each side, internally yelling at myself to get my shit together because we've got a game to win.

"You good, bro?" Dom says, skating a tight circle around me.

"Yeah, just worried this is gonna be a bloodbath." I wish I was talking about the game with the Beavers. And maybe, on some level, I am.

But mostly, I think I'm gonna destroy myself if I keep trying to protect Penny.

Chapter 5

Penny

"Hello?"

"Penny, this is Carolynn at Yesteryear Antiques," the voice on the other end of the line says.

I instantly sit up straighter on the couch, where I've been vegging this morning, recovering from last night's three-hour cheerfest by doomscrolling an online marketplace for jewelry. I shop every chance I get—pawnshops, estate sales, antique stores, auctions, you name it. Anywhere I might find jewelry, I'm there, scouring for heirloom pieces I can rework and sell. My favorite places, like Yesteryear, keep an eye out for me, calling if they get anything they think I'll be interested in.

Carolynn is the owner of Yesteryear and has become a friend, often telling me about her grandkids and her desire to retire to Florida someday. But so far, she hasn't been able to relinquish ownership of the store, which she started with a hope and a prayer and turned into a bustling business for herself and the people who rent booth space from her.

Clutching my phone tighter to my ear, I say brightly, "Hi, Carolynn! Got something pretty for me?"

"I've got a ring here . . . never seen anything like this . . . so beautiful," she whispers in a way that lets me know she's looking at it as she speaks. "I know you'll want it, so I put it back for you, but you need to get down here. Now."

I don't bother asking for details. If Carolynn says I'll want it, I will. And their hold policy is only two hours if you haven't paid and twenty-four if you have.

"Say less. I'm already on my way. Right down the street, in fact. Be there any minute," I assure her, though none of that is remotely true. What I *am* doing is pulling clothes from my closet, feeling the ticktock of my two-hour hold time as I begin doing some mental math gymnastics . . .

If I take ten minutes to get dressed, plus it's a thirty-minute trip, that's forty. I need gas, too, so add ten, but I can grab a drink at the station, so no coffee stop, which means minus fifteen . . .

"Just hurry. Don't hurt yourself or anything else." Carolynn chuckles, all too aware of my bad luck with the fragile breakables in her store. "Great performance last night too."

"Thanks, it was a good win," I murmur, trying to balance while shoving my legs into jeans.

The last period was rough, like sandpaper-on-a-sand-covered-ass-with-a-sunburn-from-a-day-on-the-beach rough. Dom and Griffin had kept the Beavers' offense at bay, and just when the game couldn't get any more tense and aggressive, Wilson had gently snuck one into the net on the Beaver goalie's left side like he was buttering hot toast. Best of all, we won.

Her laugh rings in my ear. "I don't care about those boys and their sticks. I saw you dancing your heart out while Todd was watching the game. I meant that *you* had a great performance, Penny."

Touched, I freeze, mid-pantsing, to say, "Oh. Well, thank you." And like I couldn't control my mouth to save my life, I blurt out, "I haven't even left home yet."

"I know. Just get on down here. I'll have the ring for you."

I stare at the ring I've slipped onto my finger, speechless. The center diamond is round and easily five karats, surrounded by smaller baguettes set in thick bezel-style gold. And when I look through my monocular pocket loupe, it's nearly colorless and flawless. It's a truly amazing piece of art.

Honestly, it doesn't belong at a store like Carolynn's. It belongs at Christie's or Sotheby's, being sold to the highest bidder. But stranger things have happened.

Over the years, I've learned not to judge people's relationship with their jewelry and, more importantly, with the jewelry they inherit. Grandma Betty might've thought her wedding ring was the bee's knees, but when her granddaughter, who doesn't always have that same sentimentality, inherits it, she might want something vastly different or just the money it's worth. Sometimes it's even the original owners themselves who want to purge their jewelry boxes when they realize their remaining days are more likely to involve bingo at the nursing home than fancy galas. And they're happy to sell their beloved pieces to someone who will breathe new life into them.

So, though it's odd to find a piece like this at Yesteryear, it's not unheard of.

"Who wears something like this?" I wonder aloud as I snap a picture for my "before" of the ring, imagining an elegant older lady holding court at the head of a fancy dinner table with a wave of her bejeweled hand.

"Someone who walks like this." Carolynn drops one shoulder dramatically as if the ring weighs so much that wearing it would make you walk funny. I snort-laugh at her demonstration.

"And who's really good at sucking dick," she adds unapologetically.

"Carolynn!" I hiss, but I'm laughing too. She's not wrong. I just didn't expect her to say something so blunt. Carolynn is in her sixties, with a sharp gray bob and huge owllike glasses, a penchant for overalls and gardening, and a predisposition for ladylike turns of phrase. To be honest, I'm surprised she even knows the word *dick* and doesn't call a penis something charmingly nondescript like a "you know what" or, at most, a "Lord Johnson."

"She must've been a Hoover," she adds, still going. "Shoot, if Todd gave me a ring like this, I'd take care of him every day." She pauses, her smile evaporating as she feigns sadness and says, "For the rest of his suddenly . . . unexpectedly . . . very short life." She dabs an invisible tear at the idea of being a quick widow with a rock this size on her hand.

I'm basically rolling at this point because this conversation is a new and unexpected turn in our friendship. "I'm sure Todd would understand," I say with a wink.

"He wouldn't give a good goshdarn if he went to the pearly gates if it was *that* good," she surmises, giving the ring a serious glance of consideration.

As hard as I'm laughing, I do not want that image in my head, so I get back to business. "How much is it?" I'm scared to hear the answer, but I'm already falling in love with the ring, so a healthy dash of reality seems prudent. She's right about one thing: This is a family-money type of ring, not your run-of-the-mill engagement ring. It's more like a "thanks for putting up with me for the last thirty years" type of jewelry, blow jobs included.

"Ten thousand," she whispers.

I gasp, both at the risk of that expense and also the potential reward. It's honestly a great deal for a stone like this, but buying it will max out my credit line, making it hard for me to buy the smaller, less expensive pieces I can easily turn around. And the market for resale on something like this is so teeny tiny, it's nearly infinitesimal, which means it might take me a while to actually sell it to recoup my costs and earn a profit.

All good, valid, responsible reasons not to buy it.

But if I reset it just right, and find the right buyer, this sale could set me up financially for several months. Plus, something like this would take my custom-design work to the next level, bringing in customers at a new, and higher, price point, and I want to grow my business—*need* to grow it, actually.

I've been steadily improving my bottom line, but at some point, I'd like to make enough to adult on another level, one where home ownership and a Roth IRA aren't pie-in-the-sky dreams. You'd think with two jobs that would be possible, but being a cheerleader doesn't pay much—it's a labor of love that I won't be able to do forever, so

PLDesigns is it for me. My only real shot at the future I want. A future that could start with this beauty on my finger.

I should hesitate, give it a second and maybe third thought, but I can't let a chance like this pass me by.

I'm talking myself into it, but mostly, I've already made up my mind. I have the utmost faith in my ability to work magic with a diamond this special, so I'm choosing . . . me.

"I'll take it," I say before I can stop myself.

"I knew you would," she answers with a supportive smile.

While I shakily pull out my credit card and tap it to the device on the desk, she puts the ring into a box, carefully wraps the box in tissue paper, and places the bundle into a cute little brown bag with the store name stamped on it. She even loops ribbon through the bag handles, tying a bow, but truthfully, it's ridiculously plain packaging for something so valuable. Somehow, the contrast seems fitting, though, because I'm going to take the simple design and turn it into something spectacular.

"Promise you'll show me a picture of it when you're done?" she asks, giving me a warning look, as if I'd consider saying no.

"Of course," I agree easily.

"Hope you find someone who appreciates their Hoover enough to reward them like this." She wiggles the bag pointedly.

"Me too. Your mouth to the universe's . . . dick?" I laugh at the strange decree, and she taps her nose like it's not weird at all, but rather a spot-on manifestation.

When she hands me the bag, I immediately grip it to my chest protectively, a huge smile on my face. There are champagne bubbles of giddiness rising inside my belly . . . well, either that or my breakfast is gonna make a reappearance, but I'm hoping it's the former.

I tell Carolynn thank you and goodbye before stepping out into the spring day, where the bright sunshine balances the slight chill in the air. Walking down the sidewalk, I can't help but think about how this is going to be a new benchmark in my business and in my design skills, and the ideas are already spinning in my mind.

Chapter 6

Penny

Should I redo the setting in platinum instead of gold? That'd instantly make it feel brighter and more modern. What about a halo surround? Though, at five karats, it's already a door knocker of a stone and doesn't need more to seem large and in charge. Maybe I turn it into a set, using the baguettes for the wedding band and the round diamond as the engagement ring? That'd increase my buying audience. Not to sound cynical, but love-drunk people are usually more willing to invest than sorry-I-fucked-up people, and if I can get someone both love drunk *and* rich, I'll be skipping my happy self all the way to the bank.

I'm nearly skipping already, so lost in my own musings that I don't notice the refrigerator-size shadow approaching until it's nearly right on top of me, blocking my way and the sunlight.

"Are you talking to yourself? I guess what they say is true . . . simple minds can entertain themselves for hours with nothing more than the dust bunnies in their heads."

I flinch, becoming aware of my surroundings in a whoosh and seeing Griffin standing directly in front of me, almost taking up the entire sidewalk. His arms are crossed over his chest in mocking sternness, and his eyes are filled with laughter.

He's laughing at me.

Not on the outside—he rarely does anything as jovial as that. But deep inside that black heart of his, he's laughing that he caught me mooning over seemingly nothing.

"Better than any conversation with you," I snap back, then offer, "Wait, need me to dumb that down for you? You, no good talkie. Me, better without you." I wave a hand dismissively like I'm shooing him away.

"That's definitely true," he mutters under his breath.

I'm so surprised at his agreement that I bark out a laugh. He usually doesn't agree with anything I say, to the point where I think he's just decided to be on the other side of any fence—as far away from me as possible, verbally speaking—no matter the topic. I could say the sky is blue, and he'd argue that sometimes it's gray, or I'd say that cake is delicious, and he'd make a face of disgust, though I know he eats cake because I saw him put away a slab of the three-tiered chocolate-sprinkle one Mom made for Dom's birthday.

So his easy agreement, especially with the hint of an almost sad smile at the corners of his lips, puts me on edge. There's a shoe drop coming in three, two, one . . . but nothing happens.

I even glance around to see if I can find the hidden camera, because there's got to be something weird going on. He doesn't chitty-chat with me. He's genetically averse to small talk. And he certainly doesn't smile, or almost smile. Because he hates me.

He wraps a hand around his neck, pulling on it like he's uncomfortable or nervous, two things I don't think he's actually capable of experiencing. "What're you doing down here?" he finally asks.

And it is a question, not a demand for information. He almost sounds like a normal guy making conversation. Except we don't do that, so I'm automatically on high alert, still searching for the trick.

"Shopping," I reply slowly. "You?"

I can be conversational too. Hell, I'm one of the most talkative people you'll ever meet. I just don't talk to . . . *him*. But at this point,

I think Mom would be proud of my politeness, given I haven't told Griffin to fuck off . . . yet.

"Oh, uhh . . . there's a place . . ." He looks over his shoulder, and I lean over to see what or whom or where he's looking. But all I see is the sidewalk, the usual stores, and a few people who aren't paying us any attention. When his eyes come back to mine, he seems even less sure about what he's saying. "Right around the corner, that I go to sometimes . . ."

He's dragging out his answer like there's an entire novel-length explanation for what he's doing downtown, and suddenly it hits me. "You've got a booty call down here."

"No!" His eyes widen, and the barked word is enough to tell me that I'm spot-on with my guess.

"All good, Honey," I say, purposefully using his team nickname. The official story on that is that he's sticky on the ice. The unofficial, probably truer story is that puck bunnies stick on him like flies on flypaper, so I'm not surprised he's got a woman here. I'd be more surprised if he didn't. "I won't tell Red about Downtownie, or tell Downtownie about Red." I mime locking my lips with an invisible key and throwing it over my shoulder. Then, ignoring the locked lips, I open one tiny crack on the side of my mouth to ask, "Wait, are Red and Downtownie the same woman? Probably not, huh?"

"What?" His brow furrows as he shakes his head like that made less than zero sense, but it did. And we both know it.

"Or Blondie either."

And that's when recognition dawns on his face. I can see the light of understanding in the depths of his dark-brown eyes. For the tiniest second, he almost looks shocked, and then a sly grin forms on his face. "You jealous, Pen? You don't need to be. I didn't go home with that woman at Pro-Bowl."

I hate it when he says my name. No, I hate it when he says it like *that.* Like I'm an annoying brat he has to put up with, not a whole person with feelings that get hurt. Ignoring that, I also notice he didn't argue about having a fuck buddy downtown again.

"I'm not jealous." I stomp my foot to prove that point, which in retrospect, probably does the opposite, because his grin grows even larger and the light in his eyes turns into a twinkle of teasing in a blink. He knows I'm lying through my teeth, since there's one thing I'm not good at . . . well, there's a lot of things, because I also can't do calculus, but that hasn't come up as often as the undeniable reality that I'm an awful liar. "Just worried about you passing the STD screening at next month's physical exam."

I know the guys on the team get physicals all the time, including a full panel of lab work every month, because Dom always whines about the needle stick. Some guy full-sending a puck right at his noggin? No biggie. A teeny-tiny needle prick? Terrifying. My brother is such a baby.

"I always pass. No worries there." He chuckles like that's funny for some reason.

I shrug like it's not my concern either way. "So if you're not here for a hookup, what're you doing?" I don't know why I ask again. Maybe because it seems like he really doesn't want to tell me, and that makes me that much more curious? Curiosity might've killed the cat, but at least he died with answers to his questions.

"You really want to know?"

I nod, but doubt is starting to creep in at the return of the taunting tone in his voice. "Unless it involves spiders. Hate those things." I feign horror, although it's only half feigned. I do hate the little fuckers. "I shouldn't have told you that, should I? You have to promise to never put one in my bed. I will freak out so bad that I'll jump out my apartment window to my death, my last action on this earth being to light the building on fire to destroy the spider and save the world like the hero I am."

Griffin stares at me in confused silence, which I wish I could say was a unique reaction to the things I say, but it's not. "No spiders, promise."

"Good," I say, whooshing like I'm utterly relieved at that. I tilt my head and quietly confide, "I'm actually not that scared of them, but they are creepy-crawly, you know? All itsy and bitsy . . ." I wiggle my fingers like spider legs and promptly lose my grip on the brown bag I've been clutching tightly for the whole run-in with Griffin.

He catches it easily and hands it back to me. "What's in the bag?"

Shaking my head vehemently, I taunt, "Nuh-uh, you first. Tell me about this quote-unquote 'place around the corner,' and maybe I'll tell you about the absolutely, most amazing, awesomest thing I've ever bought." I hug the bag to my chest, all too aware that I've got my life in my hands, literally . . . well, financially.

"It's jewelry, isn't it?" he says flatly.

"Okay, that was a good guess, but you still have to show me yours before I'll show you mine."

He makes a choking sound like his spit went down wrong, so I step around him to pat him on the back. "You okay there, big fella?"

But rather than worrying about him choking to death on a city sidewalk and me being publicly responsible for the death of one of our city's favorite hockey players, I'm suddenly acutely aware of how high I have to reach to hit his upper back, and how muscled that back is, and how hot he is even through the light jacket he's wearing over his white T-shirt and black jeans.

Not appreciating my life-saving maneuvers the way a civilized person would, he shrugs me off and grunts, "Come on, let's get this over with. I've got shit to do today that doesn't involve an impromptu tour of downtown."

"I've got shit to do, too, you know," I say.

My busy schedule involves such exciting things as unwrapping my newly purchased ring, staring at it with naked eyes and then again with loupes, and then squealing in excitement and nerves as I dance around my apartment, imagining what I'm going to do with it. After that, I'll have an existential crisis, hyperventilating as I worry that it's too much and yelling at myself for maxing out my credit card. Eventually, I'll move to phase three: calming myself down with a bag of sour-cream-and-onion chips before I pull out my sketch pad to start forming some ideas. So yeah, we're all busy, bucko.

I should tell him never mind, that I don't care where he was or what he was doing anyway. He can fuck off, and I'll continue on my merry way, happily talking to myself like I was before he so rudely interrupted me. But I don't. His initial reluctance to tell me makes me really want to know.

Which is why I let him lead me down the sidewalk and around the corner, eying every storefront sign, apartment window, and person we pass like the answer might be right in front of me. When Griffin stops, I still look around, not sure why he's no longer moving unless it's to let my short-legged steps catch up with his long-legged strides.

He squints down at me, his expression something along the lines of *let me have it.* Confused, I look around again, finding that we're in front of an ice cream shop called Kitty's Creamery. Even though it's mostly adult clientele, it looks like something out of a little girl's imagination, with pink-on-pink-striped awnings, a cartoon cat logo on the door, and through the window, I can see delicate-looking turquoise iron tables and chairs, bubble-style light fixtures, and a pink display case with handwritten labels for the flavors.

"This is where you go sometimes?" I ask, repeating his earlier words.

Am I judging him? Hell yeah, I am. There's got to be fifteen different ice cream shops closer to his house, and at least thirty kinds he could buy at the grocery store, but he comes here? To the pink princess palace of ice creameries? That's fucking hilarious. I can imagine him sitting on the teeny-tiny chairs, which probably only fit one of his ass cheeks, licking at a cone the size of one of his fingers and trying not to get it everywhere. Like Alice after she eats the cake in Wonderland and grows into a giant. Not to mention it's kinda chilly out. I mean, I eat ice cream in the dead of winter, but I do it at home, wrapped in a blanket, with sweats and socks on to stay warm, like a normal person.

"They have my favorite flavor," he declares.

I raise my brows questioningly, needing to hear this. If it's something like Yumilicious Boo-Berries and Dreamy-Creamy, I will lose my shit and he will never hear the end of this.

"Death by Chocolate," he grumbles.

I smirk, sensing the lie. "Death by Chocolate, you say? Sounds good." I move toward the door, grabbing the handle—the one shaped like a kitten's paw with pink-painted claw nails—and pull. Suddenly, the door slams shut in front of me, and I look up to see Griffin's big paw—with naked, trimmed nails and thick fingers—holding it closed.

"Fine, that's not what it's called."

Now totally committed, I pull on the door handle harder, and he relents, even grabbing the door and holding it open for me so I can go inside. Behind me, I hear his mutters of displeasure and sighs of irritation, but since I always seem to have that effect on him, I ignore them.

"Hi!" the lady behind the counter greets me. Then she says to Griffin, "Back for more already?"

I cut glee-filled eyes to him. At least I know he's telling the truth now. There'd been a part of me that thought he might be fucking with me, because who would think a guy like him—all grumpy asshole—would hang out at a place like this?

"No. She just wants to try it," he grunts, making me sound like the annoyance I probably am to him.

"Sure thing. Any friend of Griffin's is a friend of ours. Did you want to try anything else or just dive into the Chocolate Orgasm?"

I look to where she's pointing, seeing the stainless-steel tub filled with deep, luscious dark-chocolate ice cream, then look at Griffin, who seems to be in actual pain now. I decide to poke that hurt, and purr, "Oooh, let's go straight for the orgasm. I can't wait. Been on edge since Griffin told me about it. He screams about how good it is, says it's the best he's ever had, and you know I need that kind of thick, rich cream in my mouth."

The lady is fighting a losing battle with her laughter and gives in. "Oh, I like you. Come back with or without this guy anytime." She scoops up a ball of ice cream and plops it into a plastic cup—pink, of course—and then adds a spoon, also pink.

I grin, not promising until I've actually tasted the ice cream. No matter how tasty it is, I'm not sure it'll be as good as the look of mortified horror on Griffin's face.

As the lady rings me up, I reach into my purse, but Griffin taps his phone to the reader, paying for me before I get the chance. "Thank you," I say, puzzled at the niceness. I would've thought he'd order himself another serving, maybe even double- or triple-size it, and then leave me to pay as punishment for prying this gem out of him.

"Bye, Felicity," he tells the lady as he opens the door for me to step back outside.

Once we're out of the way of the door, I take a delicate bite. As soon as the flavor hits my tongue, I close my eyes and moan. "Uhmagawd, Griffin. Thissus soo guud."

It is. The perfect balance of sweetness, and is that . . . "Izz salt-y?" I say around another mouthful.

"Felicity sprinkles a little sea salt on the top," he informs me, pointing at my cup.

I look at the ice cream in my hand, seeing the tiny sparkles of the crystalline salt on top, and glance up at him with a happy grin. His eyes look weird—his pupils are dilated, and there's a softness there I never see. But he blinks and it's gone. Probably just my imagination anyway. Or maybe he wants another Orgasm for himself, but I'm not sharing. This is mine, all mine.

"Good, huh? It's your turn now: What's in the bag?" He points at the bag I'm clutching in addition to my ice cream.

"Jewelry," I tease, taking another bite. He glares at me and I chuckle, giving him more information, but only a tiny bit. "It's a ring with the most gorgeous diamond I've ever seen. I can't wait to redesign it."

"I'm sure you'll turn it into something magnificent."

The compliment—and its pure sincerity, with no sarcastic bent—has me swallowing hard in surprise. Usually, our conversations are filled with insults, eye rolls, and snappish comments Dom ends up having to referee. This one has been different. Easier, more comfortable, more . . . real, maybe? Or at least it feels less like he hates me.

"Thank you. You want to see it?"

It's stupid. I know it is. But I'm so excited, and I want to share that buzzy feeling with someone else, even if it's Griffin.

I shuffle the bag and my ice cream around in my hands, trying to undo the carefully tied bow Carolynn made around the handles without spilling Chocolate Orgasm everywhere. Squirting, if you will. With a scowl, Griffin tries to help, reaching for the bag.

I jerk it back, not ready to let it go. It's my future, and I don't trust him like that. Not after one polite conversation amid years of near-bullying ones. He holds his hands up in surrender. "Sorry, just trying to help. Watch it—" He points at my ice cream, where a drip is running down the cup and over my hand.

I give him a narrow-eyed warning. "Don't take it out, just peek inside the bag and open the ring box, okay?" He nods, and slowly, hesitatingly, I let him take the bag before I lick the back of my hand.

Rather than dive straight in to see the promised amazingness, he watches my mouth, and I wonder if there's ice cream surrounding my lips too. I try to Scooby-Doo lick them as delicately as I can, but there's not really a nonobscene way to do that. Griffin swallows, his Adam's apple bobbing in his throat, before dragging his attention to the bag.

He unties the bow easily with two hands, even though they're large enough you wouldn't expect him to be graceful. Some people have hands meant to play the piano; Griffin has hands meant to ball into fists and hit shit, which is exactly what he's known for.

Holding one handle, he moves the tissue paper out of the way and reaches in, opening the box. He peers inside the bag for a split second, and then his eyes jerk up to mine. "Holy shit!"

"I know, right? It's stunning," I exclaim, the giddiness of earlier returning in a flash.

He looks in the bag again and lets out a low, almost sensual whistle. I know he's admiring the diamond and not me, but it still feels like a compliment somehow, and I can't help but dance and wiggle a bit.

One second, we're standing there, the two of us on the sidewalk, Griffin smiling at my latest purchase, and me filled with excitement. The next, something happens . . .

A rush of red bumps my right shoulder, sending ice cream spilling everywhere—down my sweater, on the window beside me, to the ground at my feet, and splattering on my shoes. The movement creates wind that grabs my attention, and I jerk my head, trying to see what it is. What it was.

"Hey!" Griffin yells.

When I look back at him, he's staring open-mouthed behind him. And his hands . . . they're empty. The bag is gone.

Chapter 7

Griffin

"That did not just happen." Penny's voice is oddly flat. I'd expect a drama queen like her to be hysterical, so it must be shock.

Reality hasn't hit her yet. It sure hasn't hit me, because I can't find a single word, or even a sound, to break the yawning void silently stretching out the moment.

I had the bag in my hand, felt the ropey handle against my palm, and then a jerk as the tiny weight disappeared and the handle broke loose. And then the guy was gone.

I think . . . I just got mugged.

Penny slaps my chest with her ice cream–covered palms, leaving a mess of chocolate handprints. "Go get him! I'll call the police!"

Right. *Right.*

I'm an athlete, and a fucking monster, so I jump into action. I take off at a sprint, initially trying to dodge people on the sidewalk, but quickly giving up on any facade of manners and barreling straight through them if they don't move at the sight of an oncoming freight train. There's a wake of shouts behind me, but none of those people matter. Only one man does—the one in the red hoodie. It seems like forever, but in truth, the delay between the guy stealing the bag and me taking off after him is probably only a couple of seconds, a head start I can easily make up.

But the guy is wily. I can see him ahead, easily sidestepping the crowd, so I yell out, "Stop that guy! Thief!"

He looks back over his shoulder, and I get a good look at his face. Early twenties, maybe even late teens, closely cropped light-brown hair, and pale skin with a heavy smattering of freckles across his nose and deep purple smudges beneath his eyes. He sees me and his eyes go comically wide. Or it would be comical if he didn't have the bag with Penny's ring in his hand.

Annoyingly, no one tries to stop the guy. If anything, they seem to not want to get involved and start moving out of his way, which gives him an even easier escape route. I growl, putting everything I've got into my mad dash to catch him, but he disappears around a corner. A split-second later, I make the same turn, but he's . . . gone. Poof! Vanished into thin air like a ghost.

I look in the doorway of the closest store. Nope. I look down an alley. Not there either. I even look up the building, thinking he might've scaled it like Spider-Man, but he's no spider. Just a run-of-the-mill, shitty human thief. I glance around, thinking someone might tell me which way he went, but they shrug like they didn't see a thing, as if they missed a guy in a bright-red hoodie, balls to the wall running from a guy the size of small European car.

"Fucking cowards," I snarl, and a few of them cower back, shuffling their feet as they hurry to get farther away from me. Like I'm the one in the wrong here, not the other guy who stole.

Right. Out. Of. My. Fucking. Hand.

Shit. There's no coming back from this. Penny is never going to forgive me. I saw how reluctant she was to let me hold the bag, like it was precious, and how worried she was that I was gonna do something juvenile like hold it over her head, playing keep-away with something important to her. I'm an asshole, but I wouldn't do that. I understand that her work is everything to her. And she's damn good at it.

And I just fucked that up. Majorly fucked it up.

But I'm not a coward. I'll take my lumps. I'll figure out how to make it up to her. Somehow, some way, someday, she'll forgive me for this.

I trudge back to where I left her, but she's not there. For a moment, I panic that something happened to her, too, but logic starts to prevail as I retrace our steps. When I find her back where I originally ran into her, close to an antique store I know she frequents, she's staring at the door, slack-jawed, her eyes vacant as she squeezes them shut, then pops them open, staring at the store across the street.

"What are you doing?" I ask carefully. It's entirely possible she's lost it. I know Dom jokes about it sometimes when she gets going on one of her weird tangents, but right now, she looks like she might've actually broken her brain.

"Rewinding the last thirty minutes so this never happened. Did you catch the guy?" She looks at me with hope-filled eyes, but when she sees my empty hands and sour expression, she sags. "No, no, no . . . this can't be happening. It's not real. Just a nightmare I'm gonna wake up from . . . right now." As she declares it, she pinches the shit out of her arm before I can stop her and then cries out at the sharp pain, glaring at her arm like it's betrayed her too. "Fuck. Fuck a motherfucking duck."

"It's okay, it's okay," I say soothingly, catching her in my arms and preventing her from doing further damage to herself.

But she fights me, jerking around like an electrified worm. "No, it's not, Griffin! That ring was everything! Literally everything! And now it's gone. And it's your fault."

It's not. It's the thief's fault, but from her perspective, I can see why she'd think it's mine. I even feel guilty . . . for not seeing him coming, for not punching him when he got too close, for not catching him.

"I'll fix it. I'll figure something out," I mumble, not sure what in the hell I'm saying, but willing to say or do anything that'll stop the tears that are now running down Penny's face. She's getting heavier in my arms as the reality hits her harder and harder with every passing moment. "I'll pay you back for the ring. Whatever you paid, I'll give it to you."

That's apparently the wrong thing to say, because she snorts in derision, finding her feet to stand against me. "Ten thousand dollars, Griffin," she snaps. "You got that floating around in your savings account? 'Cause I don't. It's on a credit card that'll be due in a few weeks. I'll have to sell everything I have to pay that bill. I'm gonna end up selling feet pics on OnlyFans, and you know I have wonky toes from skating my whole life. Nobody's gonna pay ten thousand dollars to see these jacked-up piggies."

She holds a foot up in the air as if proving her point despite having on tennis shoes that hide her not-at-all ugly feet. Not that I'm into that. Or care about people who are. I've just noticed everything about Penny over the years. And her feet are fine, cute even, but now doesn't seem like the time to remind her of that, especially if she's thinking of selling pictures of them.

I make good money as a professional hockey player, but it's not as simple as a lot of folks seem to think. After taxes, agent's fees, and more, a big chunk of my game checks are eaten up before I ever step foot on the ice each week. But I have long-term investments and savings, thanks to my accountant, who makes sure I'm not going to end up one of those guys with more debts than brain cells after I retire, so I can swing it. It's just going to take me a bit to get that kind of liquid cash to give to Penny. But I will.

"I do. I'll pay the credit card, and it'll be like this never happened."

She looks at me warily, probably thinking I'm fucking with her, and I get it. This isn't me, not the way I've treated her for five years. "It'll always have happened. Even without the financial loss, I was so excited to redesign that ring. It was going to be the masterpiece that took my business to the next level."

The anger I can deal with.

I've dealt with it my whole life—from my parents, teachers, coaches. And I've got plenty of my own, too, and am used to tempering the fiery flames and heat. But the hurt and pain in Penny's voice now? The sound of her hopelessness and glum outlook on her future? That guts me. And I can't wipe that away with a stack of cash.

"What about the police? You called them?"

She lets out a bitter huff as her eyes roll hard. "Yeah, they said 'sorry that happened, go to this link on our webpage,'" she replies, throwing her voice into what I'm guessing is an approximation of the coldhearted officer who answered her call. In her own voice, she continues, "Basically told me too bad, so sad, and that I could complete their automated form to get a case number for my insurance."

"Insurance, that's a good thing, right? It'll pay for the ring."

Penny's lips twist into a sarcastic grimace before she snaps, "You'd like that, wouldn't you? But no. I have business insurance, but for a piece I literally just bought and have no certification on, I don't think they're gonna cut me a check like that." She snaps her fingers. "Besides, my insurance already costs enough. With a big claim like this, it'd either drive my premiums through the roof or they'd drop me altogether. So no, the police were no help, and my insurance is useless too."

Fuck. We're hitting the boards at every turn.

"How about this? Let me go talk to the store owner. I can see where she got it. Maybe that'll tell us something about who took it? Or where we can find another one?"

"We?" Penny snorts in derision. "There is no *we*, Griffin."

Though she's absolutely right, it hurts to hear her say it so bluntly. She might as well tell me she hates my guts. Normally, that'd be all I need to *nope* out of this situation and ditch her on the sidewalk, but I don't. This is Penny, and it's different. So fucking different with her.

"Let me try. Wait here," I say, holding up my hands and hoping that, for once, she'll do what I'm asking. "Just let me try."

When she buries her face into her hands and starts openly sobbing, my heart shatters into a million pieces. I have got to fix this, one way or another. Any way that I can.

I force myself to leave her, striding across the street and not giving a fuck about the cars coming. They can stop or they can take me out like a real-life *GTA* game, I'm not sure I even care at this point.

A tiny bell tinkles above the door as I enter the antique store. I look left and right, having never been in a store like this, but thankfully, the counter is in the middle, right in front of me. There's an older lady in overalls behind the counter, but my beeline for her is thwarted by the two customers she's currently helping.

As out of place as I am in this store, so are the two guys she's talking to, and I'm instantly suspicious. I lock my gaze on them, studying everything. They're close to my height, so easily over six feet, broad shouldered, and well dressed in suit pants, button-downs, gold jewelry, which should all be fine, but the expressions on their faces are all wrong, making them stand out. They're pissed and taking it out on the kind-looking woman.

I move a little closer but stay several feet back—far enough to not draw attention but close enough that I can eavesdrop to make sure the woman is okay.

"A ring. Huge, gawdy diamond with a thick, ugly gold band. I know it's here." Goon One slams a hand to the wooden counter like the woman is hiding it in one of her many overall pockets. Goon Two bumps him out of the way with an added side-eye that says *cool it.*

Oh shit. I've seen a ring like what he's describing. Not the ugly part necessarily, but the rest? Yep, I saw a huge diamond in a thick band . . . in Penny's bag, right before it got snatched.

"I apologize for my *friend* here," Goon Two says politely, playing the part of the good cop to the other guy's bad. "He's upset because the ring shouldn't have been here in the first place. It holds . . . um . . . *sentimental* value, so we'd like to get it back. We'll even purchase it back because we understand this isn't your mistake. It's ours." He arches an accusatory brow at Goon One like he's daring him to disagree, and I get the feeling he's the one to blame.

"I wish I could, but I sold it already. Less than an hour ago, actually." To her credit, the cashier does look sorry the guy has lost a piece that is important to him.

"You sold it?" Goon One repeats, looking surprised that a store would dare to sell merchandise, as if that's not the sole purpose for their existence.

Goon Two takes a steadying breath. "Who did you sell it to? Maybe we can purchase the ring back from them?"

"Oh, I sold it to Penny. She's a jeweler that reworks heirloom pieces into custom designs. I'm sure she'd be happy to sell you some of her work. It's stunning. She's very talented." The cashier bends down, looking for something beneath the register, and then returns with a business card. "Here you go. PLDesigns. Give her a call."

Goon Two takes the card, grunting some attempt at a polite thank-you.

"Excuse me, could you help me with this trophy cup? Is it sterling silver or plated?" a voice calls from down the main aisle. A woman is pointing at a piece high on a tall shelf, and the cashier nods, acknowledging that she heard her.

"Oh goodness, hold on one sec," she tells the guys, holding up a finger. "Ma'am, let me get that down for you. I've got a step stool right here," she says to the woman, who's trying her best to reach the large trophy and has a very real chance of dying by head trauma if the piece is as heavy as it looks to be.

I should probably offer to help, but I don't. I step back, staying out of sight and listening to Goon One and Goon Two.

"No worries, Tommy. We'll get Miles's ring back before he realizes it's gone," Goon Two says.

"Boss is gonna kill me if we don't," Goon One—a.k.a. Tommy—answers.

"We will. How did it even end up in a dump like this?" Goon Two peers around the antique store in distaste.

I have absolutely nothing to compare this store to, but I feel like it must be okay if Penny frequents it. I mean, dusty, crusty chipped paint is someone's thing, right? I've seen commercials for entire TV shows about it, like "old as fuck" is an aesthetic people actually want.

But while I'm thinking about the weirdness of decorating, my brain has been crunching on the nuggets the goons just said. Huge diamond worth at least ten thousand. Miles. Boss. Kill.

Holy fuck. And no fucking way.

The realization hits me like a two-ton wrecking ball right to the gut. The ring Penny bought, the one that was stolen, the one these guys want and think she still has . . . belongs to Miles Conniver. As in the Mob boss of the city, Miles Conniver.

Sure, things aren't like the old movies where the Mob kills people in broad daylight or gives them concrete boots before dropping them into the river. Miles shows up to mayoral inaugurations, has box seats at the Hawks games, and if you didn't look too closely, you'd think he's just a rich businessman.

But if you know, you know. He didn't make his millions with good business deals. He did it with intimidation, threats, bribes, and if you believe the rumors, probably an occasional murder to keep things working in his favor. He might appear slick and fancy now, but there's a darkness beneath his expensive suits, and he's not someone to mess with.

Before I've even made the decision in my mind, my feet are moving, making a mad dash for the door. Running on instinct, I know Penny, and I need to get the hell out of Dodge. Immediately.

But my cardio is not what I would've thought it to be, and two back-to-back sprints is doing a number on my heart rate and breathing. Or maybe that's the fear.

I'm a beast on the ice. I break rules when needed and don't hesitate in throwing punches. But that's different. It's a world where that's expected and accepted.

Miles Conniver lives in an entirely different world. One where losing something he values can result in much more than a few minutes in the penalty box. It can cost everything.

It could cost Penny her life.

As the bell over the door tinkles above me, I hear the cashier say, "Oh! There she is. On the bench across the street."

I don't need to turn around to know she's pointing out the window to Penny, who's sitting in full view in the sunshine right where I left her, wiping her tears away as she tries to rally some positivity the way she always does.

Two seconds, and I'm across the street.

One second more, and I'm in front of her. "Up, up, get up. Let's go. Now." I grab hold of her arm, pulling her to her feet.

"What'd Carolynn say?"

Another second of delay that we can't have. "Later. Let's go. Move it, or I'm gonna move you, woman."

She jerks her arm out of my grip. "What the hell's gotten into you?" Her fire is back, thankfully, even if it's for the wrong reason. She can use all that anger to run, because we need to go.

"Penelope." I'm hoping using her full government name, something I've never done, will turn that fire into an inferno. "Move your ass . . . now."

And with that, I physically shove her down the sidewalk. Which means that, Penny being who she is, she promptly trips over her own feet. I catch her before she tumbles to the ground but keep the momentum, throwing her over my shoulder and catching behind her knees with my arm, holding her securely.

"Upsy-daisy," I declare.

"Griffin Mahoney, you put me down right this second. What the fuck, man?" she shouts, drawing eyes from all around us. When she starts kicking her feet and pummeling my back with her fists, a few people give me concerned looks.

"She's into that BookTok stuff, you know," I mumble, rolling my eyes like I'm annoyed by her little fantasy flirtations. The concern turns to wolfish grins.

"Lucky girl. Make sure to smack her ass," one lady suggests with a wink and a knowing nod.

Figuring it couldn't hurt, I slap my palm against the ass that has been the object of my dreams . . . and my nightmares.

Penny gasps in shock, but she does still.

"You did not just do that," she sputters. But she doesn't sound angry or, well, not any angrier.

Huh, maybe she is into that.

I'll have to save that for later. It can't matter right now, because we've got to get out of here. I'm making long strides to move us farther away from the antique store and the goons who are now going to be looking for Penny. I turn the nearest corner, and then another and another, trying to zigzag away so they can't follow us.

Until finally, the coast is clear.

And that's when shit really goes sideways.

Chapter 8

PENNY

"What the actual fuck are you doing?" I demand as Griffin slowly lowers my feet to the ground in an alley. At least he avoided the dumpster I can smell from here, and my cute shoes are nowhere near any puddles of questionable origin.

My cheeks—both sets—are heated. I don't need a mirror to know they're pink, but I tell myself it's not arousal from being manhandled and spanked. And it's not embarrassment from the whole street seeing me hanging over his shoulder. It's anger. And since I was literally hanging upside down, it's probably gravity working its magic.

Thanks for nothing, Isaac Newton!

"Uh . . ." Griffin rubs his jaw, the scruff of his beard making a scraping sound I'd like to feel myself . . . against my palm . . . as I slap the audacity right out of him.

"Who do you think you are? You can't go around picking people up and moving them where you want them." I poke my finger into his chest to emphasize that point but get slightly distracted by the hard muscle beneath my fingertip. "What are you made of? Steel?" I poke him a little harder.

"Penny."

The rough gruffness in his voice irritates me anew, and I remember why I was mad in the first place. "You also can't spank them without permission. That requires discussion of hard limits, soft limits, safe words, and consent." I count out the rules on my fingers, wiggling them in his face.

Griffin's eyes widen, and he makes an odd sound that kinda sounds like a chicken getting strangled—or what I imagine that'd sound like, because the only chicken I've ever been around comes vacuum-packed from the grocery store. He also immediately starts coughing.

"Shit," I hiss, moving to pound on his back. "You okay? Why do you keep choking like that? Do you have reflux or something? The team doc could give you a scrip if you need one."

"What the hell are you talking about safe words for?" he manages to force out.

I throw my hands in the air. "That? You spanked me, ergo, ipso facto, safe words. The two are obviously related."

"Ipso what?" he repeats, his brows furrowed like I'm speaking another language, which technically, I am. Latin, I think?

"I don't know. I heard it on a TV show. I think it means something like 'this—dot dot dot—that.' The ipso facto is the dot-dot-dot part. I think." Tilting my head, I try to remember the context I heard it in, then shake my head to clear it before refocusing on him. "You're distracting me. Why did you run away from Carolynn's like the building was about to blow? It's not, is it? If so, I didn't do it." I hold my hands up, the picture of complete and utter innocence.

I swear I can see the wheels turning in his head like the little hamster is struggle-bussing to get motivated on a Monday morning after a forty-eight-hour weekend rager. There's even a tiny squeak as the wheel gets rolling. Oh wait, that's someone pushing a cart on the sidewalk.

"I just—had an idea—" Griffin stutters.

He's lying. Right through the cosmetically enhanced smile the teams' dental sponsor, Dr. Velspur, helped create. But I decide to give him enough rope to hang himself and stay silent. Glaring doubtfully but silent.

He licks his lips and then blurts out, "A pawnshop." I arch a *gimme more* brow, and he rushes to explain. "The thief, he probably doesn't want the ring. He wants money, so where would he go to get quick cash on stolen goods?" He gives me an expectant look, assuming I can put one and one together and get Means and Methods of Common Thievery in the Twenty-First Century.

I blink, letting the idea marinate in my brain for .02 seconds, then slap Griffin's bicep—which is just as hard, or maybe even harder, than his chest. "That's brilliant! Why didn't you say so? We're wasting time. Let's go! Where's the nearest pawnshop?"

Now I'm the one dragging him, although I have no idea where I'm going.

"Wait, wait," he argues, planting his feet. Given he's a solid foot taller than me, and outweighs me by . . . an undisclosed amount (because ladies don't discuss their weight, especially after a few too many boxes of Girl Scout Cookies and a scoop of Chocolate Orgasm), I can't budge him. He might as well be a rock or a mountain, which is admittedly kinda the same thing on a different scale.

He carefully peeks around the corner like he's looking for something . . . or someone. I scoot up close to him, my side plastered to his, and peer around the corner, too, though I have no idea what I'm supposed to be searching for.

"Did you get recognized at Carolynn's?" I whisper. "Some psycho bunny begging to have your babies right here, right now? Or a middle-aged fan who 'played a little hockey in his day' telling you how to take the season all the way, like that's not literally what you're trying to do?" I'm not making those scenarios up. They happen more often than you'd think. I've seen it with Dom, and with Griffin.

"Yeah. I was recognized," Griffin says. But his voice sounds wrong. Maybe it's because he's actually talking to me and not grunting like I'm stealing his precious oxygen by being in his vicinity?

"What's she look like?" I'm going with the obvious statistical guess on who we're hiding from. An in-your-face fan? Griffin would tell him off. A woman throwing herself at him? The manners he occasionally has—with everyone other than me, of course—make him less likely to be rude to her.

"He. Two of them. Big guys. Right there."

I look to where he's pointing and see why he didn't tell off the fans offering unsolicited advice—which is almost as bad as unsolicited dick pics. Not *as* bad, though, because at least you get a laugh out of the dick pics because it's always the guys with weird-looking Leaning Tower of Pisa dicks who send pics. Seriously, who in their right mind sees that and goes, *Hell yeah, call me Bugs Bunny, because I want me some of that carrot stick*?

Point being, the fans . . . those guys . . . look like bad news partnered with *oh shit* and a dash of *uh-oh.*

"Good move on not telling them to fuck off," I praise, nodding approvingly. "I don't think they would've taken your 'when was the last time you went to the playoffs, bud' question as well as that last guy did." Because, yeah, Griffin actually did that once and turned a lifelong fan into an enemy for life. Not that Griffin gave a shit.

"Glad you agree," he says, sarcasm dripping from every word.

"Ah, there you are," I say with a twisted smirk. "I wondered when the asshole was going to show back up. Like Hulk, you can't contain him for long, can you?"

"Can we just go to the pawnshop?"

"It's fine." I wave a hand, dismissing him. "I'll go by myself." I take three steps—out of the alley, down the sidewalk, and then stop. Without turning around, I say, "You're right behind me, aren't you?"

There's a grunt. It's either Griffin answering my question or a bear, and given no one else is freaking out at a randomly appearing bear on a downtown sidewalk, I'm pretty sure it's Griffin.

"Suit yourself. I'm going to find that ring. I have to."

He mutters something that sounds like, "Yeah, we do."

But that can't be right. There is no *we* where Griffin and I are concerned, unless you're grouping humans that live in the same city. That's about all we have in common. Or people who Dominic Lee actually like, which is an admittedly small group. But beyond that, nothing, nada, no *we* to speak of.

Yet Griffin is still behind me when I find Paul's Pawn, which is the closest pawnshop according to Google, only a couple of blocks away.

"Well, *hellooo*. You just made my day better, pretty lady," the guy behind the glass display case purrs with a flirty smile as I walk through the pawnshop door. His eyes drop from my face to my feet, with extra-long stops at my breasts and hips, but that all disappears as Griffin enters after me.

Did I shut the door in his face? Yes, I did. Was it stupid and immature? Also yes. Would I do it again? A million times over. Didn't stop Griffin even a microsecond.

"Shit. Sorry, man. Didn't mean nothin' by it," the guy apologizes to Griffin, when he should be apologizing to me for being a skeevy jerk. Griffin doesn't respond, and the guy clears his throat uncomfortably, sounding much more professional when he says, "How can I help you today?"

Griffin steps forward, starting to speak, "We're looking for a ring—"

Nope, he's not in charge. Not of me, and not of this clusterfuck of epic proportions. So I shoulder my way in front of him, pushing him back . . . and promptly stepping on his foot.

"Fuuuck," he hisses, jerking his foot from beneath mine and shooting laser beams of death my way.

It was accidental. Truly, it was. But I'm not going to let him know that. I clench my teeth, snarling through them, "Back off, bucko. I've got this."

When I turn back to the pawnshop guy, his eyes are ping-ponging between me and Griffin. It's obvious who he thinks is the bigger threat, but he's dead wrong. Griffin might be all big and tough, and rough and hot—wait, *not* that last one; I mean, he is, but not to me—but I'm hell on wheels when the situation calls for it. And sometimes, even when it doesn't. No one would be the slightest bit surprised if I *accidentally* broke a display case or two. It'd be right on par with any given day in the Life of Penelope Lee. So this pawnshop guy had better watch it.

"We're looking for a ring," I say, and when Griffin mumbles behind me, "That's what I said," I willfully and pointedly ignore him. "A five-karat, bezel-band gold ring."

"That's very specific." He scans the display case between us like he's not sure what's in his inventory. If there's one thing I know about pawnshop people, it's that they know what they have and what it's worth.

"I shop nearly every pawnshop in the state, but I've never been here. Why is that?" I question, glancing around. "Paul, is it? Of Paul's Pawn fame?" I gesture to the sign on the wall behind the guy.

All polite customer service fakeness drops away, and Paul goes shrewd, his sharp-eyed gaze considering me. I know what he sees. First, I'm a woman, which is always a point against me in this type of environment. Second, I'm young at twenty-five to Paul's likely over fifty, given the elevens between his bushy brows. Third, and most problematic in this interaction, I'm short and curvy, the type of woman men like to coddle and cuddle and fuck, not meet toe to toe as equals in negotiations. But I'm a pro at this, having dealt with dozens of Pauls while growing PLDesigns from a seed of an idea to my main moneymaking career.

"I don't know. Maybe you're a shitty shopper." He shrugs indifferently but reflexively flinches when Griffin steps up to the counter at my side. He's not as unaffected as he'd like us to think. But it's because of Griffin, not me, and that needs to change.

After a slow, theatrical scan of the rings in the case in front of me, I say, "Or maybe it's because you're selling cubic zirconia as real diamonds." I tap my finger on the glass, intentionally leaving a smudge he'll have to clean, as I point out a particular ring that's reflecting light all wrong.

"I do not! All my merchandise is tested and verified, and comes with certification papers," he claims. Figuring out that he's underestimated me—fuck, I love it when people do that—he tries a new tactic, cutting his eyes to Griffin. "You sure you want to marry this one? You're never gonna have a day of peace with a bitch like her."

One second, Paul is looking pleased with himself for the cutting insult like he thinks calling me a bitch is somehow novel and shocking. The next second, his throat is gripped in Griffin's fist and he's lying halfway across the glass display case, his face turning red and feet kicking in the empty air behind him, looking for purchase.

"Apologize."

My mother's always told me that for an apology to count, it has to be sincere and genuine and come from a place of true regret. Paul's apology is none of those things, but I still feel a little thrill at getting it. Maybe I'm a little bloodthirsty too? It's probably from hanging around hockey bros my whole life. I'll have to yell at Dom for that later.

Having gotten whatever apology he can, Griffin releases Paul by shoving him back across the counter. "The ring was stolen about thirty minutes ago, less than a few blocks from here. This place"—Griffin looks around, his nose wrinkled as if the pawnshop smells—"seemed like the thief's best bet to turn stolen goods into quick cash. Do you have it? Because trust me, if you do, you don't want it here. I'm asking nicely. The next time you're asked, it won't be so polite." Griffin curls his hands into fists so tightly that his knuckles pop and crackle like Rice Krispies cereal.

Paul shakes his head vehemently. "I don't have anything like that. I've got no idea what you're talking about, man."

It's the truth. I can see it in his eyes.

I truly thought this nightmare was going to be over. That we'd hit this pawnshop, find the missing ring, and everything would be okay. But it's not.

I gambled big, and now I'm going to lose big. Financially and professionally.

The reality hits me hard. Or maybe the ups and downs of this roller coaster of a day have finally sent me retching over the side of the cart, because I collapse, sitting on cold linoleum floor and leaning back against the display case.

"I'm so screwed," I whisper helplessly, staring at the flecks in the commercial flooring. Flecks that I'm not sure if are by design or are just dirt. "Entirely, completely, totally . . . screwed." I wish I had a thesaurus right now to better express how bad this is, but the dull roar in my head wouldn't let me read one anyway.

Griffin squats down next to me, his knees splayed wide. "You're not. I'm gonna fix this. I swear."

I glance up, finding Griffin's jaw hard and his eyes cold. But there's something else. "Why are you doing this? Helping me? This should be your best day ever. Annoying Penny losing her shit and her shirt all in one fell swoop," I accuse dryly.

It's the truth. Griffin hates me and has taken pleasure in my pain more than once before, so this should be the Powerball of victories for him, except he doesn't seem all that happy about it.

He shrugs, and he cuts his eyes away. "Dom will kill me if he finds out I let your ring get stolen."

That makes sense. Griffin and my brother are close, as close as brothers without the blood relation, but Dom has a wicked sense of loyalty where I'm concerned. He would destroy anyone who hurts me, even Griffin. But there's something else in his voice, his eyes. There's more, but before I can ask him what, Paul the Pawnshop Prick spouts off, "Wait. Did you say Dom? As in Dominic Lee? Are you Griffin Mahoney? Fuck, man, I thought you looked familiar!"

With the accidentally helpful hints of our private conversation, Paul's clocked Griffin. If he says one word about how the Hawks can make the playoffs, I won't be surprised to find him lying across the display case again.

As Griffin stands, I'm holding my breath. In fear? In anticipation? Maybe both.

"Yeah, that's me. And this is Dom's little sister. She's a jewelry designer who does custom heirloom work, and one of her pieces was literally stolen out of my hand today. I need it back." He clears his throat and swallows hard. "I mean, she needs it back."

Paul seems much more interested in what's going on now, and in helping us. He glances around like someone might be listening, though it's only us in the store, and leans in close. "I don't do stolen merch here. But there are places that sorta specialize in it. And a few fences, depending on the size of the diamond you're talking about." He drops his chin and gives Griffin a meaningful look from beneath his brows.

"What do you want?" Griffin snarls.

"Two tickets to this weekend's games against the Vortex."

Paul is a salesman at heart. He has to be to run a successful pawnshop. Negotiating with people pawning their goods to give the least amount possible and negotiating with buyers to get the most amount possible. Still, I expect Griffin to refuse. He's not one to kowtow to manipulation tactics.

"Done. Tell me everywhere you'd look if a valuable ring was stolen by a white guy with freckles and brown hair, wearing a red hoodie, that knew this neighborhood like the back of his hand."

I didn't realize Griffin had gotten such a good eye on the thief, and I can't help but look at him in awe. The teeniest-tiniest bit, and then . . . anger. "You almost had him, didn't you?" I snap.

He grits his teeth, not sparing me a glance. "Penny."

Fine, he's busy doing the menacing thing with Paul at the moment, but this isn't over.

We get a list of pawnshops that aren't always so particular about the origin of their merchandise and the names of a couple of fences, and leave with Paul reminding Griffin that he'd better see those tickets before the weekend.

Back on the street, I smack Griffin's arm. "If you saw the guy, we need to call the police back. Maybe he's a serial mugger, and they know where he hangs out, looking for hapless shoppers to snatch their bags or purses or whatever." I sound like Velma having a *jinkies* moment, but a clue's a clue, right? "With this new information, they might be able to help us find the thief, or the ring, or both."

"You already said they don't give a shit, and I don't care about the thief. Just want to get the ring back."

It's the right thing to say, but he's looking around like he's distracted by something. Or maybe just done with me and looking for any way out. That's definitely more likely. He's probably wishing he'd never run into me today and that none of this shitstorm had rained down on him.

I snap my fingers in front of his face. "*Helloooo.* Crisis, right here. Care to tune in for a second?" I point at myself to make sure he knows exactly where the disaster is, a beautiful one, but nonetheless, I truly am a disaster.

He takes a slow, deep breath. "I am tuned in. Unbelievably so." He's obviously annoyed with me again, his tone harder than rock.

Well, join the damn club, buddy. I'm annoyed too. I swear, something like this could only happen to me. My mom told me once that I'm like the calm in the eye of a tornado. I don't do any damage myself, but the debris that often swirls around me can take out entire swaths of land. Or friends, or whatever Griffin is to me. Brother's best friend? Frenemy? Something like that. Whatever he is, he really needs to watch out for the next incoming cow before it swipes him off his feet and carries him away to Kansas.

"Look, it's getting late, and these places are closing right now." He holds up the list Paul gave us. "Can you just give me tonight? Let me see what I can find out."

"You're not talking to them without me," I declare.

I do not want to talk to criminals. I'll probably do something stupid or accidentally spill their whereabouts to an undercover cop at the coffee shop or something else ridiculous. But I also don't want Griffin cleaning up this mess himself. I have some pride.

Plus, I don't trust him. He hates me, and while he's been hot and cold today, I don't know that he'll truly do everything to get my ring back. He might say he tried but actually spend the evening chilling on his sofa, watching old hockey games and laughing at the fast one he's pulling over on bratty, bitchy me.

He sighs like I'm the one that screwed up his day and not the other way around but relents. "Fine. I won't talk to them without you. I'll pick you up at ten in the morning? We can hit A-to-Z Pawn first."

I'm not sure about this course of action, but it would be sort of nice to have Griffin at my side if I'm going into sketchy pawnshops and talking to people who probably won't want to discuss their illegal business model with me. I mean, not Griffin specifically. Any huge, threatening asshole who's willing to throw hands would do. Most people wouldn't have a lot of options that'd meet those criteria, but I do. Several, in fact. Notably my brother. But I don't even consider calling him and telling him what's happened.

Mostly because I don't want to hear another one of his lectures about how I make poor decisions and am too impulsive. Usually, I can tune him out and pretend I'm Charlie Brown listening to a *wah-wah-wah-wah* adult, but in this case, he might have a teeny-tiny point, and I really don't want to get kicked while I'm down. Surprisingly, so far, Griffin isn't doing that, though he'd be the first one I'd expect to line up to take his shot when I'm on the outs.

I nod, agreeing with Griffin. Except . . . "If you're fucking with me, you should know that at 10:01, I'll be heading there on my own. Don't be late. And bring me coffee. Skinny vanilla latte, hot."

He blinks, hopefully memorizing my Starbucks order if he knows what's good for him.

"Deal." He nods but pauses. "Don't answer your phone or your email tonight. Or your door. And don't ask me why."

"Why?" I ask immediately.

He tilts his head, giving me a hard look. "Take it or leave it."

I have no idea what he's up to, but a semi-self-imposed evening of disconnect would let me cry into a slice of pizza and soothe my loss with a bubble bath, so though I'm suspicious, I agree. "Deal."

I hold my hand out, and though he looks like the thought of touching me pains him, Griffin slips his big paw of a hand around mine and shakes, sealing our agreement. He releases me quickly, though, and I try really hard not to be offended by that, but it doesn't work.

He hates me. Always has, always will. And I need to remember that even if he's helping me, he hates me.

Chapter 9

Griffin

Shit. Shit. Fuck. Damn.

I need these people to get the hell out of my way. I dodge around a guy taking pictures of a dog on the sidewalk with a grumble, nearly crashing into a door that suddenly opens in my path, and spill Penny's latte over my hand.

Ahhh! Hot, hot, hot!

I told the barista to make it extra hot so it'd be perfect by the time I got to Penny's, but now it's scalding me. I lick it off, noticing the redness already blooming with annoyance, and glance in front of me just in time to see Penny's cute brown bob flicking over her shoulder as she starts off down the street.

Without me.

I'm gonna kill her.

"Penny!" I shout. People around me flinch at the sudden racket, and I see her shoulders lift so I know she heard me, but instead of stopping, she keeps strutting farther away. In fact, I think she speeds up. "I have your latte!"

Now we have an audience, people stopping as they realize who I'm yelling at and all of them waiting to see her response. *Me, too, people.*

When Penny holds up a middle finger high in the air and keeps moving, I growl. I'm not late. Or not *that* late, and it's not my fault the line at the coffee shop was long. I texted that I was on my way. I glance at my watch: 10:04.

Seriously? She's this pissed over four measly minutes?

"That's it? You're not gonna go after her?" a guy mocks from beside me. I cut my eyes his way to find a thirtysomething suit dude smirking at me cockily. "If it was easy, it wouldn't be worth it. You gotta be strong for the ones that're worth it," he advises. "Unless that's not you. If that's the case, good for her for ditching you." He turns wisdom-filled eyes back toward Penny like he's considering giving chase if I'm not man enough to go for it.

He doesn't know me, or what the hell he's talking about, but the cut hurts all the same. He's right. Not that Penny and I are romantically involved the way he thinks, but she is too good for me. She's too good for everyone.

Which is why I can't let her go to sketchy pawnshops and talk to actual criminals on her own. "Fuck," I hiss as I take off at a trot, trying to keep the latte from spilling again. This time, people do get out of my way at least. I step in front of Penny, forcing her to stop, and hold the latte out like an olive branch. "Here."

Her amber eyes drop to the cup and then lift back to mine. "No, thanks."

She tries to step around me, fully intending to walk away from me, but I block her. I'm a hockey player, after all, and have blocked tougher opponents than a pissed-off Penelope Lee. "Take it. I told you there was a line and I'd be here."

She frowns. "Told me how exactly?" She pulls her phone from the back pocket of her jeans and holds it up. "Because I promised someone that I wouldn't use my phone, so how would I know that you hadn't ghosted me? Huh, Griffin . . . how would I know?" She taps a finger to her chin like she's pondering the greatest question of all time.

"I said not to answer your phone. I didn't mean not to read my text." It's a stupid argument, and I know it, but mostly I'm too focused on the fact that she really didn't use her phone all evening. That means she probably didn't check her emails or answer her door either. And given she's standing in front of me, full of fire and sass, she's okay. The goons didn't find her, contact her, or most importantly, hurt her. The fear that weighed down on my chest all night dissipates. But while I'm finally relaxing, Penny's ramping up to argue the semantics of our agreement, and in a last-ditch effort to thwart her, I blurt out, "I'm sorry." She recoils like that's the last thing she expected, so I say it again. "I'm sorry I'm late. I did text. You can check."

She rolls her eyes doubtfully but clicks a few times on her phone screen and then says, "Huh," before roughly shoving her phone back in her pocket. "Fine. You texted."

It's the hardest win I've ever made, and it's not even on the ice. It's against Penny Lee about a damn text message.

"Can we go? A-to-Z Pawn opens in twenty minutes, and it's a thirty-minute subway ride."

"It's a fifteen-minute rideshare trip." I've already opened the app and ordered before I realize that she's glaring at me again. So much for the apparently short-lived win. "What?"

"You're out here throwing around rideshare money to the girl who's worried about next month's credit card bill and can't split the cost with you. I know you're a *pro hockey player* and all," she says, making it sound like *hot pile of dog shit*, "but it's not like you'd get swarmed on the subway. Dom rides it all the time, and no one even recognizes him, much less bothers him."

I ride the subway too. Hell, I rode it this morning to get to Penny's. And the city is filled with options, from the subway to parking garages to various rideshare services and even those scooters you can rent on street corners. But I'm not taking any chances with Penny. I want her locked in, safely at my side, so I can make sure the goons don't try to find her.

"You're saying you'd rather take the subway and get to the pawnshop later? That's what I'm hearing." I show her my phone screen, hovering my finger over the Cancel Ride button. "Or we could be there when it opens and get this taken care of, whether that means getting the ring back or hitting the next shop, and the next, and the next, before it's sold to someone else." I draw the list out intentionally, emphasizing that this might take all day, and that's if we're lucky enough to find the ring.

Penny's lips press into a thin line, and the fiery glint of a begrudging surrender appears in her eyes. "Fine," she huffs. "But you're paying."

I never asked her to pay, not even half. She assumed. And if she tried to give me money for the rideshare, I would refuse it, but I decide to keep that to myself and let her think she's won this battle. Sometimes, the more important fight is the war—which is getting the ring back, by any means necessary.

Paul's Pawnshop, on the edge of the booming downtown square, was Saks Fifth Avenue compared to A-to-Z Pawn, which is farther out in an area best described as "don't go there at night." The bent steel bars on the dirty windows out front tell me everything I need to know. The ring isn't here.

Still, we go inside. There's a big guy lounging in a folding chair close to the door, and he looks Penny and me up and down critically, his coldly vacant eyes saying everything his mouth doesn't. I don't like putting him at my back, but I stay close to Penny, keeping me between her and the big guy. Security guard? Bouncer? Whatever his professional title, he's the muscle of the place.

The store has an air of dust and despair, like the pain and poverty of its clientele are carried in every item spread about. There is truly everything from antique-looking lamps to zebra-print purses, and more, but Penny approaches the display case first since we're on a singular mission for jewelry.

The woman standing there sets down her phone in favor of watching our approach, sizing us up with every step, which is fair, considering I'm doing the same. She looks wary, like she's both seen and done some shit in her life and came out the other side because she's willing to do whatever it takes. She's not the rise-and-grind type, she's the survive-and-thrive sort.

"How bad did he fuck up? One karat, two, five?" the woman asks Penny with a sly grin like they're two girlfriends spilling the tea. She leans over, glances me up and down, and then whispers to Penny, "Go for the five. The watch alone says he can afford it, and that's before the leather boots, designer jeans, and expensive shirt."

I'm not used to being visually added up into walking, talking dollar signs, and don't particularly enjoy the experience now. It makes me feel dirty, like I'm callously flashing cash around in a spot where people are starving. I don't dress fancy compared to a lot of the guys on the team. But when you grow up with nothing, being able to buy a luxury item here and a quality thing there is something you enjoy. Responsibly.

Penny's eyes light up. The girl has zero poker face. "Do you have a five-karat ring? Round cut, smaller baguettes, in a bezel setting?"

"Picky thing, ain'tcha?" the woman scoffs. "I don't have anything like that, but I've got this." She taps a long nail to the case, pointing at a multistone ring. It's big to the point of gaudy, but nothing like Penny's ring.

"Enough with the pleasantries," I grunt, interrupting the sales pitch that's wasting everyone's time. "We're looking for a specific ring. One we were told might come here due to its . . . um, 'questionable acquirement' by a guy on the sidewalk downtown yesterday." I hear a creak behind me and peek at the convex mirror above us to see that the big guy is now standing by the door. "No judgment there," I rush to explain. "We just want the ring. I'll even buy it if you have it."

Penny pushes her phone under the woman's nose to show her a picture of the ring on her finger. "It looks like this. Have you seen it?"

The clerk barely ticks her eyes down, the glance so quick I would've missed it if I'd blinked, before she shakes her head. "Nope, never seen it. Gus can get the door for you." She jerks her head toward the big guy, who pushes the door open for us. It's definitely more of a "get the fuck out" move than anything resembling politeness.

"Well, shit. Now what?" Penny asks once we're outside, looking at me like I'll have an answer.

I don't have a damn clue. I don't know how to find stolen jewels, or track thieves, or hide from Mob guys, but that's not what I say. I hold up Paul's list and offer, "Hit the next one?"

"Fine. I think it's close enough we can walk there."

Penny marches past me, giving me a good foot of berth, and I traipse along behind her, feeling like a lost puppy. No, I feel useless . . . which rolls right into my old friend, worthless.

In my head, I'm screaming at myself . . .

Fix this!

Do something, anything!

What was that?

I'm so caught up in chastising myself, I nearly miss it, but several hundred feet ahead, the hulking shape of a guy ducks into a doorway. Maybe it wasn't one of the goons from yesterday, but maybe it was. Maybe he went into the store, or maybe he's waiting for Penny to walk in front of him so he can demand the ring back.

It's a lot of *maybes*, and I'm likely overreacting, but I can't take that chance. Not with Penny, and not with her safety.

"You're going the wrong way. You know that, right?" My voice is intentionally cold, the tone I use to snip and snipe at her, riling her up and pissing her off. I hate it. Every time I do it, it kills a tiny part of me, but I do it anyway, again and again, because it's the only way I've found to keep the necessary buffer between us. Anything else I could try would likely hurt her more in the long run, and I can take losing bits of my soul if it's for her.

Penny stops almost instantly, and I can see her erecting her defenses before facing me, her posture straightening, her head lifting, and her intake of breath sharp.

Even so, when she does turn, she looks . . . defeated. Her amber eyes, usually so full of life and happiness, are hollow and sad. Her lips, always so quick with a friendly smile, are turned down into a pout that, while adorable, breaks my heart. "It's gone."

Her fire is extinguished. Like someone doused water on her spirit. No, like I drowned it. But there are still embers in her soul, and I can ignite them. It just takes . . .

"That's it? You're giving up that easily? Two stores, and you throw in the towel like this is a participation-ribbon peewee league where everyone gets fruit snacks and a high five after the game?" I huff out a dry laugh. "I thought you were made of sturdier stuff than that. Didn't realize you were such a weak bitch that one little setback would send you crying to your room, curled up and woe-is-me'ing about how the big, bad world was mean to you." I round my shoulders, miming like I'm sucking my thumb and pouting out my bottom lip. It's a fair estimation for how she looks right now, minus the thumb-sucking.

It hurts to do, but it works. Every word has fanned her flames. I can damn near see them getting brighter, growing bigger behind her eyes. And all the while, my soul goes darker and uglier.

"Excuuuse me?" she snaps. "You did not just say that. Take it back." She steps right up to me, her chin lifted defiantly and her eyes full of fury.

There she is. There's my Penny.

I mean, not *my* Penny. But her Penny. Herself. That's what I meant.

I lean down, getting so close that I smell the coffee on her breath and the vanilla body wash she uses. "No."

She makes a sound of offense that I take secret delight in and then plants her hands on my chest, giving me a hard shove, and nearly falling in the process. How does this woman, who is all elegant grace on the ice and ass-shaking on the cheerleaders' stage, manage to nearly fall when pushing against an immoveable mass? No idea, but she does it. Seemingly easily.

"God, you're such an asshole. No, worse! You're like a hemorrhoid on an asshole."

Her tiny growl is the cutest thing I've ever heard. And reassures me that she's still fighting . . . for the ring, for herself, for more than she realizes.

"Yep," I readily agree. "Doesn't mean I'm not right about you, ya big crybaby." This time, it's teasing. It's the cutting remarks we always engage in as I work us back to the safety of treating her like an annoying brat the way Dom does. It's the only safe space for us. "Ready for the next store now?"

I half expect her to continue stomping away in the same direction she was going, which I'll have to stop because, though I've been teasing Penny, I've also noticed that the hulking guy hasn't reappeared down the block and could still be lurking in wait for her. Thankfully, she seems to have heard my initial question about going the wrong way and walks back past me in the opposite direction.

"Coming?" she throws over her shoulder.

I glance down the street once more, questioning if I overreacted in the first place. Still not seeing anything, I rush to follow Penny. Her ass, covered in denim that hugs her curves just right, is swinging side to side, taunting me with every step.

"I wish," I mutter under my breath.

Chapter 10

Penny

It's the same story at the next two pawnshops. We go in, ask if they have the ring, show them the picture, and they say no. My ridiculously optimistic, high hopes of recovering the stolen jewelry are falling further and faster with every minute.

And though I did have that one moment of weakness earlier, I've done my best to stay positive, promising myself the next store would be the one and cheering myself up after every no and invitation to get the fuck out. On the upside, I'm solidly maintaining my streak of being wrong, and so far, I'm zero for four—striking out at Paul's, A-to-Z, Cash-a-rama, and a no-name place that really set Griffin off.

He's usually grumpy and snappish, but he was downright hostile to the clerk at that last store. Okay, so yeah, the guy was flirting with me, but I can handle myself.

Usually.

Except right now, I really don't want to deal with guys who try to "c'mon, baby" me into giving them my Instagram handle so they can "slide into my DMs and maybe me" later. *Blech.* Which is what I literally said out loud to the guy. That apparently hurt his *wittle feelwings*, and he had to let me know that I wasn't "that cute" anyway. As if. I'm fucking adorable and I know it. I'd been ready to hair flip out the door and head to the next stop, but Griffin had already nearly taken the guy's head off, calling him a Fleshlight fuckboy.

Yeah, it was kinda funny, leaving both me and the clerk slack-jawed in shock, but peeling Griffin off other guys is getting to be exhausting. On the ice is one thing, but in day-to-day life? I mean, has he heard of therapy? It'd probably do him some good to work on communication that doesn't involve threats of violence when things don't go his way.

It was kinda hot, though.

Sigh. Maybe I need some therapy, too, because growly, asshole, fight-first types are not my type. Never have been, never will be, and one day with Griffin certainly isn't enough to change that given all the times he's acted like my very existence was bothersome. My body's probably just confused from spending all day surrounded by his cologne and weird kindness, which is probably his intent anyway. I wonder if it's some new tactic in our ongoing battle of who hates whom more?

Why does he smell like sex and pine trees, and why do I like that? And I love—I mean hate!—that he opens doors for me when I'm perfectly capable of doing it myself.

Pulling the now folded-and-refolded list from his pocket, Griffin looks at it thoughtfully. His full lips are pressed into a hard, flat line, and his eyes are squinted like he's staring at one of those hidden-image pictures where you have to stare through it to reveal the secret. Unfortunately, I don't think there's any mysterious message in Paul's chicken scratch.

Scrubbing a hand over the scruff on his jaw, Griffin peeks up at me through lashes so thick and long they make me jealous, and asks, "Where to next?"

"My internal toaster just popped with one of those irritating buzzy sounds that threaten possible electrocution if I don't stop." I wiggle my hand by my ear like I actually hear buzzing, and Griffin looks at me like I'm speaking gibberish, which, to be fair, I might be because he looks really sexy right now, and that's a sure sign that my brain has turned to mush. Because while he is obviously objectively attractive, I have never considered the words *Griffin* and *sexy* in the same sentence in my life. *Griffin* and *woodchipper*? Yes. *Griffin* and *grump-apota-saurus*? Obviously. Who hasn't? But *sexy* is a new one to me where he's concerned, which is . . . *concerning*, possibly to the point of an "am I having a stroke?" danger zone.

The loss of the ring must be getting to me. It's the only explanation. Well, either that or the lunch we grabbed from a potentially sketchy food truck contained hallucinogenic aphrodisiacs, in which case, I really need to get home before the buzzy sound in my head leads me to search out another type of buzzing. One thing I know for sure is that I do not want to ride a Molly trip with Griffin as the closest human being. I once witnessed a girl dry-humping a frat boy's leg, and that was enough for me to know that wasn't for me. Especially since it wasn't even his thigh but his shin, which seems exponentially worse.

Point being, I'm coming to terms with not finding the ring. I think I started to hit the acceptance stage of grief a couple of stores ago, and now, the process is nearly complete. I just need a few minutes alone, curled up in a nest of blankets, screaming into the void . . . or a pillow, because despite Mrs. Rosenthal's opinion, I am a considerate neighbor, and I'll be okay.

Eventually.

I always am. Life pulls this shit with me all the time—handing me lemons, knocking me out, and then kicking me while I'm down. But what do I do? Handle that shit like the badass chaos queen that I am. I wake up from the dirt nap, act like that was totally on purpose by making a dirt angel, and then serve up a homemade lemonade with a smile. All without losing my crown since I've got lots of practice keeping it righted on my head amid the disarray of my existence.

And this speed bump in the road of Penelope Lee will be the same as every other obstacle I've faced, in my rearview mirror, and nothing more than a chapter in my memoir, which I've tentatively titled *What Not To Do When the Universe Sends You a Glitter Bomb of a Day*. I think it's gonna be a *New York Times* bestseller for sure.

"You're off the hook. I'm going home. I'm gonna file this under 'Lessons Learned' and hope to never get a repeat lesson." I hold my hand out, offering a handshake. "Thank you for your help."

Griffin glowers at my hand like the polite offer outright offends him. Or maybe it's just me that irritates him, because he blurts out, "Just like that? You're giving up that easily?"

"Ouch," I snap. "No, not 'just like that.' It's hard, and I'm pissed! It sucks, and it hurts, and I'm pissed—and yeah, I know I already said that, but I really, really am." I throw my hands out. "What else am I gonna do?"

I once saw a T-shirt that said something like "don't you dare tell me what to do, but also . . . could you tell me exactly, step-by-step, what to do?" That's kinda how I feel like now. If Griffin has an answer, I'd love to hear it. I'll be mad as hell that he does when I don't, but I'm also mad that he doesn't have an answer when I don't. Can he win? No. Can I? Also no. But life isn't always logical. Hell, in my experience, I've found it rarely is.

I might not have high hopes left, or an ounce of go-get-'em remaining, but apparently, I do have some fire in me. There's also the slightest chance it's arousal, but I'm going to ignore that entirely, and stick with what I know—anger, which I take out on Griffin.

"Well? If you've got a better idea, I'm waiting to hear it." I blink, waiting expectantly. When he stays silent, his glare inching closer to a warning look, I assume a smug smirk. "Didn't think so. So this—whatever this is"—I wave a hand between us—"is over. I won't say a word to Dom, which means you're free and clear. *Go on, get, you stupid mutt, I don't want you anymore.*"

"Did you just *Air Bud* me?" He scoffs.

I make a shooing motion, hoping he'll take what's not even a hint but an explicitly spelled-out dismissal, and leave me alone.

I should feel guilty about it because the truth is, he doesn't deserve it. The thief targeting the bag isn't Griffin's fault, not really, but he's become one of my favorite punching bags. This is how we are, and right now, I really need to hit something, to rage and fight against the unfairness of the whole situation, and he's standing right here in front of me, with those broad shoulders that can carry the weight of the world and thick skin that nothing gets through. And he already hates me, so witnessing my poor-me pity party won't change a thing.

Griffin has crossed his arms over his chest, taking every sharp word I spit, every bit of my anger, and giving zero reaction to any of it. His stone-cold facade never shows a single crack. "You done yet?"

He doesn't mean with the ring hunt but rather with my tantrum, because if I'm honest, that's what it was. Can you blame me, though? I've got $10,000 on the line, a guy who hates my guts confusing me by acting all sweet, and my plans for taking my work to the next level poofing into the ether. In my estimation, I'm entitled to a moment of hysterical verbal shit-slinging, and I'm taking full advantage of it.

I sigh, my shoulders dropping. "I'm gonna go home, cry my way through a box of Thin Mints with Talia—one of the prized freezer packs we save up for special occasions—and then figure out how to recover financially from this before the credit card bill comes due. I might be unlucky as hell, but I'm a businesswoman at heart, and I will figure this out."

Griffin clenches his teeth, the muscle in his jaw popping out and disappearing again hypnotically. It's obviously not the answer he expected, and I don't think he has any idea how to respond to my mercurial mood swings. After a solid fifteen seconds of staring at me like he's waiting for me to take it all back and pick another pawnshop to go to, he inhales deeply. "Okay."

And that's that. The search is over. The day is done. Our choose-your-own-misadventure is complete without a happy ending. Of any sort . . . until he pulls his phone out of his pocket and clicks around, then looks up and down the street. "There's our rideshare. Let's go."

He grabs my hand, pulling me toward the black Camry, and I jerk out of his grip. "What are you doing? I can take the subway home."

He snorts out a laugh like I've said something funny. "Get in the car, Penny. I'm taking you home."

He says it like there's no discussion to be had, but I can argue with a brick wall. Hell, I basically am considering Griffin's a blank, detached, building-size humanoid. "This morning we were in a hurry. And the other stores were far away. Home is a straight shot on the A Line."

"Uh-huh." He's agreeing with me, except I don't think it actually counts as agreement when he's simultaneously opening the car door and pushing me inside. Not to the point of alarming the driver or having me shout out about being kidnapped, but he's definitely not letting me head toward the subway station either. He even puts a hand on my head, guiding me into the car so I don't bump it on the doorframe.

In the back seat, I cross my arms over my chest. Refusing to look at him, I snap, "Girls hate it when you do that."

"Do what?"

Whipping a spite-filled glare his way, I inform him, "Push their heads down."

The driver clears his throat to cover his laugh as he pulls into the street.

"Are we talking about me making sure you didn't get a concussion from getting in the car? Because we both know that's something you'd do." Griffin lifts one brow, daring me to disagree when we both know he's right.

"And it's my head to bang against whatever I want to. Doorframes, headboards, my hand." I slap my temple against my palm to demonstrate and then let my head fall back against the headrest of the seat with a sigh. Eyes closed, I murmur, "I bet you're one of those bossy alphaholes that 'encourages' girls to suck you off by pushing them toward your dick. Trust me, she knows where it is, and if she wanted to, she would."

"What the fuck are you talking about?" he barks, harsher than I expect. I crack one eye, feeling like I've hit a particularly sensitive nerve and not wanting to miss the moment of clarity when the truth of his actions hits him. But instead of having a revelation about his own cringeworthy behavior, he's judging me and my past. "Did somebody do that to you? Who?"

He sounds furious—no, maybe lethal—but also shocked for some reason. That's probably a sign that he's not one of those guys, which is good. For the puck bunnies, I mean. Not me. I don't care at all. Not a bit, not even a teeny-tiny, itty-bitty bit.

I fight to hide the grin trying to steal across my face, the result of successfully getting a rise out of him, and instead shrug dismissively. "Seriously, it's too high of a percentage to count without fingers and toes getting involved. Don't make me math right now."

"Penelope."

What makes him think he has the right to full-name me in that warning tone? Dom doesn't even do that. Very often. Though that's probably where Griffin got the idea to push me that way. Unfortunately, it works, bringing out every bit of brattiness I possess.

"Fine. You want to do this?" I challenge. "High school boyfriend, college boyfriend, guy at a frat party, a guy from Tinder, another guy from Tinder . . ." I wiggle my fingers like counting is hard and let my voice trail off.

Unfortunately, all that is true. And then some. I haven't had the best luck with dating. I'm a lot, I know that, but I'm not looking for someone who wants me to dull my shine for them. I'm looking for someone who sees me shining and cheers louder than anyone, for someone who catches me when I trip over my own feet (literally or metaphorically) and tells me the unexpected "solo" was an exciting addition to the plan. In my limited experience, that seems to be a tall order, and an impossible find. But when you're as desperate as I am, turning to Tinder for actual dates and not just hookups, bad luck in the extreme is to be expected, and good guys are not.

"High school boyfriend Cooper? College boyfriend Tyler? Got them. Who's the frat guy and the Tinder guys?" Griffin is trying to be nonchalant about that list, but he's about as *chalant* as you can get, and it sounds more like a hit list than a recitation of my past lovers. Not that I slept with all those guys. They're just the ones that immediately came to mind with the head-push move.

Hell, the last Tinder guy had barely kissed me before he was shoving me southward and settling into his seat like he was ready to be serviced. No, just no. That was when I deleted the app and went on a dating strike that lasted until I went out with Jacob, and we all know how that turned out with Dom's Middle Ages approach to my dating life.

"Wait, how do you know my high school and college boyfriends' names?" I ask, suddenly wide awake and staring at Griffin in horror.

It's his turn to shrug dismissively. "Dom talks about you. He worries."

It feels like he's leaving something out there, like maybe he worries too. But that doesn't make sense. Griffin probably wishes my brother were an only child. If that were the case, he wouldn't get roped into going on wild-goose chases for stolen rings that will never be found with emotionally messy drama queens. Not that I'm usually this hysterical, but he hasn't exactly seen me at my best in the last two days. For completely reasonable, understandable reasons.

"Dominic is a pain in my ass."

"But you love him. And he loves you," Griffin counters.

He's right, and we both know it. Still, I steel my face, unwilling to give him the satisfaction of agreeing with him, even though it's true. I do love my brother. He's the best brother a girl could hope for. Except when he's controlling and thinks he knows better than I do what's good for me. But other than that, he's the best. And fine, even his annoying overbearingness comes from a place of love, so I can't be too mad about it.

"He talks about you all the time, you know that, right?" Griffin continues, not put off by my silence. "About how brave you are for dropping out of college and starting a business, about what a creative genius you are, seeing potential in ugly shit no one else wants, and about how you never let an obstacle get in your way. You just bulldoze right over anything or anyone that tries to block you on the path to making your dreams come true."

He watches me as he speaks, his look considerably softer than the hostile glares he usually offers me. He's looking at me like he believes what Dominic says about me too.

But I'm not brave. I flunked out of my college classes because I was already too busy trying to build PLDesigns to study for a history test or do a psychology project I didn't care about. And I'm creative for sure, but a genius? I don't need a Mensa test to know that's not the case. As for obstacles? I definitely go right over them, but it's not a bulldozer situation. It's a stumble-and-tumble type deal.

I once read a quote that said it's not about how many times you fall but how many times you get back up. Over the years, I've fallen roughly a million times. But I'm still getting up every time. Including now.

I can feel the hot prick of tears in the corners of my eyes. "Did he really say all that?" I question, wanting to believe it, but also all too aware that we're talking about my brother, Dominic, who's more prone to kicking ass than offering kind words.

"Yeah." Griffin nods. "That, and that you're unbelievably annoying, can't drive for shit, and could trip over an invisible rock a hundred yards away." He ticks off those attributes on his fingers, and I can't help but look at his hands. His knuckles are rough, showing a lifetime of impact, his fingers long and thick, and the overall size is somewhere around that of a dinner plate. "Wait, maybe it was me who said that part?"

He tilts his head like he's trying to remember if it was him or Dom. It works, I laugh, the contrast in Griffin's tone and words drying up my tears before they can fall. "Thanks, Griffin." He shrugs like it's nothing, but the momentary sweetness means something to me. So does the teasing. It's familiar like a comfy pair of jeans. "He talks about you too," I taunt, planning to say something nice to him for a change too.

He tenses, every muscle suddenly hard as a rock, and I can feel the dread emanating from him like a visceral thing in the back seat between us. I swear I can almost hear the high-alert warning sirens going off in his mind behind his sharp brown eyes. "What did he say?"

Dominic has said a lot of things about Griffin. That he had a shitty childhood and is no contact with his parents, that a high school hockey coach saved him from ending up as another juvenile delinquent or prison statistic, that he went straight to a development team because hockey was all he had, and that playing in the NHL was his one and only end goal, so now he's in a constant state of *now what*. That his walls are built up taller and stronger than a fortress, that he doesn't trust easily or fully, that he's a no-strings-attached guy with women, and that he's the only guy Dominic would want at his back if he was going into battle, because Griffin is both loyal and completely stone cold. His heart beats in his chest, but it doesn't beat in his soul because it died long ago. Okay, that last bit is my creative liberty with what Dom said, which was closer to Griffin being an emotionless zombie, but I think it's more accurate.

Griffin isn't ready to hear any of that. In fact, I think it might piss him off to know that Dominic has told me, Mom, and Dad any of his personal trauma and damage. Instead, I grin and tell him something else entirely true. "He said you're his favorite asshole."

A sprinkle of fondness, tempered with a touch of crude. Perfect.

The gruff laugh that rumbles Griffin's chest feels like a win, and after today, I could really use one. "Other than himself, you mean," he corrects.

I nod, laughing my own agreement about my arrogant bastard of a brother whom we both love dearly. We fall into comfortable silence for the rest of the ride back to my apartment, and when the driver pulls over to the curb, Griffin gets out and holds his hand out to help me from the car. It feels like a trick, so I intentionally ignore it and get out on my own, without tripping and everything. I should get an award.

"Thanks for going with me today." Mom would be proud of my manners. I might not be Griffin's biggest fan, nor he mine, but I do recognize that it was nice of him to escort me to the sketchy stores. I would've gone, with or without him—I wasn't lying about that—but it was definitely quicker and safer with him at my side.

"You're welcome."

I expect him to casually wave before hopping back in the car to go home, but instead he walks toward the door of my building. I freeze, staring at his back. His very wide, muscled back. "What are you doing?"

Annoyingly never missing a step, he glances over his shoulder. "Walking you to your door."

"Why?" I ask, more confused about that than almost anything else today. Griffin should be eager to get rid of me, especially after a day of dealing with my roller coaster of emotions, the highs of my hopes and the lows of my letdowns over and over again, especially when they're mixed with my rambling and tangents, a.k.a. *side quests*, as I like to consider them.

"Just get inside," he says with a heavy sigh.

Fine, I guess we're doing this. For no good reason. Because it's definitely not a date, where the guy walks you to your front door. And we're not friends who take care of each other. He probably just wants to make sure I don't trip walking up the stairs or something. Dom would kill him if I got hurt mere seconds after he released me into the wild. That's got to be it.

At my door, he pauses, and I search his face, trying to figure out what is going on inside that thick skull of his. Something, obviously, but his expression is inscrutable.

If this were a date, I might think he was trying to decide whether to try for a kiss since he's standing nearly toe to toe with me and his brown eyes are locked on mine. But if eyes are the windows to the soul, Griffin's are so shuttered that I couldn't tell you if his soul is even in there.

And he definitely has less than zero interest in kissing me. Not that I want that either!

Maybe there's something on my face? Or pepper in my teeth? Surely not! The food truck lunch we had was hours ago, and he would've told me before now, right? I laugh internally at my own naivete because, no, Griffin wouldn't have. He would've let me walk around with pepper, broccoli, and whole grains of rice in my teeth, smiling at everyone I passed, and never saying a word, laughing at me the entire time.

I lick my lips unconsciously, letting my tongue quickly slick over my teeth, but find no stray bits of lunch. I swear he tracks the movement, and I frown, preparing for one of his textbook-standard, jabbing insults.

"I'm sorry."

He says it so quietly that I might've imagined it, then quickly whirls on his heel, striding down the hall.

Sorry for what? That we didn't find the ring? It was a long shot. I'd hoped, really hoped, we would, but deep down, I knew it wasn't likely. Still, I don't call out that it's okay as he rounds the corner. Instead, I watch his butt as he disappears.

I don't like him. And that was weird. But a nice ass is a nice ass, and Griffin has that *gyat-damn* posterior. That I'm totally *not* into since I like . . . um, short, skinny, nerdy guys who talk a lot and are in touch with their emotions. Yep, that's *totally* my type and I'm not overcompensating at all.

Inside, Talia is sprawled out on the couch, a bowl of popcorn at her side and a glass of wine in her hand. "Hey! Where've you been?" Given her Snoopy pajamas and freshly washed curls, she's been holding down the couch for a bit, and hasn't been outside today at all.

"It's a long story, which I'll share in one second, but first—"

I head over to the window and peek out, looking at the street in front of my building. I'm not sure what little voice in my head told me to do it, but I'm glad I do, because when Griffin appears, he looks . . . mad? I'm not sure that's exactly it, but his eyes are narrowed, his jaw is set, and his shoulders are down and back like he's trying to appear intimidating. It's the game face I've seen hundreds of times. He scans up and down the street in both directions for several seconds.

"What're we looking at?" Talia says from right beside me. "Oh! Griffin," she says casually. And then I feel her eyes land on me heavily and she screeches, "*OhmyGod!* Griffin! Girl, you need to start talking."

As though she's got an ear pressed to the wall and was just waiting for us to make a peep, Mrs. Rosenthal bangs three times.

I ignore them both in favor of continuing to look out the window.

"It's not like that." But something about the way he's searching the street has my Spidey senses tingling. Like he's looking for something, or someone. It hits me with a *duh*. "He's looking for Dom, probably scared my brother would murder him in broad daylight, no questions asked, if he saw us out together."

Talia gasps. Not about the murder, because she's seen Dom in action firsthand, but about Griffin and I being out together.

"No, not like that," I rush to explain. "I need a glass of wine too. And Thin Mints."

"On it," she replies, high-kneeing it to the freezer. "Are we celebrating? Or commiserating?"

"Both."

❧

"I feel like I've missed an entire season of my favorite show, and I was only gone for three days," Talia whines, throwing her head back against the couch and staring at the ceiling after I've told her everything from Carolynn's call to striking out on recovering the stolen ring.

She wasn't really *gone* gone. She's a radiology tech at one of the local hospitals and works three twelve-hour shifts each week. It's a great way to make full-time money, and gives her plenty of time off if she doesn't take extra shifts. Unfortunately, she's still too new to get the primo schedule, so her assignments are usually spaced out and then she's sleeping at odd hours. Mix that with my work-when-I-want jewelry business plus my practice and game schedule, and we sometimes go entire weeks without seeing each other in person, even though we're coming and going from the same apartment.

"Four. It's Thursday," I correct.

Talia's eyes pop as they jerk to mine. "It is not."

Nodding, I say, "Yes, it is. We had a single against the Beavers, then the whole ring situation happened, and there are games tomorrow and Saturday. Hawks versus Vortex."

The games are how I keep track of time, and for some reason, the logic works on Talia, too, though she has no interest in hockey despite living with me and our apartment being constantly invaded by two professional hockey players. Actually, it's probably a good thing she doesn't give a rat's ass about it, because if she flirted with Dom or Griffin when they came over, we would've never made it as roommates. Or best friends. And that would be a tragedy since she's one of the best human beings to ever grace the planet as far as I'm concerned.

"It's Thursday," she says flatly. "Oh my God, I work Sunday. I have just over forty-eight hours before going back. I can feel the minutes slipping through my fingers." She groans dramatically and virtually melts into the cushions, her arms and legs askew and her head lolled over to the side.

She looks on the edge of dying right on the green sofa we nearly came to blows over buying in the middle of IKEA. Not because we didn't both love it, but because it was over our budget and she wanted to pay the extra with her sign-on bonus from the hospital, which I vehemently disagreed with. In the end, we halved it, and she's currently lying on what I consider to be my half.

Talia's reluctance about going to work is unusual. She loves her job. Like she's one of the rare people who truly, deeply loves what she does.

"What's wrong?"

She exhales heavily. "Nothing."

Something is obviously wrong, and while she might not want to share, she needs to. It's for her own good. But I don't pry, at least not verbally. Instead, I hold up a Thin Mint and lift an eyebrow, the offer silent but there. It's a surefire winner. I just have to patiently wait for her to give in to the chocolatey bribe and veiled threat.

"Bitch," she mutters with less than zero heat, surrendering easily as she snatches the cookie and shoves it in her mouth. "We had a run of really hard cases. Motor vehicle accident with a van full of kids that all needed X-rays. Crying kids gut me."

She closes her eyes, seeing the kids in her mind. I'm sure she helped them and was as gentle and caring as possible, but it makes sense that she'd want a break before going back.

"They all okay?"

Eyes still closed, she nods. "Nothing permanent. A surgery here and a cast there. They were just so scared without their parents." She shakes her head hard like she's rattling the memories out. "Let's talk more about Griffin."

"Or the ring debacle," I suggest, stating the obvious priority. "What am I going to do?"

But Talia's unswayed by my focus on the real problem at hand. "You really think he eats ice cream at a cat-themed shop all the time?"

Of everything I told her, that's what she's stuck on? Seriously? "Apparently. The lady in there knew him by name."

"It seems so cute and sweet, especially since he's all growly and grunty. *Me, hockey man. You, go away.*"

It's a fair impression of Griffin's usual gruff, short rudeness, and usually, I'd laugh. But it feels wrong to do that after he was kind and helpful. I mean, he also did kinda get my ring stolen, but he's tried several ways to make up for that and fix it, and I'm not as mad at him. The situation? Abso-freaking-lutely. But Griffin? Not as much.

Though that might be the Thin Mints talking.

"You're smiling," Talia whispers, leaning my way with a grin of her own.

Immediately, my lips fall. "No, I'm not." That lady who protested too much? Yeah, that's me, doth protesting.

"Mm-hmm." She takes a heavy drink of her wine, her brows arched high on her forehead, not believing me a bit.

Later, after we've gone through an entire box of cookies, a bowl of popcorn, and DoorDashed salads—because balance is important—I check my phone. I half expect Griffin to have texted me, but that'd be weird. Or for Dom to have magically divined that something was amiss in his universe today because Griffin and I were together without him. But he hasn't texted either.

What is in my email inbox though is an inquiry from my PLDesigns website.

> You bought a ring at Yesteryear Antiques yesterday. I am very interested in purchasing it from you. Contact me as soon as possible.

Of freaking course. I would already have a buyer for a ring I no longer have in my possession. And not just a ring but The Ring. I swear the universe must be laughing its ass off at me this week. What's next . . . an audit? Immaculate conception? Hit by a bus on the way to the arena?

"Look at this." I hold my phone up to Talia so she can read the message.

"How do they know you bought a ring?"

"Carolynn has a stack of my business cards. She hands them out to people looking to sell jewelry or have pieces redone." I roll my head around, trying to get in the right headspace to respond, because I can't exactly tell someone interested in my designs, *Hey, sorry, there was an oopsie and I lost that super-duper valuable piece of jewelry, but don't worry, you can totally trust me with your expensive diamonds.* That does not set the proper tone for the business I run, or the businesswoman I am, despite current circumstances to the contrary.

I type out . . .

> Hello. Thank you for your inquiry. Unfortunately, that piece is no longer available. I have other designs on my website available for immediate purchase or would be happy to discuss a custom piece if you'd prefer. Have a great day. Sincerely, Penny Lee

I show the message to Talia, who nods. "That's some lipstick on a pig of this suck-tuation."

That it is.

I hit send and only cry a little at the loss of what would've been the sale of the year for me.

Chapter 11

Griffin

"Where the hell were you last night, asshole? Balls deep in some bunny, putting another notch in your bedpost?" It's more of an accusation than a question, as it's followed by a round of grunts that make me worry about Dom's bedroom vocalizations, because he sounds like he's trying to pass a kidney stone more than simulate sex noises.

I ignore him, keeping my eyes on the blades of my skates, where I'm doing my precheck for any irregularities. It's a habit I established long ago, and I let the routine pull me in, tuning out everyone and everything around me.

Or I try to, until a cold hand gooses me right at my waist.

"Goddamn it!" I grumble, flinching away and slapping at Dom's ice-cold hand. He must've come straight from the cold plunge tub to fuck with me.

"Damn, who pissed in your Wheaties this morning, Honey?" Dom taunts, his easy grin telegraphing that he has no idea why I bailed on him for our pregame dinner last night. It's not a given, but it's regular enough that turning down the invite likely drew suspicion. But I wasn't sure I could face him without spilling everything that's happened with Penny.

Not that anything has happened. Other than the stolen ring, of course.

I can't avoid him forever, though, and this morning's skate is the perfect example of that. Game-day preps are a mixed bag of sorts. When we're playing at home, most guys will hit the ice at some point to warm their muscles and get a light sweat on, do a check in with sports med if needed, then head home to nap, chill, and eat before going back to the arena for the game. On the road, it's pretty similar, although the morning skates are always a team event since we have to coordinate with the home team's ice time.

Today had no come-when-you-want skate option. Coach deemed it a mandatory morning skate for the entire team, which only shows how important tonight's game is.

"Probably your mom," Brody suggests unhelpfully. In sync, Dom and I turn evil glares his way. Nobody talks about Momma Lee like that, especially Brody. She's off-limits for "your mom" shit-talking, and everyone knows it because you'll get not only one but two pissed-off assholes coming after you in her defense.

"You wish my mom would piss in your Wheaties, bro-zo," Dom throws back at him, irritated but not ripping Brody's head off just yet. "Too bad she wouldn't piss on you even if you were on fire. She'd rip open some marshmallows and pass out graham crackers because you'd finally be useful for something."

A chorus of "oooh"s rings out before turning into good-natured chuckles.

With a grunt of forced laughter, I resume checking my skates, hoping to dismiss both Brody and Dom. No luck there, though. Dom sits down on the bench beside me, lowering his voice to keep the conversation between us. "You good, man? What's up?"

Tapping my temple, I tell him, "All good. Just getting my head right for tonight."

That's not true at all.

What I'm thinking about is whether I should say something to Dom before he discovers that I was out with Penny yesterday. Not *out*, like a date, but *out* like going all over town, eating at a food truck, taking her home, and dropping her off at her door.

Like a fucking date, you asshole.

It sounds bad. I know it does, but it so obviously wasn't a date. It was a search and recovery mission, and an unsuccessful one at that. But if someone else tells Dom before I do, there will be no coming back from that. He'll see it as a complete betrayal, which it is.

I should tell him.

But I don't.

Telling him would mean sharing one truth—that Penny and I hung out without him playing buffer—but hiding a much deeper, darker, uglier one—that I was *this close* to kissing her at her door. The only thing that stopped me was my preference for life topside of the ground, because Dom would destroy me, or anyone who touches his baby sister, and currently I'm the only one who knows Penny's in danger.

Which I'm going to figure out, and fix, without anyone being the wiser. I just don't know how . . . yet. Shit, I haven't even told Penny, which I really should at this point. Not telling her is more dangerous than anything else. And yet . . . I can't.

"We've got it in the bag. You know that," Dom scoffs.

Completely lost in thoughts of yesterday, it takes me a moment to remember what he's even talking about.

The game, idiot! The fucking game!

He's speaking a win into existence, not allowing any room for doubt to wiggle into his psyche, which is more important than one would think with such a physical game. Truthfully, more games are lost in the locker room than on the ice, and a single player can sink a whole team's season if their mind's not in the right space.

And he's right, for the most part. The past few seasons, we've beat the Vortex 95 percent of the times we've played them. They're perennial cellar dwellers who have one of those batshit owners who thinks he knows more than actual hockey professionals because he's got a billion or so dollars. We definitely need to take advantage of it this season again, focusing on the nearly guaranteed wins we've got tonight and tomorrow.

But there's more to it than simple statistics. The Vortex is our geographically closest team, which means the games are always well attended. The energy of a full arena is infectious and addicting, and can make it all too easy to get distracted, and distractions can mean scores . . . for the other guys.

We need this win tonight. It'll set up our momentum for tomorrow night, and three wins this week can snowball us into next week's games against the tough-to-beat Torches, which will in turn send us right into the playoffs. That we are going to win. No questions, no hesitation, "no regrets," as Brody would say. I've never hoisted a Stanley Cup yet . . . and I'm going to fix that, come hell or high water.

"Yeah, I know. I'm solid."

Unfortunately, I am not solid. I'm liquid, gas, hell, I might be a wisp of water vapor for as hard and unyielding as I feel right now.

I can feel Dom's eyes searching my face, and fearing he might see the lie plainly written there, I get up to shuffle around in my locker.

"Honey."

"Yeah?" I bury my face in my bag, moving clothes here and there like I'm looking for something when I'm just hiding from Dom's too-perceptive gaze.

"You and me, two against the world." I don't have to turn around to know that he's holding his fist up.

All guys have some internal hype track they tell themselves, and when Dominic and I started as rookies, feeling each other out and learning how we could use each other to improve our zone on the ice, those words became our vow to each other. We hit the ice as a team, but more importantly, Dom and I skate out there as brothers, the two of us at each other's backs, no matter what.

That's why I'm loyal to Dom. In those early days, I was an angry loner with something to prove, fighting against everything and tackling anything I could. I'd shoved my damage down to the point where my rage was mostly confined to the ice, but even there, I was a wild monster. The chatter about me during the draft centered around people placing bets on how quickly I'd end up benched or banned from the league. Honestly, I loved it. It felt good to let loose and to be celebrated for the violence that seemingly came naturally to me. Guess it was the one valuable thing my dad taught me—fight everyone and everything like your next breath depended on you winning the throwdown, because, often, it did.

But pretty quickly, Dominic started helping me channel my whiplash-fast temper until I became the player I am today, still as monstrous but less wild and more intentional about my attacks. Without him, I wouldn't have made it this far, and it was a no-brainer to sign with the Hawks when free agency came around. I stuck with Dom so I wouldn't end up an often missed trivia question about that hockey player has-been who crashed out and bombed his chance at the big show. I owe him everything, especially something as small as not touching his baby sister, which is the only thing he's ever asked of me. It's the only rule our motley team stands on—jokes about moms and sisters might be par for the course, but hands off or you'll end up with your hands (cut) off.

I grit my teeth as I turn around, praying I've schooled my face enough to hide the multitude of sins I've committed, and move to tap his fist with mine.

He jerks away, and my stomach drops out my ass for a split second until he grabs my fist in both of his hands, opening and closing his clawed fingers around it to "bite" my wrist. "Baby shark, doo doo doo doo do doo, baby shark." His grin is a complete gotcha.

"Shut the fuck up, Dominic!" Coach calls out, coming out of his office with impeccable timing.

But it's too late. Brody, with a set of brass balls or maybe a death wish, starts singing off-key at the top of his lungs. "Mommy Shark, doo doo doo . . ." He grabs imaginary breasts in his hands, and guys start laughing as his show ramps up. By the time he gets to Daddy Shark with a jerk-off motion, even Howe is guffawing.

"Hit the ice and get your morning skate in," Coach orders, probably fearing the accompanying moves for Grandma and Grandpa Shark. Honestly, I'm scared of what Brody would come up with too. Probably something to do with a blow job and no teeth. "Game meeting in thirty."

"You're lucky Coach likes you," I whisper to Dom as I finish lacing my skates. I feel a bit more even-keeled after the stupid sing-along.

Are we grown-ass men, some of whom will end the night with bruises, bloodstains, and possibly a few rattled brain cells? Yes. Are we also idiots who will sing an annoying kids' song just to piss off Coach and pull smiles from the grumpiest of us? Also yes. Even me, maybe especially me.

"Ha! Everyone likes me. I'm Dominic Lee, how could they not?" He seems genuinely confused at the idea that someone might not entirely, deeply love him.

As fucked up as my childhood was, and with the resulting damage that comes with it, Dom is the opposite. Loved, supported, and cheered on as a child, his self-esteem is near unshatterable, his confidence unmatched. And he generously shares that with me in so many ways.

I will never be able to repay him for what he's done for me—with hockey, with his family, with his friendship. He took me under his wing, accepted me into his world, and rehabbed me like a feral honey badger into the slightly less rabid honey badger I am now.

Bumping Dom's shoulder as I pass him on the ice, I say, "Thanks, man."

Thirty minutes later, Coach has given us the breakdown for tonight's game, which basically consists of "you'd better fucking win, dipshits" but said in a much less poetic way. The end-of-the-season stress is getting to us all. We have a real shot at going all the way this year, and that brings tension to everything.

We can't afford any distractions. We need to stay singularly focused on winning. Normally, that'd be no problem for me. But right now, I'm more worried about Miles Conniver's goons tracking down Penny for a pretty ring than I am about a shiny trophy.

And that's the most shocking thought I've ever had.

That shiny trophy has been my goal for my entire life, the thing that will give validation to my whole existence, showing I am worth something, even if my parents couldn't be bothered to pretend they believed that for eighteen measly years. To them, I was an inconvenience, an expense, a worthless sack of shit they didn't want, as they never hesitated to tell me. I don't expect them to come crawling back if I'm suddenly on the front page of the paper, but I might harbor a secret dream of Dad seeing my face and realizing that he was wrong about me all those years ago.

After our morning skate, I go home automatically. Hell, I do everything on autopilot. First, I slug a high-calorie smoothie that's easy on my stomach and will get my carb and electrolyte count up for tonight. Before I know it, the glass is empty, and I rinse it, putting it in the dishwasher. Next, I sit in the shower for thirty minutes, letting the hot water pound my back and rain down over my head. The whole time, I play out the game in my head, watching moves I've seen from the Vortex in the past and beating them to the punch every time. After, I dry off and chug a water bottle in one go, knowing I need to stay hydrated.

Lying down on my bed, I set an alarm for three thirty, which will give me time to get back to the arena, do the press walk in, and hit the locker room.

All this is normal, just like any other game day, something I've done hundreds of times before. Except this time, lying here, all I can think about is Penny. I feel like I need to check on her.

Surely, she didn't go back out today without me? She wouldn't do that. Would she?

She absolutely would, with zero qualms or hesitation. But she has a game tonight, too, and a pregame schedule to adhere to.

I wonder what that looks like for her.

I'm ashamed to say I have no idea. I've never given a shit about the cheerleaders' schedule on game days, and while I've always cared about Penny, I've done too good of a job at keeping her at arm's length. Now that I'm worried, I don't know if I should be.

Is she practicing for tonight's performance or taking a nap? Is she doing her hair and makeup with the girls or chilling at home? Is she . . . fuck, is she being tracked down by those goons right now?

I toss and turn, staring at the ceiling and wall before repeating the pattern again.

I could call her. Apologize again, or ask if the Thin Mints helped soothe her broken heart, or just ask if she's okay. That wouldn't be weird, would it?

It definitely would be. And a move like that will only make it harder to act like the asshole she expects next time she, Dom, and I hang out. Because that can't change. Two days of uncharacteristic niceness on my part won't be enough for her to reconsider her opinion of me, but it might make it harder for me to continue being the asshole I always am. She's too real, too raw, too special to keep treating like the bratty annoyance she thinks I see her as.

But I'll have to do it. There's no other option, and ultimately, I just need there to be a next time we hang out, and for Penny to not get further caught up in whatever Mob drama has come to bear at her doorstep.

That's got to be my focus.

And, oh yeah, the fucking game.

Chapter 12

PENNY

"Five, six, seven, eight!"

Layla counts us down and, as a team, we walk onto the ice, waving our poms at the crowd. Yes, walk in tennis shoes, not skates. Why? Because *dance*, which isn't really an answer, but also . . . very much is.

Over the sound system, the announcer shouts, "And here's to the flyest cheerleaders in the league, our Ice Hawkettes!"

There's a few "ca-caw" callouts that break through the roar in my head, but beyond that, I don't hear the crowd as we take our starting positions. It's showtime, and whether they're ignoring us in favor of ordering a beer from one of the vendors that walk the arena or laser-locked on us, it's all the same to me. It's time to work . . . and *work*.

I didn't always want to be a cheerleader. Once upon a time, I was a figure skater who lived, breathed, and dreamed of spins and jumps. While Dominic would practice hockey on one end of the rink, bragging about how he'd be an NHL pro one day, I'd be at the other end, pretending I was the star of *Disney on Ice* when I was young, and later, imagining that I was competing at the Olympics. Unfortunately, only one of us took it as far as we dreamed, which is why there are people in the audience tonight wearing my brother's jersey number.

I might've gone further if it hadn't been for the coach I had the year I turned fourteen, who was strict to the point of abusive, and by the time my parents figured out why I was suddenly stressing about the puberty-driven changes to my body, the damage had been done to my love of the sport.

But I still loved many aspects of figure skating, like the choreography, the movement, and the performance. So I found a way to turn the body that was deemed too short and too curvy for figure skating into a plus by becoming a cheerleader in high school. There, I focused on power and projection, precision and passion, and with my background, I was a force to be reckoned with.

When Dom got drafted into the pros, my parents and I went to all his games, and I had another brilliant idea when I saw the cheerleaders. They were the best of everything I love—dance, cheer, and skating—and a new dream was born. When he got traded to the Hawks, I secretly tried out and became a Hawkette the next year, and this is my third season with them, making me one of the veterans.

The music starts, and we begin to move as one, our well-rehearsed routine flying by in what seems like warp speed. At the same time, it's slow motion, the movements automatic, letting me simultaneously smile and wink and engage with the audience in front of me, demanding their attention and working hard to keep it.

Somehow, I manage to do it all without stumbling a bit on the slippery ice. In my regular life, I'm a disaster waiting to happen, tripping over my own feet and attracting drama at every turn, but when I'm performing, nothing can stop me and I ooze confidence in every step. It makes no logical sense, but I've long ago given up on figuring out the hows and whys of it, and just appreciate that I haven't eaten ice in the middle of a performance . . . yet.

Too quickly, since I don't want to leave this graceful zone of existence, the last note plays, and we hold our ending pose for a beat, letting the applause sound out before we start waving and clapping our poms together. I see a little girl in one of the lower sections waving back excitedly and give her an extra-big smile.

We carefully make our way to the gate, lining up for the player announcements and entrances as the announcer starts down his roster. He begins with the visitors, calling out the Vortex players, and above us, on the jumbotron screen, the guys' pictures and stats appear. As they pass us by, we clap politely, keeping smiles plastered on our faces, though there's a fair amount of racket in here, as their fans have shown up in force.

Then it's the Hawks' turn, an entirely different experience. Our smiles are real, the claps proud, and the fans go nuts, chanting players' names and banging on the glass in front of them.

"Dominic Lee!"

As my brother passes me, I chirp out, "No mercy, Dom!" He flashes me a cocky grin as he turns to skate onto the ice backward, mouthing *no mercy here* as he thumps his chest. He's such an arrogant bastard, and though I can't roll my eyes at his antics when I'm on the ice, he knows exactly what I'm thinking.

"Griffin Mahoney!"

I flip my attention back to the monster entering the rink. With there being a solid foot of difference between our heights, Griffin always towers over me, but when he comes toward me with an extra couple of inches from his skates and several inches wider from the shoulder pads, I feel tiny. But the quick side-eye he shoots my way has me feeling ten-feet tall and bulletproof because the fire in that look is new.

Not cold. Not annoyed. Not dismissive. Nope, I might not be a body language pro who can decipher men with pinpoint accuracy, but that look was . . . something I don't have a name or label for. And while I'm considering buying one of the fancy thermal label makers to organize my work at home, I probably shouldn't make a cute pink tag that says "Honey" on it because . . . it's still *Griffin*.

And he hates me. Right?

Except that look wasn't one of hate, right? Maybe a day with me has led him to succumb to my considerable charms. And I don't mean my boobs, which are great but were covered in a T-shirt yesterday for our Tour de Pawn. I mean maybe, after years of trying and a few more years of saying, *Fuck it,* he's finally decided to like me. Or at least, not hate me, which is nearly the same thing in my book.

Are we becoming friends?

The idea doesn't seem as preposterous as it did a few short days ago.

"Good luck, Griffin!" I cheer, happy to have made some progress with the brute.

He flinches, and I swear I see his chest rise sharply like he sucked in a breath. It takes me a second to realize my mistake and correct myself. "I mean, good luck, Honey!"

I can't help but grin at the progress we've made. Three measly days ago, he was glaring at me like he wished I hadn't invaded the pregame dinner at Pro-Bowl. Now, we're on a first-name basis, and I even used his nickname, which sounds dangerously close to an endearment. Maybe by the next time we see each other, he'll actually call me Penny without it sounding like a curse word. It's a new goal, I decide.

I don't get to plot that out any further than deciding the colors of the friendship bracelet I'm going to make him—obviously Hawks black and gold—because it's time for the players to warm up and for the cheerleaders to either get up to our stage area for game-time performances or to put on skates to join the crew that clears the ice during breaks. Cheerleaders rotate between the roles, taking turns either performing or doing shovel skates, and tonight I'm headed up to dance for the whole game.

"I hate you, you know that, right?" Layla whispers once we're clear of the ice and the crowd and can be ourselves for a moment instead of our cheer-sonas.

I jerk my eyes her way. "What? We're besties. Like this, you and me." I cross my fingers and immediately drop my pom, of course kicking it straight into a security guard's booted foot. Making a sound of suffering, I mutter an apology as I quickly bend down to grab it, never missing a step.

"You hang out with two of the hottest guys on the team all the time. Eating dinner with them, going to the gym with them, sitting on the couch to watch *Bachelor Island* with them." Between the blissed-out smile, lovestruck eyes, and awestruck tone, she makes it sound like I've got a MFM throuple going down on the regular.

A laugh escapes hard and loud at her very wrong assumptions. "First of all, they don't watch *Bachelor Island*. Second of all, one of those hot guys"—I pause to stick my tongue out and gag—"is my brother. And the other one is like a brother. That's all kinds of ick."

She tilts her head, her brows fighting their Botox to furrow as she stares at me.

"What?"

"I'll give you that Dom is your brother. But Honey? He doesn't look at you like any brother I know. He looks at you like he wants to devour you. Did you hear that grunt he let out when you called him *Griffin*?" Her eyes roll back, her lashes fluttering. "God, I bet that man is a beast in bed."

"La la la la la," I intone, covering my ears with my poms. "Seriously, I wouldn't know. Now or ever. And if you find out, please don't tell me. I don't want to sit across the table from him at Pro-Bowl and pretend I don't know that he sweats like a wildebeest when he has sex."

She purses her lips like she's imagining that. And totally unprompted and unwanted, a vision pops into my mind—of Griffin hovering over me, his teeth gritted, his neck muscles popping out, and his eyes locked onto mine as he thrusts into me deep and hard. There's not a bead of sweat in sight, just pure, raw sex appeal. I shake my head, wishing I could unsee that image because it is dangerous . . . and stupid . . . and pointless.

We're barely becoming friends, like on the tippy-tappy fine line between forced acquaintanceship and friendship. So there's zero need, like *negative* need, for me to have even one little dirty thought about Griffin.

"Of the two of us, I think you're the one more likely to get that answer."

"Huh?" I almost missed what Layla said, but in the time it takes me to question her, what she's implying registers, and I act quickly to correct her. "Don't. Be. Ridiculous."

"Okay. If you say so." There's a glint in her eyes that says her words and her thoughts on this don't match up at all.

I'm not the one who'd get that answer. Griffin is barely starting to tolerate me. The last few days are probably like an allergy shot, exposing him to the thing that irritates him the most in the hopes that he'll start to be a little less reactive to it. That's all. What Layla has mistaken for a desire to devour me is merely not outright loathing.

There was that moment at the door where you thought he might kiss you.

The whisper in my mind sounds like the devil trying to confuse me. I did think that. For one blink of an eye. And then I remembered who he is and who I am, and how much he hates me. Add in the way he virtually bolted down the hall like he couldn't get away from me fast enough, and I was obviously misreading all the signs. It wouldn't be the first time that's happened. Just the worst person to have it happen with.

Oh God! What if he thought I wanted *him to kiss me?*

Maybe I was unintentionally sending signals, and that's why he skedaddled? That'd be just my bad luck. Hell, he probably told Dom that I threw myself at him like a standard-issue puck bunny and he had to let me down easy since me and him are an absolute no-way-not-happening thing. I bet they laughed and laughed at pitiful Penny.

Belated embarrassment at what's a much more likely possibility than what I'd considered last night runs through me, instantly making me hot and sweaty even though the arena is chilly.

As we get to the stage area that sits a level above the Hawks' goal, Layla and I split the middle line, the rest of the team falling into place around us. We prep for the next few hours of action. I start by fanning myself with my poms, plastering a fake smile on my face while my mind races.

The game begins with action from the first puck drop and never slows. It's like the Vortex and the Hawks are out for blood, a chance at the playoffs, or maybe both. Whereas the Beavers game was primarily played on their goal's end, tonight both teams are everywhere, looking for openings and dashing through them with precision. Each rotation is vicious, each opening exploited hard. Howe has blocked two shots on goal before we even hit the first media break.

The media breaks are when the fans watching at home will see a commercial or two. And while the game might not be continuous, in the arena, the activity never stops. Teams rotate players on and off the ice, making sure a fresh line is out, and coaches bark orders to their teams. The cheerleaders on the stage do short routines to the music pumped through the arena, hyping the crowd to keep the energy up, and the ice crew quickly shovels the ice's surface, clearing it of loose shavings.

Tonight, I'm thankful to be dancing because being too close to Griffin seems like a really bad idea. What if he reads into my casual use of his name the way Layla did? God, he is never going to let me live it down if he truly thinks I've suddenly gone all ooey-gooey, googly-eyed for him the way the puck bunnies do.

And he absolutely does not look at me like he wants to devour me. Layla is totally, 100 percent wrong about that. Mild non-loathing, that's all it is. Which is great, considering its progress, but there's definitely no eating of any sort going on here.

Still, poking the grumpy grizzly bear that seems to live inside Griffin is a bad idea, especially during a game this important. So, yep, it's a good thing I'm up here, cheering my heart out and shaking my ass . . . far, far away.

I only watch Griffin a little bit, all the while telling myself that I'm really watching Dominic play, the same way I have my whole life, as his biggest cheerleader. I almost believe it too . . .

"Ooooh!"

The audience reacts to a particularly aggressive play on the ice, where a duo of Vortex players try to sandwich Dom against the boards with a borderline blindside check. Griffin's right there, and he's pissed. I mean, *Honey*. Dom and Honey, the badass hockey players who have each other's backs.

"Shit," I whisper under my breath.

Griffin—I mean, Honey—throws his gloves to the ice and goes in on one of the Vortex players. Patterson, the larger of the two, of course. Meanwhile, Dom and the other player are fighting, but it's for show, some shoving and sweater pulling but nothing major. The real battle is Honey and Patterson.

My breath catches as I watch him do what he does best. Annihilate.

I'm torn between staring at the close-up on the jumbotron and the real action on the ice. Both are violent, and I find myself caring if Griffin gets hurt in a way I never have before.

Because we need him for the playoffs.

I don't even believe my own lie. Griffin's more than a caricature of an asshole to me now, more than the annoying jerk my brother brings around. He's Griffin, the guy who helped me yesterday when he didn't have to, and was mostly nice about it. And also, the guy I need to relieve of any misunderstandings about what happened at my door before he spreads that gossip any further.

"Get him!" I shout, sounding a bit too bloodthirsty for a proper cheerleader.

Thankfully, Layla doesn't scold me for it and instead gives me a knowing look as she mouths, *Beast*.

The whole thing feels like minutes but is actually only seconds, and when Honey pushes Patterson away, they're both grinning around their mouth guards like that was the most fun they've had in ages. Grabbing their gloves, they both skate to the penalty box, ready for their mutual five-minute time-out.

Play resumes, both teams shorthanded, and I finally breathe again.

By the final buzzer, I'm a wreck inside. Griffin has always been the enforcer for the Hawks, and I've seen him fight hundreds of times. Never has every single shoulder check, punch, or slam against the boards sent my heart rate skyrocketing and opened a pit in my stomach. But tonight? It felt like I was the one engaged in the violence on the ice. Well, probably not that painful, given I've seen some of the bruises and black eyes Griffin has had over the years, but my whole body is tight in a way that has nothing to do with the dancing that's second nature to me.

But the Hawks win, two to one, which is what matters, and I shake my poms overhead, smiling widely as I watch the players celebrate. Through the crowd of guys, I swear I see Griffin glance up toward the cheerleader stage, but I have to be wrong. There's no reason for him to do that.

No reason at all.

❧

At home, after I've showered and put on pajamas, I text Dom the same way I have after every game he's played in the NHL.

Great game! Congrats on the win!

The reply comes back almost instantly.

Thanks. You get home okay?

Who needs Mom and Dad being all up in my business when I've got a brother like Dominic Lee? Actually, he's more protective than Mom and Dad have been in years. They realize I'm grown and need to stretch my wings. Dom, not so much.

I think he'd rather I be a pretty bird in a gilded cage, safely tucked away where nothing and no one could hurt me. I'm not sure why or when he got such a burr in his ass about me being a delicate little thing. Or maybe he doesn't think I'm fragile, but rather that I'm a mess?

That seems more likely since I can be messy—current predicament as evidentiary example one—but it's not like I call him to bail me out of jail at three in the morning on the regular. It was just that one time, *years* ago, when I snuck out to go to a party at some kid's house and it got raided. I'd used my one phone call to wake him up, and as a legal adult of all of nineteen, I'd been released into his care since our parents were away on vacation, which they totally hadn't been. Dom never ratted me out, though, just made me promise to never go to another high school drinking party again. I kept that promise, at least until college, but sometimes Dom acts like I'm still a wild child teenager, not the stable, independent, responsible adult I mostly am.

Nope. Went to a bar for a celebration margarita, met a cute biker named Deadshot, and ran away to Vegas. We're getting married in the morning. Can't wait to introduce you.

He sends back a straight-faced emoji with one eyebrow raised.

JK. Home, safe and sound. GN.

You're an idiot. Good thing I love you. GN.

I smile and set my phone on the couch beside me, picking up the remote instead. I'm always too hyped after a game to go straight to bed and will spend a couple of hours watching reruns of whatever stupid show is on so that my brain will finally settle enough to sleep.

Tonight, it's not the television or my bed calling to me, though. It's my phone.

I pick it up, telling myself this is a bad idea. Maybe the worst idea I've ever had.

Still, my fingers hover over a new text. One to Griffin.

"Don't make it weird, Penny. Just say the same thing you said to Dom. Totally normal, brotherly congrats."

Great game! Congrats on the win!

Send.

"See, it's fine," I tell myself. Except my fingers are still going.

Are you okay after that fight with Patterson?

Surprisingly, I don't mean the one from the first period. Griffin and Patterson went after each other a couple more times during the game, and the last one, when the Vortex was getting desperate, resulted in Patterson going into the penalty box.

New phone. Who dis?

I swear to God, I'm going to kill this man the next time I see him. I knew I shouldn't have texted. Dom's right, I'm such an idiot. My phone dings again.

I'm fine, Penny. And thanks.

Okay, he was teasing me, just like always. Because everything's fine between us. Nothing weird, nothing flirty, just normal. So why am I hugging my knees tighter, gripping my phone harder, and grinning at the screen?

Did you send Paul the tickets you promised?

Keeping things all business seems like a good idea.

Yeah. Left tickets for tonight and tomorrow at will call.

Okay, well, that's that. Conversation over. Ding!

What are you doing?

I stare at the four little words that could mean so many different things. Is he asking if I'm available for something like an ice cream run or a booty call? Or maybe both? Is he asking why in the hell I'm texting him? Is he being literal, like wondering if I'm watching TV or lying in bed?

I have no idea how to answer that, so I tell him the truth.

I have no idea. Like if an idea is a lightbulb, mine's completely dark. It probably has that weird rattly sound when it's burned out too. I might be drunk. Or drugged. Or sleepy. Probably all three, so I'm gonna go now. Forget this happened.

Penny . . .

Those three dots are no more helpful in deciphering the male brain. And if I can't dissect that simple thing, I have no chance at figuring out my own. I blame Layla.

I'm going to bed. GN.

A second later, I send one more text.

I'm not really drunk or drugged. And I'm wide awake.

I know. GN.

Chapter 13

Penny

I sleep in on Sunday, not crawling out of bed until eight in the morning. I know that's not late for everyone, but it is for me. If I snooze past six thirty, I feel like I've missed seizing so much of the day. I'm looking to *carpe diem*, not *carpe sleep-'em*.

The Hawks have back-to-back games almost every weekend, but the cheerleaders only perform at home games, and these weekends take a toll. It's like running a marathon two days in a row. I'm sure the players would argue that they have it harder, and they probably do, but this morning, I feel like I got hit by a car. Not a big mom-mobile minivan but a small Fiat at least, with sore muscles and a raging desire for sugary cereal to make up for the energy I expended.

Instead, I throw some berries and granola in a bowl of blended cottage cheese and sit down on the couch to eat a healthy breakfast in peace.

But peace doesn't come.

We won again last night, beating the Vortex three to two in the second action-packed battle of our double-header weekend, which is amazing. That part was fine. It was the rest . . .

The hours spent watching Griffin play. Cheering a little harder for him than everyone else. Worrying every time a play went violent and he was right in the middle of it the way he always is. Telling myself that I was being stupid and that Layla was seeing things that aren't there. Replaying the text exchange in my head on repeat and feeling stupid for even texting him in the first place when I never have before.

That's why I didn't do it again.

After last night's game, I went home, showered, got food, and stared at the television for a couple of hours. I sent my usual check-in to Dom so he wouldn't worry, and then stuck my phone under the couch cushion and sat on it so I wouldn't do something embarrassing like text Griffin again. My plan worked, but I felt unsettled about it all evening.

Which is ridiculous. We don't check on each other despite me doing just that Friday night. We're like one degree of Kevin Bacon, with my brother being the only thing connecting us. If it wasn't for Dom, I wouldn't give Griffin a second thought, and his only reaction to not seeing me anymore would probably be a hallelujah and a significant lowering of his blood pressure from the lack of annoying brattiness in his life.

After finishing my breakfast, I wash my bowl and leave it in the dish drainer to dry. I've got the whole day ahead of me with a wide-open schedule. Glancing at Talia's closed door, I decide she's likely still asleep and that I shouldn't bother her and instead choose to do some work since I need to create as much as possible as quickly as possible to make some money before my credit card bill comes due.

Trying to be quiet—for Talia's sake, not Mrs. Rosenthal's—I pull out a ring I picked up at an estate sale a few weeks ago and spend the next three hours hunched over my desk. First, I take photos from every angle. These will be key for my social media, where people love to see the before-and-after shots of my makeovers.

Then I designate a clear plastic box for this piece, tagging it with a handwritten label and again considering adding a label maker to my workstation. That'll have to wait, though, since I don't have a spare cent to spend on something I can do with a pen and an erasable sticker. I free the tiny rubies that comprise the ring and start moving them around on the box's gridded mat to play with placement. At the same time, I'm sketching on a notebook at my side.

It's an imprecise process, but it's mine. I like to let the original design speak to me, but also the stones themselves. Sometimes they'll tell me exactly what they want to be. With others, I have to coax it out of them with ultrasonic baths and silly pep talks about how pretty they are and how they're going to love their new homes.

Talking to gemstones? To gold and silver? Out loud like they're going to answer me? Yes, I know how crazy that sounds. But that's what artists do, and yes, I consider myself an artist. One whose medium happens to be jewelry.

Once I'm satisfied with my initial plan for the rubies, I move to my computer to create a digital 3D rendering. I look at it from every angle, imagining it on someone's hand and double- and triple-checking my design choices. Is the setting correct? Is it unique enough? Is it the best way to showcase the stones? But also, is it sellable? Usually, I don't worry about that. I do what feels right and trust that each completed piece will eventually find its perfect buyer. But with bills looming, I can't wait for an eventual sale. I need to design, complete, and sell multiple pieces, preferably within the next three weeks. And that's a tall order. No, a venti order.

Mmm, coffee sounds good.

I do a check of the stones, making sure each one is securely stored in the box, and take off my loupes, putting them into their case for safekeeping. Stepping away from my work desk, I stretch my arms over my head, then roll my head around to release the tension building in the back of my neck.

In the kitchen, I start the coffeepot and stare at the *drip-drip-drip*, willing it to go faster. After only a minute, I move the pot and replace it with a mug, letting it fill straight from the source. If I could, I'd tilt my head under the drops and let them fall directly into my mouth. Or even mainline it if that was a possibility.

I didn't sleep well last night, hence the late wake-up. I kept dreaming about Griffin, alternating between nightmares where he was outright laughing and pointing at me for some unseen embarrassing move on my part and fantasies where he kissed me at my front door . . . and then came inside my apartment . . . and then, me. Those had kept me tossing and turning more than the bullying imagery because . . . it's Griffin.

Who's not my friend. He's a forced acquaintance who begrudgingly puts up with me. And he's not my type despite being a literal demigod of a man.

Demi? I think wryly. *There's nothing* demi *or* semi *or* hemi *about him. He's a walking, talking beast like Layla said.*

Who I have zero attraction or interest in!

I laugh at my own ridiculousness.

"What're you laughing at?"

I jump a foot in the air at the unexpected voice, knocking my breakfast bowl from the dish rack, and it falls to the floor, loudly shattering on impact.

"Shit!" I shout.

I automatically wait for the banging on the wall we share with Mrs. Rosenthal to start, but nothing comes. Maybe she's asleep? Or gone to the grocery store? Or dead in her apartment? There's no telling, but I'll take the rare win, because last time we broke a dish—and by *we*, I mean *me*—she called the police, telling them Talia and I were fighting and to please hurry. The police responding to the call had been really confused when it was only me at home, with nobody to fight with but my own butterfingers and the ramen-noodle-covered floor.

Like the calm, cool, collected medical professional she is, Talia is completely nonplussed by the shards of bowl, despite being barefoot, and is staring at the now almost-full mug of coffee beneath the dripping filter. "I will fight you to the death for this, so don't try me."

She's not kidding. Never get between a shift worker and their caffeine. You'll end up needing medical attention, and you'd best not need it from the person you prevented from getting their dose of java because you'd be shit out of luck. Their motto is "no mercy," and they can hold grudges better than the Furies.

"Go ahead," I offer graciously, "just slip another mug under there for me while I clean this up."

She happily does, and while I clean up the broken dish, she takes a deep draw of what's now her coffee and sighs. "Sorry for scaring you," she says after the caffeine hits her. "What were you laughing at?"

It's what she asked in the first place, and I kinda hoped she would've forgotten with the shattering dish, but no such luck.

"Nothing, just something Layla said." I shrug like it's no big deal, not worth talking about or even mentioning again, as I dump the remains of the bowl into the trash.

She thankfully takes that at face value and doesn't dig deeper. *Go me!* "Hawks win?"

"Yeah. Friday's and Saturday's games."

"Dom and Honey do their thingy?" She's nothing if not precise about the ins and outs of hockey.

"Yep. Teamwork makes the dream work."

"You fuck Griffin yet?"

My jaw falls open, and I stare at her, stunned into absolute silence. And then I get my brain firing on enough cylinders to refute that ridiculous idea. "There is no fucking here. Griffin or otherwise!" I realize that she wasn't asking questions about the game because she gives a damn but rather was trying to set me off-kilter enough to answer off the cuff, without even attempting to lie, and I walked right into her trap. Luckily, there wasn't anything to tell, otherwise, we'd be having an entirely different conversation now.

Behind her mug, I see Talia's lips tilt up ever so slightly. "Pity. Let me know when you do."

I snort out a laugh, aiming for offended and landing somewhere closer to *pshaw, nuh-uh*. "Nothing is going on with me and Griffin. I swear you and Layla must be comparing notes. He just feels bad about the ring getting stolen and is scared Dom will blame him like I did,"

I explain in exasperation. "Do?" I correct myself, but then admit the truth. "Did." I don't blame him anymore. It was just bad luck, and if anything, that's my all-too-familiar territory.

"That's what Layla said that had you chuckling to yourself? Something about Griffin?" She nods like that makes perfect sense. I stare at her because it doesn't. "Pen, if he hated you, he'd take pleasure in your pain, but he's not doing that, is he?" She doesn't wait for my answer, steamrolling ahead to plead her case. "No, he spent a whole day running around town to pawnshops with you. And he's not scared of Dom. Griffin's bigger, meaner, and more violent than your brother could ever be."

She's wrong. And so is Layla. Not about the bigger, meaner, more violent part, because that's true, but the rest of it, totally off base.

But all that gardening they're doing, planting those little seeds of doubt, is slowly working. "But he always acts like I'm a brat that annoys him, like he wishes I wasn't invading his time with Dom."

"Boys are stupid. And men are stupider." She shrugs like that's some great, deeply sage wisdom, and honestly, in the face of a lifetime of evidence, I can't argue with her.

"Men can be stupid. But I'm not. I refuse to be one of the puck bunnies who fall at the players' feet, thinking they're different from all the others. I have some pride." Based on last night's dreams, that's not true at all, but I'm not going to openly admit to having sexy, slutty dreams about Griffin. Talia would have to pry that secret out of my mouth with copious amounts of alcohol and/or chocolate. Even then, having those fantasies doesn't mean I'll act on them.

I'm just confused, that's all. And probably horny. Maybe I should order a battery buddy off of Amazon to help take the edge off? Or reactivate my dating apps and get back out there? Find a nice, sweet, non-pro athlete guy who likes to talk about the stock market or *Star Wars*, and can scratch the itch that's apparently making me susceptible to the slightest kindness from a total asshole. Yeah, that's a good idea.

I pick up my phone and click into the App Store to download Tinder again.

"Are you texting Griffin to come over for a hookup?" Talia asks hopefully, coming over to stand beside me. When she sees what I'm actually doing, she sighs in disappointment, her eyes rolling hard enough to click in her skull.

"Mom says your face'll get stuck like that if you keep doing it." My mother's never said that, but a mom somewhere did.

"Sometimes what you're looking for is right in front of you." Talia pushes the phone down before I can hit reinstall on the white fire logo where I might find my knight in shining armor, or at least a dick without Griffin attached to it.

"Sometimes what's right in front of me is a jerk with a cute butt and anger management issues," I correct.

"Sounds hot."

"Ugh," I groan. But it has nothing to do with Tinder or Griffin or Talia this time, and everything to do with the notification I just received from my website. I click into my inbox to read the email.

It's from the same person who messaged before, and reads . . .

> That ring shouldn't have been at the antique store. It was a regrettable, accidental mistake. The ring has deep sentimental value and I need it back. Will pay any price. Please.

The tone could be read as clipped, or it could be desperation.

But either way, it relights my desire to find the ring that started all this. I have a buyer on the hook, which would solve my credit card issue, and it's someone who has a heartfelt attachment to it, which is always good for an emotional boost. It's also a very welcome and needed distraction from trying to figure out what's going on in my head—and farther south—about Griffin.

I need to find the ring. I have to find it. And get it back.

I've talked to several pawnshop owners. Now it's time to talk to the even seedier fences and see if anyone has tried to sell them the ring. My ring.

Gulp.

"So, Mr. Mad Dog, have you seen this?" Trying to keep my hand from shaking, I hold up my phone to show him the picture after I finish explaining why I've approached him on what's apparently his street corner. "It's very important, and I promise I have no interest in however you might've come into the ring's possession."

I can't see Mad Dog's eyes behind his dark sunglasses, which he's wearing despite the spring sun being mild at best, but I hope he's looking at the picture of the ring.

"It's possession? Like by a demon? Or bad juju?" Since the question is asked in complete seriousness, like we're on the set of the latest horror film, I decide to roll with it.

Nodding, I lean in close enough to smell his Old Spice and the underlying body odor he was likely trying to cover with the generous dousing of cheap cologne. Lowering my voice, I confide, "Yeah. The ring's possessed. If you're not the rightful heir, it's . . . *scccchrrrrit—*" I draw my finger across my throat to make sure he understands how serious the situation might be. "Only the family can wear it without deadly consequences, and anyone who keeps the ring from them will be cursed for eternity."

He lowers his sunglasses down his nose with one finger, revealing dark eyes filled with doubt but also a fair amount of consideration as he stares at me. But then he chuckles, the disbelief winning out. "Girl, you're crazy as hell."

Shit. I thought I might be getting somewhere with the fence from Paul's list.

But I can't give up, so, unwilling to let go of the one possible path to Mad Dog admitting he has the ring, I dig in my heels and go harder. "No, really. A few days ago, I was totally happy, my life was great. Now, I'm in financial ruin, I've got a weird crush trying to develop on a guy who basically hates me, I'm out of Thin Mints, and . . . and . . . *I got hit by a car.*"

Okay, that's a stretch. I feel *like* I got hit by a car, but despite there not actually being any car-to-body contact, I'm willing to lie my way into getting the ring if that's what it takes.

Mad Dog's eyes drip over me. "You don't look like you got hit by a car. You seem fine to me."

"Well, I am . . . this time," I intone cryptically. "But there's no telling what could happen next time. That's why I need the ring. You gotta help me. Please!" I grab his arm, shaking it in desperation, and suddenly realize that beneath his designer tracksuit, Mad Dog is jacked. His bicep is so large that my hands don't fit around the muscle.

He jerks out of my grip with a grunt, his whole vibe changing. Looming over me, he has me attempting a backbend to get away from his finger, which is pointed right in my face. "Bitch, don't you fucking touch me. Nobody touches Mad Dog."

My heart racing and my breath stuck in my throat, I hold up my hands in surrender, realizing how severe of a misstep I've made. I mean, approaching a criminal named Mad Dog was scary enough to have me second-guessing my life choices, but he'd seemed nice enough to listen to my story, and my hopes had risen exponentially that, while the pawnshops had been a strikeout, this was going to work.

I was wrong. Dangerously wrong.

"Sorry. Sorry, Mr. Mad Dog, sir. I just really need the ring. My bad. Sorry."

He takes a slow breath, and I can virtually see him packing the threatening aura back behind his facade of chill. When he leans back, giving me some space, I feel like I can breathe again. Shallowly, but at least my oxygen isn't being choked by fear.

Mad Dog glances up and down the street, then pins me with a look. Or I assume he does, because he's pushed his sunglasses back up his nose, and I can't actually see his eyes, but I freeze all the same. "I don't have your ring. Honestly. It looks like more than I'd handle from an unknown source I haven't personally vetted, you get me?"

I nod. He doesn't know the thief, so he wouldn't trust him. My hopes dash into ruins again.

"Not everybody has the same scruples I do, though. Who else you got on that list of yours?" He jerks his head toward my phone. When I first approached Mad Dog, I showed him the picture I sneakily took of the list Paul gave us to explain how I found him. He hadn't been happy about it, but it'd at least gotten him to talk to me.

My eyes widen and a smile blooms on my face. "Really?" I quickly pull up the picture again and show him.

Mad Dog isn't nearly as forgiving as I am, though, and warns, "Don't get your hopes up, girl. None of these guys are gonna want to talk to you, but if you've got balls enough to hit me up, I think you'll be all right."

I should take the compliment, but my mouth does what it does best—talk shit. "I don't have balls. Those sensitive, useless little things? *Pshaw.* I've got ovaries. Tough as a mother, explode on a monthly basis, and like a Timex or a bomb, keep on ticking." I tap my hips with my hands like *take that*. "Tick, tick, boom!" I make an explosion move to emphasize my point that I'm totally a badass who can talk to a few fences who don't want to talk to me.

Mad Dog stares at me like I'm weird as hell. Unfortunately, it's a look I'm all too familiar with from receiving it on a near-daily basis my whole life, and I worry I've gone too far. But he refocuses on the list, then hums. "Shit. If it was me, I'd ask Johnny K. He's got a hard-on for diamonds. If I had one to move, he's who I'd go to."

I check the list myself, finding Johnny K. "Thanks, Mad Dog! You ever want to see a Hawks game, let me know. I'll get you a couple of tickets. Cheap seats, but I'll make it happen. I can be your secret ticket source." I wink like we're a couple of old friends conspiring together. Then think better and hold up a finger. "One time offer, no playoffs," I amend.

"Better." He laughs proudly. "Be smart, girl. You're diving in shark-infested waters. And save the Hawks tickets for Johnny K. He's the hockey guy. I'm more of a basketball guy myself."

It's not until after he's wished me luck and I've walked away that my bravado fades and it fully hits me how stupid what I just did was—approaching a known criminal, asking questions about his business, grabbing him.

What the hell was I thinking?

I was thinking about the credit card bill I'll have to pay. I was thinking about the potential buyer who could make all that a moot point.

But when Mad Dog squared up at me, not one person on the street blinked an eye or made a move to help me. In fact, I think they actively pretended not to see, completely unwilling to get involved in what could've been a really dangerous situation.

And I'm about to do it again. With Johnny K.

I hesitate, but I know I have to do this.

But maybe . . . I don't have to do it alone?

Chapter 14

Griffin

I'm riding my favorite kind of high—victory. The last two nights, the Hawks kicked ass on the ice and came out the winners both times. Not only that, I scored a goal, a rarity for someone whose job is to lock down the right side of the ice like the pro I've worked hard to become.

Pride hasn't always been a familiar feeling. For most of my life, I felt ashamed, overlooked, and like the world would be better off without me in it. But finding my space, the one place I fit perfectly, changed all that for me, and now, I'm damn proud of who I've become and what I've accomplished because it wasn't easy. I fought for this feeling. I'm still fighting for it.

There's one tiny problem on today's high, though. An asterisk that's an approximately five-foot-two brunette with amber eyes, a smart mouth, and a penchant for catastrophe.

When Penny texted me Friday night, my first reaction was almost immature excitement. The smile on my face was so unfamiliar that my cheeks fought against the unusual expression. And then I'd thought . . . *oh shit*! Because Penny can't text me or call me or hang out with me. Well, maybe she could handle that and be fine. But I can't. The only way to keep from fucking up my whole life is to keep her at arm's length. So I'd sent a teasing text back, and played off the whole exchange.

She didn't text again last night. *Which is good,* I remind myself for the hundredth time because I spent last night staring at my phone, conversely willing it to ding and willing it to stay silent at the same time.

But while I personally need to keep my distance, I also need to figure out what to do about Miles Conniver's ring. It's out there somewhere, and his goons are going to track Penny down eventually. If they haven't already.

Why haven't I told her about the whole situation? I'm sure she'd understand, right? But something keeps stopping me. Maybe it's because, for once in my life, I want to be the so-called white knight. It's a selfish desire, but it's there, deep in the dark recesses of my mind, especially given that protecting Penny is nearly written in my DNA after all these years. Maybe I'm worried that Penny would hear the news and march right downtown to Conniver's office and try to talk to him directly, and I definitely don't want that. She'd either end up a pale figure at the bottom of the river, or hell, knowing her luck (and mine), he'd fall in love with her the way everyone else does. Or maybe I'm afraid that somehow, someway, she's going to blame me for it. Which, if she gets into trouble because of me not saying anything, is exactly what she would rightfully do.

But I can stop all those possibilities from happening by doing one thing—finding the damn ring. And action over analysis, particularly self-analysis, is always at the top of my playbook.

That thought is what gets me moving today. Penny might've given up on finding it, making her peace with the situation through tried-and-true wine-and-cookie therapy, but I haven't given up. I can't because if anything happens to Penny, I will never forgive myself. Dom won't forgive me either.

I'm staring at Paul's list, trying to decide which fence to hit first—literally or figuratively—when my phone rings. "Hello."

It's silent for long enough that I pull the phone from my ear to check the screen, expecting it to say *Telemarketer* or *Spam Risk.* But it doesn't. It says *Penny Lee*. This has never happened before. Penny hasn't called me a single time since the day we met. But she is now.

A million new possibilities run through my mind in an instant. Miles's goons found her. She got hit by a bus. She accidentally joined a cult, or started one. She led an impromptu parade that stopped traffic for blocks. She won the lottery. She found the ring. With her, it could be literally anything.

"Penny? Are you there? Are you okay? What's wrong?"

"Um . . . heeeeyyy there, Griffin, old pal, chummy-chum-chum. How're you?" she drawls out, sounding weird even for her.

"Are you drunk for real this time?"

She laughs too hard, too brightly, like what I said is super funny. Or maybe like she's drunk at twelve thirty on a Sunday. It might be five o'clock somewhere, and there's nothing wrong with a bottomless mimosa brunch, but Penny usually does her drinking at night, at home, something I'm thankful for because the thought of a drunk Penny in a seedy club, dancing with some dude, would have me in handcuffs before sunrise, and not in the fun way.

"No," she scoffs. "I haven't been drinking. Can't a girl just call up a friend and see what he's doing? If he's busy or, I don't know, just sitting around, twiddling his dick or something? That's normal, right?"

My brain stuttered when she called me a friend, but I got completely lost about the time she said "twiddling my dick," because said appendage perked up like Penny was calling attendance and he wanted to be sure he was counted as here. I shift on the couch uncomfortably, reminding my dick that there will never be a time where Penny wants him. "Twiddling *thumbs*," I correct.

"Tomato, potato, same thing," she says. Her voice is airy, breathy, like she's aiming for no big deal, but there's a fair to mid chance she just ran from a bear. Or, more likely, a goon.

"Penny! Are you okay?" I bark. It's rude, abrupt, and demanding, but my stomach is trying to crawl up my throat as the need to make sure nothing goon-ish has happened to her grows.

"Yeah, fine. Why?"

I've had years to study Penny, her mannerisms, her voice, and every emotion that flits across her expressive face, and though I usually get anger from her, I'm familiar with the whole spectrum that comprises her heart and brain. So from her tone alone, I can picture her cute wrinkled nose of *don't talk to me like that* along with her total obliviousness to why I might be angry. That's enough to reassure me that the goons haven't found her.

"Because in the five years I've known you, you've never called me once." Another thought hits me. "Is Dom okay?"

"Oh!" she says, both relieved and a little surprised, but still sounding weird. "Yeah, fine. I think. I mean, I haven't talked to him today, but probably? That's not why I'm calling, though."

I take a deep breath, gritting my teeth to keep from shouting, *Why are you calling me, then?* My default asshole mode won't do me any good right now. Penny would probably hang up on me just to further piss me off and do a happy dance over my rising blood pressure. "Why are you calling?" I manage to say in barely a growl.

"I wondered if you might, if you're not too busy, maybe go with me to talk to someone about a particular missing ring?" If she hemmed and hawed any more before getting through that question, I would've crawled through the phone and strangled her myself, saving Miles Conniver's goons the trouble.

"Are you tracking down the fences?" I shout.

"If you're gonna be like that, never mind."

After clearing my throat, I try again. "Do you want to talk to the fences?" There, totally calm and collected, if not a bit grumbly.

"I already did," she informs me cheerfully. "Mad Dog said the man to go to is Johnny K, but he's a hockey fan, and I figured you might be my ace in the hole there. Plus, there was that whole moment when Mad Dog got a teensy bit irritated with me and kinda got in my face, so I realized it might be better to do this with a buddy. And since you already know what's going on, and I wouldn't have to catch you up on the whole story like I would Dom, you're the obvious choice to go with me. That is, if you're not too busy twiddling your dick . . . or your thumbs."

She didn't take a single breath during any of that. But despite the rambling, there was a lot of information, like that I now need to track down somebody named Mad Dog and give him a taste of his own medicine, because how fucking dare he threaten Penny? Also, she's asking me for help. Not her brother, not her parents, not a friend. Me, Griffin Mahoney, the guy she hates who fucked this whole ring thing up for her from the get-go.

That pride I felt over my goal feels small compared to what's growing in my chest now. Penny reached out to me in her time of need. Sure, it's partially because Dom would give her shit for not being careful with such a valuable piece of jewelry, but it's also because she wants *my help*. In some twisted way, when shit hits the fan, she's coming to me.

"I'm on my way. Where are you?"

❧

I'm going to kill her. No, I'm going to kiss her and then kill her.

No, you're not. You're not gonna do either of those things. You're gonna help, that's it.

I argue with myself the whole way to meet Penny, and when I finally lay eyes on her, my sigh of relief is soul deep. She's okay.

More than okay, she's sitting at a café table outside a coffee shop, petting a dog and talking to its owner like she's got nothing but time and friendship to offer. Selfishly, I wish she could offer that to me.

Actually, that's not true. She would've offered that easily when we met. What I wish is that I could've accepted her friendship and reciprocated it instead of shutting down any and all potential relationship we might've had, friendship or otherwise. But I chose Dom then, and though I've questioned that choice a million times since, I can't go back to unring the bell on years of asshole behavior now.

Could this ring deal be the start of that? A chance to turn a bad situation into something good?

The hope that lights inside me at that idea is a dangerous thing. It'd be too easy to let it grow into an inferno of something much more than friendship. At least for me.

I tamp down my feelings the way I have so many times before, deliberately hardening my face into barely controlled annoyance as I approach her. "Penny?"

She turns light-filled amber eyes to me, her smile bright and her whole body relaxed until she sees me and my stony expression. The light dims, her smile fades, and her shoulders inch up toward her ears. "Hey! Thanks for coming." She turns back to the dog, "Sorry. This is my friend I was telling you about, so I have to go. You're such a good boy. You have a good walk and a good day, and make sure you get two yummy treats when you get home." The dog wags his tail like he understood every word, and I realize she wasn't talking to the owner, offering friendship I greedily wish I could have, but rather the dog.

Meanwhile, the dog's owner is eyeballing me like I've interrupted the meet-cute with Penny that he's going to wax poetic about at their wedding reception. I meet his glare with an unveiled threat in my cold eyes, silently ordering him to get the fuck out of here. Little does he know, I'm saving his life. Because if he doesn't leave, and take the admittedly cute dog with him, I'm going to kill him.

But he heard Penny's dismissal and has taken in my considerably larger size and hostile warning and wisely, albeit with disappointment, walks away.

"You couldn't sit here for thirty minutes without flirting with some rando?" I accuse. I know I sound jealous as fuck, but I can't help it. I am jealous . . . of anyone who gets the relaxed, happy, vibrant version of Penny that I want. Especially when I get the bratty, annoyed version. It's what I deserve, but it still stings.

"Clover came up to me," she replies, throwing her hands wide.

"Not the dog. The guy." I'm assuming the guy's name wasn't Clover, though, these days, who knows? I went to school with a guy named Pine. He was a hell of a math whiz who helped me cheat my way through trigonometry, so who am I to judge? But seriously, that guy's name isn't Clover, like the weed, right?

She looks down the sidewalk where they disappeared like she's only now realizing that the dog had a guy holding the other end of the leash. She has no idea how gorgeous she is, how her radiant spirit shines out of her, attracting the attention of every Tom, Dick, Harry, and Clover in a one-mile radius.

Most of all, she has no idea that I see that beauty in her.

That's how it has to be. It's for the best.

When she looks back at me, I see how tired she is, and I twist inside. I should be helping her, and instead I'm a fucking vampire, sapping her strength. "This was a bad idea, wasn't it? Never mind. I'll be fine. You can go back home or wherever you were, to whatever you were doing. Just return to your regularly scheduled programming, and I'll figure this out on my own."

I snort out a humorless laugh. Fine, I'm a vampire, but I won't let that continue. I need to fire her up again. "If you think for one second that I'm letting you talk to criminals by yourself, you're crazier than I thought."

"Letting me? Nobody *lets* me do anything." She stands up, bowing up to me in the fiery way that is such an unbelievable turn-on. "And I'll take *crazy* as a compliment, thank you very much. Capable, relentless, awesome, zesty . . . um, yee-haw'er. Okay, that last one needs work, but you put me on the spot, so give me a break."

I stare down at her, my breathing too quick for the short exchange, and consider my options. Whether I'm leaving or staying isn't up for debate. Instead, I'm pondering how to get her to *let me* stay by her side for the sketchy shit on her agenda today.

"You're right. You can do whatever you want, but I would like to help. Please," I force out, the conciliatory tone foreign and difficult to fake.

"That's more like it," she says, flipping her hair over her shoulder haughtily. A moment later she caves, offering, "Because I really think going alone was a bad idea, not that I would ever admit it."

She totally just admitted it, but I don't call her out, having learned my lesson for the day. "I was going to talk to some of them today too," I confess. "When you called, I was already looking at the list."

She backhands my chest with a beaming smile. "Great minds, huh? It's like we're on the same wavelength!"

I nod slowly. "Yeah, thinking alike, that's us."

It's so not us.

On the way to Johnny K's, she tells me more about her conversation with Mad Dog, claiming he's a misunderstood good guy with ethics and morals and business standards. "He said he wouldn't work with an unknown source he hadn't personally vetted." She makes that sound like high standards, not a bar on the floor to keep from getting arrested in a sting operation or scammed by another criminal.

I'm expecting a seedy, bars-on-the-windows-type place at the address she has for Johnny K, but I'm wrong. I even confirm the address with the rideshare driver because I'm nearly certain he's dropping us off at the wrong place.

"Ooh, fancy-schmancy!" Penny coos as we get out of the car.

Johnny K's isn't a sketchy place at all. Or doesn't appear to be. It's a storefront, with vinyl lettering on the windows proclaiming "By Appointment Only" and fake topiary trees on either side of the gold-handled door. It looks bougie, not dangerous. But sometimes that's the biggest mask of all.

I look like someone people should fear. But for the most part, I'm not. I may throw hands here and there, both on and off the ice, but I wouldn't consider myself unsafe. I have a code of ethics that I follow—mainly don't fuck with what's mine, and I won't fuck you up. On the other hand, Miles Conniver doesn't look like someone you'd worry about. I've seen his picture in the paper, and he appears to be a typical wealthy guy—precision haircut, white teeth, tailored suit, and manicured hands that have never seen a day of work. Yet, of the two of us, he's the one who'd kill you, or have you killed, so the "store" look of Johnny K's place isn't all that reassuring.

Penny, on the other hand, is getting more and more excited, like she might find a new favorite shopping locale.

"Stolen merchandise," I remind her quietly as we approach the door.

"I know. But this is a bajillion times better than Mad Dog's corner," she explains. I'm not sure she's right. This place is a pitcher plant, one of those places where flies go in and don't come out.

The door is locked, and through the window, the place looks deserted. One glance around, though, and I spot a camera above the door. "You said this guy's a hockey fan, right?" When Penny nods, I step up to the camera, lifting my chin so my face is fully visible. "Hey, I'm Griffin Mahoney. I play for the Hawks. I wanted to see if we could have a conversation about jewelry." I pointedly cut my eyes toward Penny, implying I want to buy her something. If Johnny K is a salesman, I just showed my whole hand, and hopefully, that's not something he can resist.

"One minute."

I'm not sure where the disembodied voice came from, but it elicits happy claps and a few hops of joy from Penny. "It's here. I can feel it. It's gonna be here," she chants. And though I'm not nearly as sure as she's trying to be, I hope she's right.

It takes a few minutes, but eventually, two guys come into sight. One stands behind the glass cases, which are shaped in a U facing the door. The other guy is obviously the muscle and comes to open the door and greet us. "Welcome in, Honey. We're big fans. Loved the way you put Patterson on the boards last night."

I nod my appreciation—they're clearly not bullshitting if they know my nickname—but focus on the man we're here to see. "Johnny?"

"Johnny K? Mr. K? Or just Johnny?" Penny asks, rushing forward with her hand extended. "Thank you so much for seeing us. I really appreciate it."

For his part, Johnny looks taken aback by Penny's effusive greeting, but after a quick visual check-in with me, he shakes Penny's hand politely. "Of course. How can I be of service?" I can see the facade of customer service slipping over Johnny K's core thoughts of what-the-fuck *Twilight Zone* have I entered into?

He's a man accustomed to dealing with rich people, that much is obvious, but there's a sinister aura to him despite his expensive slacks, designer shirt, and gold chains. Honestly, I feel like he might be a bit of a kindred spirit. Rough to the core but forced to play dress-up and act nice in an unfamiliar world, like me with the Richie Rich team owners, who want us to monkey dance for their entertainment; the media, who expect the players to perform verbal tricks in interviews fawning over the opportunities we receive; and the fans, who think we owe them something because they bought a shirt with our number emblazoned on it. For me, I play along because hockey was my way out, and for that, I love it. For Johnny, I think he just loves money, which can also be a way out of whatever situation you're in.

"We're looking for a ring," Penny tells him, glancing down at the jewelry in the glass cases. "A special one."

She's getting better at this, not jumping right into accusations and hopeful demands for her ring the way she was doing at the pawnshops. It's working too. Johnny smiles warmly at her, respectfully saying, "Of course. Everything here is special . . . to the right person."

Ironically, I think this is the time for blunt honesty. I step up to Penny's side and instinctively place my hand on the small of her back. She straightens reflexively at the delicate touch, and I take the briefest of moments to appreciate the intimacy of the connection before turning hardened eyes on Johnny. "Can I be straight with you?"

He dips his chin deferentially, his face impassive in preparation for me to say something outrageous. I'm sure he's heard it all—nipple rings, connecting chain rings, diamond teeth inlays. I bet he hasn't been told a story like this, though.

"We bought a ring a few days ago. Gorgeous, unique piece that she absolutely loved. But it was taken, right from my hands, on the sidewalk downtown by a guy with freckles that was wearing a red hoodie." I observe Johnny closely, watching for the smallest tell that he might know what I'm talking about. And I see the slight dilation of his pupils—he knows who I'm talking about, I'd bet on it. "We were told that this guy sometimes does business here. To be honest, I don't give a shit about him, or you, or your business. All I care about is the ring. I'll even buy it again because I understand you've got money invested in it."

I'm making it sound like I already know he has it in the hopes that he'll believe I have more intel than I do. Or maybe Penny's eternal optimism is wearing off on me, turning me into a hope-filled believer too.

But Johnny's a better businessman than that. A smarter one too. "I don't have it. Don't know what you're talking about," he clips out, his eyes cutting past us to the guy at the door.

"You haven't even seen it yet," Penny pleads, holding up the picture of the ring on her finger, where Johnny can't help but look at it. I get the sense that with the barest glance, he could tell you the karat weight, quality, and value of virtually any piece of jewelry. "*Have* you seen it?" she asks, doubt creeping into her tone.

Johnny shakes his head. "I don't have that ring. Perhaps something else would be an acceptable replacement for it?" The consummate salesman, he gestures to the cases between us, which are filled with stunning, sparkling diamonds and colorful gemstones.

"Penny, can you give me a second?" I say out of the side of my mouth, never dropping my gaze from Johnny. "Look around or something."

She gives me a huff of displeasure but does step away, thankfully. I lower my voice, leaning in toward Johnny. "Look, we need that specific ring. It's important. I saw your reaction and you know the guy. Could you give me his name or where I can find him? I'll pay a finder's fee, and if you give a shit about him, I'll even promise to not hurt him. I just need the ring." I can see the refusal in his eyes, so before he can speak it, I offer, "Or if you don't want to tell me, can you reach out to him? Be the middleman between us, and I'll buy it from you so you get your cut of the profit. Whatever you want. Cash, hockey tickets, signed memorabilia. I just need the ring."

The words virtually stick in my throat, because begging isn't in my nature. But for Penny, I'll do it. I'll do anything.

Knowing he's got the upper hand, Johnny takes a slow, deep breath, letting a smug smile lift his lips. "I know the kid. I'll see what I can find out."

"Thank you. Appreciate it."

Johnny laughs as he pulls out an iPad from below the counter. "I'm not running a charity here." He clicks a few times and then lays it on the case in front of me. There's a $1,000 payment pending.

I grit my teeth, swallowing the argument. If there's any chance he actually knows the kid and will reach out, it's money well spent. I tap my phone to pay and a tip screen pops up. "Seriously?"

Johnny's grin is filled with pure satisfaction. "Tips are customary for quick service."

Sighing in resignation, I click the 20 percent option. "Call me as soon as you know anything," I say, scribbling my number on the paper he offers. He takes it back, and without a look, slips it into his pocket.

I hold my hand out, and when he shakes it, he turns into Mr. Congeniality. "Nice doing business with you, Honey."

I squeeze his hand a bit harder, not letting go. "Griffin. And our business has just begun. I'll be waiting for your call."

He nods his agreement, and I feel like he has a grasp on how urgent this matter is. "If you'll excuse me, I do have a scheduled appointment today I should prepare for."

I release him and turn to Penny, who has somehow gotten completely distracted by the pretty, shiny things and doesn't seem to have paid a bit of attention to the conversation between Johnny and me. "Ready?"

Once we're outside, she starts laughing. "You know he just scammed you, right? He probably doesn't even know the guy that stole the ring, but he saw your wallet coming from a mile away."

I guess she was paying more attention than I thought.

Shrugging, I say, "If there's any chance, it'll be worth it, though." Glancing her way, her observation belatedly clicks in my mind. "I figured you would be all hopeful and optimistic that he was gonna call the thief, get the ring, and have it waiting and ready for us with a fresh cleaning by tomorrow."

Her lips turn down into an uncharacteristic frown, and her gaze drops to the sidewalk. "Reality sucks sometimes. True story."

I risk bumping her shoulder with my arm, the move friendlier than I'd usually dare, but we've moved well beyond that at this point. "Who'da thunk I'd be the optimist and you'd be the cynic?"

Her laugh is more breath than humor, but when she looks back up at me, there's a bit more life in her eyes. "Maybe you're rubbing off on me."

I don't want that to be the case. I want Penny to keep her idealistic, good-hearted view of the world, and not be jaded by my ugly, fatalistic one. I guess that's one more reason why we're not a good fit. Will never be a good fit. She deserves someone as bubbly and bright as she is, someone who floats through life seeing opportunities and possibilities, not someone who views the world as a war to be waged, filled with potential adversaries that have to be fought to get every scrap they receive. She doesn't need someone who will drag her down to his depths. She deserves someone who will lift her up to new heights.

The reminder is bitter, and I force my focus ahead of us, watching where we're going in the hope I can prevent Penny from tripping over her own feet. It's the only reason I see them . . . Miles's guys, coming right at us.

"Shit," I hiss. I glance left and right, instantly looking for a way out. They can't see Penny. How'd they even know where to find her? Because there's no way it's a coincidence that they're on this street, at this time, right when she is. No way at all.

"What?"

"Um . . . here . . ." I don't explain anything. I just shove her into the alleyway between the two buildings beside us and push her up against the brick wall, blocking her from view with the expanse of my body.

"Griffin, what the fuck? What're you doing?" Penny exclaims, her palms pushing against my chest like she has any hopes of moving me.

"Shh . . ." I glance over my shoulder toward the sidewalk, but Penelope isn't one to take orders from anyone, least of all me.

"What? Move!" She pushes against me harder, her nails digging into my flesh where she tries to grab at my shirt, and her voice getting higher and louder to the point where she's drawing attention.

I have to shut her up so the goons don't see her. One second, I'm shushing her, and the next, though I'm not sure how it happens, I'm . . .

Kissing Penelope Lee.

Chapter 15

Penny

I do not know what is going on.

One second, Griffin is teasing me for being a skeptic about the flashy, trashy fence we were talking about, and the next, he's cursing and bodily moving me again. He's really got to stop doing that. Despite my small stature, I'm not a kid he can just pick up and put wherever he wants me to be.

And then, my demand for answers has his eyes darting all over the place, from my face to the sidewalk behind him.

How in the hell does this end up with Griffin Mahoney kissing me?

Seriously, universe, what is going on? Is Mercury in retrograde, or did my pheromones kick in at the most inopportune time with the least likely person? Maybe Johnny K put a love spell on Griffin? I don't believe in magic potions, but that's as logical as what's happening right now.

But it's not really a kiss.

Oh, his mouth is on mine, and his body is pressed against me so tightly that I can feel the bulge in his jeans, but this is no kiss. It's a mashing of his lips to mine to shut me up. Hard, unyielding, forceful power against my frozen shock.

Fighting for oxygen because I've stopped breathing, I push him away, and this time he relents and gives me the smallest amount of space. He seems to be breathing just fine, though a little fast for an athlete. He should really up his cardio before the playoffs.

"Sorry, you need to be quiet," he whispers into the air between us.

I rear back and slap his cheek . . . hard. "What the ever-loving actual fuck, Griffin?" I spit out. He had no right to do that. It's a complete violation of the tenuous friendship I thought we were building with this whole fiasco. It also lit a fire inside me that I do not like or appreciate in any way.

Except . . .

I reach up, grabbing his face and pulling him back down toward me, kissing him again. This time, I make sure to move my lips against his, feeling the unexpected softness of his mouth as he submits to me so much better than I did to him. It makes me feel powerful, even though I know it's a false sense of control when he's so much larger than I am.

The kiss turns into something more, his hand snaking between us to gently caress my throat. He doesn't squeeze, but the feeling of his large palm over my tripping pulse has me opening my mouth for him. The heat of our shared breath mixes, and I don't know whose oxygen I'm taking in any longer. It doesn't matter, my entire brain is just shouting *more, more, more* like a greedy bitch who hasn't been kissed in way too long, which is exactly what I am. I lift to my toes to get closer to him, very nearly climbing him like a tree, and then wrap my arms around his neck, teasing at his nape with my nails. He groans against me, and the vibration is sexy as hell. I think I smile, but I definitely clench my thighs together, feeling the aching thud of my heartbeat in my clit.

Something is happening in my chest. A heart attack maybe? But no, that's not it. Nor is it the flutter of butterfly wings, nothing so poetic and pretty as that for a girl like me. Instead, my heart is thudding against my rib cage like a herd of flightless penguins flapping their wings around wildly like they've forgotten evolution did them dirty.

Griffin's hands land on the brick wall on either side of my head with a resounding slap, breaking the spell woven around us.

I dip my chin, ducking out of the kiss that just entirely reset everything I thought I knew about Griffin Mahoney. Cold and robotic? Two minutes ago, I would've said yes. Now that I've felt the heat and need churning right below his stoic surface? Absolutely not.

"What was that for?" he says, his voice husky and rough.

I lick my lips, feeling the slickness there from the kiss. "I didn't want you to think I'm a shitty kisser who just stands there with frozen, tight lips. Now, it's my turn . . . Why did you kiss me?"

I want him to say that he couldn't withstand my charms any longer. That he's been holding himself back from me for ages and finally succumbed. That I'm sexy as hell and he needed to taste me. Because that'd be hot as fuck.

Except it's Griffin and me, and none of that is true.

"It's a long story."

He rubs the back of his neck, suddenly looking exhausted, and I remember that he played an intense, tough game barely more than twelve hours ago and is likely still feeling the effects. I should be kind and let him off the hook, but how can I after *that*? I need answers, pronto. I roll my hand at the wrist expectantly, like *get on with it, then*, and Griffin lifts his face to the sky like he might find answers there, or a way to delay my inevitable demand for his body, or hell, maybe he's hoping aliens will beam him up. None of that happens, obviously.

"Can we . . . I don't know . . . go somewhere and talk?" he finally says.

I blink in surprise, reconsidering my earlier quick dismissal of aliens. "Did you get body snatched this morning or something?" I poke at his chest with a finger. "If you're really Griffin, let me hear the special growl you make when I piss you off?"

"Penny," he rumbles.

"Pretty close," I say with a twitch of my lips, and he steps farther away from me, obviously irritated. That's something I'm used to dealing with. "Can you blame me for doubting that you're you? Griffin Mahoney—textbook silent, broody sort—wants to talk, like with actual syllabic words, not grunts and grumbles, to me, Penelope Lee, in private?" Not a bit of that makes sense—because of the sentiment, not the words themselves. I'm a master speaker, so it's not that, for sure.

"I don't *want* to," he corrects. "If you're fine pretending that never happened, I am too." His gaze drops to my lips like I might need a reminder of what he wants me to forget about.

As if that's a remote possibility.

Forget that Griffin kissed me? Forget that the hands that cause so much damage to others were gentle on my throat in a way that made the constant noise in my brain disappear for a moment? Forget that he tastes like sinful sex and bad decisions? Forget that my clit is pouting at not receiving the much-needed attention she thought she was going to get?

Unlikely. I'm going to be replaying that kiss over in my mind for masturbatory sessions to come for a very long time. Not that I'm going to tell Griffin that. With that type of ammunition, he'd gloat every time we see each other for the rest of our lives.

"Talking, it is. Your place or mine? Talia's at work today, so it'd just be the two of us." I wiggle my brows, teasing him mercilessly, because I know exactly what it sounds like I'm proposing. Not that I am. But also, I'm not *not-proposing* that either. I mean, either way is fine, *just fine* by me.

Ah shit. I'm doing it, aren't I? I've turned into one of the puck bunnies, so starved for affection and attention that after a couple of days of kindness and one knock-my-socks-off kiss, I'm forgetting—or willfully choosing to ignore—all the asshole behavior and insults he's hurled at me over the years.

Slut, party of one? Me, right here, I think, mentally raising my hand.

I don't feel bad about it, though. There's no reason to. I'm a woman with needs, ones I've been ignoring for too long. And Griffin's a man, a sexy one who wears cologne that drives me mad, helps when the shit hits the fan, and makes one of his rare smiles feel like the ultimate reward for my weirdness.

"Mine," he finally says.

Ready to get this show on the road, I instantly jump up and down, clapping my hands in triumph. Unfortunately, he wasn't prepped for that reaction—which he really should've been, and is absolutely in my way—that's his fault, too, and that's how I end up clocking him in the chin with the top of my head. Totally his oopsie-doopsie, not mine. At all.

"Motherfucker!" he grunts, reflexively jerking back and pressing his palm to his chin to ease the sharp pain. Eyes squinched shut, he glowers at me through one tiny crack in his lids, but when he sees me rubbing my head, he immediately forgets his own pain and replaces my hand with his, caressing the sore spot. "You okay?"

"Yeah, sorry! I was just excited because I've never been to your place. Is it like Bruce Wayne's lair or an empty, personality-less Airbnb?" Griffin looks pained by my suggestions, and I wince. "It's a bachelor pad, isn't it? With a black leather couch you can wipe the jizz off of and a movie-theater-size television?" He flinches when I say the word *jizz*, which makes me laugh. "I can't wait to see what Home de la Honey looks like," I summarize, rubbing my hands together in eager anticipation.

"It's . . ." He looks confused at the concept of describing his home as if adjectives aren't specifically designed for just this type of situation. "A place to crash," he settles on, not giving me a single clue.

"I guess we'll see, won't we? Let's go." I grab his hand, pulling him back toward the sidewalk, but he wraps his big hand around my wrist and stops me.

At the edge of the alley, I'm struck by déjà vu when he peeks out like he's looking for something, or someone. It's what he did after throwing me over his shoulder, and how he looked up and down my street after dropping me off. Like he was worried Dom might see us together.

But Dominic has no reason to be here.

It's a postgame day. He usually sleeps in late, watches television, and does recovery yoga, though I'm not supposed to tell anyone that. I don't know why.

Point being, Dom's nowhere to be found, so why is Griffin acting like he might be?

I wasn't wrong. Griffin's condo is plain and simple like I expected, but it's not devoid of personality if you know where to look. The couch is cognac-colored leather (not black), and the pillows on either end are solid cream, but they have tassels on the corners. There's a black-and-white-patterned rug beneath the couch and a long, low television stand holding a large flat-screen. There are also a few framed art pieces, which surprises me for some reason until I see something that completely shocks me.

"You have a picture of Mom and Dad!" I exclaim, pointing at the only framed picture on the TV stand. In the image, my parents are smiling at the camera, arms wrapped around each other, and the background tells me the picture was taken at the hockey arena where Dom and Griffin played when they were on their former team.

Griffin strides over, slamming the frame face down like that'll undo me seeing it. His nervousness at having me in his private space is palpable, and when he scans the room like he's looking for anything else he doesn't want me to see, I rush to reassure him.

"You don't have to be embarrassed! It's cute! They're basically your parents too at this point."

He snorts a humorless laugh. "I don't have parents."

The statement is harsh, the meaning even more so. It makes me want to ask about a million and two questions about his history all at once, but knowing Griffin, that's a surefire way to have him close up tighter than a bank vault, and I don't want that. So I dance around the deep waters he's treading in, and tease, "That makes sense. You probably spawned right from the depths of Hades like a demon." Raising clawed hands and snarling in an approximation of a hell-born creature, I act like I'm gonna scratch him. It's maybe a bit more T. rex than Beelzebub, but it gets the point across.

A tiny smile lifts one side of Griffin's lips. "Feels like it sometimes."

"Well, then, I'm happy to share my ridiculously awesome parents with you. Be warned, though, once they decide you're theirs, there's no escape. But you already know that, considering you've been to every holiday dinner for the last five years and are the only non-Lee in the Lee group chat."

Something about that causes his smile to melt away until he's frowning so hard that lines bracket his mouth.

"Penny for your thoughts?" I gesture to myself, using the quip I've used for so long that I don't remember when it started. "Specifically your thoughts about a kiss that may or may not have unexpectedly knocked my socks off." I hold my foot up, showing him that I'm not wearing socks beneath my sherpa-lined slip-ons.

"Jesus." The epitaph is a curse, not a prayer, and he collapses to the couch, his head cradled in his hands and elbows on his spread knees. "How the hell did I get mixed up in this mess?"

I hold up a hand, helpfully answering that question as I sit on the other end of the couch, thinking distance is probably a good idea. "Probably me. I do have a tendency for messy drama. Which is totally not my fault! This time. Well, actually, I did kiss you, so maybe it is?" I tap my chin, staring off to the side like I'm considering that, then shake my head, "But you kissed me first, so definitely not my fault. Now that that's decided, tell me why."

"I needed you to shut up."

He says it like that's explanation enough, but it's totally not. If it were, it would've been enough in that alley when he said it. Wasn't then, isn't now. "Needed me to shut up because . . ." I prompt.

"There are these two guys that are kinda, sorta, maybe . . . *fwabakingku.*" He swipes his hand over his mouth, distorting the mumble so that I don't catch what he's said.

"I've heard of five guys"—I lift my eyebrows pointedly, assuming he's seen the memes too—"and Five Guys, good burgers. But what about two guys?"

He doesn't want to say it again, and he glares at me, furious I'm trying to make him. Or maybe it was my reference of five guys. I definitely don't think it was the mention of burgers.

"Guys fucking me?" I suggest, trying to get the sounds he made to shape into words. "Fighting me? Feeding me? Something *eff-ing* me. Maybe try charades? I'm really good at it, though I haven't played since high school at Mary Beth Lomer's sleepover. But I kicked ass, figuring out Patrick Star from *SpongeBob SquarePants* in record time, which was harder than you'd think. At first, I guessed Mary Beth was being a dead body, because she just laid out on the floor, spread out like a star," I demonstrate, sticking out my arms and legs at odd angles, "but I got there, and we beat Preston Barnes in the final round. Served him right. Guy was a prick."

Griffin abruptly pushes to his feet, looming over me. "Following you," he spits out. "Two guys following you."

"Like in an IG fan sorta way, or a stalkery way?" I ask the question, but my mind is already rolling as I replay the videotapes in my head of the people on the street today. It doesn't take long before I find the guys Griffin is talking about. One more second, and I realize that I've seen them before. "They're not following *me*. They're following *you*! Those are the fans you said tried to talk to you at Yesteryear."

He sighs heavily, sitting back down. "About that . . ."

I can read him like a book. His shoulders are tense, his jaw set, and his eyes cold. "I'm not gonna like this, am I?" I guess.

Griffin shakes his head. "No. And let me start by saying I'm sorry for not telling you sooner, but I thought I could handle things and you would never have to know."

He might as well have slapped me. I don't like people hiding things from me, like they know what's good for me better than I do, or like I'm not capable of making choices for myself. I feel lied to, which makes me feel stupid for not realizing I was being lied to, and I don't like this feeling. Not one bit. "Apologies don't really work when you're doing it because you purposefully hid something from me," I snap.

Griffin doesn't flinch a bit, taking the verbal blow like a champ, though it's a much more direct hit than any of our usual banter. "I went into Yesteryear to ask about the ring, remember?"

I nod because, yeah, I remember—I was there, sitting on a bench, crying my eyes out at the unfairness of the world after having been mugged. It's not the kinda thing a girl simply forgets.

"In there, I saw two guys talking to the lady behind the register. They were asking about your ring, said it was sentimental and an accident it was there in the first place, so they wanted it back. She gave them your card and then pointed you out. That's when I got you out of there because I had a bad feeling about those guys." He grits his teeth, making the muscle in his jaw appear and disappear, but his eyes are vacantly staring at the coffee table like he can't look me in the eye while confessing his sins. "And then today, it seemed too coincidental for them to be on the same sidewalk, at the same time, as you when you just as easily could've been home today. I think they followed you. Have you seen them anywhere else? Near your apartment or the arena or the coffee shop, anywhere you go. Think hard."

I replay my mental tapes again, and given they stand out with their size and vibes, I pretty quickly confirm that, until today, I haven't seen them since outside Yesteryear. If I had, I probably would've guessed they were athletes, likely hockey players, since that's the world I live in, and tried to figure out what team they play on. But that hasn't happened, so I know I haven't seen them. I shake my head, but Griffin doesn't look convinced.

"How would they even know where I live?" I muse, thinking through everything he's said. "If Carolynn gave them a card, it has my website and email, that's it. No phone number, no address. And my website lists my PO box. I'm not a total idiot, I know how to be invisible. Basic business practices coupled with being a single woman in the city. Leave no trace isn't just for national parks, you know?" I explain sagely.

"Okay, so maybe they don't know where you live," Griffin echoes, making it sound like he came to that conclusion all by himself and wasn't baby-stepped there by my awesome plan-ahead business skills. But at least I know he's listening, because he looks on the verge of crashing out, running his fingers through his hair and his eyes bouncing around like he's worried one of those guys might've followed us here and will burst through the door any second.

I'm mad at him—furious, actually—for lying, but I also care if he winds himself up into a panic attack when I'm safe. I mean, I'm sitting here in Griffin's apartment, a place I've never been to, with a man who would apparently go to extreme lengths to protect me against some vague threat. It's not the worst place I've ever been. That'd be in a dark closet, playing Seven Minutes in Heaven with Preston Barnes at Mary Beth Lomer's sleepover after that charade game. He wasn't only a sore loser but an octopus who suddenly couldn't understand the word no, at least until I kneed him in the balls the way Dom always told me to do. Comparatively, Griffin's couch isn't half bad.

"If they were actually following me, why would they wait to approach when you're with me? They could've intercepted me anytime today—on my way to Mad Dog's or when I was talking to him, or while I was waiting for you at the café. There's no reason for them to have waited to approach me until I was with someone like you."

"What's that supposed to mean?" he sneers, angry eyes jerking to mine.

I stare back at him like he's an idiot because, surely, he's not serious. Has he ever seen himself in a mirror? Waving a hand around to encompass all of him, I explain, "Big and muscly and obviously on the verge of a throwdown at a moment's notice. Your presence turns what could've been a chill 'hey, about that ring . . .' conversation into a 'don't speak to her without my permission or I'll end you' vibe. And that doesn't make any sense. So maybe it's just a coincidence?"

Some people don't believe in coincidences. They think fate or God or the universe conspires to put things into place, exactly as they're destined to be. I've been in too many weird situations to believe that's true. Unless the universe has a really twisted, sick sense of humor. Which I guess might also be a possibility, but I'm going with weird *coinkydink* this time. Griffin doesn't look convinced of that.

"Hey! Someone messaged me through my website about the ring too. I wonder if it's one of them? Probably, right? Unless there's someone else out on the hunt for the elusive Cursed Ring of Bad Luck-landia."

"They messaged you? And you didn't say anything?"

I recoil, confusion and a don't-yell-at-me bitchiness warring on my face. "Why would I tell you? Considering I didn't know there was any reason to be concerned because you didn't warn me?"

He pinches the bridge of his nose, his eyes closed like he's praying. It's a look I've seen before, many times, from many people. He's annoyed with me and trying not to lose his shit. But my point is valid. We've never really talked about my business. I mean, he hears it when Dom asks or my parents brag, and he's been super helpful with this whole ring deal, but there was no reason for me to bemoan my continued misfortune with him specifically. I handled it myself, the way I always have.

"Can I see?" He holds out his hand, expecting me to give him my phone simply because he asked. Though *ask* is a relative term. There might've been the littlest question mark on the end of what he said, but it was an order all the same.

I could refuse. I could get up and leave. I could just wash my hands of this whole catastrophic episode of season twenty-five in Penelope Lee's life. Instead, I pull my phone from my pocket and, after a few clicks, show him the messages and my responses. He nods as he reads like he approves. Not that I care, and not that it matters, but a tiny piece of me wants to show him that I'm a businesswoman who can string together a professional email in an unfortunate circumstance. I'm not a complete clusterfuck, current situation notwithstanding.

"I haven't responded to the latest message. When I saw it, I got inspired to try to find it again. That's why I went to talk to Mad Dog this morning. Maybe I should respond, though?" I hover my fingers over the buttons on my phone, trying to figure out what to say.

"Just tell them it was stolen. It'll get their attention off you, which is the most important thing."

I'm already shaking my head before he finishes the never-been-a-business-owner advice. "I can't tell them that. It makes me sound like an irresponsible, unreliable flake, which I'm not. At the end of the day, it's still a potential client."

"Or a potential murderer," Griffin deadpans.

"Har har har."

Griffin scrubs a hand over his jaw, thinking. "Why don't you wait? Maybe Johnny K will come through on this and we can get the ring back?"

I can't help but grin. "Look who's the optimist now? You're downright Hopeful Harry over there." But it does sound like a good idea, probably because it's delaying an inevitably uncomfortable conversation with the potential client-slash-murderer. I put my phone down and risk poking the bear, which is probably stupid, but I want to do it anyway. After all, I've never been accused of playing it safe, so why start now? "Now that that's figured out, are we going to talk about the second kiss?"

A devilish smile lifts his lips so high that I see a rare flash of white teeth, or at least a rare happy flash. Normally he only bares his teeth like a predator ready to rip into a victim. "You mean when you kissed me?" He arches one brow, the arrogance he normally possesses rushing back into his entire aura. "And tried to hang on to my neck like a monkey so you could wrap your legs around me?"

My jaw drops open and I make a huffing sound of *nuh-uh*, but he's not exactly wrong. I'm just not ready to admit that maybe he's right. "I meant the one where you pushed me up against the wall and I could feel your dick digging into my stomach and your hand on my throat made me want to do wicked, nasty, dirty things."

"Fuck, Penny. Don't talk like that around me," he hisses, shifting his hips and making me feel victorious in our never-ending war of words. Then he waves his hand. "Scratch that, don't talk like that at all. It's dangerous."

"I'll talk however I want to. About all the sexy, naughty things I like or might like if I had the chance to try them," I argue, realizing something revolutionary. At this moment, Griffin wants me. Drawing a tally mark in the air, I inform him, "Hand necklace, two thumbs up, ten out of ten, would do again. Think there's a place on Yelp to write that review?"

"Jesus," he hisses again. This time, I think it's a prayer. But for what? Salvation? Forgiveness? It hits me like a ton of bricks. It is forgiveness. He doesn't think hiding the whole situation with the guys at Yesteryear is something to apologize for, but kissing me, the little sister of his best friend? Yeah, that's against bro code, which is something Dom and Griffin take seriously. It's something all the Hawks take seriously.

My teasing mood vanishes, and more seriously, I say, "Don't worry, I won't tell Dom. He'll never know. I promise."

He looks relieved . . . for approximately .02 seconds before resignation washes over his face. "I will. Eventually. You're the one rule he has, and I would never disrespect him or your parents that way, no matter how long I've wanted you."

I don't think, I react, jumping to my feet and then around the coffee table to loom over him. "How long you *what*?"

Chapter 16

Griffin

I did *not* mean to say that. Ever. And certainly not to Penny herself. I planned to take that secret to the grave for both our sakes. But it slipped out, and I can't take it back.

Fuck, I want to take it back.

But do I really? Isn't there some small sliver of relief in my cold heart that's glad it's finally out in the open? Yes, but that doesn't mean I should've given in to that weakness. I've fought it for so long, doing my damnedest to hold it deep inside, because I know the damage this truth bomb is going to cause.

I've played it out in my mind hundreds of times. Sometimes, I imagine it wouldn't be that bad . . . that Penny would leap into my arms and say, *Me too*; that Dominic would be mad at first but would then hug me tight, saying that he's glad I'm the one to capture his beloved sister's heart because he can't imagine anyone better than his best friend with her. Even in an imaginary fantasyland of my own making, that pretty picture doesn't seem probable. The much more likely response would be Penny saying something cruelly dismissive and Dominic beating the shit out of me, which I'd let him do because I'd deserve every hit. In that scenario, I never see Penny again, which is untenable.

If she doesn't know how I feel, at least I get the joy of seeing her, knowing her, and watching her succeed. From one small step away, I can witness everything as she lives the life of happiness she deserves.

But now I've fucked it all up. I'm good at that. Always have been, always will be.

"Nothing, never mind." I get up from the couch, walking into the kitchen (a.k.a. running away from Penny and the clear look of shocked horror that's written all over her face). Threading my fingers through my hair, I pull harshly at the strands. The pain is a much-needed punishment for ruining everything, but it's not enough. I slam my hands onto the counter, the sound sharp and too loud. "Fuck!"

"Griffin?" Penny says from the doorway, her voice quiet and unsure.

I don't look at her. I can't. I don't want to see the revulsion on her face. It'll be there—I know it will be. I've done too good of a job at becoming the asshole she hates. There are years of insults, of pushing her away, of making her feel beneath me, when the truth is, I'm the one unworthy of someone as amazing as her.

"I thought . . . well, I've always thought you hated me? Right? You hate me?"

God, I can't stand it anymore. I can't fucking stand it.

I don't decide. I don't choose. Or maybe I chose a long time ago and have been denying the inevitable, even to myself. My feet move of their own will, getting me closer to the one thing I want the most—Penny. "Does this feel like hate?"

Not giving her a moment to answer, I take her mouth with a kiss. She jolts in surprise, but I cup her cheek, keeping her at my mercy. It's such a relief . . . a *release* . . . to finally touch her the way I've wanted to for so long. She's somehow familiar, the Penny I've known for years—and new, the Penny I've never experienced like this. When she gently falls against me, the small surrender ignites every ember I've kept at a slow burn, cranking my need up to the point of desperation. I reach down, wrapping an arm around her lower back and picking her up easily. She hangs on to my neck, but she's so short that her legs dangle, her toes bouncing against my shins.

Spinning, I deposit her on the kitchen counter, shoving her knees open with my hips until there's enough space for me. Her hands explore my chest, and I lift into her touch, wanting the invisible branding of her fingertips. She's already unknowingly tattooed her name onto my heart; she might as well claim my body too. Because it's hers. It's *been* hers.

And she will be mine.

Even if only for this one ill-fated moment. I know this is madness, but I can't stop it now. I don't want to. And unless Penny herself tells me to stop, I won't. I'm seeing this through, even if it leaves my life in ruins and my heart in pieces.

I move a hand to cup her throat, remembering how much she said she enjoyed that. I almost expect her to giggle at the obvious callback, or make a joke of it, but her breath catches, so I put the slightest pressure, squeezing the tiniest bit, and I feel her pulse flutter rapidly against my fingers. Fuck, she *does* like that. My other hand drifts even lower, finding the fullness of her breast, and though she's wearing a sweatshirt and a bra, I can feel the hard nub of her nipple. I tease my thumb over it, and it responds, pearling up even more.

Using my hold on her throat to lift her chin, I press heated kisses down her neck and simultaneously slip my other hand beneath her sweatshirt, wanting to feel her soft skin. She struggles at my waist, fighting to raise my shirt. If that's what she wants, she can have it. She can have anything, everything. I force my hands off her for the one second it takes for me to rip my shirt off and drop it to the floor, and then they're back on her. I pull her sweatshirt up, too, and she ducks out of it. Her fingers dance over the bare skin of my biceps as I cup her breasts, taking my fill. I could dive into the line of her cleavage and live there for the rest of my days as a happy man, surrounded by her scent and the beating of her heart.

I've seen her in a swimsuit before. It nearly killed me because I wanted to lay her over my legs and smack her ass for daring to let anyone see that much of her, but I also desperately didn't want her to cover up. I wanted to see—and memorize—every inch of her that I could, from the freckle on her rib cage to the small heart tattoo on her right hip bone. This bra has more coverage than her favorite swimsuit does, yet this feels more intimate. Swimsuits are for the public; her lingerie is private. Just for me.

That thought has my cock surging demandingly in my jeans, but he'll have to wait. I want to taste more of Penny—more of her mouth, her breasts, her pussy, anything she'll let me have. I would beg for scraps of her attention, worship any inch of her body.

"Jesus," I growl, "you're so fucking beautiful." I press a kiss to the fullness above her bra on one side and then the other, my thumbs swiping over her nipples. She reaches behind herself, easily undoing the fastener in the back, and with the slightest dip of her shoulders, her bra falls. She throws it out of the way like the damn thing is cursed. And Penny Lee is topless on my kitchen counter. I know exactly what I want to eat first.

I trace a circle around one of her nipples, then tease over the nub with my tongue. Penny arches into me, and I suck more of her flesh into my mouth as her arms wrap around my neck, holding me to her. The barest brush of my teeth has her whimpering needily, so I do it again on the other side. I want to learn every single thing she likes and doesn't like. Hell, I can't wait to hear her Yelp ratings.

Her fingers splay over my chest and move down my abs, which clench and flex beneath her touch. *Fuck, is she . . . ?* When she cups my cock, I instinctively buck into her touch with a groan of pleasure, cursing the barrier of my jeans. Her movements turn frantic, her fingers working at the button of my jeans. "Off, take them off," she orders.

I press my forehead to hers, eyes demanding her full attention even though fire is rushing through both of us, burning any shred of logic we might have under different circumstances. "Penny, are you sure?"

"Don't make me question myself. Just do it," she gasps, her fingers still struggling to undo my jeans. But then she freezes. "Unless *you're* not sure?"

The insecurity is deafeningly loud. And entirely my fault. Every cruel word I've spat her way, every grumble of annoyance, every dismissive glance has made her doubt me. I wanted her to think I hated her, *needed* her to think that, but for just a moment—this reckless, dangerous moment—I want her to understand the truth.

"I was sure the second you walked into your parents' kitchen wearing a pair of jeans that fit your ass like a second skin, a team shirt, and a smile that made it feel like there might actually be some good in this world. I was sure then, and though I'm going to burn in hell for it, I'm sure now." For all the sweetness in the picture I'm painting, I might as well be telling her to fuck off, because my voice is rough with desire, the words gritted out like they're being forced from the depths of my soul without me wanting them to be heard.

She blinks, and I think she's realizing that's what she was wearing the first time we met. In truth, it'd been Dominic's team logo, and she'd been supporting her brother. But in my twisted head, it was always for me.

I deliberately slow my movements as I reach for my jeans, giving her every chance to stop me while praying she doesn't. Instead, she goes for her own waist, making quick work of her zipper and lifting her hips to shove her jeans over her hips and down, taking her panties with them. While she kicks her legs, trying clumsily to get her shoes and clothes off, I rush to do the same.

As soon as we're both naked, I'm back on her, melding my mouth to hers and letting my fingers explore the new territory of her thighs, her hips, and then down toward her pussy. All the while, her fingernails scratch a path toward my cock, claiming every inch. The gentlest brush of the backs of my fingers over her clit sends a shudder through her, and her thighs spread even farther apart to give me better access. "I have dreamed of what you taste like."

"Really?" she whispers on a breath, still sounding like she thinks this might be a dream of her own. Later, she'll realize it's not. That it's real, and that the fallout is going to be a nightmare. If I were an honorable, good, worthwhile man, I'd have the strength to remind her. But I'm too far gone to sacrifice this chance. I need it so bad. I need *her* so bad.

I rumble into the sensitive shell of her ear, "Really," before slowly dropping to my knees. I grab her hips roughly, yanking her to the edge of the counter, and push her legs wide, spreading her bare for my hungry gaze. Penny leans back, her hands propping her up and her head resting on the upper cabinet like it's the softest pillow. Taking the shortest moment possible to appreciate the beauty before me and inhale her intoxicating scent, I'm finally able to fulfill one of my most recurrent fantasies by tasting Penelope Lee. She's as heavenly as I dreamed, sweet and musky . . . and *mine*.

Dipping my tongue into her, I savor her, and then moan as I take her clit into my mouth, sucking it as I play with finding out what she likes . . . what she loves . . . and what drives her fucking wild. That's what I want—full-throttle, no-holds-barred Penny. Later, when she regrets this, I want her to at least know that, for one moment, it was worth it. That *I* was worth it.

I devour her, I possess her, I claim her, even leaving my mark on her thigh right next to the crease where her leg meets her pussy. Is it an asshole move? Yes. But I never claimed not to be, and the primal need to leave proof of my presence here, at her most private of places, is riding me hard.

Getting close to the edge—of her orgasm, because her hips are hanging well over the edge of the counter at this point—she begins to buck, searching for what she needs to fall. Wanting to give her more, I tease my fingertips over her entrance, feeling her slickness. One finger slides in easily, so I give her another, fucking her with them.

I can feel her pussy clenching down on my fingers, her walls quivering, and I need her orgasm like I need oxygen. Not only seeing and hearing Penny come but also being the person who makes her shatter is a gift I will fully appreciate the significance of. I work her mercilessly, roughly demanding her body take everything I have to give it—my mouth on her clit, my fingers inside her pussy, and my other hand reaching up to pinch her nipple.

She inhales sharply through clenched teeth, her whole body going stock-still for the longest second of my life, and then spasms rack through her. Her cries are music to my ears, the juices that flow from her pure honey, and I become an instant addict to her pleasure. When the shudders slow, I pull my fingers out and suck them clean as I stand.

My cock is standing hard and ready, desperate to be inside Penny, but now that the edge is taken off for her, I fully expect her to say never mind and leave me fucking myself and spitting out her name as I spill over my hand the way I have countless times before. But she reaches for me instantly, her nails digging into my biceps, and she jerks me in for a kiss. Penny's taste on my tongue and her mouth on mine is a level of intoxication I never fathomed could exist, but here I am.

"Fuck me," she mumbles against my mouth, never stopping the kiss.

I should stop. I should at least put on a condom. I should do countless other reasonable, rational things. I do none of them.

One hand on her hip and the other on the base of my cock, I find her opening and thrust balls-deep into her in one smooth motion. Her head falls back, hitting the cabinet door, but the cry she lets out is of pure bliss, not pain. Finally inside her the way I've always wanted to be, I pause for one heartbeat to let her adjust, but she's already grabbing my hips, encouraging me to get on with it.

Not needing to be told twice, and praying she won't hate me later for this, I give her everything I have, everything I am. Years of pent-up desire, secret hopes I've harbored deep inside, and pure need flow through me as I thrust into her again and again. Penny locks her legs behind my waist, limiting my range of motion, but I make the most of it, staying deep—so *deep*—in her pussy and thrusting shallowly but fast.

"Goddamn it," I spit out through clenched teeth. She feels so good that I'm already teetering on the verge of coming. I have to change things or I'm gonna blow too soon, and I want more of this, more of Penny.

I wrap my arm around her lower back, lifting her into the air and basically impaling her on my cock. Her arms scrabble around frantically, looking to grab on to something. She finds the handle on the cabinet and holds on to it for dear life like the damn thing might stop her from falling. But she's not falling, she's not going anywhere. She's mine.

I grab her throat again, squeezing a little harder this time. "Look at me, Pen. Look at me so I know you know full well who's fucking you."

Her lids flutter, trying to close, but she fights hard to open them and meet my gaze.

"Griffin. I know . . . Oh God . . . Griffin."

Fuck. My name on her lips, in a breathy, sexy voice I've never heard from her before, is my undoing. I pound into her harder, faster, rougher, too desperate for this to pretend I have an ounce of gentle and sweet in my soul.

"Pen?" I grit through clenched teeth. I need her to tell me to stop if she doesn't want this to happen. I'm seconds away from spilling inside her, and while the thought of painting her walls with my cum is all too powerful for me, I don't want her taking risks she doesn't want.

"Mm-hmm," she mumbles, nodding wildly.

It's enough for me, and with one more stroke, my balls pull up tight, electricity sparks through my spine, and I explode. Pulses of my hot cum shoot out, filling her pussy, which is squeezing me like a vise. I think she's coming again, too, but I'm too lost in the blackness behind my closed lids to look at her and find out. Still, I continue thrusting until the sparkles fade and the waves of ecstasy recede.

When I breathe again and open my eyes, Penny is smiling at me weakly. "Whoa. Plot twist, huh?"

I can't help but chuckle in surprise. "We are so fucked."

"Kinda the point, right?" She wiggles her hips slightly like I might need a reminder of what we've just done. But a shadow passes over the brightness in her eyes. "Unless . . ." She trails off, the question of *now what?* written all over her face.

I wish I knew. But I have no idea. I never intended for things to get this far, for this to happen. I figured I would never know the reality of what fucking Penny is like. Now that I do, I mostly just want to do it again, even though I'm still inside her.

I don't say anything. I brush a stray hair back from her face, my eyes searching hers for a hint of what she's thinking. Usually, I can read her like a book because she never hides a single thing. Every hope, fear, and thought is displayed on her face without reserve, but right now, I can't tell what's going on in her head.

I know my own head, though. "Pinch me."

She frowns but reaches for my arm and pinches me hard. The sharp bite is a welcome pain. "Huh, not a dream. You're real." I smile, knowing it probably looks cocky as hell, but I am feeling pretty damn pleased with things. Her mouth rounds into a shocked O, which I press a smacking kiss to.

"You're such an asshole," Penny teases, her grin playful.

"Never claimed otherwise."

Chapter 17

Penny

We do the awkward dance of getting cleaned up and dressed in silence, and find ourselves back on the couch in the living room, where I look at the man sitting beside me.

I don't know who he is.

He grunts and growls like Griffin. He basically pushed my hand out of the way so he could swipe at my center with a warm rag himself and pulled my sweatshirt over my head like I was incapable of dressing myself.

And he looks like Griffin, with blond hair that's currently sex tousled, scruff on his jaw that I can feel the delicious burn of on my thighs, and dark-brown eyes that are uncharacteristically soft. He's shirtless, so I can see his broad shoulders and the tattoos on his biceps that I've long wondered the story of but never dared to ask. His jeans are unbuttoned, showing the tease of a happy trail that disappears behind the zipper, and his bare feet are propped on the edge of the coffee table. He looks like a model shooting an editorial ad for some designer cologne or maybe a Stars of Hockey calendar. He'd be January, like a frozen lake, solid ice on the surface, but the coldness covers a deep, hot spring of raging waters I never knew existed.

So yeah, very much like Griffin—stoic and detached but also . . . nice? That's so weird, and if there's one thing I'm an expert in, it's weirdness. It's gotta be the orgasm. That's the only explanation. My pussy's so good that it turned a monster into a man in—checking my invisible watch—twenty-seven minutes.

Was that really all it was? Less than a half hour of desperate, wild, spontaneous sex that has forever changed my expectations of what sex can be? Apparently so. Because I'm not the same Penny from a half hour ago either.

His voice breaks the silence of the room, low and almost amused. "I can hear you freaking out."

"*Pshaw*, me? I'm not freaking out. You're freaking out. No big deal. Just a bit of wienering, some totally normal sexing between two people who apparently *don't* hate each other as much as we thought. Unless that was hate sex? Was it? I've never done that before. Might have to think a bit before I rate it, since I don't have anything to compare it to." I nibble my bottom lip, thinking. "In the moment, nine-point-four. Being passionately swept away, eaten out, and roughly fucked on a kitchen counter are definite wins. I can see what all the gossip is about where you're concerned." I give him a thumbs-up, nodding knowingly. "After? I've gotta say, maybe a seven-point-eight because this is hella awkward. Should I go? I should go."

I make a move to get up from the couch, and Griffin stops me, basically clotheslining me back into the cozy embrace of the leather. "Penelope."

"That's my name, don't wear it out. Ha ha." I don't laugh, I literally say the words.

He stares at me flatly like he doesn't even have the words to express how exasperated he is with me. With this whole thing. Finally, he mumbles, "I'm sorry. I knew better, knew that was a bad idea. I'm usually better at restraining myself, but spending all this time together is messing with my head." He taps on his temple. No, it's too hard to be a tap. He hits at his temple like he's punishing himself.

"Gotta say, the rating is gonna fall to a six-point-seven if you keep saying fucking me was a bad idea. That's not exactly what girls like to hear when your cum is still inside me."

He moves so fast that I don't have time to react. One second, I'm sitting on the couch, and the next, he's jerked me into his lap in one smooth move, settling me over him like I weigh nothing with my legs folded beneath me on either side of his hips. I have a split-second thought of saying, *Yeehaw, cowboy*, but like he knows it's my newly discovered kryptonite, his hand wraps around my throat again. Every thought banging around in my head—and there are a *lot* of them right now—simply ceases to exist when he touches me like this. Eyes fixed on mine, he silently demands my full attention.

"A bad idea for you. It was my every fantasy come to life. But *I'm a bad idea for you.*"

Wait.

Gruff, snappish tone aside, that sounded sweet. Like he's not wishing to turn back time and undo what we did because it was a mistake, but that he's worried about me. Yet he's scowling at me like I broke his favorite hockey stick.

If mixed signals were a person, there would be flashing neon signs over Griffin.

One thing I do know for sure is that no one tells Penelope Lee what to do. I've fought that battle enough in my lifetime, with people thinking I can't handle my own business, my own dating life, my own life period. But I can, I have, and I do.

I push his hand from my throat, not wanting him to have any semblance of control over what I'm going to say next, totally as my damn self. "How's about you let me make my own decisions—good, bad, or otherwise—and stop trying to make them for me? How about that, hmm?" He's close enough that I could kiss him, but instead of finding his lips, I intentionally aim for his nose, placing the softest boop of a kiss there. It's teasing, lighter than the dark, heavy place he's trying to take this to, which is why I do it, secretly afraid he might be right about the whole bad-decision thing.

He is my brother's best friend. And doesn't exactly have a history of treating me well, so that's not gonna go over easily. Not with Dominic, but more importantly, not with me. He's got some 'splaining to do.

He crinkles his nose, then swipes a finger across the tip.

"Are you wiping off my kiss or rubbing it in? Answer carefully."

His answering glare is all too familiar. I can feel the judgment, the accusation, the virtual name-calling—bratty, annoying, unwanted. I've felt and heard it too many times, basically every time we're in the same room.

"You always act like you don't want me around, but then you recite exactly what I was wearing the day we met. Those are some serious contradictions. Care to explain?"

"Not particularly." His eyes drift to the side like he's trying to avoid a conversation that I suspect is getting too close to the danger zone in his mind. His stupidly, sweetly, messed-up mind.

But I have a trick up my own sleeve. Or at least an idea of one. I grab his jaw in my hand, turning his face back to mine. His nostrils flare, and I know I've got him. "Explain it anyway. For me."

"Fuck."

He lifts me, dropping me back on the couch before getting up. Pacing across the living room, he runs his fingers through his hair in frustration. Looking everywhere but at me, he mumbles, "I don't know what you want me to say."

"Do you hate me as much as you act like you do? It's a simple yes-or-no question."

His laugh is a bitter, mirthless huff. "That is not simple."

Staring at his back as he makes another lap across the floor, I don't move. I don't breathe. I sure as shit don't ask again. Because while not a yes or no, his answer is crystal clear.

I thought I knew who Griffin Mahoney is, but I don't think I know at all. The image I've had of him is the man he wanted me to see, but

I suspect the real Griffin Mahoney is an entirely different man, one I could like. But I'm not going to beg him to want me, to like me, and definitely not force him to admit to the barest minimum of non-hate. I have some pride. Or I did before it took that nuclear missile–level hit right to target center.

"I think you might've been right earlier. We should've pretended the kiss never happened. Then whatever this was wouldn't have happened. It's not too late, though. We can still course correct. Let's just pretend it was a little oopsie, like you fell dick first into me and we accidentally ended up puzzle-pieced together. *Whoops!*" Getting up from the couch, I reach for my shoes, slipping them on as quickly as possible. "It'll make family dinners awkward as hell, but that won't even be that different. You can do your customary frowny-face thing like you wish I wasn't there, and I'll annoy you by breathing wrong or whatever it is I do that bothers you."

I want him to stop me. Deep down, I know that's what I'm hoping for. It'd be a sign that I haven't totally fucked up my life in a newly spectacular way. But he doesn't.

I get all the way to the door before he says a word.

"I won't let dinners be uncomfortable for you."

Yeah, as if that's the major issue here. Not the rest of this whole debacle.

And to think, just this morning, my biggest problem was a damn ring. Now? I've managed to implode my whole life with what amounts to be both the best and worst sex I've ever had. How ridiculous is that?

I know everything happens for a reason, but c'mon, universe . . . what the fuck?

Glancing over my shoulder, I snipe, "How are you gonna do that? Your usual glare-and-growl show over Mom's infamous spaghetti and meatballs isn't gonna cut it when you've been guts deep inside me."

"Goddamn it, Penny! Fine, then I won't go anymore. Is that what you want?" he shouts, his hands thrown up in what looks like exasperated surrender.

I whirl, feet planted and arms crossed over my chest, doing my best Griffin impersonation and not answering the question.

Shaking his head, he declares, "I was fine without them before, and I'll be fine without them again. I'll lose the only family I've ever had, my best friend, and you in one fell swoop. It was bound to happen eventually anyway. It's what I deserve."

"Oh, quit with the poor-me pity party." I play the tiniest violin with my thumb and index finger. "Come to dinner, don't come to dinner, do whatever the hell you want. You're a big boy, so fucking act like one."

"I'm fucking trying!" he roars. "I've been trying my hardest for five years, doing the one and only thing Dominic asked of me." He holds up a finger, then points it at me. "Stay away from you. I couldn't even do that right." His shoulders fall as his gaze drops to the floor.

"You're right about one thing."

He doesn't lift his face, but he looks up through his lashes at me. "What?"

"You do deserve to lose me. You've treated me like shit, and even if it was some noble gesture to respect Dom's wishes, it still felt shitty. He told me once that any man worthy of me wouldn't be scared of him. He's not always the best brother, but in this, I guess he was right."

With that, I open the door and walk out, leaving it wide open behind me. Not so he'll chase me but so he'll have to be the one to close the door on whatever this could've been. If it could've been something at all.

Chapter 18

GRIFFIN

"What the fuck is wrong with you?" Dom demands. Even though he's skating by, staying in perpetual motion, behind the glare of the arena lights on his face shield, I can see true concern in his eyes.

Tonight's game against the Torches is turning out to be an unexpected bloodbath. All thanks to yours truly. I've gone from defending the right side of the ice and keeping the puck out of Howe's zone to seeking out other players to wail on. I need to slam into something, full body contact followed by a fistfight that'll get all this pent-up anger out. Anything that'll make it stop, even if it's for only a second.

"Done with this shit."

The puck drops, action resumes, and I scope out my next target. They'll never know what hit them.

Unfortunately, I know exactly what hit me. Penelope Lee.

It's been four days since she walked out of my apartment.

The first day, I waited for Dominic to come beat the shit out of me. When it didn't happen, I slowly started to realize that Penny hadn't told him anything. I wasn't sure if that made me feel better or worse. Mostly, it'd just made me *feel*, and it was fucking awful. A black eye or bruised rib would've been infinitely easier to deal with than the growing sense of betrayal and guilt.

That night I texted her, needing to make sure she was okay, but she didn't respond, leaving me on read. I even tried asking about the ring, because I haven't forgotten about that problem, but she didn't reply to that either.

Walking in for introductions tonight, I immediately began searching for her. For one too-brief and delusional moment, I held on to the ridiculously hopeful idea that she might chirp at me the way she did before the Vortex game. Alternatively, at the other end of the old-fashioned spectrum, I expected things to be the way they were before, with her doling out easy smiles for everyone else and spite-filled glares for me. Instead, she stayed deathly silent, not even letting her eyes land on me as I skated by. She looked past me as if I wasn't even there. To be fair, I feel like a ghost of myself, a mere shell of a man, so I shouldn't have been surprised by her non-reaction, but I was. Especially since my heart had been pounding in my chest with excitement just from laying eyes on her.

And since the game started, I've done my best to tune her out. But it's damn near impossible when there's so much that I want to say. Well, not *that* much. Mostly just that I'm sorry.

I do a quick check of the cheerleaders. Penny's up on the stage, just to the home side of the red line, her brown hair flipping around as she dances. I want to watch her, to soak in every second of seeing her that I can get. But the play moves toward our end of the ice, drawing my attention back where it should be. The fury is instantaneous. I'm ready to plow into whomever I can, as hard as I can. I'll fuck them up, and I don't give a shit if I get fucked up in the process too.

I'm mad at myself for getting distracted, I'm mad at losing a moment of watching Penny, I'm mad at . . . everything and everyone. Most of all, myself.

After the game, the locker room is full of celebratory shouts. Even Howe and Brody are hugging as they sway to some remixed, fake-twang version of "Take That Puck and Shove It."

"You ain't scoring here no more, don't stand in my way as I'm shooting on your goal, so take that puck and shove it. You ain't a winner here no more."

Yeah, we won, knocking the division-leading Torches down in the rankings and guaranteeing our matchup in the first playoff round. I don't feel like celebrating, though. I feel like bodychecking a few more guys.

"Honey! How's your finger?" one of the sports medicine guys shouts.

I dislocated my right pinkie finger when it caught on Cavanaugh's sweater during a scuffle. It didn't turn into a full fight because we couldn't risk the fighting penalty in such a tight game, but getting your finger caught on someone's gear and twisted out still sucks. But I popped it back into place before the next play started and it's fine. Besides, I know the drill and have anti-inflammatories at home to take before bed tonight.

I hold my hand up in the air, curling and uncurling my hand. It's the closest to an exam he's gonna get from me. My bruised knuckles crunch like Rice Krispies cereal, but from across the room, the trainer can't hear the gross noise. He dips his chin and writes on his clipboard. That's what I am to him . . . a check mark on a list. A weapon to be aimed and fired. And that's what I'll do again tomorrow night.

I'll take on the Torches the same way I did tonight—mercilessly, with minimal regard for penalties or my own safety.

"Get dressed," Dom says, suddenly right beside me.

Frowning, I hold my arms out, highlighting that I've literally got my pants on and my shirt is in my hand.

"You and me, we're going out." He doesn't give me a chance to argue or refuse. Pointing a finger at my chest, he declares, "And that wasn't a fucking question. We've got shit to discuss."

Fuck.

Maybe Penny told him after all.

What are we doing here of all places?

If Dominic wants to have a man-to-man chat about my misdeeds with his sister—which I fully expect to involve more fists than words—I wouldn't expect it to be at a golf driving range, but here we are. I figured he'd lead me to his place or maybe mine if he's feeling generous, so I could collapse into bed after he fucks my shit up.

I park beside him and get out, on high alert despite the unusual locale for a smackdown.

Inside, Dominic charms the hostess as she leads us to a bay far away from anyone else. I roll my eyes when she tells Dom there's no need to reserve the two bays on either side of us for additional privacy because they're happy to give us the space as "special guests." Part of that is a Hawks privilege, the other is that they're only open for another hour so it's unlikely they'll get a rush of guests this late. Either way, it works in our favor.

The manager comes over before we've even settled into our seats. "Hell of a game tonight, guys. We're gonna do it again tomorrow, too, right?" He smiles one of those fake customer service grins, making it seem like he's a Hawk, too, and we're all in this together, kumbaya-style. If that's the case, I'd like to see his knuckles. I bet they're not nearly as swollen and bruised as mine are. "We can do anything you need. Just let me know. I'm Andrew." He points at his name tag like we'll remember that.

I've already forgotten. His name doesn't matter when I'm about to lose my best friend.

"Thanks," Dom tells him. "Can the kitchen do something high protein for us? Whatever chicken or beef and rice type thing they can put together. We don't care what it tastes like. It's fuel to us."

Andrew looks offended at the idea that something his kitchen staff would make wouldn't be delicious. "How about a spin on breakfast tacos? It's not on our late-night menu, but for you we'll make it happen. Chicken, eggs, grilled peppers, roasted potatoes, guacamole, salsa on flour tortillas?"

"You can skip the tortillas. Just pile all that shit in a bowl, and we'll be good." Andrew nods like he's making a mental note of Dominic's order. "And water. Just bring us the biggest pitcher you've got. We've gotta rehydrate."

While Dom handles the pleasantries with the manager, I sit there sullenly, wishing we could get this show on the road, because something tells me the manager isn't going to be quite as accommodating when Dom and I start throwing punches.

When Andrew leaves us alone, I'm ready. Well, as ready as I'm going to be.

"What's up?" I already know the answer to the question, but I figure I might as well open the door and let Dom in. I'm a shitty friend who's broken his trust, but I'm willing to face the consequences for my actions head-on. I deserve every last one of them.

"What's up? Are you serious, man?" Dom snaps, his public charm falling away. "I saw you on the ice tonight. You were distracted as hell and violent as fuck. And before you argue that's your job as enforcer, that is *not* what tonight was. You were on a search and destroy mission, and whether the Torches will be feeling the effects of that or not, you were taking risks that should've gotten you kicked out of the game. You're damned lucky you didn't end up on the injury list," he says. "The way you were going after the Torches? Normally I'd ask if one of them fucked your mom, or your sister, or wife, but since that's not an issue, what the hell is?"

He's not yelling at me about Penny? But about the game? Okay, that's also unexpected, but I don't argue with him. There's no point. He's right.

My jammed-up finger wasn't the worst of it tonight, just the most obvious injury since I popped it back into place on ice. Hell, they showed the replay of me doing it on the jumbotron. But getting my head bounced off the plexiglass during one of my little body checks will definitely have them hunting me down for another concussion check before tomorrow night's game, even though I already passed one mid-game. Not because I'm in real danger, but again, it's a check mark on someone's list. *Is Mahoney safe to take another shot for the team?* As if I'd ever say no.

"Nothing. Just playing."

"No, you weren't. You were out there trying to destroy yourself. And I'm not gonna let that happen," Dom declares, as if he alone can stop that from happening. "The season is too important for you to fall apart now, so whatever's fucking up your mind, you need to let that shit go. Pull an Elsa outta your ass or whatever you gotta do. But let. It. Go. The team needs you. I need you."

He's right. Hockey is what I'm good at. It's basically all I'm good for. I've got to focus on the season, on winning against the Torches again tomorrow and prepping for the playoffs. I can't let my team down.

"You're right," I concede, still expecting him to pick up one of the golf clubs and knock me over the head with it. That would definitely have me sitting out on concussion-watch protocol.

"You need to hit something? Hit those." Dominic points at the golf ball teed up in front of us.

Is that why he brought me here? To hit something, to unleash my anger in a healthy way? It sounds like it.

I'm not a golfer. I didn't grow up with a father who took me to the country club to hit balls, and though I worked in school, it sure wasn't as a caddie. But a club isn't so different from a hockey stick, and a ball is like a small puck, so what the hell.

I get up, still hesitant to give Dom my back, considering the Penny situation, but I'm beginning to think she really hasn't told him and this isn't some ploy to get me to lower my guard so he can sneak in for a death blow.

I line up the shot and do a couple of practice swings, getting a feel for the club. *Thwack!*

The ball goes sailing through the air in a long arc, landing just shy of the back net. I bounce my shoulders, the controlled hit feeling good. It did release some of my anger.

"Feels good, huh? Do it again." Dom sounds like Mr. Miyagi telling the Karate Kid to keep practicing.

I hit another ball, then another, and another. Each time I line up the shot, I take a deep breath, letting my focus center on the ball before swinging as hard as I can. I'm not going for precision, trying to get the ball into some tiny hole. I'm going for distance by hitting with as much power as I can generate.

Andrew arrives with our food, and I sit back down across from Dominic. When we dig in, the only sounds breaking the silence are us chewing and swallowing as much as possible as fast as possible.

"Now that that's out of the way"—he points at the tee with his fork—"what's really going on with you?"

"What do you mean?" I say slowly.

Shit. I knew it was too good to be true. Gut punches on a full stomach are gonna hurt even worse. Maybe that was his diabolical plan all along? Knowing Dominic, probably so.

"You're not only acting like a monster on the ice, you're blowing me off left and right. Skipping pregame dinners? That's not like you. What's up?" This isn't about hockey and being teammates that count on each other. His question is deeper, more personal than that. He's asking as my best friend.

"Nothing. Just a lot going on in here, none of it good." I tap my temple.

He tilts his head, looking at me shrewdly. He knows me better than anyone and can probably see the guilt written all over my face. But what he asks is, "Did your parents come out of the woodwork or something?"

"What? No. I haven't talked to them in years. You know that."

He nods, not giving up yet. "Yeah, just checking. You know they'll try it eventually. You're getting too much press for them not to try getting back in your good graces, and wallet." He rubs his thumb and two fingers together. It's a sad truth that when you get that prized NHL contract, one of the first things teammates and coaches warn you about is to watch out for people coming after your money. Too often, it's the people you love most, like family. Thankfully, mine wouldn't even know how to get in contact with me if they wanted to. My phone number, address, and email are top secret like the rest of the teams', and even if my parents did somehow track me down, I wouldn't respond to people who are effectively dead to me. "So if it's not them screwing with your mind, what girl has you this fucked up?"

My heart rate skyrockets and a lump appears in my throat. But I manage to force out, "There's no girl."

There is *so* a girl. But if he doesn't already know, I can't tell him that. He's the one person I've always talked to about everything, and the one I'd trust to give me the best advice, but this time, he's the one I can't talk to.

"You are such a shitty liar," he taunts, smiling and laughing around his mouthful of chicken. "But before the first round kicks off next week, Pro-Bowl's calling our name, and I won't take no for an answer."

I doubt he'll want to have dinner with me by then. There's no way I can keep this quiet that long. The guilt is already eating me up inside, as evidenced by the way I behaved on the ice tonight. Hell, by the way I'm acting right now.

Dominic is my best friend, and when he finds out I fucked Penny, it will be the end of this friendship. I know that down to my bones, which is why I'm too much of a coward to tell him. Penny's words echo in my head—that any man scared of Dom isn't worthy of her. As if that was some breaking news flash. I've never been worthy of her, that's been the issue all along.

Besides, I'm not scared *of* Dominic. I'm scared I don't know what I'd do without him at my side. For five years, I've chosen him over and over, reminding myself that I would be nothing without his friendship, his support, him reaching into the depths of hell I was existing in and saving my worthless ass. When I didn't know what Penny felt like, tasted like, sounded like, I could make that decision and live with it. But now? I don't think I can.

I want her too much. I'm a greedy, selfish bastard, and I can't stop myself anymore.

Maybe I can become worthy of her? Is that even possible? I don't know.

When I don't answer, he stops eating to give me a calculating look. "Is it serious?"

I shrug noncommittally. "You know me."

"I do. And I have never seen you give a woman a second thought. So what's going on?"

This is real talk. Not the shit-stirring locker-room antics we usually stick to. Knowing that I'm writing my own death warrant, I sigh. "I'm pretty fucked up."

"As we've established," he offers supportively.

"What if I'm never good enough for anyone? I don't know how to do emotional shit. And communication?" I ask, unconsciously tapping into my soul as I wave a hand between me and him with a look of misery. "I never learned how to do any of that. All I learned was how to hide emotions. Happiness, not that there was much of that, but if something made me smile, it'd get snatched away. Sadness meant I'd get called a crybaby and Dad would threaten to give me something to cry about. Anger only incited my dad's, and he was bigger and stronger than I was for a long time. Even when I grew, he was still meaner than me. I just don't know what to do with all the stuff inside me." I pull at my shirt over my heart, wishing I could rip the damn thing out and stomp on it. That'd solve everything. "I learned to turn it all off, and not care about anyone, because they didn't care about me either."

"Fuck you," Dom spits out, offended. "I care about you."

"I know. And I appreciate that. You have *no* idea how much. But I don't want to fuck you." It's the smallest sliver of lightheartedness in the heavy dump of my trauma.

"But you want to fuck her?" he guesses.

I lick my lips, trying to figure out what to say. "I want *everything* with her. But I'm not good enough for her. For anyone."

"*Pshaw*, you're the best, so first you have to believe it. Then give her a chance to know it. And if she can't see it, she's not the one for you." He smiles like that's a done deal, and I tilt my head, challenging his Pollyanna advice. Relenting, he concedes, "Okay, so yeah, you're a little complicated, but aren't we all?"

"You're not."

Dom stretches his arms up and out and leans back in a parody of jackassery. "Well, I'm special."

"So is she." Yeah, special enough to also have grown up in the Lee household, with all the love, support, and kindness of a good family. And without all the unhealthiness of the Mahoney one.

"Not special enough if she can't appreciate the great man that you are and see you working to be even better. I'm not saying that's gonna be easy, or quick, but one day, if you work hard enough and really believe with all your heart, you'll be half as awesome as I am."

"You are such a son of a bitch," I growl even as I laugh. "Fucking self-help book quackery? Really?"

"That's why you love me," Dom quips, nodding with a certainty that only he could possess.

"I do. Thanks, man."

He points a warning finger my way. "But don't do all this talk therapy and psychoanalysis mid-playoffs. Those are too important. To the team, and to you. I know how much you want that Cup. The rest of this can wait until it's in your hands. If she's the right one, she'll understand that hockey will always be your first love. Then me, then her." He's held up a finger with each priority, one for hockey, and one for him, but instead of a third finger, he switches to flipping me off, like the fucking part is still the main thing this unnamed woman has on me. His shit-eating grin makes things feel . . . normal.

They're not, but for just a little while longer, I really want to pretend they are.

Chapter 19

Penny

"Good morning, sunshine!" Talia sings as she comes into the living room, but I can feel her eyes. She's studying me like I might burst into tears, a curse-laden rant, or an interpretive dance combining both at any moment. To be fair, she was the unlucky-ducky recipient of a rage-fueled, tearful rehashing of what went down at Griffin's last weekend, and since then has heard several different versions of "Can you believe this asshole?" all week when he's texted me. So her expecting more of the same is reasonable.

"Hey," I reply dully, not lifting my gaze from the ring I finished yesterday. Part of it is that I don't want to unfocus my eyes, which are adjusted to the brightness of my work light. Most of it is that I don't want to risk crying again.

Not because I'm sad. But because I'm mad. Okay, and a little sad. But can you blame me? Great sex followed by "that was a bad idea" would crumble anyone's self-esteem.

"Coffee?"

Shaking my head, I tell her, "No, thanks. I need to finish my final checks on this so I can post pictures before I go to the post office. There's always that chance someone will buy it instantly and I could send it out today with the other packages." I gesture vaguely at the two boxes I've already prepared for today's shipping.

When I first started the PLDesigns online shop, I would literally publish an item for sale and then stare at the screen, refreshing every five seconds—yes, I counted—while obsessively watching the site traffic. I was sure someone was waiting on the other end of the internet, ready to click Add to Cart the instant I made something available. Now I know better and usually post and run. But with current circumstances, I'm back to watching my order page like it's a pot of water I'm waiting to come to a boil.

"How much have you sold?" Talia asks, coming back from the kitchen to sit on the couch. The strong scent of coffee comes with her, and I don't need to look up to know she has a steaming mug in her hands.

"Just over two thousand dollars." Normally, I'd be over the moon and dancing a happy jig at those sales. Two thousand in this short of time is a good chunk of change. But with the looming credit card bill, it's not enough. Not nearly enough. Especially when I've already gone through my small backlog of pieces to see what I can redesign quickly. I've got the pink topaz ring I'm currently examining, and that's it. Having consistent turnover and listings that sell quickly is usually a plus, but after this, I'll need to source more as quickly as I can.

Being the amazing friend that she is, Talia already offered to loan me the money to cover the credit card bill. Twice, in fact. I thanked her for the willingness to help but assured her that I would figure this out on my own. In fact, the second time, I told her that I would sell my soul to the devil before I took her savings. I think she believed me when I started listing all the heinous things I would let him do to me for the 10K, which must be why she hasn't offered again.

"That's good." She knows it's not, but her support is still appreciated. "How was the game last night?"

Okay, guess we're digging right into the nitty-gritty without lube.

I blink hard a few times, letting my eyes adjust to find Talia on the couch, where she's curled up in a nest of blankets, coffee mug cradled in her hands and covered by a handknit mug cozy that one of her patients made. It always makes her smile, but today her face is the picture of worry.

"We won." She doesn't give a shit about the team standings, so "win or lose" isn't what she's really asking. She wants to know what happened when I saw Griffin, when he saw me, and whether there were fireworks or a nuclear bomb in that moment. But that answer does actually lie somewhere in the game report.

"Aaand . . ."

I don't know how to explain last night's game to a non-hockey person. Griffin had been on a rampage, spending way more time than usual in the penalty box and going after people more than the puck. The highlight moment—or technically a lowlight one—was when he fixed a dislocated finger on the jumbotron. I gasped at the gruesome sight, and Layla jerked her head my way, demanding to know what the hell I'd done to our boy.

Ours, as in the Hawks. Because he's not mine, not in any way that matters. He made that abundantly clear when I asked if he hated me and he didn't have an answer. I wasn't looking for him to confess some deep, dark, long-hidden love for me. Simply non-hate. Yet, after five years of family holidays, countless pregame meals, helping me move, and dozens of other interactions, he couldn't do that. After reciting what I'd been wearing the day we met and screwing me stupid, he couldn't say, *I guess you're kinda-sorta-maybe all right–ish sometimes*.

What the hell was up with that? It's not like I'm a stage-five clinger by any stretch, but some human decency and manners are the bare minimum. And I do mean *bare* minimum. My actual standards are considerably higher. Giving in to lust had been a moment of weakness on my part. I'm chalking it up to the unexpected chemistry in that first real kiss, and then the firestorm between us when Griffin asked if his kiss felt like hate. For the record, no, it did not. It felt . . . hot, sexy, and exciting in a way I'd never considered. Mostly because I've never considered Griffin to be anything other than Dominic's asshole friend.

The last few days, though? Oh, I've been doing some *considering*. Lots of it. But it would take more than a good dicking for me to accept the way Griffin treated me after. I don't know what it'd take, and honestly, I hope to never find out. Because, again, I have standards.

"Let's say he threw himself into his work the way I've been throwing myself into mine," I finally answer Talia.

"Shiiit. Are the other guys still breathing?"

"Probably. Guess we'll find out tonight when we do it all again." I hold my hands up, shaking invisible poms, and fake a smile that feels more like a grimace than anything remotely cheery. I will definitely have to get my act together before tonight's rematch against the Torches, or Layla will bench me.

"I don't envy them. Or you. Physical battering? Emotional?" She holds out her hands, weighing the two options and not finding an obvious loser. Or winner.

"Gee, thanks, what would I do without your analytical breakdown of the situation," I say wryly. Luckily, Talia's a great friend and doesn't hold my bitchiness against me . . . too much. She simply tilts her head, giving me that trademark Mom stare that asks, *You done yet?*

And yes, I am. I need to pull my head out of my ass and start focusing on the positive here, like . . . I've sold enough to make the minimum payment on my credit card bill. I had a stellar orgasm that wasn't machine made. I have a new favorite ice cream shop and a potential shopping ground of new pawnshops. I won't have to sit across from Griffin at any more family dinners or pregame meals if he knows what's good for him.

See? It's practically glittering with good news in Penny Land.

Fortifying myself with a deep breath, I list out, "Mission one, take pictures of this bland, boring eternity band of a ring and post them." I curl my lip toward the gorgeous ring I've made, wishing I'd had the time to create the cluster effect I'd first imagined. But time isn't on my side, so I went with a surefire seller. Pink eternity band? It's perfect as a push present for a girl mom, or as an anniversary band. The options are endless and buyers nearly countless, which is good for my money situation but bad for my creative muse. Sacrifices must be made, though, and I promised my muse that she'll get to play after I pay off this bill. "Two, make a run to the post office before the noon pickup. Three, get ready for tonight's game. Aaaand break." I clap my hands like we've completed our daily huddle and force another smile. This one is at least real, because I like a plan. It makes me feel like I've got goals and can achieve them step-by-step.

"Good luck," Talia says warily, taking a sip and settling a little deeper into her nest. Guess I know what she's doing today.

I kinda wish I could plop onto the couch beside her and binge-watch *Drag Race*, but I don't have the luxury of time the way she does because she didn't screw up by losing the biggest investment she's ever made and then follow it up by screwing her brother's best friend.

That'd be me. Way to go, Penny!

❧

I slip the two small boxes I'm shipping out into a ridiculously oversize tote bag, then slide the straps onto my shoulder. Gripping the bag tightly, I scan the parking lot before getting out of my car. Am I overly paranoid my precious cargo might be stolen right out of my hands? Yes. But that doesn't mean I've gone full tinfoil hat. In fact, I think it's a perfectly logical response after it quite literally happened.

I keep my head on a swivel walking across the lot, looking for thieves in red hoodies, along with anyone else suspicious. Thankfully, I only see other people like me, trying to make it before the noon pickup.

Inside, I check my PO box first. I don't get a lot of snail mail since most of my business is conducted online, but there seems to always be a stack of junk mail and catalogs I never subscribed to, so I like to keep it cleared out. I shove all the randomness into my bag, keeping my shipping boxes where I can obsessively confirm they're still there every two-point-three seconds. And yes, I'm counting.

One-and-a, two-and-a, check. One-and-a, two-and-a, check.

Getting in line to ship my packages, I start going through the envelopes while keeping my bag clutched to my front. I've got a nifty sorting system happening, with the stuff to be opened to the back of the boxes and the stuff already opened to the front.

Slowly, I one-step my way closer to the front of the line.

Until, nose down in my bag, I start to hear grumbles of annoyance in front of me. "Back of the line, buddy!"

I glance up to see what the fuss is about and quickly jerk my face back down to my bag.

It can't be. There's no way they're here.

It's the two guys Griffin said were following me. What are the chances they're at the post office on a Saturday at noon? Since they have no envelopes or boxes in their hands, slim to none.

"One second. I have a question," one of the guys barks at the woman I'm guessing told him to wait in line like everyone else is doing.

"And I need to mail this before my morning MiraLAX kicks in. Back of the line," she says, not conceding an inch.

My heart starts racing in my chest as fear trickles through my veins. I really thought Griffin was overreacting and it truly was a coincidence that those guys had been at Yesteryear and then near Johnny K's. It's a big city, but also people tend to stick to the relatively small portion that's closest to their homes. Or at least I do, and I figure that's the same for most people. Plus, we didn't see them go into Johnny K's. They might've been shopping at any number of stores on that block, or live in one of the apartments above the stores, or been out for a stroll to take advantage of the good weather. Any number of possibilities that have nothing to do with Griffin's bad feeling about them.

But a third appearance? Is that beyond the scope of coincidental? It feels like it might be.

Keeping my face down, I peek through my hair, and see that one guy is talking to Ms. MiraLAX. The other guy is talking to the post office clerk. "I need to find out the home address of someone who has a PO box here. How do I do that?"

"You don't," the clerk answers, her voice monotone with a complete lack of concern about his question or the fact that he cut in line, which Ms. MiraLAX is still complaining about. "Next!"

"It's your turn," Ms. MiraLAX tells the man in front of her, who had been impatiently toe tapping while waiting for his chance at the counter but is now standing back like he's not in such a hurry after all. I can understand why. The two guys are significantly larger and more intimidating up close and personal, especially now that I think they might actually be following me.

But me? Why me? I'm nobody. Yeah, the ring is a one-of-a-kind piece, but I already told them it's unavailable. That should be that.

"Look it up. It's box 4862," the guy tells the clerk, taking away any residual doubt I may have still had. Because PO box 4862 belongs to PLDesigns, a.k.a. me, and is what's listed on my website.

I have to get out of here.

I duck my head again, nearly shoving it into my bag, as I turn around. "Excuse me," I whisper to the lady behind me as I get out of line. I force my feet to walk despite a very strong urge to sprint. It feels like one of those National Geographic documentary moments . . .

Though the faster female lions are known as the primary hunters, males are better suited for ambushing larger prey, and these hungry lions have stalked this guileless prey for days across prairie flatlands and through tough terrain, their patience growing weary with every passing day. Until now, finally . . . they're ready to pounce. Sensing an invisible danger, the prey reacts instinctually, bolting away. The lions give chase, wearing the prey out as they direct it toward a lone tree. The prey foolishly takes the bait, seeing the tree as a safe reprieve and climbing as high as possible to find cover. Not realizing that was the lion's plan all along, the prey is now trapped. There's no way out. The lions simply have to wait out the doomed prey.

I can't let myself be stuck in a tree.

I fight off the fear building in my gut and climbing my throat, telling myself . . . *Don't run. Don't act suspicious. Don't draw attention. Don't. Run.*

So, of course, as soon as I'm through the door, I sprint for my car. It's instinct. I can't help it. As I cross the parking lot, I'm scrambling in my bag for my keys. Once I find them, I press the unlock button over and over like that'll make it extra-unlocked for me to jump right in.

I swing the car door open and climb in, but because it's me, of course I bang my head on the doorframe. Pained tears instantly spring to my eyes. "Owwww!" I hiss, rubbing the tender spot on the side of my head with one hand and double-locking the doors with the other.

But I made it out alive, and thankfully un-chased by big, scary guys who are apparently looking for me. And trying to find out my home address.

Oh my God! I have to get home.

But some sanity reigns, plus I'm kinda seeing double from the head bang, and instead of peeling out of the lot on two wheels and laying down a line of rubber, I slouch down low in my seat. Heart still pounding and my breath fogging up the windows, I wait for the guys to come out. I need to see their faces. Not because I haven't memorized them at this point but because I need to see if they look happy or disappointed. That'll tell me if they know where I live.

I pray the post office's lack of give-a-shit served me well this time and the clerk refused to be bothered into looking up my address, which I was assured was entirely private since that's the whole point of a PO box. But I don't know if I trust their process that much.

I'm staring fixated at the door, waiting, and when it finally swings open, the two guys come out, their faces thunderous as they yell at each other. I can't hear them, but I can read the situation well enough to know one thing for sure . . . they didn't get my address. Yet.

It's a huge relief. But if they went this far, what else will they do in search of this ring? I swear it really must be cursed. And unfortunately, I think the curse has extended to include me.

Chapter 20

Penny

Busting through my apartment door, I'm already talking to Talia. "Oh my God, you are not gonna believe what happened at the post office!"

Expecting her to be ready to hear my crazy story, I'm completely unprepared for hers.

"He says he's here to apologize." Talia holds her hands up, though I'm not sure if it's in surrender or to stop me from attacking the man sitting on our couch, who also looks concerned I might launch myself at him, and not in a good way.

Griffin.

I cannot believe the audacity this guy possesses. Showing up after what he did? Fuck that, and fuck him. Not literally, obviously, but in the fuck-off way. In my mind, I flip middle finger after middle finger at him. *Fuck you! Fuck you! Fuck you!*

I don't speak to him, but to Talia instead. "Well, you can tell him to apologize to someone who wants to hear it, because it's not me."

I drop my bag on my desk chair, glaring death at the son of a bitch, who's sitting with his elbows on his spread knees, eyes locked on me. At the post office, I felt like prey and those scary guys were predators. But I was wrong. How Griffin is looking at me now? That's predatory. His brown eyes are dark, intensely focused, and I suspect that if I went for the door, he'd beat me there because he's watching my every move that closely.

"I'll leave you two to it," Talia says uncertainly. And then, traitorous bitch that she is, she picks up her purse, shoots me a look of *sorry*—or maybe it's *don't be too loud or Mrs. Rosenthal will call the super*—and vanishes out the door, abandoning me to this rapidly sinking ship.

"She did not just do that," I say to no one in particular, because I am not talking to Griffin. Like ever again. Silent treatment? Try invisible treatment. No talking, no looking, no acknowledgment. That's what he gets.

"I brought you ice cream. It's in the freezer."

I whirl on him, incredulous. "You think ice cream is gonna fix this? You must be stupid if you think I'm that easy."

So much for the invisible treatment.

He flinches instantly at my sharp tone. But the shadow that passes over his eyes when I call him *stupid* sends regret through me. I'm not mean and cruel that way. I'm not the bully. He is, and I refuse to stoop to his level. "I'm sorry. You're not stupid. But ice cream isn't going to undo what you've done."

"I know. Brody just always says . . ." He shakes his head, and pushing on his thighs, he rises from the couch. "Never mind. I shouldn't have come."

Curiosity piqued, I ask, "Brody says what?" Jordan Krivosky, a.k.a. Brody, is the youngest player on the Hawks, with a reputation for being in the throes of his oat-sowing days. He's definitely not the type Griffin would typically take advice from, on anything.

Griffin slowly lifts his eyes to mine, his frown creating deep lines around his mouth. "That he takes girls their favorite treat, whatever it is, because it's a surefire way in. I knew you wouldn't want to talk to me, so I was willing to do anything. I figured you would've already had coffee this morning, and I couldn't find any Thin Mints at the three grocery stores I went to, and some lady finally took pity on me and said they don't even sell them there, but I knew you liked the ice cream at Kitty's Creamery, so that's what I got in the hopes you'd at least talk to me."

He shrugs like it's no big deal.

It's *so* a big deal.

It's not some huge, overly grand gesture, but it is sweet. Especially on a game day when I know he has an entire routine to stick to, but he's ignoring all that to go to three grocery stores on an errant cookie scavenger hunt, bring me ice cream, and, according to Talia, apologize. So yeah, it doesn't fix everything, but it does soften me a little. Like the tiniest sliver of a single percent softer. "Thank you."

Hearing the opening, Griffin rushes to add, "And I am sorry. That's what I came to say. I'm sorry for not having the balls to tell you the truth."

"Which is?" I arch one brow expectantly. He's the one that said he wants to talk, so he should get to it before I change my mind.

"Oh, uh—" He pulls on the back of his neck, nearly cracking it in the process, it looks like, and his eyes drift up to the ceiling. It feels like he didn't think he'd actually get this far into the possible conversation and isn't sure what to say now.

Meanwhile, I've played out approximately eleventy-three bajillion possible conversations in my head over the last few days. None of them went quite like this, but those scenarios did tell me one thing: Regret is pointless. We can't go back and unfuck each other. Even if I could, I'm not sure I would. Not that I'm telling him that.

"It's fine, Griffin. We'll pretend the other day never happened. No harm, no foul. I won't say a word to anyone, especially my brother, and we'll just go back to family dinners, hangouts with Dominic, and it'll be fine. I don't need to be coddled like some emotionally fragile, delicate flower. I'm tough, I can handle that what happened was obviously unexpected by both of us, and take it as what it was . . . a one-off, casual fuck."

"No."

That's it. One word. I get that silent and grunty works for some girls. I'm not one of them. I snort a humorless laugh and deadpan right back, "Yes."

Griffin takes three steps across the room until he's standing directly in front of me, and I have to crane my neck to look up at him. He takes my upper arms in his hands, his touch gentle despite the pain on his face. "You asked me if I hate you as much as I act like I do. No, the answer's no. And no, I don't want to go back to acting like I do. No, I don't want to act like I never tasted you, like I was never inside you, like I never heard my name on your lips when you came."

Stay strong, Penny.

"That's great and all, but it doesn't change the fact that you've hurt me. And I don't want to pretend that a couple of weeks of being nice fixes years of you treating me like I'm either invisible or annoying. I don't want to act like a good fuck negates how cruel you were after being inside me, because that shit hurt. I refuse to accept that a half-assed apology with no explanation changes everything."

"Goddamn it, Penny," he spits out harshly. He releases me, spinning away to cross the room like he needs space from me. But I think what he really needs is distance from the truth. "I'm fucking trying here."

"Try harder. What's going on in your head? Today, last weekend, for the last five years," I challenge. "What do you think about me? Feel about me? Want from me?"

I'm not playing games. I never was, and I'm not going to start now. I might be a living, breathing disaster, and have enough flaws of my own to write a *War and Peace*–size novel, but he's fucked up too. And while I might be able to withstand whatever he's got lurking in his depths, I shouldn't have to do it without an explanation. I refuse to.

He turns back to face me, his eyes full of fire. "I love you. Is that what you want to hear? I've always loved you."

I did not expect that. Not in a single one of those eleventy-three-bajillion possible scenarios did Griffin Mahoney confessing his love for me come up as an option. Except it's not a sweet-nothings type of admission. It's an accusation, like his feelings are somehow my fault. As if I'm flying around in a diaper and wings like baby Cupid, shooting arrows at him to make him fall in love with me no matter how hard he doesn't want to be. News flash: I haven't done a damn thing but live my life.

"You have a funny way of showing it," I accuse right back.

"I know!" he roars. His eyes are jumping left and right, like he's seeing something, but it's damn sure not my living room's wood flooring. Maybe the past? Or whatever inner monologue is running in his head?

As for me, my brain's singing "Tubthumping," à la getting knocked down, but getting up again. This whole thing with Griffin is one more dramatic moment in an otherwise drama-filled life for me, and I'll get through it the same way I have everything else—one breath at a time until it's a funny story I relate during a family game of Never Have I Ever. Dominic will be pissed when I win with a blindside of *slept with my brother's best friend.*

Then, shaking his head, Griffin quietly confesses, "I don't know how to do any of this. I've never loved anyone. Hell, I've never *been* loved by anyone."

Those few words change everything. I think I might be seeing the real him for the first time, because I think that might be the most real thing he's ever said. All my weird thoughts stop, and the desire to angrily lash out abruptly evaporates, replaced with genuine concern. Gently, I ask, "What do you mean you've never loved anyone? Never been loved by anyone?"

He scrubs his hand over his mouth like he doesn't want to say any more, but after a few seconds in which the air in the room feels heavy with history, he lowers himself to the couch, his elbows on his spread knees and hands hanging between his legs. "What has Dominic told you?"

Not a lot, to be honest. But even if he'd told me everything there was to know about Griffin Mahoney, it wouldn't matter. I sit down beside him, my crisscrossed legs between us so I can look at him directly. "I want to hear it from you."

He swallows thickly, and for a moment, I think he's going to clam up again, or throw out angry words instead of being real. But he doesn't. Instead, he slowly begins to speak. "My parents weren't like yours. There were no loving hugs or encouraging words in my house. My parents just didn't love me. As an adult, I can see that maybe they weren't capable of it? But as a kid . . ." He shrugs forlornly, sighing. "I don't know, I always assumed it was because something was wrong with me. That I was born unlovable. I quickly learned that it was safest for me to stay out of sight and out of mind." He cocks his head a bit so he can see me in his periphery. "I wasn't always smart enough to be safe. Sometimes I needed attention, and it didn't matter if it was good or bad, or how much it hurt in the end. I just wanted to be seen for a change."

A dark picture is developing in my gut, of a little boy version of the monster I'm now sitting beside. "What do you mean *safest*?" I ask carefully.

I don't want him to say it. I'm praying that I'm wrong. But when Griffin runs his finger along the bridge of his nose, tracing the slight bump of a poorly healed break there, the hope washes away in a flood of horror.

"Oh my God, Griffin!" I gasp. I try to gather him in my arms, wanting to wrap him up in the hug I think the boy inside him still needs, but he pushes me off.

"It's fine. It was a long time ago," he says, dismissing it like a parent breaking his nose is a totally normal thing. "I was thirteen then. I'd had a big growth spurt over the summer that year and was taller than my mom and nearly as tall as Dad. I thought I was finally a man." He flashes a bitter smile. "So the next time they started arguing about groceries and my dad turned on me, shouting that he wasn't going to keep wasting his hard-earned money on feeding a worthless bastard like me, I stood up to him. Figured out I wasn't a man yet pretty quick. Mom told me I got what I deserved for being such an ingrate, and I went back to being invisible. For a while anyway. Unfortunately for Dad, I kept growing, and broken ribs hurt a hell of a lot more than a nose, as he found out."

The smile that steals across his face now is full of successful vengeance, and sends a chill down my spine. I think I should feel shock, or maybe be repulsed. The violence in his family is not something I'm at all familiar with personally. My parents are great, and I've always known that. They show up, they're supportive, they encourage me and Dominic to dream big and take risks. They *love* us unconditionally.

It sounds like Griffin has never had that a day in his life, so I can't hold him to the expectations I would have for myself, or for Dom. Griffin's different because his life has been different. And after revealing that his dad broke his nose when he was a literal child, I think Griffin could tell me that he'd killed his dad and buried him in the backyard under the toolshed, and I'd high-five him and take the secret to my grave. "Whatever you did to him, he deserved it, and worse," I declare.

"He would probably disagree, but I wouldn't know. Haven't talked to them since the day I turned eighteen. I'd like to say I left, but the truth is, they kicked me out once their 'parental obligation was done,' as if they ever fulfilled that." He huffs out a caustic laugh, and I feel like he's quoting exactly what was said to him.

For never having met his parents, the hatred toward them that fills me is a surprise, because I was raised not to hate. But Griffin didn't deserve any of that. No child does. And I'm bloodthirsty enough to kinda wish I could have a couple of minutes alone with Mr. and Mrs. Mahoney to punish them for what they did to Griffin.

"My hockey coach let me crash on his couch until I finished school that year, and then I moved out, started busting my ass in amateur and minor leagues, killing myself to get an NHL contract. That was when I met Dominic."

Knowing Griffin didn't have a family of his own is very different from the full picture I now have, and I'm starting to understand why Dominic was so adamant about bringing Griffin into our family. "Who loves you, and who you love?" I offer, finally getting why Griffin is so loyal to my brother.

"In a totally bro way," he clarifies.

Nodding, I give him a tiny grin. "Of course. But that's what brings us to the 'bros before hos' situation we're in now." I hold up a finger. "Not that I'm a ho, but you know what I mean."

"Dom made you sound like a cute little chaos goblin, so I was expecting . . . well, I sure as hell wasn't expecting you that day when you walked into your parent's kitchen. You took my breath away." He looks at me fully for the first time in the last few minutes. His eyes are brighter, like getting all that off his chest lightened the weight he's been carrying all this time. "You were so damn beautiful, with this light that radiated from you. You felt like the fucking sun. You still do." He reaches up to take a lock of my hair between his fingers, twisting and twirling it mindlessly, and his breathing steadies out like touching me has somehow soothed the last few minutes away. "My whole life was hockey, and then I saw you. And you were the one person I could never have. You *are* the one person I can't have."

"Because of my brother?"

He doesn't answer directly. But he releases my hair and leans back on the couch, his arms splayed along its back. His grimace is answer enough.

"He doesn't decide who I date or don't date," I argue.

"In general, that's true. But with us, yeah, he does. I owe him, Pen. He pulled me out of this deep, dark, self-destructive place, and I decided all those years ago that I would repay him by doing basically anything he asked of me. And in all those years, do you know the only thing he's asked?" He gives me a hard look, and before he says it, I already know. "Staying away from you. So I did. I treated you the same way he did, trying to keep you at arm's length, while secretly obsessing over you at the same time. Living my life on the outskirts of yours, asking Dom about you anytime I could without raising his suspicions and hoarding stories about you like an addict. I've memorized your every look and gesture, studied your smiles, and cursed every man you dated. Hell, I encouraged Dom to run them off because I was so fucking jealous that they could date you, touch you, be with you."

Okay, that paints the last five years in an entirely different light. Not necessarily a favorable one, but all our interactions are starting to morph and twist a little into something other than the hate I thought they were founded in.

"So to summarize, you're basically a stalker?" I expect him to roll his eyes, or maybe crack a smile. Instead, he agrees with a slight jerk of his head, his eyes darkening like he's daring me to do something about it.

Penelope Nicole Lee, get your shit together, because that is not hot! It's creepy, and scary, and . . . kinda hot. God, I am such a mess.

"I know it makes zero sense, but for a long time, I thought I was acting like an asshole to protect you from me and my shit." He taps his temple, reminding me that the damage that's shaped him still lives rent free in his mind. "But now I'm realizing I was protecting myself. I didn't want to lose the only friend I've ever had, the only family to ever welcome me into their fold, and so, selfishly, I chose them and told myself that it'd be okay. That I could love you from afar and it'd be enough."

"And has it been?"

"Fuck no," he admits heavily, his eyes looking down. "It's been absolute torture."

I can't help but chuckle, because wrong or not, that does make me feel better. Griffin hasn't been kind to me for a lot of those years, but I can see how he treated me much the same way Dominic does. It was just without the underlying history and siblinghood bond between us, so it felt harsher, meaner, more hurtful. But with his explanation, I can understand why he was doing it. It still doesn't make it okay, but I can understand how we got to that point at least. And though it probably makes me a bit evil, I like that it hurt him, too, because there were numerous times he hurt my feelings. Tit for tat might not be healthy, but I never claimed to be that. Doesn't seem like Griffin is either.

"So why tell me all this now? Why not just pretend the other day never happened and go back to the status quo? It'd be a hell of a lot easier than all this." I wave a hand in his general direction, knowing that spilling his guts this way had to be beyond difficult. Especially for a bottled-up man like Griffin.

He runs his fingers through his hair like he's exasperated, but this time, it feels like it's with himself. Not me. "Because you're the first thought I have in the morning, the last one before I go to sleep, and you fill every moment in between. I can't escape you at night, either, because I dream about you too. You're this big, important force that's controlled my entire being, and finally touching you the way I've wanted to for so damn long has broken every last grip I had on my sanity."

Wow. The power behind his words feels like the smallest taste of the depth of his feelings. This man I thought was cold and emotionless is anything but. "I had no idea," I whisper.

He pins me with an intense look, his jaw set in stone. "I didn't want you to. I never wanted you to know. But it feels like fate took it out of my hands along with that ring. Some stupid part of me keeps trying to whisper in my ear, saying this might be my chance. That it might be *our* chance."

Slowly and deliberately, as though he's expecting me to stop him, he lays his hand on my knee. His thumb immediately begins tracing a path there, and even through my leggings, I can feel the heat of his touch.

Griffin is blowing my mind on so many levels, I've lost count, and I'm trying to keep up with the whiplash speed in which he's rewriting our history. He doesn't hate me. He likes me. He's stalking me. He's protecting me. Okay, that last one is confusing as hell, because how does being mean equal protection? But given how Griffin sees himself as some unlovable monster, I guess I can kinda connect those dots, in a very roundabout, indirect path that's basically a toddler-esque crayon scribble.

"Chance to what?"

"Whatever you want," he answers, not clarifying anything. "Use me. Tell me to fuck off. Hurt me the way I've hurt you. I deserve it."

Sighing in disappointment, I tell him, "If you've been paying attention the way you say you've been, you know that's not who I am."

"You are sunshine and light, tackling everything life throws at you as though every moment is an adventure to be experienced to the fullest, and never letting anyone or anything hold you back from chasing your dreams, not even yourself." He sounds sure and confident in that appraisal.

I can't help but smile because if I were going to write the perfect blurb about me, that's what I'd want it to say. "I think that's the nicest thing anyone's ever said to me." I have cheerleaders in my life—my family, my friends, my teammates, and myself—but having Griffin, someone who I didn't think ever saw me in a positive way and who has never had a cheerleader in his corner, list out the things I value most in myself is powerfully seductive.

"I'm not good enough for you. Nobody is, but I'm definitely not. I'm fucked up, like really fucked up, and I don't know how to do any of this. Feel? Talk?" He shakes his head like those are entirely foreign concepts despite having just done a lifetime's worth of feeling and talking. "But I'm willing to try, willing to learn, if you'll give me time to get there, to where, one day, I might be good enough for you."

"You make it sound like you're damaged goods, but you're not." I scoot a little closer, and his touch moves up my inner thigh the skinniest inch. "I have hated you, wondered what Dominic saw in you as a friend—or even as a human on occasion—and cursed your name dozens of times. But I've also seen you be loyal and kind, helpful and caring . . . just not to me. That hurt, but now I understand." I tilt my head, thinking. "Though I still have to process all that now that I know why you've treated me the way you have. The point is, there's a good person in there." I point at his chest, barely touching him, and he grabs my hand, desperately pressing my palm over his heart. I can feel the *thud-thud-thud* pounding beneath the muscle.

"I really don't want to fuck this up, Penny. Please don't let me fuck this up, okay?" he begs. I don't think I ever considered that a man like Griffin, with his size and reputation as the fists-first type, would beg for anything, so that he does it for me gives me a heady sense of power. It's a feeling I haven't had before with him, and I think . . . I like it. "I'm risking everything here, for you, because you're worth it. Just don't let me ruin it." He shoots me a glance filled with promises and hopes, like my eternal optimism has rubbed off on him.

"I'm definitely worth it." I take my hand back, patting my own chest proudly. His lips lift the tiniest bit into what is technically a smile. Well, the beginning of one anyway. "But I'm risking my heart, one you've spent five years bruising, so make sure you're worth it. Or it won't be Dominic you'll have to fear. It'll be *me*." I want to set that expectation up front. I don't know what I'm doing, but I know what I won't do, and that's let Griffin backslide into bad behavior. Not a single time.

He nods solemnly, taking that vow seriously.

"What do we do now?" I whisper, hoping he has a clue, because I sure don't.

Is everything fixed? No. Of course not. But I can recognize that what Griffin's shared with me today is big, and I'm willing to forgive the other day as momentary postorgasmic panic because I was doing a fair amount of panicking myself too.

The last five years is another subject, though. Even understanding why Griffin acted the way he did, I'd be stupid not to recognize the red flags. He's been wounded, and I'm not in a position to play nurse to a wounded heart and soul that may be beyond healing. I can't allow myself to be sucked into a toxic relationship, even if Griffin isn't guilty of causing his own toxicity. But he deserves a chance, at least that's what my heart's telling me.

Just a cautious one.

"I was thinking I still owe you an apology." His eyes darken and his voice goes husky and rough. "A very long, detailed one outlining all my mistakes and correcting each and every time I made you feel . . . How did you put it? Invisible and annoying?" He stands, taking my hand and pulling me to my feet.

"That's a lot of apologizing," I tease, flirting my ass off because seductive Griffin is doing strange things to my belly. And lower. Things asshole Griffin never did.

He cups my face in his big hands, lifting my eyes to his so I can see the genuine truth shining there as he says, "Penny, you have never been invisible to me. You're the only damn thing I see most of the time. And the only thing annoying about you is that I haven't been able to touch you. But I will apologize as long as you need me to and as many times as you want to make up for each and every time I hurt you."

I'm not 100 percent sure about this. I'm a strong 69—ha ha!—percent at best. There's a lot of history between Griffin and me, but also, it feels like I just met the real Griffin Mahoney. And while he's throwing around words like *love*, I understand that it's not that deep yet, because for all he knows *of me*, he doesn't know *me*. But he wants to. And I want to know more of this Griffin, the man who has been cruel in a twisted attempt to be kind. The Griffin who was misguidedly protecting me from himself. The Griffin who is willing to bare his soul, however dark and damaged it might be. The Griffin who has been unwaveringly at my side through my latest catastrophe, showing up and having my back even as I do stupid, sketchy things while never once calling me out or blaming me for the situation. The Griffin who makes the noise in my head, that's always so very loud, simply cease to exist with his touch.

This isn't what we should be doing. He has a game to prep for, and I have a performance to get ready for. Most importantly, this is too new, too fresh and confusing. But good decisions and responsible living are boring, especially compared to Griffin Mahoney offering to make me come multiple times.

So while it might not be the best plan, I make a choice for myself. Selfishly wanting the world to fall away and to fall into the arms of the one man who can make that happen, and knowing it might make everything worse, but hoping it makes things better, I ask, "What time do you have to be at the arena today?"

"I was supposed to be there thirty minutes ago. Coach has been blowing up my phone. But this conversation is more important than that."

"Than hockey?" I shout, dumbfounded. Then I start shoving him toward the door. "Oh my God! You have to go!"

He grins, catching my hands to stop me, though my puny pushes weren't moving him at all. "More important than anything."

That's ridiculous. Hockey is Griffin's life.

His mouth finds mine, and he nips at my lip like he's trying to make sure I'm real. And I feel it . . . I feel important. This moment feels important. Like the start of something big.

Chapter 21

Griffin

"Mahoney! Where the hell have you been?" Coach bellows through the locker room, overwhelming every other conversation and plunging the whole space into silence. He's not a yeller, so I've obviously severely pissed him off by showing up late and missing his pregame pep talk.

All my teammates studiously focus on their skates and sticks, trying to stay out of the line of fire. Even Brody stays mostly silent, just quietly humming, "Dum-dum-dum-dummm," under his breath to mourn my impending demise.

"Got caught up in something. I'm here now." I'm not even half dressed yet, still working my socks over my shin guards with my pants sitting on the bench beside me.

"We'll talk about this more later," Coach says, clearly pissed, "but for now, get ready to play. You don't have time to screw around."

That conversation is not going to end well. Coach is clear on expectations, and I just shit all over them. But I had to. I was not going to cut that conversation short for anything. The game could've started, and I would've still been sitting with Penny, if that's what it took for her to give me a shot.

As soon as Coach disappears back into his office, Dominic appears, looming over me in his full gear minus his skates. "I told you to wait till after the playoffs to figure out your shit with this girl."

He's making an educated guess, because I sure as hell haven't told him where I was or why I was late. "Later," I declare. "We need to focus on the game."

He huffs out a humorless laugh. "Yeah, you seem focused as fuck, asshole."

I'm not. Not at all. I feel lighter than I have in years. Maybe lighter than I've ever been. I feel like my conversation with Penny healed some shit that's been tearing me up inside my entire life, and that kiss goodbye promised a bright future I've only ever dreamed of.

The anger that usually simmers just below my surface is simply . . . gone. Which would normally be a good thing.

But for me, the team enforcer, a mere thirty minutes out from what promises to be a very physical, aggressive game in which I'm going to have to fight like a monster? Not so much. I need to find that anger, draw it back up from the deep, dark well in my center so I can use it to unleash hell on the Torches in defense of my Hawks.

"I already hate her, you know that? She's got her claws all up in your head, and we have a damn Cup to win," Dominic sneers.

And there's the anger.

Instantly, I rise, grabbing his jersey in my fist. "Shut the fuck up, man. You don't know what you're talking about."

He tries to push me off, but I'm bigger, heavier, and madder than he is. I will also not let him talk shit about Penny, even if he doesn't know that's who he's talking about.

"I know enough," he spits out.

Howe and Brody join forces, pulling Dom and me off of each other until they're standing between us. Howe's lucky he's the one with a staying hand on my chest. I respect him enough to not throw him off. Brody wouldn't be so lucky.

Dominic points a finger at me. "Get your head in the game. Don't fuck this up for all of us over some pussy."

"It's not like that!"

Dom stomps off, his slides squeaking on the tile floor as he heads to the bathroom. A second later, the slamming of a door echoes through the locker room. Brody immediately spins around, his bright eyes nearly dancing. "Honey's got a honey?"

"Shut the fuck up, Jordan."

"Oooh, must be serious if you're using my government name," he taunts. But he's not as stupid as he looks, and though he has a shit-eating grin on his face and makes some *did you hear that?* eyes at the other guys, he goes back to getting ready, leaving me to do the same. Thankfully, no one else says a word to me either.

I don't see Dominic again until we're lining up for our entrance. We usually fist-bump before we take the ice, saying our motto of "you and me, two against the world," but this time, he shoulder checks me as he steps in front of me to take his place in the lineup. Staring at the back of his helmet, I can feel it all slipping away.

Our friendship is never going to be the same once he knows about me and Penny. But I've chosen him for five years—over myself, over Penny, over any chance at happiness. And I can't do that anymore. I won't.

The only thing I can do for now is make sure we win tonight.

❧

The game starts hard and fast, with Jack Off and the Torches' center going at it right from the drop, sticks flashing as they fight for the puck. I hold back, letting them handle their shit, but keep a close eye, ready to step in if things progress from hard hockey to cheap shots. We do get the puck as Jack Off gets it out to Dom, who sends it up to Brody, but nothing develops during the rotation, and the Torches get it back just as Coach rotates us off the ice for the second line.

The next rotation isn't much smoother. Or the one after that.

Last night's loss is still hot and fresh for the Torches, fueling their every move. They're aggressive but sloppy, their rage doing them no favors. On the other hand, we have the luxury of a secured spot in round one of the playoffs. Tonight's game effectively doesn't matter for the Hawks, but we never play like that. Every game is a chance to dominate, to shine, to win, and we attack it as such, showing no mercy.

Play after play, I hold the defensive line, sacrificing myself bodily to keep the Torches away from Howe's goal. And while Dominic and I are mad at each other, it doesn't matter on the ice. Our moves have been practiced for years, to the point where they're automatic. I don't have to look at him to know where he is, and anytime I need him, he's there, and vice versa. It's a dance between us.

There's just one extra little problem.

Penny.

She's on the ice crew tonight, so she's constantly on the edge of my field of vision with a few other cheerleaders and the rest of the crew. And I can't keep my eyes off of her.

She has on the skirted uniform that's always driven me crazy, paired with tall green-and-white-striped socks and hockey skates. I don't know why seeing her in a tiny skirt and hockey skates does something to me, but it always has. Tonight it's sending my blood flow to my dick, and my jock doesn't exactly have space for an erection.

Dom is going after Campbell, one of the Torches' forwards, who's making a play toward the goal, and I defend the passing lane, making sure that nobody can slip behind for a dink-and-dunk-type deflection goal. I'm not worried, Dom's got this guy handled. He's a beast on the ice in his own right. And like she's pulling them, my eyes tick to the right for the shortest of split seconds, directly to Penny. I see her intense gaze as she watches her brother battle, and then her brows climb high as her mouth rounds.

I jerk my eyes back to the action just in time to feel Jenkins, the other Torch forward, slam a shoulder into the solid mass of my chest, knocking me almost onto my ass as he skirts by me for exactly what I'm supposed to be preventing.

"Tired, old man?" he chirps. I'm only two years older than Jenkins and not tired at all. But I was . . . distracted. And that distraction let Jenkins make an unchallenged shot. Howe does his best, doing the splits to the ice, but the puck slides into the net, lighting the lamp behind the goal.

The Torches just scored, and it's my fucking fault. The crowd boos loudly . . . both at the opposing team's goal and at my whiff.

"What the fuck, man? Where were you?" Dom snaps, as if he didn't let Campbell get that wrist pass off. But that doesn't matter when I should've had the lane, intercepting the pass to clear it out to Brody or Jack Off.

I don't answer, other than banging my stick to the ice. He's right. I have to focus. My whole life might've changed this afternoon, but I can't forget that I'm in the middle of a game. I won't let my teammates down. Again.

Attention locked on the ice, I find the anger I need to play my best. It's directed at myself, but it'll do. Any anger gives me the edge I need.

By the end of the period, we've tied it up. As the ice crew comes out to clear the ice, we skate to the exit and make our way to the locker room, where Coach beelines directly for me.

Going almost nose to nose despite the three inches my skates give me, he demands, "Do I need to pull you?"

"No! I'm in."

With his eyes locked on mine, I can see the questions lurking in his. Being late isn't like me. Missing a play like that definitely isn't. But he's trusting me.

The second period starts, and I attack the ice, the Torches, and even the puck, sending it sailing back to the other end at one point. It's an icing call, but the boom of a puck banging off the glass almost fifty yards away brings people to their feet.

The cheers from the crowd fade into nothing as my focus locks onto the puck and the players on the ice. The world doesn't exist outside the rink. Me and my teammates. Rotate in, rotate out, defend our ice, and make plays on the Torches' goal.

"Griffin!"

It's not my name that breaks through the fog. It's the sound of Penny's voice shouting my name in a tone that has nothing to do with cheering me on. She sounds . . . scared, and that sends a jolt of terror through me.

I lift my head, and though she's standing with the ice crew, I find her instantly. She points above her head at the crowd. I don't know why at first, don't see anything amiss. And then . . .

I see them. Miles's goons are working their way down the aisle, getting closer to Penny. It doesn't look like they've seen her yet since she's blocked from view in the tunnel under the stands, but they're looking for her. One even gestures toward the Hawkette stage with a jerk of his chin.

"Fuck."

I need to get her out of here. Now.

But I'm in the middle of a game. I don't know what to do.

Like fate heard my plea, Jenkins intercepts a deflected pass meant for Brody to try to break away for another go at our goal. Not this time. I bodycheck him hard and fast, completely unprompted, and he falls to his ass, spinning out on the slippery ice.

The crowd roars, surging to their feet to better see the unexpected fight, and two refs skate up, whistles blaring. But it's not enough. I need off the ice.

I throw my gloves and shout, "Who's tired now, fuck stick? Come on. Get up, Jinx."

Jenkins hates that nickname, and he heaves himself up, throwing his gloves too. He's not their enforcer, he doesn't normally fight, but in a blink, we're going at it. I need this to happen faster, so I throw one straight for his temple, knowing it'll get me the five for fighting that I want.

Whistles scream by my ear, and I push Jenkins away, looking expectantly to the ref. "Major penalty, five minutes."

Perfect.

I don't bother glaring at Jenkins. He had nothing to do with that fight and was just the unlucky target closest that'd I could hit and get off the ice. As a ref escorts me to the penalty box, my eyes stay locked on Penny. I jerk my head, telling her to come here.

Is that allowed? No. Talking to players in the sin bin will get us both in trouble. But she ducks down and gets as close as she can.

Go to the locker room. Get out of here before they see you. I mouth the words and point down the tunnel back toward the locker room, where there is security that will keep the goons away from her.

She shakes her head, her brow furrowed as she looks around like I don't know it's the middle of a game. "I can't leave."

The fuck she can't.

But she doesn't know what she's up against. For everything I told her today, I stupidly still haven't told her that the guys who're after that ring work for Miles Conniver. She doesn't understand the danger.

"You good, Honey?" the box attendant asks.

No. I'm not. I'm about to do the stupidest thing I've ever done. Which tracks because, of course, it's Penny driving me to madness.

I stand, dropping my stick, gloves, and helmet before grabbing the top of the plexiglass wall that surrounds the penalty box and bench area to vault myself up and over. The crowd closest to the box reacts instantly, cheering and saying, "Whoa." But they don't matter. Only Penny does.

Her eyes widen as I come barreling toward her, my skates clattering on the concrete. Grabbing her arm, I push her. "Come on. You have to get out of here."

"Griffin," she argues over me.

I don't have time for this. My five minutes is going to be up soon, and I have to be ready. The only way to do that is to have Penny somewhere safe.

So I scoop her up, throwing her over my shoulder. My gear is hard plastic and probably poking her, but there's no time for comfort. Besides, she's kicking her feet and slapping at my back anyway, so I don't think she's looking for a cushy first-class-level ride.

"Put me down!" Her cry echoes through the tunnel, but when I start jogging down the padded floor toward the locker room, it changes to an angrier, "Don't drop me!" as she grips around my waist, hanging on for dear life.

At the locker room's door, I lower Penny to the ground and lock eyes with the security guard standing there. "Tim, nobody gets in other than Hawks. And don't let her out either."

"What?" he asks, confusion marring his usually jovial face. He's a retired cop, but he's still got the instincts in there somewhere.

"The fuck?" Penny finishes, slapping at me.

And though I can't feel it through my padding, I whirl on her, grabbing her hands to stop her. "Penelope. They're looking for you and they're here. That means they know you're a Hawkette."

Her face goes slack as the blood drains. "I saw them at the post office today. They were trying to get my address, but I don't think they did."

Holy shit! She didn't tell me that!

Like you didn't tell her about Miles?

"Stay here," I order. Thankfully, she nods her agreement. I press a quick kiss to her lips, give Tim a glare of *don't fuck this up*, and tear off back down the tunnel toward the ice.

I hop over the wall and back into the penalty box with half the goddamn bench and arena looking at me like I've lost my mind. Which makes sense, because I have. You don't leave in the middle of the game unless you're forced to or sports med takes you out. "Ahhh . . . your five's up," the attendant says, opening the gate. Guess they decided not to penalize me again.

I hit the ice like a demon-possessed monster, ignoring Coach as he screams for me to rotate off the fucking ice, goddamn it. I don't have anger filling me now. It's cold dread mixed with hot fear, and the combination isn't something warm and toasty but rather an explosive need to fuck shit up. And since I can't go into the crowd and attack the goons, the Torches will have to do.

Still, I do a quick scan of the crowd, finding the goons easily. They're smooshed into two seats beside each other, just below the cheerleaders' stage. And while they're watching the game, they're spending an inordinate amount of time turning around, looking for Penny up onstage.

"The fuck was that?" Dom shouts over his shoulder as he flies by, his eyes watching the action as Jacofovich fights to get a clear angle on the Torches' goal.

"Later," I snap back.

Jack Off shoots and scores, putting us one up. While the crowd cheers and Jack Off does a tight victory lap around the net, the crowd laughs at something I can't quite make out. I glance up to the jumbotron and see that they're replaying me jumping out of the penalty box, throwing Penny over my shoulder, and running down the tunnel with her. Thankfully, it only shows her face for a split second, and when I quick cut my eyes at the goons, they seem to have missed it.

But Dominic didn't miss anything. He may have missed it live, focused on defending the Torches' power play, but he sees the replay, and is putting pieces together in real time.

"I can explain," I rush to tell him, holding my hands out.

But he's a freight train that won't be stopped. "You son of a bitch!" he snarls. Before anyone can react, he's on me. My best friend—hell, my only real friend—is beating the shit out of me.

His gloves are gone, his bare fists pummeling my body. With a sharp smack, my helmet's gone and he's landing punches on my face.

Knowing I deserve it, I take every single one. I don't block them, I don't duck, I simply let him destroy me, leaning back against the boards so I don't go down to take a knee or a blade to the face.

Bam! I feel my nose crack and blood run down my lip.

Bam! My jaw takes a shot, and red-tinged spit flies onto the ice.

Bam! I lurch forward as he uppercuts my gut.

Whistles are blaring loudly, fans are screaming, and I can feel hands on us, other Hawks clearing the bench to try to pull us apart.

Finally, they manage to separate us, but I think, to everyone's surprise, it's Dominic they're trying to control. The refs confer for a long time as the trainer holds a towel to my face. Sure, we were fighting, but fighting your own teammate? How do they deal with that? Coach is arguing that it's an internal thing, that at most a refusing-to-start-play bench penalty is all that's required, but the refs shake their head, and I can hear them. "Lee, Mahoney, game misconduct. Both are ejected."

"But—"

"Be glad I don't make it a match penalty, Coach!" the ref says, and Coach shuts up. He's right, that would incur an automatic suspension for both me and Dom. We probably don't deserve a match penalty, especially since, as Coach said, it was between teammates, but I'm not going to argue with it because this is one fucked-up situation no matter what.

Dominic and I are escorted to the edge of the ice by two refs and half the Hawks between us as human shields, with marching orders to keep going to the locker room. And though Dom's the one that went ballistic, Coach is glaring at me. He knows I'm the loose cannon, and if steady-as-a-surgeon Dom gave me a beatdown, I deserved it. That talk with him is shaping up to be a fucking doozy.

I push my way into the locker room, already jerking my sweater over my head. Dom's at my back, which I hate because I can feel him glaring at me, still deciding if he's gonna take another go at me. But now that I'm out of the game, my only mission is Penny. I need to get her out of here and stashed somewhere safe.

I'm pulling off gear as quickly as I can, not caring about getting it in my bag. Hell, I'm barely tossing it toward my locker. Jersey, flung. Pads, dropped. Skates, ripped off, and fuck me, they're probably half ruined from stomping on the fucking cement. Pants and socks, shoved down as one.

"How could you?" Dominic demands, his voice echoing sharply through the empty room. "I fucking trusted you."

"I know," I answer, not glancing his way or pausing my speed strip down. Finally, I'm naked as the day I was born, digging for sweats in my locker.

"Put your dick away so I can beat the shit out of you some more," Dominic barks at me.

I yank my pants on, free balling it to hurry a little more, and Dominic steps up to me again. He's still geared up and stands several inches taller than me in his skates. His pads will protect him, too, except I won't be throwing any punches his way. If he needs to hit me again, I'll let him. As long as he's quick about it.

"Can we do this later? I promise you can beat me to a pulp later. Right now, I need to make sure Penny is safe."

That brings him up short, his entire face morphing to confused concern. "What do you mean *safe*? What the fuck's going on, man?"

"Griffin?" Penny's voice comes from the sports med room, drawing both my and Dom's attention instantly. "What are you two doing in here? The second period still has a few minutes, right?"

I turn my face toward her, and she sees my bleeding nose and swelling eye, eliciting a gasp. "Oh my God! What happened?" I say nothing, but Dom's face must give him away, because Penny plants her hands on her hips. "Dominic Lee! What the hell did you do?"

Shocked by her indignation, he stutters, "D-defend you?"

"Guys, let's do this somewhere else. We need to go," I tell them both.

"Go? Go where? There's still another period, and Coach will want to talk to us after the game," Dominic exclaims.

Ignoring him, I catch Penny's eyes to say, "They're still here, Pen."

"Oh my God!" Horror washes over her face, but is quickly followed by true fear. I think that's the only thing that gets Dominic moving, straight to her.

"I don't know what's going on, but I've got you, Penny-Nickel-Dime," he says, trying to calm her down. Waving me off, he sneers, "I'll handle whatever this is. You can go."

I laugh outright. "The fuck you will. I'm going with her. If *you* want to come, you can."

It's a line in the sand. It's always been the two of them as siblings and me on the outside. I guess, to Penny, it was Dom and me as friends, with her on the outside. Now there's a new dynamic. It's me and Penny as whatever we're becoming, with Dominic on the outside.

Penny comes up to my side, looping her arm through mine and peering up at me. "Can we go?"

I watch as Dominic realizes everything has changed. "Mother*fucker*!"

Penny unhelpfully whispers, "Technically, he'd be a sister-fucker." Dominic shoots her a deadly glare, and she squeaks, "Right. Not the time. Definitely not the time."

Chapter 22

Penny

Griffin and Dominic spend a ridiculous amount of time arguing about whose house we should go to, with Dominic insisting we go to his place, even though he has no idea what's going on and Griffin countering that his would be safe and is closer.

Quickly done with all that noise, I stomp off toward the exit. "I'm going home. Feel free to come with me or not, your choice." Secretly, I really hope they come with me because I'm scared to go outside with those two guys hunting me down.

What if they did get my address?

Thankfully, like the good guys they are, Griffin and Dominic follow along like my own personal, overly protective, Velcro-level guard dogs. Though without looking behind me, I can tell they're elbowing each other for position so their fight isn't remotely over, but as long as they don't start punching again, I'm not going to intervene. Who am I kidding? If they start throwing punches, I'll absolutely play referee, whistle or not.

The few team staff members in the locker room don't try to stop us, thankfully, but I'm sure they'll be telling tales after the game. God knows what the fallout from that's going to be.

Once we get to my apartment, like the big-brother-slash-dictator he is, Dominic decides he's in charge. "Tell me what the hell's going on."

"With what specifically?" I question, noting that there are two separate but connected issues here. One, the ring and stalker guys. Two, me and Griffin.

"Penny," Dominic says in that warning tone I hate.

"Dominic," I echo in the same tone because I can mimic Mom and Dad just as well as he can.

Irritated with me, he sighs deeply before leveling Griffin with a hard look that promises painful blood loss. Right when I think he's going to ask Griffin for the lowdown on what's happening, he slowly turns back to me for the answers he wants. I guess Dom's decided to give Griffin the silent treatment. That lucky bastard. "Safety first. Why aren't you safe, and who was at the game that scared you?"

"So, it's kind of a funny story . . . about that whole situation . . ." I say, dragging it out. "I got myself into a teeny-tiny dill pickle of a situation, like one of those cute little cocktail gherkins. But I had some help this time." I glance toward Griffin, intending for it to be a compliment, but given Dominic's grumbling, I'm pretty sure he heard that this is Griffin's fault, not mine, despite knowing that I'm nearly always in some sort of trouble. "You see, it all started with Carolynn at Yesteryear—you know the antique store I like to go to?—calling me about this amazing ring—"

Griffin cuts me off. "She bought a ring. We got mugged. There are two guys who want the stolen ring. They're stalking her."

Well, okay, I guess the story wasn't quite as long as I thought.

"You were mugged?" Dominic shouts, eyes filled with fury. If the thief were in the room with us, I have no doubt my overly protective brother would tear him into a million pieces, spreading his entrails like confetti. But anger quickly morphs into concern as he scans me from head to toe as though I might be hiding some bruising or broken bones. "Are you okay? Did you call the police?"

"Yes, *Dad*. I'm fine. And of course I called the police. They didn't care, just told me to fill out an online form to get a report number."

I roll my eyes, still really annoyed with that. "And we think the guys who want the ring have been messaging me through my website. I told them the ring isn't available, but they keep emailing. And today, they were at the post office where my PLDesigns PO box is. I heard them trying to get my address from the clerk and skedaddled out of there as quick as I could."

I rub the faintly tender spot on the side of my head where I hit it, testing for a bump. Griffin and Dominic both zero in on the unconscious movement, knowing exactly what it means, considering my history of clumsiness. I wave a hand dismissively. "I'm fine. But when I saw the guys at the game tonight, it raised up all the little baby hairs on my neck because I don't think that's a coincidence." I shoot Griffin an apologetic look because I really did think that at first.

"So we need to call the police again and tell them these guys are stalking you," Dominic declares.

A bark of laughter escapes as I say, "Dude, have you ever seen a single true crime show in your life? Well, I have, and they don't care unless the guy hurts you, and even then, it's doubtful they'll do much. At this point, what have they done? Send a few emails? Walk down sidewalks in areas I happen to be in? Show up to one of the most well-attended sporting events in the state? Yeah, don't think any of that's gonna qualify as suspicious. And the post office? I'm pretty sure they didn't get my address, so technically, all they did was ask a question and get told no. Believe me, I hate to say it, but they haven't done anything illegal. The police are gonna smile and nod, and tell me to lock my door. Which I'm going to do obviously." I glance at my apartment door, noting the two dead bolts with a small sense of relief. "I'm just really glad I got out of there tonight." I walk over to Griffin and thread my arms around his waist, hugging him tightly. "Thank you."

Griffin's strong arms wrap around me, and I feel him drop a quick kiss to the top of my head. "Of course. I'll keep you safe."

"Get. Your. Fucking. Hands. Off. Her." Dominic spits the order out through clenched teeth as he stomps toward us. Griffin immediately releases me, not because Dominic said so, but to put himself between me and potential harm's way.

But I'm not afraid of my brother, so I step right back between them. "Don't tell me what to do," I snap at Dominic.

Dominic's lips lift into an evil grin. "I didn't. I told him what to do." He looks at Griffin, his best friend, with pure, unfiltered hatred.

One second, I'm standing between them, planting my feet on the solid ground of my own adult independence. The next, they've stepped around me like I'm nothing more than a speed bump on their roadway to mutual destruction.

Dominic's hands land on Griffin's chest and he pushes him hard. "I fucking trusted you."

"I know!" Griffin answers. "I tried to stay away from her. I tried so fucking hard."

"Not hard enough."

They're yelling, pushing, and grabbing at one another.

Bang-bang-bang. Mrs. Rosenthal hits the wall, and I hear her shouting for us to be quiet. For once, she has a point.

I watch in horror as Dominic and Griffin start fighting again, seeing exactly how Griffin got the bloody nose he showed me in the locker room.

What has happened? They've always been such good friends. I knew this would be explosive, but I didn't expect my brother to turn on Griffin so completely.

It hits me. Dominic is doing what he's always done as my brother. Protect me. He thinks he needs to protect me from Griffin, and I can understand why. He's seen how Griffin has treated me too. And while he might've been okay with it before as nothing more than a teasing friend, he's obviously not okay with it if Griffin is more. But he doesn't understand, he doesn't know why.

"Stop!" I shout, but they don't listen. Mrs. Rosenthal bangs on the wall again, and I glare at the white surface like she'll see me through it and realize that I'm doing my best here.

I jump onto Dominic piggyback style, yanking on his shoulders as I try to pull him away from Griffin. "Leave him alone."

But I might as well be a fly on a donkey because Dominic easily shakes me off. Griffin notices me sprawled on the wood floor and rears back, punching my brother for what seems like the first time, landing a massive blow to Dom's stomach that has my brother reeling. "Don't fucking hurt her."

"I'm not hurting her! You're hurting her," Dom gasps painfully from his doubled-over position, his hands cradling his gut.

Woo-hoo! My man can pack a punch, I think to myself proudly.

What? Is Griffin my man?

That's a question for another time. What I do know is that he's not going to not be my man just because Dominic says so. The only people who can decide that are Griffin and me. And let's be real . . . the only one who can truly decide that is me, because if I put my back into it, I could seduce Griffin like *that*, although that's not the sort of woman I am. If he wants to commit, then I'm going to make sure he's committed, no influence allowed.

And I'm about to say as much, using my cheerleader projection voice to break through their melee, when Dominic surges up, landing a solid uppercut to Griffin's chin. So instead of shouting, I decide it's high time for me to get a little farther away from this battle. Neither of them would intentionally hurt me, but with the way my luck runs, I'm likely to accidentally catch hands from one or both of them. And they're tougher than me and will be fine after all this hitting. Meanwhile, I'd probably end up needing a nose job, and I happen to like my cute, swoopy nose and don't want it changed.

But they have to stop. And shut up before Mrs. Rosenthal calls the police. I have no doubt they'd show up for something like this. Hell, they'd probably arrest Dom and Griffin just to say they took down two famous hockey stars, asking for autographs and photos while simultaneously booking them in and taking mug shots.

An idea strikes me. It's crazy, but I think it'll work.

I dash for the kitchen, grabbing the sprayer hose from the sink. Turning the cold water on full throttle, I whisper a quick prayer of thanks for excellent water pressure and thumb the trigger. The spray arcs across the room, dousing them. I play firefighter, swooping the sprayer back and forth to drench them both.

"No, bad boys!" I call out, chastising them like wayward dogs.

"What the fuck?" they both sputter as they stop fighting and their anger-filled eyes find me.

I release the trigger but keep the sprayer locked on Dominic, silently threatening another spray as I inform him, "This is happening." I swing a finger from myself to Griffin to make it clear what I'm talking about because my brother likes to play stupid when it suits him. "This."

Dominic immediately starts shaking his head. "No, it's not."

"Quit with the bossy big brother act and be a better friend," I tell him, ignoring his refutation. "Now."

"It's not an act," Dominic answers flatly. "And I have been the *best* friend. You don't know this guy like I do." Sneering, he lifts his chin toward Griffin.

Dom's talking about Griffin like he's not standing right here. No, he's talking like he wants to make Griffin feel like shit, and he's using me to do it.

Well, he can fuck off if that's his grand plan.

I press the trigger, squirting him again, and he sputters in enraged shock.

"I know enough!" I declare. "You and Griffin are best friends. He's the one you want at your side and at your back, and who you love like a brother. And he's done the same for you. Respecting you so much that he squashed down his feelings for me in some misguided bro-code bullshit."

"Bro-code bullshit? Is that what he told you?"

"He told me a lot. Enough that I'm willing to give him a chance." I cut my eyes to Griffin, a soft smile stealing across my face. "Because he's worth it."

"You deserve better," Dominic spits out.

I watch the light in Griffin's eyes dim and his jaw clench hard. That hurt him. He said as much about himself today, but hearing it from Dominic cuts a lot deeper. I wonder how many times he's heard that in his life. His parents told him he was worthless, and now, even as an adult, his best friend in the whole wide world is essentially doing the same. His dad, the man who was supposed to love him unconditionally, hit him so hard that he broke his nose. And now, his best friend has done that too.

My heart breaks for Griffin, which is something I never thought I'd say or think or feel about the stone-cold man but is absolutely true in this pivotal moment.

"Dominic Lee, I have never been so disappointed in you as I am right now," I reply evenly, totally seriously, and absolutely disgustedly. "If you know anything about Griffin, have ever had one real conversation with him the way a friend would, I want you to think really hard about what you just said and what you've done tonight."

I'm channeling every bit of Mom that I can, from the glare to the stance to the frown shaping my lips. Dropping the sprayer hose, I beeline straight to Griffin. Grabbing his cheeks in my hands, I force his eyes to mine, pulling him down until he's nearly nose to nose with me. His skin is wet, chilled by the water, and there's bruising blooming beneath both eyes from his clearly reinjured nose. "You are a good man. Deep inside that fortress of a heart, you care. And I see that in the way you protected me tonight. I see it in the way you let my asshole brother—"

"Standing right here," Dominic interjects.

Ignoring him, I forcefully repeat, "The way you let my *asshole brother* beat you to a pulp in some stupid attempt to punish yourself. And you are worth everything. Friendship, love, family, friends. I deserve the best, and I think I've found it."

Dominic snorts in disbelief, but Griffin is locked onto me, listening intently and absorbing every word.

"If you kiss her . . . cross my cock and swear to balls, I will kill you right here, right now."

He won't. I wouldn't let my brother kill Griffin. And not only because Talia and I wouldn't get our security deposit back. But because I'm in this thing. Earlier today, I was reeling. Hell, I still am, but for entirely different reasons. Because I see the way Griffin is trying so hard to respect Dominic while also wanting me with every fiber of his being. And he left a damn hockey game—twice!—for me. If that's not an indicator of how important I am to him, I don't know what is.

And I'm sure Dominic won't kill me—partially because he loves me, but for sure because Mom and Dad would have his ass. So I make the move, lifting to my toes and pressing my lips to Griffin's. I can feel him holding back, the tight grip on his restraint returning, and when he doesn't fully give in to me, I crack open one eye to find his eyes opened fully as he looks past me. My lips still pressed to his, I ask, "Is he mean-mugging you?"

"Mm-hmm," Griffin answers, not moving away.

I let go of his face, sliding one hand behind my back to flip my brother the middle finger. I don't know what Dominic does, but Griffin chuckles against my lips and then kisses me properly. His arms wrap around my waist, and he lifts me, my feet dangling in the air as he stands to his full height. His lips soften, melting against me as he leaves gentle smacking kisses across my mouth.

The surrender we both make to the moment settles something in my soul. Things are going to be okay . . . eventually. They have to be. Unfortunately, like all great things, the kiss is over too quickly, but probably not fast enough for Dominic, judging by the furious look on his face when I turn around.

"How long?" His eyes cut from me to Griffin.

"A couple of weeks," I answer.

At the same time, Griffin grunts, "Five long years. For your ungrateful ass."

I press my lips together to hide the smile trying to lift them. Rushing to explain the latest turn of events, I say, "For me, it's a couple of weeks with this whole ring fiasco, and Griffin helping me with it."

The mention of what brought us all here tonight is another cold-water damper and kills my smile.

"What're you doing with that?" my brother asks. Dominic is a doer. He needs a mission, and I think for a long time, I've been his number-one mission. Protect Penny. Not that I needed his protection. And he thought he was doing that by fighting Griffin. I don't think he's done with that mission, but sensing he's losing the battle, he's retreating to fight again and win the war. He won't, but I'll gladly take the momentary reprieve of focusing on another mission where I could use his help.

"Hiding?" I suggest unhelpfully.

"Yeah, no. That's not good enough," Dominic declares.

"Well, I'm open to suggestions. What'cha got?"

But Dominic doesn't look to me. He turns to Griffin. "What have you been doing?"

Griffin grabs a hold of the back of his neck and cuts his eyes toward me. His voice is rough in that way that says he's ashamed of something when he finally says, "There's a little more to the story that you don't know yet."

"Oh yeah, Johnny K said he'd call Griffin if he found out anything about the mugger. He's supposed to be scouring the dark underbelly of the city to see if he can suss out any intel, but more likely, he scammed Griffin out of a thousand dollars." I report that as if I'm summarizing the latest *Law & Order* episode, with all the dramatic retelling I can muster.

"Johnny K? Who's that?" Dominic asks.

I almost clap in excitement because he asked Griffin, not me. See? They're talking again like the bestie bros they've always been. I knew Dom couldn't stay mad that long. Well, I hoped. And it seems like I was right!

"Sketchy pawnshop-owner-slash-stolen-goods-fence we talked to about the ring and thief," Griffin answers.

"You took my baby sister to some dangerous hole-in-the-wall pawnshop?" Dom rumbles. Well shit, that didn't last long, because he's quickly ramping back up.

I hold up a finger. "To point, Johnny K's was fancy, and Griffin didn't take me anywhere. I was going there based on Mad Dog's recommendation. He's the super-helpful but kinda scary fence I talked to first on my own without telling Griffin, and when it went a teeny-tiny bit sideways—" Dom's eyes widen and he opens his mouth like he's going to cut me off, so I keep on chattering away, not even pausing to breathe in the hopes that he won't interrupt. "I smartly called Griffin for reinforcements. So no, he didn't *take* me. He *went with me* because I asked him to. If he'd said no, or tried to stop me, I would've gone without him, and there's no telling where I'd be now . . ." I trail off, playing up the danger factor to get my brother to realize that Griffin did right by me, and he should be thanking Griffin, not blaming him.

"Seriously? Why the fuck do you even care about this ring that much?" Dom finally asks. "It sucks it was stolen, but can't you just design another one?"

My jaw falls open as I glare at my brother. "You did not just tell me to make another one, as if each piece I make isn't one of my precious babies." He rolls his eyes, acting like I'm being dramatic, and maybe I am, but my work is important to me. "Yeah, if you couldn't play hockey anymore, you could just get another job. It'd be no big deal, right?"

"That's not the same thing and you know it."

"It's exactly the same thing!" I protest. "Plus, that ring was special. It was gorgeous and I had so many ideas for it. And it was really expensive. Redesigning it was going to take my work to the next level."

But all Dominic hears is the money issue. "I'll pay for it. Whatever it cost, and you can just walk away. Tell those guys it's gone and be done with it."

"Believe me, I tried to pay for it," Griffin tells Dominic, commiserating over my refusal to take his money.

I want them to reconnect, but not over my annoying tendencies.

"Griffin tried. Talia tried. But I'm paying it off myself. Because it's not about the money. It's about what's right."

"It's not that cut and dry," Griffin says quietly. He has a weird look on his face that I can't place. The closest thing I can relate it to is . . . regret. After an audible deep breath, he starts pacing. Oh shit. He seems to pace when he's about to drop a bomb, and I already don't think I like this. "There's more to the ring, more to the guys."

"What do you mean?" Dominic asks slowly, like he can sense something's wrong. And he probably can because, despite tonight's demonstration to the contrary, Dominic is usually a good friend and likely knows his bestie's tells too.

Griffin sends me a remorseful look and then licks his lip before saying, "When it first got stolen, I went into that antique shop to see if I could find out anything about the ring. I thought I could just buy another one. That's when I saw those guys talking to the owner."

"Carolynn," I fill in helpfully.

"But she walked away, and those guys were setting off alarm bells in my head, so I hung back to eavesdrop on them. According to them, the ring wasn't supposed to be at the store in the first place. I think one of them fucked up or something, but it belongs to their boss, and they're trying to get it back before he realizes it's missing and gets angry."

"Wait, so I bought stolen merchandise?"

"Not stolen, just accidentally sold," Griffin corrects, though he doesn't sound sure of the technicality of that.

Dominic narrows his eyes, reading Griffin like a book. "Who's the boss?"

Griffin swallows thickly as though the answer is stuck in his throat. "I'm pretty sure it's Miles Conniver."

And there's the bomb.

"What?" I shout as fear whooshes through me. I've heard the expression "turns your blood to ice" and always thought it was a poetic liberty to describe true fear. It turns out it can actually happen. Well, I'm sure my blood is still coursing through my veins, but my entire body has gone frigid, frozen in place like a deer in the headlights of an oncoming car.

"Fuck," Dominic hisses.

I don't know a lot about Miles Conniver, mostly just the news articles that tout him as a local business hero, but there's always a "read between the lines" vibe to everything you see about him. I do know he's not someone to fuck with, and apparently, he thinks I have his misplaced jewelry. If I did, I'd just give it back. But I don't.

I feel like I'm hyperventilating. Or having a panic attack. Maybe both at the same time. All I know is that I either have too much oxygen or not enough oxygen. So I pinch the middle of my nose, the pain forcing me to take a deep breath, figuring either the inhale or the exhale will help.

"What am I going to do?" I mutter. But I don't wait for my brother or Griffin to give me the answer because I'm not really asking them. I'm asking myself. "I know, I'll just tell him I don't have his ring anymore. I can even give him a description of the thief. And if he gets mad at his guys for it ending up at Yesteryear, then that's their problem. It's not my fault they screwed up."

It's a good plan.

Well, except for the part where I have to talk to Miles Conniver and be the delivery person for some bad news. People do tend to shoot the messenger. Usually that's metaphorical, but I think with Mr. Conniver, there's a chance it might be literal.

Shit.

"No fucking way," Dom declares, pointing a finger at me. It's as though he heard my mental arguments against that idea too. Then he whirls on Griffin. "You've known this all along?"

Belatedly, I catch up to that little chicken nugget of information. "You didn't tell me," I say flatly, not looking Griffin in the eye but rather staring at the wood floor. He knew from the beginning that these guys were dangerous, and he's protected me from them, which is sweet. But he also put me at risk by not telling me that I was in very real danger, and that's some bullshit. If I'd known the damn Mob was after me, I wouldn't have gone to see Mad Dog by myself. I wouldn't have gone to the post office by myself. I would've made so many different choices, about so many different things, over the last couple of weeks.

Okay, I probably would've done some of those things, because I'm stubborn, but I would've done them with the understanding that it was stupid. I wouldn't have been wandering around the city all willy-nilly, thinking life was hunky-dory other than a stolen ring.

Griffin reaches out to me. "I should've told you, but I thought I could protect you from them. I didn't want you to—"

I jerk away from him, staring at him disbelievingly. I don't know what he's about to say. It doesn't matter. He kept vital, life-altering information from me, *again*.

"You should've told me. You should've told me how you felt a long time ago. You should've told me about this as soon as it happened." Shaking my head, I say, "I want to try, Griffin. But this . . . I can't be with someone who thinks they need to shield me from every little thing like I can't handle reality. Despite what my brother thinks"—I send him a glare, too, because he's created this cursed bubble around me—"I do not need protecting. I can handle myself and whatever catastrophe I get myself into. Been doing it for twenty-five years and plan to keep on doing it."

"Penny," Griffin says, recoiling. The hurt is written all over his face, his eyes filled with sadness. But I'm hurt too—hurt that he thinks I'm so weak.

"You heard her. You need to go," Dominic says as he steps up to my side.

But I move away, putting space between myself and both guys. "Both of you, get out," I order.

"I'm not going anywhere," Dominic scoffs, plopping himself on my couch and crossing one ankle over the other knee, making himself at home. "I didn't do anything wrong. I didn't know anything about this, and if there are Mob guys out there trying to find out where you live, I'm not leaving you alone here. You can be as mad as you want, but I'm not leaving. Unless you're coming with me to my place."

Reluctantly, I admit to myself that he has a point. I do need to be smart about my safety and not just reactive. But I need a minute away from Griffin to process.

"I'm sorry I didn't tell you. Let me fix this," he pleads. "I can fix this."

He said earlier that he would fuck up. He was right. I thought he had yellow flags, but maybe I was wrong. Maybe they're red flags.

"I can't do this," I say, pulling away when Griffin reaches for me again. "I mean, I can, but I need to overreact dramatically for a minute before I can get my head straight. Just give me tonight. I need to think. Today's been a lot."

It has been. Just this morning I was consoling myself with work and had no idea that Griffin had feelings for me or that I was being stalked by the Mob. My brain laughs at that thought, not sure which of those I would've considered to be less likely because they seem equally ridiculous.

I'm just me. Admittedly amazing, but nothing special enough to blow up a five-year friendship over or go on a cross-city manhunt for.

I leave the two guys in my living room, too exhausted to care if they start fighting again. If I'm a grown, independent woman who can solve her own issues, then they sure as hell can solve their own too.

Numb, I go into my bathroom and strip down, carefully folding my uniform. Dazed, I stand under the hot water of the shower, letting it wash away the sweat of tonight's performance and my makeup. Shocked, I pull on pajamas and fall into bed, where I immediately begin crying softly into my pillow.

I have really gotten myself into a mess this time.

Chapter 23

Griffin

I don't want to leave, but one look at Dominic's face tells me that staying is only going to make things worse. "I'm sorry, man, but I love her. I've always loved her. I've tried my hardest to stay away from her—for her sake, for your sake, fuck, for my sake—but I can't do it anymore. I love her too much."

"She's who's been fucking with your head?" He points toward Penny's bedroom door, then at me. "Who you're not worth?"

I dip my chin, agreeing, because tonight has made that abundantly clear to us both.

"Then be better for her. *Fucking be better,*" he tells me harshly, making it sound so damn easy. "Start by fixing this mess so she's safe."

It's as much of a blessing as I'm going to get from him. It might also be a one-way ticket to my own ruin—which could be what he's hoping for—but if there's even the smallest chance that I can fix this, I'll do it. I'll do anything for Penny, and he knows it.

I leave, my decision already made. Johnny K hasn't gotten back to me with any new information about the thief or the ring, and I can't wait around any longer hoping he will. I have to go directly to the root of the problem.

❧

The hostess at the stand inside Aqua Est Vita is a hockey fan. Or at the least, a Griffin Mahoney fan, because she doesn't even flinch at my obviously not-to-dress-code sweats, Hawks T-shirt, and tennis shoes. Or my face that still looks like pulped hamburger.

"Griffin Mahoney! Oh my God, how can I help you?" she gushes.

I look past her, scanning the tables inside the restaurant, looking for one man. If he's not here, I don't know where I'll go next. His residence is unlisted, likely one of dozens of properties he owns in the city, and his office is the same, possibly anywhere or simply wherever he and his laptop may be. But this restaurant is his haven. That's a known fact.

I don't see Miles Conniver himself, but I see a man in all black standing guard near a table in the back. That's got to be his security, which means . . . he's here. Thank fuck.

I want to charge into the depths of the restaurant, slide into the chair across from Conniver, and demand he call off his dogs. But that'll end up one way—with me thrown out the back of the restaurant, and then probably off the closest dock.

So I play it smart. One step at a time, with the first being getting closer to Conniver.

I lean down, keeping my voice between me and the hostess. One glance at her brass name tag tells me her name. "Amelia, I need one minute of Mr. Conniver's time."

Her smile all but evaporates. "Do you have an appointment with him?" she clips out crisply.

I flash the cocky smirk that's led to many an opponent calling me a bastard. "I have something to discuss that he will be very interested in."

Looking uncertain, she glances over her shoulder. "Oh, um, well . . . he doesn't see people without an appointment."

"Just ask him. Please." I could spill the whole thing to Amelia and see if her relaying the information to Conniver would get me an audience with him, but I think dangling an enticing carrot has a better chance. "Tell him it involves a diamond ring. A very *special* diamond ring."

Amelia's eyes widen, and though she still seems doubtful, she holds up a finger, telling me to wait one moment, and hurries toward Conniver's table. I watch as she bends down, whispering to a man whose face I can't see. He says something back to her, and she nods.

As she comes back, it takes every bit of willpower I possess to root myself to the floor and not cut the distance in half. Because her answer doesn't matter. If he said yes, that's where I'm headed. And if he said no? I won't listen and that's still where I'm headed.

"He said you have one minute," she informs me, waving for me to follow her. As she leads me to Conniver, she informs me, "To be up front, I don't think it's because of any ring. You cost him a lot of money by getting kicked out of the game tonight. He had a personal wager riding on that game, I'm certain. So be careful."

I appreciate the warning and give her a tight nod, thanking her. Five seconds later, I'm standing in front of the most dangerous man in the city. The one his own people fear. And I'm doing it voluntarily, serving myself on a silver platter like I have a death wish. But if it'll save Penny, I will gladly make that sacrifice.

His crisp white shirt is open at the neck to show a gold chain that matches the rhinestone-encrusted watch on his wrist. Or hell, maybe those are diamonds too. His hair is perfectly coiffed, and there's an air of ostentatious largesse surrounding him—thank you, long bus rides in the minor leagues, where I had to read books to fill the fucking time. But his expression seems bland enough, thankfully not openly furious over whatever bet he lost.

"Mr. Conniver, thank you for seeing me." I'm not sucking his dick, but manners seem appropriate. He gestures to the seat across from him, and I sit down, mindful of the security guard standing just to the side.

"Mr. Mahoney, I understand you would like to discuss a ring. I, however, would like to know what happened on the ice tonight. And if I can expect it to happen again?" He arches a sharp brow, blatantly asking for insider information to shape his gambling on the Hawks' next game.

"If you'll give me a bit of leeway, I think you'll see that the ring and tonight's game are interwoven."

Judging by the way his eyes flare in surprise, it's not the answer he expected. I also don't think he's surprised often, because he seems quite intrigued. "Do tell."

"About two weeks ago, I was downtown when I ran into Dominic Lee's sister." Conniver's lips purse, and though I suspect he already has several new questions, he stays silent, letting me speak. "She's an amazing custom jewelry designer that works primarily on heritage pieces, and she'd just bought a new ring. Unfortunately, it was stolen right out of my hands by a mugger on the sidewalk."

"That is unfortunate." It's lip service at best, and as he takes a sip of his liquor, his eyes drift away like I'm boring him.

He thinks he's got it all figured out. Tonight's fight with Dom was because I let his sister's ring get stolen, end of story. But that's not even the CliffsNotes version of what's happened.

"The ring was a five-karat diamond, surrounded by baguettes, in bezel-set gold. And it shouldn't have been at the antique store Penny bought it from, according to the two guys who were there, desperately searching for it." I level him with a hard look. "The two guys who have been messaging her, following her, stalking her, and that showed up at the game tonight looking for her because they think she still has the ring. The ring they want to find before their boss realizes it's missing."

Conniver's face has gone perfectly blank, his eyes cold. It's eerie, like he simply turned off his emotions. They're shark's eyes, a predator ready for the kill possibly. "This ring, do you have a picture of it?"

I move to reach into my pocket for my phone, but the guard instantly steps forward, grabbing my bicep. I glance up at him, slowing my movement and showing him that it's just my phone, not a weapon. Cleared, I cut my eyes to Conniver, who shrugs. "He's my defense. I'm sure you understand that."

I do. I understand defending a goal. But not a man. Especially not a man most people need defending from.

Not commenting on that, I find the picture of the ring on Penny's hand and turn my phone around to show Conniver the screen. He barely glances at it before his eyes lift to mine. "Where did you say she bought this?" The question is sharp, his tone accusatory.

"Yesteryear Antiques. I don't think anyone there knew the ring's history. Or owner." I lift a brow in question, wanting to confirm that I'm right and the ring is his.

"It was my mother's." He looks at the photo again, this time his gaze longer and considerably warmer. "You said it was stolen?"

"Yes, we talked to several pawnshops, and a few fences, trying to find it. The mugger was a young guy with freckles, wearing a red hoodie. Johnny K said he might know the guy." I don't bother explaining who Johnny K is, figuring he probably already knows or can find out. "But my concern is the guys following Penny. They've tried to get her home address, and they were obviously looking for her at the game tonight. That's why I had to get her out of there. Which made Dominic realize that something's going on between us before we were ready to share that with him."

"Hence the fight," Conniver summarizes. He sighs, his finger tracing the rim of his glass. "These guys, what do they look like?"

I cut my eyes to the security guy standing beside the table. "Like him. Big, tough. One of them is named Tommy, I think."

"Thomas and Mark," he says instantly.

The names don't really help me, though they do confirm that I've been right this whole time. The ring? Conniver's. The muscle? Conniver's. Penny? In danger.

"I just want them to leave Penny alone. I'm really sorry about your ring, and if Johnny K finds out anything, I'll let you know. But Penny has nothing to do with this. She was just in the wrong place at the wrong time, and bought a ring she thought was beautiful that she was excited to redesign."

"She was going to redesign the ring?" he snaps.

That's not the important part, not at all, but I have to play nice to some small degree. "You can look her up—PLDesigns. She repurposes old jewelry, like heritage stuff. Turns them into modern pieces of wearable art. But what about the guys? You'll call them off?"

I frame it like a question, a request, tailored to a man like Conniver. But it's most definitely a command, and he knows it. He stares at me for a long moment, his face expressionless, and I'm almost certain I've signed my own death certificate, but then he slowly turns to the security guard. "Tell Thomas and Mark that I'd like to see them first thing in the morning at my office." The guard nods, silently acknowledging the order. Conniver turns back to me, his tight smile still making him look like a shark. "It's handled. Miss Lee won't come to any harm."

That easy? I mean, sitting across from this guy isn't easy despite the fancy restaurant. "Just like that?"

The corners of his lips lift into what might be considered a smile but feels more like a threat. "Is there anything else, Mr. Mahoney?"

"No. I guess not. I just want Penny to be safe."

"And she will be," he says with a wave of his hand as though he's a magician that can simply make it so. And I guess, despite the lack of a top hat and wand, he is.

"Um, well . . . thank you."

I go to stand but freeze halfway when he adds, "I trust there won't be any further issues on the ice between you and Mr. Lee during the playoffs?"

There will definitely be issues between me and Dominic. Lots of them. But on the ice, we'll keep our shit together. We're solid players, and we want that Cup, for ourselves and for the Hawks. And for the city.

I nod. "No problems."

"Good." He manages to make the single word sound like *if you know what's good for you, you won't fuck up my gambling, or I'll be forced to take my losses out on you.*

Just like that, I walk away from the table, feeling the security guard's gaze follow me and all too aware that I just sat with the closest thing to the Grim Reaper that I hope to ever meet. It was surprisingly uneventful, at least on the surface, but I would hate to be Tommy and Mark tomorrow morning.

Up front, Amelia smiles as she holds out a napkin. “Can you sign this for me?”

“Sure.” I take the marker she holds out and scribble my name. When I glance back up, she’s holding her phone up, already leaning into me to pose for a picture. I fake a smile, and she clicks the button on the screen.

“What’s your number? I’ll send it to you,” she purrs, her gaze slowly dripping over my face, down to my chest, and lower. I know I look like hell, bruised and swollen with dried blood on my shirt, but she makes it seem like I’m dressed to the nines and looking my best.

“Thanks, but I’m good,” I tell her gently but firmly.

I’m not good. I haven’t been good in a long time, maybe ever. But I’m not looking for a quick fuck with a hostess. I want Penny, only Penny.

She gives me a shrewd look. “Lucky girl.”

But I shake my head, correcting her gently. “I’m the lucky one.”

I hope that’s true, and that, in keeping this secret from her, I haven’t fucked up everything beyond repair.

Chapter 24

PENNY

I promised Dominic I would stay in my apartment with the door locked and not answer it for any reason. Not even the DoorDashed brunch I whined about wanting this morning. But seriously, after a night like last night, a girl deserves some eggs Benedict with an extra side of hollandaise sauce and a freaking mimosa. My brother, who will henceforth be known as the taste-bud-hater, disagreed vehemently, going so far as threatening to tie me to a dining room chair if that's what it took to keep me safely locked up. He probably wouldn't actually do it, but I didn't feel like testing him today. Still, my promise was definitely made under duress, and even then, he didn't want to leave me.

But duty calls. Duty, which also goes by the name Coach Leverson, head coach of the Hawks, made the not-a-request call requiring Dominic and Griffin to attend a meeting at the arena.

And now I'm alone with my thoughts again, waiting on my DoorDash delivery because I totally lied to my brother about that and am going to take my troubles out on a Styrofoam box of deliciousness. And like the adult I am, I will absolutely hide the evidence before he returns so I don't have to listen to another of his lectures about safety.

As if Dominic—a six-foot-plus-tall, muscled-up mountain of a male celebrity known for violent on-ice beatdowns—would have a better grasp on safety than I, your average everyday woman, would. Yeah, something tells me he's never walked a city block checking out the store window reflections to see if anyone's behind him, but I've certainly done that. Countless times, as has every woman. Being hunted by the Mob definitely adds a new level of danger, but it's not like I couldn't get a stalker on a random trip to the grocery store or through an appearance as a cheerleader.

So yeah, I ordered brunch, *and* I'll check the peephole before opening the door to make sure it's the DoorDash delivery and nothing more. Because I freaking deserve it, the same way I deserved the Chocolate Orgasm ice cream I picked at until it melted last night, refusing to share a single bite with Dominic. Nope, kept it to myself, all while reliving the up-and-down emotional roller coaster I've been riding for the last twenty-four hours, trying to make sense of it all, and then dumping the liquid chocolatey goodness down the drain, pointedly making sure Dominic saw me.

My grand revelation from hours of deep thought? I just have to keep putting one foot in front of the other, fixing my crown when it goes off-kilter, and getting up every time I get knocked down . . . again.

After that self–pep talk, I started to make a plan. Because this girl likes a plan. In no particular order, my to-do list is . . .

One, a come-to-Jesus talk with Griffin, in which I tell him to stop the secretive shit or I'm out. Those yellow flags of his are now screaming blood orange, and that's not continuing. He screwed up big-time, but in a twisty way, it was for a good reason. Well, he thought it was. But this is the last time I'm going to give grace on that. Nor am I going to spend my life perpetually wrapped in Bubble Wrap. My spirit would suffocate. So if that's what he wants, it won't be with me.

Two, tell Dominic to get off his high horse because, despite him thinking he's the boss of the universe, he can't control me or Griffin. He should be thanking Griffin for the five-year reprieve. Because the truth is, I remember my thoughts when I saw Griffin in my parents' kitchen all those years ago. Before he opened his mouth and ruined it,

I was thinking I'd like to ride that ride. Raw, rough, and repeatedly. So really, the delay is a gift because I was an entirely different woman then. Young, full of dreams, and so stupid about the reality of life that with nothing more than the barest crook of Griffin's finger, I would've happily let him smother me in Bubble Wrap. Now I know myself, my heart, and most importantly, my strength. So I'm glad to have had that time to grow up. And Dominic should be glad, too, because I'm better for it. I'm more *me* now.

Three is the hardest step in this new plan and the scariest conversation of them all. I have to talk to Miles Conniver. I suggested it last night and promptly decided it was a horrible, no-good, dangerous idea, but I think it's the only way to stop the threat his guys pose. Maybe if Mr. Conniver knows I don't have the ring, they'll leave me alone. Because none of this is my fault. All I did was buy a beautiful ring. The rest is the universe pulling a sick prank on me again.

Four, did my pink eternity band sell?

That being the easiest question to answer, I pull up my website's back end to see that yes, the ring did sell. Woo-hoo! That's another $500 toward my credit card bill! A few clicks later, the buyer has been sent an email thanking them for their purchase and I've got a shipping label printed. Even though the post office is closed today, I box the ring up beautifully, prepping it to begin its trek to its new owner in Oregon tomorrow. The small win restores my sense of control in some small way, reminding me that I can handle the rest of my to-do list too.

Even though I'm expecting my food delivery, the knock on my door scares the bejesus out of me. I jump a foot in the air, clutching invisible pearls at my neck, before laughing at myself. One glance at my phone, and I see the notification that my order has been delivered. Still, I peek out the peephole, checking the section of hallway that I can see.

The coast is clear, and heaven in a box waits just on the other side of the door. I open it slowly, already bending down to grab the bag when footsteps sound out on the stairs a few doors away.

I glance up as the two people I want to see least come into view. Not my brother and Griffin. I wish it were them. But no, my life couldn't go that well. It's the guys from the game.

I gasp in startled shock. They've found me!

How and why do things like this keep happening to me? Did I piss someone off in a former life, and now I'm doomed to catastrophe after catastrophe as punishment? Is there some sage-infused penance I can do to make it stop? Hell, I'd snort the whole damn sage stick if it'd help at this point.

But I don't think that'd really work either.

"Shit!" I hear one of them mutter, and then he's running toward my door.

I abandon my food, slamming the door shut as fast as I can and locking the dead bolts, wishing we had more than the two, which have always seemed perfectly adequate until now. Today, with the Mob bearing down on my door, I'm thinking steel core and twenty locks would be better, and then I'd only lock half of them so that if they tried to pick them, they'd be unlocking some and relocking others.

Back pressed to the door, fear dumps into my veins. What am I going to do?

I need to call the police. I need to call Griffin. Those are the only two things that come to mind. Only then do I belatedly consider grabbing a knife.

I hear a muffled voice in the hallway and press my ear to the door, listening. "We didn't mean to scare her, boss. We were coming up the stairs, and there she was." The voice goes silent, and I assume he's listening to someone else talk that I can't hear. Another glance through peephole tells me the taller of the two guys is on the phone. "Yeah, will do."

A loud knock on my door sends me scurrying back like their break-in is imminent. "Miss Lee, we're here to apologize. Mr. Conniver would like to have a word with you."

I let out a nearly silent laugh, wondering if that actually works on people. Yeah, sure, a *Mob boss* wants a word? Pretty sure that word is *murder*.

"Miss Lee?" He knocks again.

I look around as if a solution will appear out of thin air, and when it doesn't, and unsure what else to do, I fake a bad accent and say through the door, "No Miss Lee here. Wrong apartment."

"Your food is sitting here with your name on it. And we know who you are," he answers dryly. Silently, I mouth, *Shit.* "We're here to apologize for scaring you. We just wanted the ring, and we understand you don't have it anymore. We're sorry."

If you look up *insincere* in the dictionary, you'll find an audio clip of that apology. But I'm not looking for us to braid each other's hair and do a few trust falls like besties. I want them to go away. And I want my eggs Benedict, which is probably going all soggy in the box because of them.

"Okay, apology accepted. Bye now!"

"Mr. Conniver still wants to speak with you."

"No thanks."

On the other side of the door, I hear his voice again, but he doesn't seem to be talking to me. I risk looking through the peephole again and see that he's back on his phone. "I said *sorry* and told her you want to speak to her. She said *no, thanks*." He shakes his head at the other guy, who shrugs. "Do you want us to take her by force?"

"I can hear you!" I shout through the door. I'd still prefer an inch of steel core for a door, but my current door does have this as an advantage.

"Shit, she heard that," he says to whom I'm assuming is Miles Conniver on the line. "Okay, okay. I'll tell her." He hangs up and says through the door, "He says to answer your phone."

I have two seconds of confusion because my phone is completely silent on my desk before it rings, scaring the shit out of me.

Let's get one thing straight, I'm not answering that phone, because that's creepy as hell on a good day. On the day after some scary guys try to get your home address from a public servant, show up to your job, and then show up at said address? Hell no, I'm not answering. Nope, not talking to a Mob boss. So I go over and decline the call.

It rings again instantly.

Guess Miles Conniver isn't used to being ignored. Well, we're all learning new things, I suppose. I send it to voicemail again, then pick it up and bring it closer to the door, where I can keep an eye on Dumb and Dumber in the hall.

And still, it rings again.

"Lady, you'd better answer it."

"Or what?" I ask, watching them through the peephole. The two guys look at each other in confusion. They're probably not used to people refusing their boss either.

"Pretty sure you'll lose the biggest customer your little jewelry business has ever had," he quips, laughing like this whole thing is some joke and not the most terrorizing experience of my life.

Instead of ringing again, a text message comes through.

Please answer your phone. I'd like to discuss my ring. —M.C.

That's totally step three of my solidly thought-out plan, but I was going to leave it for last, procrastinating while I figure out what the hell I'm going to say. But apparently, I'm doing the hard things first.

I glance at my little framed cat art with the "Faith Over Fear" motto. I have no faith this is going to go well. And I'm full of fear that I'm going to disappear and end up on milk cartons all across the country.

Still, when my phone rings again, I answer. "Hello?" In breaking news that solidly demonstrates what a completely brave, total badass I am, my voice only cracks a little.

"Miss Lee?"

"Yes?"

"This is Miles Conniver. A mutual acquaintance of ours told me that we have a piece of jewelry in common."

I frown in confusion, because what did he say? "A mutual acquaintance?" Then it hits me. "Oh, did Johnny K find your ring?"

The other end of the line goes silent for long enough that I pull the phone away from my ear to make sure we didn't get disconnected. "He has. It will be back in my possession within the hour. The ring is what I'd like to speak with you about."

"Okay," I drawl out. Honestly, even though I already decided to return the ring to its rightful owner after Griffin told me it was essentially stolen to begin with, I'm still disappointed that I won't get to work on the gorgeous ring.

"I've looked at your work and find it to be quite unique."

"Oh, uh . . . thank you."

"I understand you had already created designs for my ring, and I would very much like to see them if you'd be willing to share?"

Excitement shoots through me, but is quickly tempered by my entrepreneurial spirit and business acumen. Plus, a healthy dose of "yeah, sure, buddy," because that sounds like code for "come into my white panel van and see the cute puppies." "Of course, I'd be happy to share those with you. For either a consultation fee, if you intend to have another jeweler complete the work, or with a deposit, if you'd like my custom, concierge-level experience from design to completion on the piece."

Saying that to one of the wealthiest, most powerful people I've ever spoken with is truly terrifying. That he chuckles is worrisome. "How much did you pay for the ring initially?"

Normally, I would never tell a customer what I paid for the piece they're purchasing. Mostly, because it doesn't matter. What they're investing in is my vision, my design, my work, my art. This is a unique situation, though. "Ten thousand dollars."

"One moment."

My phone dings in my ear, and I pull it away to look at it. There's a notification at the top of the screen alerting me that I've received a $10,000 Zelle payment. I should be over the moon thrilled about that because it'll clear my credit card balance, but there's a bigger issue. "How did you do that? How do you know my username?"

"Miss Lee, I can know anything I desire to know." I hear a smile in his voice, like he finds my confusion and shock to be quite amusing. But he's all-business when he speaks again. "Now that we've handled that, I would like to see your ideas. As I said, the ring will be in my hand within the hour. Depending on your designs, it could be in yours shortly after if you're available for a commission piece."

A commission piece for a Mob boss? Definitely not. But how do you say no? And truthfully, I don't want to say no. My creative muse is begging to get their paws on that ring and reminding me that I promised free rein after that blah-boring but beautiful pink eternity band.

"Okay," I say, at least 50 percent sure of this plan of action. "When and where?" I figure I can ask Dominic, Griffin, or both of them to come along as my bodyguards. Hell, maybe the whole Hawks team, just to be safe.

"Now. Thomas and Mark have a car waiting for you."

The bark of laughter that escapes my chest is tinged with hysteria, because there's absolutely no way that's happening. "I am not getting into a car with those two. I'd end up on milk cartons, with my parents on the nightly news, begging for my return. Which, by the way, if anything happens to me, the police will be on your doorstep first because lots of people know about the missing ring. *Lots of people*," I emphasize. Okay, so it's more like three—Griffin, Dominic, and Talia, but that doesn't sound nearly as threatening.

He chuckles again, the sound just as worrisome this time because I'm not exactly known for my top-shelf humor, and his even-keeled voice and formal demeanor don't make me think he is either. "I mean you no harm, Miss Lee. You have my word, which can be trusted."

"People, especially men, telling me they're trustworthy is kind of a big red flag. Especially when they have a reputation like yours. I'm sure you understand."

"Indeed," he concedes. "My men are there to apologize, genuinely, and then drive you to my restaurant. Nothing more. Believe me, they have been suitably chastised for scaring you."

Chastised for scaring me? He makes it sound like they got a good, stern lecture, which isn't nearly enough. But also, a lecture from Miles Conniver would definitely be enough to scare me straight.

I'm still not stupid or blindly trusting enough to get in a car with them, though. I have some sense of self-preservation. "I'll take a rideshare."

"As you wish." He gives me the address for the restaurant, and a moment later, the two guys in the hallway walk away. I'm still plastered to the door, watching through the peephole to see if they make a move toward busting it down.

Aqua Est Vita is gorgeous, fancier than any place I've ever eaten, for sure. Inside, the hostess greets me warmly. "Miss Lee? Mr. Conniver is waiting for you."

As I follow her, her stiletto heels *click-clack* on the tile floor, while my Sambas squeak. Because you can bet your ass that I wore tennis shoes after the ridiculous amount of running from Conniver's men I've had to do over the last few weeks. I'm dressed for a business meeting, in slacks and a blouse, hoping for the best, but with touches of personality . . . and safety in mind.

As we walk deeper into the restaurant, I search for anything that sets off my alarm bells, but there's nothing. People are dining happily, with black-outfitted servers bustling about. A bouncer-looking guy, who isn't either of the ones who've been following me, stands near a table in the back, clearly my destination.

When we reach it, Mr. Conniver politely rises and extends a hand. "Ah, Miss Lee. Thank you for coming. Please sit," he says, making no mention of what it took to get me to agree to this little chitchat, the promise of getting to work on that gorgeous ring. And a $10,000 deposit. Apparently, I do have a price and am a total slut for a special diamond.

He looks . . . wealthy. Manicured, coiffed, well dressed, with an air of elegance and importance. He doesn't look scary, but looks can be deceiving, so I'm careful as I shake his hand and sit across from him.

A hint of a smile ghosts across his lips before he covers it by sipping his coffee. "Again, I assure you I mean you no harm. Nor do my men. I am truly interested in your designs."

"And again, forgive me if I don't believe that for one second, when they've been stalking me, literally hunting me down across the city."

He tilts his head, agreeing. "Fair point. All in a vain attempt to hide their mistake with the ring in the first place."

"How did the ring end up at Yesteryear? Carolynn would never sell something without permission." Does it matter? No, but it's been bothering me, and given the curious kitty at least died with answers, I'm asking questions.

Mr. Conniver cuts his eyes left and right as though someone might dare to eavesdrop on him, which is laughable. Even his table has a wider berth around it than the other tables. And no one is sitting at the four closest ones surrounding us. "Oddly enough, that's related to why I've asked you here. You see, I'm going to propose to my beloved, so there's been some reorganization at my home in preparation for her moving in. Some items for donation, some for resale, and one special piece of my mother's was meant to go to the family jeweler for resizing. I'm afraid there was a mix-up, but thankfully it's been corrected now."

He reaches into his pocket and pulls out the gorgeous ring that started this whole debacle. I gasp and, like the jewel hound I am, proceed to gush over it. "It's so beautiful, just like I remembered, even though I only had it for a little while."

Mr. Conniver smiles fully, a look that's oddly boyish on him, softening the harsh lines of his face. "That's why I'd like to have you redesign the ring for Georgina. My jeweler was simply going to resize it, but I've studied your work, and I think you can turn it into something truly special. And she deserves something as unique as she is." He sounds genuine, his love for his bride-to-be apparent in every word.

Georgina must be unique, because I can't imagine many women signing up to marry a Mob boss. On the pages of a book, maybe. But in real life? It'd be terrifying in a way I'm not sure the fancy dinners and clothes could make up for.

I search Mr. Conniver's face, looking for any hint of a lie, any tell that he might be deceiving me. But now that he has the ring in his possession, there's no need to harm me. That was the only possible reason a man like him and a woman like me would even cross paths.

So I take the leap, deciding to believe him. "Then let's create something gorgeous for Georgina. First, tell me about her so I can tailor the piece to her."

Chapter 25

GRIFFIN

Two Hours Ago

"No more issues," I vow to Coach.

"Everything's good," Dominic echoes.

We're both lying through our teeth. Things are not good between us. They might never be again. But we can't let that ruin our careers. Sure, we've built our careers on a bond of brotherhood, but we've both been in hockey long enough to have experience playing with teammates we hate. It's almost mandatory, especially when you're a pro.

Still, even considering that idea makes my gut churn.

We've already explained our sudden and unprecedented mid-game departure as a family emergency, taking care to keep Penny's name out of it as much as possible so it doesn't affect her status with the Hawkettes. She'll have to take her lumps for leaving, too, but we're not adding fuel to that fire, because Coach would immediately go to the Hawkettes coach to discuss why her cheerleaders are ruining games for the team.

Because without Dom and me, we lost that game against the Torches. Thankfully, our playoff seed is locked in at this point, but the win gave the Torches some bragging rights I wish they didn't have and created some doubt moving forward into the playoffs.

"We need you two. Whatever's going on, it stays off the ice. Or you'll both be off the ice." Coach is no idiot, seeing right through our lies. I'm amazed that he hasn't decided to put us on separate rotations, keeping us away from each other at least temporarily.

"Heard."

"Yes, Coach."

Dismissed from his office, Dominic and I walk through the locker room and out to the parking lot. I can feel his anger, sense his betrayal, both surrounding him like a heavy blanket. Trying to head his explosion off, I admit, "I went to see Conniver. Told him everything."

He whirls, his eyes wide, to shout, "You *what*?"

"You told me to fix it, so I did." I lock eyes with him. "I fucked up, but I want to be better for her. I want to be worthy of her."

We both know I'm not, and may never be.

Dominic lifts his eyes to the sky and sighs heavily. "Why didn't you tell me? I thought we told each other everything."

I don't shy away from the question. He needs to understand this, so I'm going to let him judge me all he wants. "I don't know what to say, man. I knew the first time I saw her, but you were my only friend, and staying away from her was the one thing you asked of me, so of course I was going to do it. But I didn't know how to act, so I acted . . . like you." I shrug, seeing that it was the wrong choice to make, but not sure what I would've done things differently. I didn't have a lot of choices back then, and I sure hadn't seen how good life could be yet. "Love felt like one more thing other people deserved and got easily, that I would never have. I was . . . bitter?"

Labeling an emotion beyond *happy*, *sad*, or *mad* is a big step for me, but bitterness feels accurate for what I'd felt then. Hell, I've felt it for years, every time I saw teammates with girlfriends and wives, or even with casual hookups, because at least they got to be with the person they wanted.

But not me. Not Griffin Mahoney.

Dom stares at me, his eyes hard and his jaw set. "You're not just fucking around with her?" he demands, the question accusatory.

I tilt my head, glaring at him, and he glares right back, waiting for an answer expectantly. "Well, I do want to fuck her."

His fist balls, and his jaw clenches so hard I can see the muscles bulge at the corners where I never can shave right on the first pass. "I'm gonna kick your ass again."

"Fair warning," I tell him, my own fist balling, "this time I'll fight back. The passive shit is over."

That brings him up short, and I can almost see him replaying the fight on the ice and the one at Penny's. "You didn't fight back," he echoes, stunned. "Not until she accidentally fell while trying to ride me like a bucking bronco. Why not?"

I shrug. "It needed to happen. I deserved it."

"Holy shit, man. You are such an asshole." He huffs, shaking his head like he didn't already know that. Like he hasn't always known that. "You've actually been pining away for her all these years? Like some lovesick puppy?" A hint of a smile teases at his lips.

He's laughing at me. Normally, I'd tell him to fuck off, but he has a point. "Woof, woof," I deadpan, sounding as pathetic as I am. But he deserves an answer, a real one. "Seriously, I do want to fuck her—" I admit playfully, and once Dominic's brows lift the way I knew they would, I add, "And love her, take care of her, see her succeed. I want to have babies with her and grow old with her. I want a life with her." I blink dumbfoundedly, shocked at my own rambling. Dominic seems just as surprised. "I never listed it out like that, but yeah, I want everything with her. I want what your folks have. It's as simple and as complicated as that."

He nods slowly, and I watch as he swallows hard. "Okay. I hope you haven't screwed things up too badly, then." He shows me his crossed fingers and twists his lips like he totally thinks I have.

It takes a second to register what he's said. It's his version of acceptance. "That's it?" I ask, throwing my hands wide. "Yesterday you're beating the shit out of me, and now you're just all 'good luck with that'?"

He grins evilly. "Hey, if you want to take that on, she's your problem now." He stretches his arms wide like he's flying free for the first time in his life. "Wow, that feels good. If she blows something up, that's you. If she breaks a leg, that's you too. If she ends up with a stolen ring from a Mob boss"—he leans my way and gleefully informs me—"you."

He has a point. Penny might be the death of me, literally, but she's the only woman I'd plead with a Mob boss for. Hell, she's the only woman I'd do lots of things for.

"I told her I'd be back after my meeting with Coach. You coming with?" Dom asks.

And like that, we're okay. Or at least some version of it. Still, I say, "I'm sorry, Dom. I didn't mean to blindside you with it, especially not mid-game." I push my jaw left and right, rubbing it to show that it's still sore from his punches.

But that's not what he questions. Instead, he looks at my nose and the raccoon eyes I'm sporting right now. "Your nose okay?"

I inhale, showing him it works, which is all that matters. We're hockey players, not fashion models. "As okay as it ever was," I answer with a shrug. "I set it last night, trainer looked at it before we talked with Coach. Little lidocaine cream, and it is what it is."

Honestly, his punches aren't what hurt the most. It was his words, which is always the case. The verbal beatdowns from my parents are what still echo in my head, much more than any ache or pain from a fist. Which reminds me that I have some deeply, brutally honest apologies to make to Penny to rewrite some of the things I've said to her over the years. Never anything as hurtful as my parents, but enough that she's not sure about me yet. But she will be.

"You deserved it." He huffs, frowning. "But I'm sorry too. I didn't know how you felt and thought you were doing the puck bunny thing with my baby sister. That wouldn't be cool, man."

"I know. Trust me, I'm not doing that."

"All right, then, let's go see what Penny-Nickel-Dime has gotten herself into now," Dom says, shaking his head, because truthfully, even within the confines of her apartment, there's no telling. "Whatever it is, it's on . . . you."

I roll my eyes. I think he's going to get a lot of mileage out of that one. "I can handle it."

"I know you can. If there's anyone who would know how to handle her, it's you."

I think it's his way of saying I'm worthy of her, and I appreciate that more than he could possibly know. But there's one important distinction I need to make. "I can handle whatever disasters come her way, but she doesn't need handling. She's good on her own. I just want to be the lucky bastard who gets to watch her shine from the good seats."

Dominic laughs and points a finger at me. "Use that. Tell her that. It's some good shit."

He thinks I'm spitting game, but it's the truth.

"Speaking of disaster," Dominic says, letting out an exasperated sigh as we come up the stairs at Penny's apartment to see a bag sitting in front of her doorway, "I told her not to order food."

He picks it up before knocking on the door. We wait a few seconds, but she doesn't answer. I pull at the receipt stapled to the bag, scanning it. "This is over an hour old," I say, dread starting to build in my gut.

"Shit." Dominic knocks on the door, harder this time. And as soon as he stops, I start.

"Penny?" When I don't hear her coming or unlocking the door, I ask Dom, "You have a key?"

"No, she told me she didn't want me walking in on her with some dude between her legs." He glances up and down the hallway like she might magically appear from somewhere other than her apartment.

I growl, not liking that image at all, and Dominic chuckles. "This could be fun."

The tease promises a future full of torment, mostly for me, but Penny will be collateral damage. Not wanting that, I go back hard. "You think so? Because I'm going to be the only man between her legs from now on," I inform him with an arrogant smirk. That wipes the smile off his face right quick. Back to business, I knock again as I ask, "What about Talia? You have her number?"

"Yeah, but if she's not here to answer the door, she's probably at work. You think we should wait?"

Arriving at the same conclusion I've already accepted, he asks, "We're breaking down her door, aren't we?" I nod. "Okay, but when Penny gets mad, it was your idea, not mine. On three?"

"Like Mississippily?"

"Is there any other way?"

"One, Mississippi . . . two, Mississippi . . . three . . ."

We both lunge at the door, but Dominic stops short, and I'm the only one that hits the solid surface, shouldering it with all my might. It gives way with a concerningly easy crack of the frame that's definitely going to need repair.

"Your idea and you did it. I'm totally in the clear," Dominic brags, pumping his fist. "How's your shoulder?"

I don't care about the blame, and I sure as hell don't care about the dull ache in my shoulder. I need to lay eyes on Penny and make sure she's okay.

Please let her be taking a shower and have not heard us knocking. Or have fallen asleep and forgotten about her food delivery. Hell, I'd take something like she fell and can't get up at this point, because I would happily carry her wherever she needs to go, even if the hospital is the first destination.

A quick scan of the living room, no Penny. A glance toward the kitchen, empty. I dash toward the bedroom, where her unmade bed taunts me. The bathroom is the last place to check, but that dread is growing rapidly.

She's not here. Penny is gone.

Back in the living room, I meet Dominic's eyes, his face a mask of concern the same way I'm sure mine is. "Do you think she would've gone out for something?"

"And left her food? That was damn near all she was talking about this morning. She wouldn't just leave."

Pursing my lips, I glare at him, because he knows as well as I do that she absolutely would. She'd leave simply because Dominic told her not to.

"What's all this racket?" a voice grumbles from the hallway. An older woman in a ratty bathrobe, slippers, and glasses appears in Penny's doorway, seeing us at the same time we see her. She gasps, clutching her robe closed at her neck before remembering that she's the building's resident Grumpy Bitch. "I swear these girls are running a whorehouse over here. Guys coming and going all day," she complains, her lips curled up in distaste.

"Guys? What guys?" I bark.

She scrunches her face, and I fully expect her to tell me to watch my tone, but she just waves a hand toward Dom and me. "Two big guys like you."

I cut my eyes to Dom to find him looking at me too. We're on the same page. It had to be Miles Conniver's guys. And after that bastard told me Penny would be safe.

"They were out here in the hallway earlier, talking with the cheerleader through the door. Loud as you please, like they didn't give a rat's patootie if they were disturbing other people's peaceful afternoons."

"Then what?" Dominic demands.

"They left," she answers, and I'm not sure if she means the guys or Penny or both. Could they have snatched her in broad daylight and this woman have not done a damn thing to stop them? "She left a few minutes later."

Okay, that at least tells me that Conniver's guys didn't kidnap her. It's a small consolation from the worst-case scenario forming in my mind. Still, wanting to be sure, I clarify, "She left on her own? The guys weren't with her?"

"Yeah," she says, nodding. But then she pauses dramatically before drawling out, "Weeell, up here. But I watched out the window. I like to keep an eye on things, you know?"

Does she want a cookie for being the neighborhood snoop? "And?"

"Cheerleader got in an Uber. The guys were driving one of those big, fancy SUVs. They followed her after the Uber pulled away."

"Shit!" Dominic hisses.

"Come on," I tell him. "I know where she went. At least I hope I do."

"What about this door?" the neighbor tuts. "You can't leave it wide open like this. They'll get robbed blind." Is she expressing actual care for Penny and Talia? Hell, that's as much of a shocker as anything else, considering she's always banging on the wall like they're the most annoying pests in her life.

The door is a concern that'll have to be addressed, but it's not the priority when Penny's in actual, real danger at this very moment, so we pull it closed behind us . . . well, as close to closed as it will go with a cracked frame. "You like to keep an eye on things? Make sure nobody but Penny, Talia, or us goes in there, and I'll make it worth your while."

Her eyes flare, looking something other than grumpy for the first time, and she smiles, revealing pristine dentures that contrast oddly with her unkempt appearance.

"Okay, I'll see what I can do," she agrees.

The ride to Aqua Est Vita seems three times as long as it was yesterday. Probably because I'm terrified that something has happened to Penny, or is happening right now, and I'm not there to stop it.

I pull up to the restaurant, not even bothering to park in a space but just leaving my car double-parked in the street. I toss my keys to the valet, unconcerned about if he'll actually move it or not. It can get towed for all I care.

Inside, I bypass the hostess stand, marching straight for the back with Dominic hot on my heels. "Penny?" I shout, disturbing the restaurant full of people loitering over their brunches.

"Griffin?" I hear her a split second before she comes into view, and even the smallest hint of her voice tamps down my fear a few notches. But seeing her sitting across from the most dangerous man in the city isn't the least bit reassuring despite the fact that she looks perfectly whole and more than a bit confused at my sudden and loud appearance.

"Mr. Mahoney, lower your voice," Conniver orders sharply, coming to his feet. "This restaurant is not the place for that sort of behavior."

Is he for fucking real?

"You said you'd leave her alone," I accuse, pointing a finger into his chest and not giving a shit about the security guard rapidly moving my way. Conniver doesn't flinch and instead holds up a hand, stopping his guard.

"Griffin," Penny hisses, her tone gone severe as she glances around at all the attention my entry has garnered.

"I believe my words were that she would come to no harm, and I think you'll find that to be the case. Correct, Miss Lee?"

He looks expectantly at Penny, and when she turns confused eyes from him to me and back again, what she finally says is, "You talked to Griffin? About what?"

His lips twitch as though he's fighting a smile. "I may have misled you to some degree. While we do apparently have Johnny K in common, we have another mutual acquaintance. Mr. Mahoney." He gestures toward me like he's Vanna White and I'm a letter he needs to spin around. "He came to see me last night to inform me that two of my men had been misbehaving in an attempt to correct their unfortunate mistake. He was quite persuasive in his request that I leave you alone." Conniver arches a brow, giving me a tiny smirk. "To point, I had nothing to do with any of that and was wholly unaware until the issue was brought to my attention."

I didn't persuade him in the slightest. I begged, I demanded, I would've gladly laid down my life if it meant keeping her safe, and both Conniver and I know that. Penny hears something else entirely.

"You came to see him without me? And without telling me? Damn it, Griffin, you can't keep hiding stuff from me and keeping secrets. What else is there? What else haven't you told me?" Penny demands.

Is she fucking serious?

I've laid my heart bare for her, all the ugly, traumatic broken shards I have left. And she's throwing it back in my face that I didn't tell her sooner. As though there's some acceptable timetable of when to reveal your darkest shame or deepest feelings, and I've totally fucked it up.

"Nothing," I spit out. "I've told you everything, more than anybody else knows. Even Dominic. And I would've told you about this when I saw you today, except when I got to your place, *you weren't there*. So, hi," I say, waving a hand like we're buddies who haven't seen each other in a long time, not people in a really bumpy start of a new relationship, "last night after I left your place, I came to see Conniver, and told him what's been going on. He was surprisingly understanding, and said you'd be okay and he would handle getting the ring back. Now it's your turn. What are you doing here? With him?"

I'm not jealous. I'm scared of Conniver and don't want him this close to Penny, especially when he's watching our back-and-forth like it's a daytime soap opera playing out in front of him. To be fair, he's not the only one. The rest of the restaurant is doing the same thing because we're making quite a scene.

She blinks, still processing what I've said, and is probably about to fillet me wide open for daring to speak to her in such a harsh manner. I can't say it's the smartest thing I've ever done when I want her to give me a chance, but there was no right answer here. If I'd texted her last night, I would've been smothering her when she asked for space. Same thing if I'd shown up on her doorstep this morning. And now? I've blown everything by apparently *not* telling her? There's no right, only wrongs.

Maybe that's all I'm capable of, all I'll ever do. No matter how well intentioned I am, I just fuck up.

"Redesigning the ring for Mr. Conniver?" Penny says, her voice unsure. Of me? Of him? Of herself? I'm not sure.

"Johnny K come through with the ring?" I ask Conniver, and he nods. I almost ask if the unluckiest thief in the world is still alive but quickly decide I don't want to know the answer to that question. Not that Conniver would tell me anyway. I'm sure he's well versed in speaking precisely to stay out of legal trouble.

Turning back to Penny, I clarify, "And you're going to redesign it the way you wanted to do in the beginning of this whole thing?" She gives a tiny shrug. "Great. Everything's golden, then. Guess my work here is done."

Chapter 26

Penny

I watch Griffin spin away. See Dominic give him a sad puppy-dog look. In a second, all I can do is study Griffin's broad, muscled back as he simply leaves.

What just happened?

"Sis, I told him that I hoped he hadn't screwed things up too badly with you, but now, I think you're the one screwing up. That asshole *loves* you," Dom says as soon as the door closes. "He was damn near reciting sonnets about you, waxing poetic about how cute your babies would be and looking forward to matching rocking chairs when you're old and gray. And after he cracked open his cold, dead heart, you just told him it wasn't good enough. That he wasn't good enough." He pins me with a glare of barely restrained anger. "And I think you know how many times he's heard that."

My mind spins, the world turning upside down. Is Dominic on Griffin's side? I thought he was mad at Griffin? It seems like the tables have not only turned but entirely flipped, and my brother is protecting Griffin from me rather than the other way around now.

"He can't keep secrets from me, hiding things like I can't handle it," I argue.

"Agreed. And he knows that. You know he does." When I don't disagree, Dominic continues, his voice a bit gentler. "But that's not what this was. He told me about his late-night rendezvous as soon as we walked out of the meeting with Coach. I'm guessing he would've told you as soon as he saw you too."

He was going to tell me? He wasn't hiding it?

Confused, I glance from my brother to Mr. Conniver as though either of them might have insight on what I should do.

Mr. Conniver leans back and says in that same almost predatory way that I'm starting to understand he has when he touches on the seedier side of his profession, "Miss Lee, I think you'd agree that I am not an easy man to approach. Yet Mr. Mahoney came to see me, telling me potentially upsetting information without regard for his own safety. His only concern was . . . you. If I may say so, it was quite romantic."

I'm sure, to a man like him, a protective streak a mile wide would be romantic. But to me? I don't know.

Sensing my doubt, Mr. Conniver adds, "If I thought my Georgina were in danger? Let's just say that I am not a man who would merely fight the world for her. I would set the world on fire to keep her warm and leave it in ruins to ensure her safety. Without hesitation. Such a primitive mindset is not an easy thing to understand, and some would consider it monstrous. She simply sees that as . . . me. She understands that our life will come with harsh realities and hard situations, mostly with my own inner demons, to be honest, and she loves me, not in spite of them but because they have shaped me into the man I am. She accepts me, sins and all. And in return, I love her more deeply than any other man possibly could." He pauses, making sure he's caught my gaze before finishing with, "I think Mr. Mahoney and I have much in common. If you can understand the love behind his actions and forgive, he could be your best ally, and you would be his biggest strength."

"Yeah, what he said," Dom echoes, pointing at Mr. Conniver. "Ditto, or whatever. Fuck, I should have studied more in college. That was some insightful shit."

My brother is right. The words Mr. Conniver just spoke are poetic in a way I wouldn't expect from someone I'm afraid might actually murder me. He's a study in contrasts, though I guess I shouldn't be surprised that a man who can control the city from the shadows is keenly intelligent. He'd have to be, or he would've been overthrown, violently and dramatically. I'm sure, in his line of work, the value of a well-spoken turn of phrase is priceless, whether a threat or, in this case, advice.

The two men stare at me, waiting while I hotly debate with myself. Mostly mentally, of course, but there's some talking to myself, too, which I'm sure looks a bit crazed.

"OhmaGod, what have I done?" I finally whisper, hands covering my mouth as I realize the truth. All my talk about flags this, flag that . . . I want Griffin—the good, the bad, the ugly, the mistakes, and the sweet gestures. The man I've fallen for, exactly as he is.

"Nothing unfixable, but I can't keep playing couples' counselor for you two. I know I'm good, but you're going to have to figure out your own shit eventually, and quit depending on me to solve all your problems," Dominic teases. "Plus, I expect a special thank-you toast at your wedding for bringing the two of you together."

Our what? my mind screeches.

I stare, about to argue with so much of what he just said, but ultimately decide Dominic can have his illusions of grandeur. Rising to my feet, I try to maintain some semblance of professionalism, but I'm pretty sure I sound hysterical when I say, "Mr. Conniver, could we possibly reschedule this meeting to discuss your ring's design?"

He's a busy man. One who's probably unaccustomed to being blown off for personal drama. But he nods easily, unperturbed. "Far be it from me to stand in the way of love. Especially when it appears this ring has already brought together the two of you. I hope it will do the same for me and my Georgina."

"I'll make sure it does. I'll send you some sketches?"

"Go!" Dominic shouts.

I jump, a smile blooming on my face. I'm going after Griffin, and we're going to get some things straight so we can move forward . . . together.

"He probably went home." Dominic holds up a finger, cautioning me. "Oh, and tell him not to worry about your door and the neighbor. I'll take care of them today."

I freeze. "What's wrong with my door? And what neighbor?"

Dominic waves me off with a shit-eating grin. "Long story. Ask Griffin. More importantly, blame him."

"You have to let me up," I tell the security guard in the lobby of Griffin's building. I'm basically hanging on his desk, pleading with my whole heart, and he thinks I'm some rabid puck bunny fan.

"I'll call upstairs," he says blandly, picking up his phone.

"No!" The shout echoes through the empty lobby, making me sound more desperate than I am. Well, okay . . . maybe *as desperate* as I am. "I'm mid–romantic gesture here, and you're screwing it all up!"

Behind me, the elevator dings as someone exits. The security guard and I both glance that way, thinking the same thing.

"Ma'am—"

His warning tone won't stop me. Nothing will stop me!

I bolt for the elevator, slipping through the closing doors at the last second. I push at the buttons, hitting ten for Griffin's floor, along with nine and eleven in my overexuberance. And then . . . nothing happens. No whoosh up into the air. No beeping. The elevator simply stays put, the doors closed, mocking me.

"Come on, come on, come on," I chant, hoping I can cheer it into compliance.

Instead, there's a ding of doom as though the call button outside has been pushed again, and the doors slide open to reveal the security guard.

He's standing with his hands on his hips despite not having a weapon, his feet planted firmly, and a sour frown on his face. "Come with me."

Sighing, I stomp back toward the desk, feeling like the moment is particularly anticlimactic when the guard points at a chair and returns to his desk duty station. The least he could do is put me in handcuffs like I'm a threat.

I plop into the chair, my legs askew, my arms crossed over my chest, and my mouth downturned in a pout. "Now what, Paul Blart?"

The security guard arches a brow, obviously not pleased with the uncomplimentary comparison. I hear the tones of him pushing buttons on the phone as he dials. When the call connects, I hear Griffin's gruff hello before the guard launches into a completely inaccurate retelling of the last five minutes. "I've got a woman down here who claims to know you and is trying to come up without permission. She made a run for the elevator, but I stopped her. You want me to call the police?"

"Five three, brunette, probably glaring at you right this second?" Griffin says, which is nothing more than a lucky guess.

"Griffin, tell this guy to stop heart-blocking me!" I shout in the general vicinity of the phone. Quiet enough that Griffin won't hear, I explain to the guard, "It's like cockblocking, but with the heart."

"Send her up," Griffin clips out before hanging up with a sharp click.

I stand up to my full height, trying my best to look righteous. "See? I told you he'd want to see me," I tell the guard snottily. He sighs heavily as I do my best to strut back to the elevator. The effect is only slightly squashed by the squeak of my tennis shoes. At least, this time, when I push the button for the tenth floor, the doors close and I begin the expected whoosh into the air.

When the doors open, I take a deep breath before heading toward Griffin's condo. When I turn the corner, he's already waiting on me, his back leaning against the doorframe, his arms crossed over his chest, and his mouth firmly set in a hard line. The purple bruising beneath his eyes only highlights the anger in them. "What are you doing here, Pen?"

"I came for an apology," I inform him primly.

Rolling his eyes, he huffs, "Fine. I'm sorry. Is that what you want to hear? I'm sorry I didn't tell you about the guys following you, I'm sorry for not telling you what I suspected about their boss, I'm sorry for talking to Conniver without clearing it with you first, I'm sorry for busting into your lunch with him today, I'm sorry for . . . everything." By the end, he sounds gutted and essentially sorry for his own existence.

And I'm the one that's made him feel that way.

"No," I say, shaking my head. But then I reconsider. "Okay, yes to some of that. But I'm not here for you to apologize to me. I'm here to apologize to *you*." The surprise on Griffin's face hurts my heart. "I'm sorry for taking my fear out on you. I'm sorry for making you feel like you're not enough. You are, Griffin. You're amazing, and I think I understand why you did what you did."

"Could you explain it to me, then, because I feel like I'm always fucking up at every turn?" He forces out a small chuckle, but it's a front, a way to try to hide the negativity he's heard so many times before that he's internalized it, now hearing it from the narrator in his head. His brain says that negative self-talk is wrong, but his gut says differently.

"Mr. Conniver actually did a great job of that, but Dominic's going to claim it was his speech that got me to pull my head out of my ass."

"We're gonna let him keep thinking that, right?" Griffin asks, this time sounding genuinely amused.

I nod, grinning that he gets it. "Can I come in?"

He steps back from the doorway, letting me in. As he closes the door, silence reigns between us, awkwardness enveloping each of us individually. I'm trying to figure out how to right our course when we've gone so far astray. I think Griffin is just waiting to see what I'll do.

Hoping that what started this in the first place can restart it, I step into him. He moves away like I might attack him, not stopping until his back is pressed to the front door.

He's right. I am going to attack, but not the way he thinks. Because he's also wrong. I'm not angry anymore. I'm sorry, I'm hopeful, and I really want to kiss him. I lift up to my toes, letting my hands find his chest. His heart pounds beneath my palm, beating just as fast as mine.

"Griffin," I murmur, then take his mouth with mine.

He doesn't move for a split second where I fear I'm the one who's fubared us. But miraculously, he groans in relief—or maybe desperation—and takes control of the kiss. His hands cradle my face, his lips move against mine, and he tastes faintly of mint and chocolate. One quick move, and he spins us, pinning me to the door. One hand to the door's surface and the other at my throat, he devours me while the world blissfully slips away and my entire focus becomes him and the desire building inside me.

But this is not only passion, it's promises. Promises to do better, to be patient with one another, to not let ourselves get in our own way as we learn how to love each other.

When he presses his forehead to mine, I force my lids to open, finding him staring at me. His eyes have gone dark and hungry, but there's pain flickering in their depths. "Penny, are you sure?"

"We should talk," I say gently. Disappointment flashes across his face as he steps away to give me space, but I grab his shirt, gripping it in my fist and using it to pull him back, demanding he look at me again. "To set up some expectations and boundaries so this doesn't happen again in the future," I clarify.

"The future?" he echoes dumbly.

Smirking sassily, I boop his nose, being gentle because I'm not sure if it's still sore from my brother's punches. "You didn't think you could get rid of me that easily, did you?" Not waiting for—or wanting—that answer, because I'm well aware that I have the potential to be a stage-five clinger-on-er where Griffin is concerned, I sit down on his couch, pulling a pillow into my lap and then patting the surface in invitation.

He lowers himself slowly, peering at me like he doesn't trust me, which, to be fair, is understandable. "I truly am sorry," he starts, running his fingers through his hair. In just the last few weeks, his hockey flow has gone insane. The Hawks are superstitious and won't cut their hair or shave during the playoffs, so it'll be interesting to see how mountain man he gets. I think I might like it on him.

I wave a hand dismissively. "I think we've both apologized enough. Mistakes were made, tears were shed, voodoo curses were chanted over NHL-authorized bobblehead figurines." His eyes widen in shock. "Oh, was that one just me?" I tease, smirking like I'm just kidding. I'm actually not. I already have the bobblehead of Griffin, with his teeny-tiny signature printed on the bottoms of the feet like Woody in *Toy Story*. The collectible has come in handy a few times over the years, like when he pissed me off or said something particularly hurtful. "By the way, for no reason at all, how's your butt feeling? Any tingling, numbness, or sharp poking pains . . . say, around midnight last night?"

His brows climb sharply, his eyes saying, *Seriously?*

"Huh, guess it didn't work, then. Noted." I scribble in the air like I'm actually taking note of that chicken nugget of information. "To the matter at hand, or at *heart*, as the case may be—" I grin and his lips twitch like he's fighting off a smile. "Are you done pretending like I'm not the love of your life?" I ask airily, flipping my hair over my shoulder.

He barks out a laugh. "Pen, I never wanted to pretend. I felt like I had to. So yeah, I'm done. I love you. I've always loved you. Even when I was acting like an asshole and making you think I hated you, I loved you."

"I'm gonna hold you to your promise of a long, detailed apology to make up for some of that," I warn, running a fingertip on the pillow's tassel while sending a flirty look his way. "Because I'm done pretending too. I'm scared this could get messy, and it definitely has the potential for dramatics, but 'messy drama' is basically my middle name, so I might not know the difference. And you're signing up for this knowing that I attract all manner of uncontrollable chaos, so that's your poor decision-making in action." He's definitely grinning now, and so am I. "Besides, I wouldn't want to face down scary shit like love with anyone else but you. I mean, you took on the Mob for me." The praise is well deserved because I don't think anyone else would've done that for me.

But Griffin did. Without hesitation, and without wanting a trophy or applause or a cookie. "We can figure out this whole relationship thing together. Starting with brutal, complete and total, no-holds-barred honesty. Don't hide anything from me, ever."

I can see the hope trying to grow inside him, making his face seem boyish and his smile happy. But he tamps it down, still fighting, still doubting. "Deal. And on that note, while you're making it sound all cute like we're getting matching shirts—"

My whole face lights up at the idea of getting us those airbrushed shirts that say "I'm with him" and "I'm with her" with big red arrows pointing at each other, but before I can suggest wearing them to Thanksgiving at Mom and Dad's this year, he keeps talking. "You need to understand that I'm gonna make it hard to love me. I overthink and obsess. I don't trust. I'm gonna need pretty constant reassurance that you're not screwing with my head and that this isn't some sick prank. Be patient with me. I'll figure it out—how to love you the way you deserve, I mean. I'll figure it out and do my damnedest to make sure you never doubt the way I feel about you."

He pins me with a hard look, admitting, "Even with the best of intentions, I'm still gonna fuck up. I told you I would, I already did, and I will again. But I'll do my best to never make the same mistake twice. I promise you that."

This man still thinks he's some sort of consolation prize I'm settling for, when he's the biggest stuffed animal at the carnival, one of those you have to pay too much for and work smarter, not harder, to win by throwing softballs at a clown's gaping but too-small-for-the-ball mouth hole.

"Of course you'll make mistakes. You're fucked up." I tap my temple the way he so often does, smiling softly. "But I will, too, because I've never done this relationship thing either. And I'm just as fucked up as you are." He tilts his head, glaring at me doubtfully. "All right, maybe not *as* bad, but I've got my own issues. Like did you know that I apparently have a thing for mean guys who are secretly obsessed with me? Or that I always wonder if my ass is too big the way my skating coach told me it was, but then I remember that it's where I keep my superpowers because a timely hip roll from me can do a whole lot of damage or basically solve any problem?" He shakes his head, fighting to hide a laugh, but I can tell it's there, right in his chest, because I'm irresistible. "And that's okay. I think everyone's a little messed up. Nobody's perfect."

There's no reason to bemoan that fact. It's just the truth. Everyone's got baggage. The important thing is how we deal with it. Like you shouldn't stuff it under the seat in front of you, acting like it fits when it's obviously too big to be a carry-on and should've been checked into the cargo hold. For Griffin and me, I intend to address any issues together, possibly naked, and with Chocolate Orgasm ice cream involved.

"Dominic, a.k.a. Mr. Perfect, would disagree with that on principle."

"Which is an issue in and of itself." The mention of my brother brings up another point. "Are the two of you okay?"

He nods hesitantly. "He told me you're my problem now. Seemed kinda thrilled about it, honestly," he says, completely deadpan.

"Rude," I say, pushing him playfully. And annoying monster that he is, he doesn't move an inch.

He laughs. "I didn't say it. He did."

"What's up with my door?" I ask, remembering Dom's order to ask Griffin.

Griffin's eyes drop to his lap as he ducks his chin. "Um . . ."

"Nope, not doing that. The truth, the whole truth, and nothing but the truth, so help you God, or I will—" I stumble, not sure how to finish that threat. And then I know. "Tickle it out of you."

"I'm not ticklish," he retorts, unconcerned.

"Challenge accepted," I say gleefully, clapping my hands and already planning a sneak attack where I goose him and drop him to his knees, where I'll then put that apology promise to good use. "Now, the door."

If I didn't know better, I'd swear Griffin Mahoney is blushing. But that can't be the case. What in the world would embarrass a man like him? I reach out to touch his cheek, testing the warmth, and find him burning up. He catches my finger, presses a quick kiss to the fingertip, then releases me. "You were supposed to be there and you weren't answering, so we got scared something had happened to you. Your DoorDash was sitting there, cold and old, and the Mob was hunting you, so it was a reasonable assumption."

"My eggs Benedict!" I wail, having forgotten all about that.

"We can order more," he offers. "And you can eat it while I fix your door, because I busted through it to check on you. Where'd you order it from?" He picks up his phone from the coffee table, finger poised to order a replacement eggs Benedict, but I didn't miss that middle meat-and-cheese part of his sandwich speech.

"You broke down my door?" I repeat hollowly. That's a lot. Like, *a lot*. He must've been so scared. "So it's standing wide open right now?"

He shakes his head vehemently. "Of course not. Your neighbor came over to yell at us about being noisy. She's the one who told us about Conniver's guys being there. I told her I'd make it worth her while if she kept an eye on your place today."

"Mrs. Rosenthal is babysitting my apartment?" I say doubtfully. "She's probably having a yard sale on the sidewalk, selling all our stuff and pocketing the money for herself."

Griffin blanches. "She wouldn't."

"Oh yeah, she would," I argue. "But it's okay. Dom said he was going over there. I'm gonna trust that he'll handle it, and if anything's missing, I'll take it out on him, never letting him live it down."

"Do that. Blame Dom," he readily agrees. "Do you still want me to order a replacement eggs Benedict?" He waves his phone, reminding me.

But I'm hungry for something else. Well, maybe two things. "Why do you taste like Thin Mints?"

He laughs. "I've been searching for them and finally found them. They're in my freezer, and when I got here, I thought I'd try your method of eating my feelings. You want some?"

That is so sweet, and yes, I do want a celebratory cookie, but when he tries to get up from the couch, I launch myself at him, stopping him.

"Later. First, I want you," I purr.

Chapter 27

Griffin

I don't think I've ever heard anything as sexy as Penelope Lee saying that she wants me.

Me. Griffin Mahoney—good for nothing, worthless, only useful as a battering ram or a punching bag. Except, to her, I'm more.

And I vow to myself to always find a way to be more for her. Starting now . . .

"Come here," I growl, pulling her into my lap. She squirms, settling herself right over my already hardening dick. I grind against her, and even through my sweats and her pants, it feels ridiculously good and dangerously addictive.

I would do terrible things for this woman. I would do depraved things for her. Hell, I'd let her do them to me if she wanted to. Anything at all, anything she wants, I'll make sure it's hers.

Leaning in, she whispers in my ear, "Is that a hockey stick or are you just glad to see me?" When she sits upright, she's grinning, proud of her own silly joke.

In my mind, I've gone dark and ominous, and with one little question and her cute smile, she brings light and levity like a fucking magician.

"I don't know whether to be flattered you're calling it as big as a hockey stick or insulted because I'm definitely thicker than one," I quip, arching a brow as I try to meet her mood.

"How thick is a hockey stick?" She holds her hand up, peering at the circle she's made with her thumb and finger and wiggling on me like she's measuring by feel.

"Do you want to compare? I've got a stick in the closet by the door." The offer makes her laugh, but then I add truthfully, "And I'm definitely glad to see you."

Her smile melts into something more meaningful as she comes closer for a kiss. She's careful, avoiding my nose thoughtfully as her lips meld against mine, and I taste my future. A future with Penny, something I never thought could actually happen, but now . . . is.

Wrapping my arms around her, I pull her in tighter before exploring her back with my palms. She reaches for the hem of her shirt, interrupting our kiss to yank it over her head and drop it to the floor before fixing me with a heated look. Her pupils are dilated with a desire I never thought I'd see from her. But there it is, for me.

Penny is mine, the way I've always dreamed. The way I never dared to hope.

I reach up to cup her jaw, and she tilts into my touch, closing her eyes. "You are so fucking special, Pen."

She inhales a jagged breath before meeting my gaze once more. "You're pretty special too," she replies. It's not the truth, but the way she says it, I can almost believe it. Maybe one day, it will be true.

I trace a line along the edge of her bra, down to her cleavage, then back up the other side. Through the satiny fabric, I can see the outline of her nipples hardening in response to my touch. "You like that?" I ask.

In answer, she reaches behind herself, undoing her bra and dropping it off her shoulders. Her tits fall free, right into my hands. "You like *that*?" she asks right back.

"Yeah, I do." My voice is barely a rumble, rough and gritty with desire. When I tease my thumbs over her stiffening nubs, she arches for more, so I dip my head down to take one into my mouth. She adjusts, scooting up my body as I scoot down the couch until we find a position where I can reach her better and give her what she wants. With her hands on my shoulders for leverage, I suck and lick one nipple, then the other, slowly building up the intensity until I nip and nibble, drawing a sharp intake of breath from her.

I don't think she realizes it, but her hips have started moving, grinding against my stomach with her ass teasing the tip of my cock. After dropping a hand to the button at her waist, I make quick work of it and her zipper to give me room to slide my hand inside her pants and her panties. She's so soaked and slippery that two of my fingers slide into her easily.

Her fingertips have been tracing lines over my chest, but now she plants them firmly, using the leverage to lift her hips so I can finger-fuck her deeper. I suck her nipple, wrapping an arm around her waist to lift her more securely, and move my fingers in and out of her with a curling, stroking motion that seems to set her on fire. I find a rhythm she matches with the faint bucking of her hips, and with every stroke, the base of my palm hits her sensitive clit. The sound of her slickness fills the room, a symphony of her desire that's only matched by the increasing pace of her breathing.

I can feel her walls quivering, getting closer and closer, and I nip at her breast again. Judging from before, she likes to ride that sharp edge of pain and pleasure, and this time seems the same, because she cries out a breathy "yes" as she arches for more. I bite a little harder, suck a little deeper, but pull my fingers from her to focus my thumb on her clit. I swipe her slickness over her whole mound, coating her in it and knowing that I will lick up every last drop before I'm done with her. When I circle the hard nub again, a shudder instantly shoots through her. Not an orgasm, just a prequel, but I can't help but preen at her pleasure.

I'm proud to be the man she wants to touch her this way. I want to be the only man who's ever given this gift again, for the rest of her life. Intimacy is more than sex. I know that. It's who you trust enough to share your hopes and fears with. It's who you want at your side through every moment, big and small. It's a connection felt in the soul. And for me, that's Penny. I want to be that for her too.

But my mind has become nothing more than a driving beat of primal urges where poetic words are a foreign concept.

I want Penny's orgasm. For her, of course, but also, selfishly, for me.

As I move my fingers faster over her clit, she wraps an arm around my neck, holding me to her so tightly that I might suffocate, but if I took my last breath while making her come, I would die a happy man, that's for damn sure. I feel her whole body go tight and freeze, right on the edge, then I nip at her breast once more.

She explodes, her whole body spasming wildly. I dip my fingers down to her entrance, spreading her cum up to her clit, over and over, to prolong her pleasure while she rides my hand spastically. As she finishes and releases her hold on my head, I rumble, "Good girl. Now, get up here so I can taste it."

"What?" she utters, spent.

But I'm just getting started. I help her stand for a moment, shoving her pants and soaked panties off, and she gets with the program, toeing off her tennis shoes until she's naked before me. With a hungry eagerness, I slide to the floor, my back against the couch, and gesture her over. Standing over me, she steps her feet out, straddling my legs, and I lick my lips as her pussy comes closer.

"I already—"

I chuckle darkly, tracing the heart tattoo on her hip. "Once. You think that's enough? No fucking way, Pen."

Using my thumbs, I spread her lips to reveal her sweet little clit. An evil smile ghosts across my mouth. I can't wait to taste her. But I glance up, meeting her eyes. "Watch me. Don't close your eyes."

She bites her lip uncertainly, but nods.

My first lick of her is like coming home, and my cock surges painfully in my sweats, demanding attention. But it'll have to wait. I want at least one more orgasm from Penny first. I tease my tongue over her clit, dipping down to her entrance, and then back up to circle her clit.

"I can't . . . I don't think I can . . . It's too much . . ." she gasps, her mind arguing but her body complying, bucking against my mouth desperately, demanding more.

I spread her lips wide with one hand so I can suck her clit into my mouth, where I flutter my tongue over it. At the same time, I fill her with two fingers from my other hand, curling them to pet the spot that quickly has her moaning my name.

"There you go. Come for me again." I glance up her body, finding her eyes open but her brows furrowed in doubt, keeping her from orgasming. Pulling my fingers from her pussy, I lift them to her mouth. "Taste how much your body wants this."

She opens her mouth obediently, and when I slip my fingers in, she sucks at them hungrily, her tongue teasing along their length. My mind immediately translates that to what it would feel like for my cock to be in her mouth, and my balls pull up so tight that I worry I might come without her even touching me. Eyes locked on hers, I slide my fingers back inside her, and she clamps down on me instantly. "See? You can do it. Show me you can do it."

She nods with a whimper, and I reward her by fucking her with my fingers again as I go back to torturing her clit with my mouth. She gets there even faster this time, the doubt no longer holding her back, and when she seems to be on edge, I shove my fingers deep, focusing on that spot inside her, and suck her clit into my mouth. The moment stretches, her orgasm right there for her to fall apart over, and when she finally gives in, spasms rack through her as her juices flow messily over my hand. She grabs my shoulders for support, lifting up to her toes on wobbling knees, and I have to reach into my sweats as fast as I can to squeeze the base of my cock to hold off my own orgasm.

When she comes back, there's a blissed-out smile on her parted lips, and she's panting rapidly. I expect her to say something sexy—not *thank you*, because, believe me, it's my pleasure, but a *wow* wouldn't be unexpected. Instead, she says, "I'm naked and boneless, and you still have on shoes."

She's right. But I definitely didn't expect her to say that. I laugh. "Want me to take them off?"

"All of it. Take it all off."

She collapses onto the couch, eyes locked on me like I'm going to put on a show, but I just stand up and rip my shirt over my head. I do the same quick removal of my shoes and my sweats. As naked as she is, I finally take my cock in hand, giving myself a tight stroke of warning. Precum oozes from my tip, running down over my hand.

"My turn?" she asks, a sparkle in her eye.

"If you so much as look at me sideways, I'm going to come, and I have every intention of getting inside that pussy before doing that, Pen."

"Once? You think that's enough?" She throws my words back at me, and then she gives a pouty frown, her eyes dancing. "Or can you only go once?" She holds up a finger, then lets it fall, implying that my dick's a one-go-rounder.

I growl, grabbing her throat and lifting her chin so she has to look me in the eyes, because her looking at my cock is going to make me embarrass myself. "I will always be ready to fuck you. Anytime, anywhere, as many times as you want it."

I've awakened the devil. And this time, it's Penny who gives me a look that would make the horniest succubus in hell quiver in heat.

She licks her lips, her lashes lowering as she looks back down at my cock. I don't release her throat, keeping my hand there the way she likes as she teases the tip of her tongue over my crown. When she moans at my taste, precum rushes out for her, my body eager to satisfy her however she'd like.

She sips it, savoring the flavor with soft, fluttery kisses, before she takes me into her mouth fully, inch by inch slipping past her lips until I feel the back of her throat. My stomach muscles clench as my body tries to curl in on itself, the pleasure amazing, but my tenuous grip on my restraint keeps me upright. She moves back up my shaft, her tongue leaving erotic patterns on my skin before she circles my tip, grinning like the little chaos fairy she is.

I shudder, knowing this woman's going to be the happy death of me. I expected it to be a long, slow process, taking our whole lives, but it's going to be in the next sixty seconds if she keeps teasing me like this. "Please, Pen," I beg, completely at her mercy. "I need—"

She pulls off completely. "Take my mouth. Show me how much you want to come." Without pausing, she swallows me to my base again.

Mother. Fucker.

My restraint is shredded, any remaining gentleness in ruins. I hold her throat in one hand and her jaw in the other as I fuck her mouth, hard and deep and fast. She tries to keep suction around me, the slurping sounds evidence of her efforts, and that only adds to my need to show her exactly what she does to me. Embarrassingly quick, my balls pull up tight as lightning shoots through my spine, and I explode harder than I've ever come before in my life. Pulsing jets of my cream fill her mouth, and she swallows it down eagerly as I force myself still, not wanting to choke her.

When I can see again, I find her grinning happily, obviously proud of herself. I run my thumb over her lips, gathering the mess of our mixed bodily fluids that escaped, and slip my thumb into her mouth, feeding it to her. She sucks it clean, grinning even more now. "Still got another one in you, Honey?"

I shake my head. "Don't call me that. That's for them." I wave a hand toward the door, indicating the rest of the world. "To you, I'm Griffin. Or *asshole* or *bastard* or whatever you want to call me when I fuck up."

"Griffin." She sounds like that's it, the only thing she'll ever call me. "And you didn't answer the question."

"Woman, flip over and get on all fours."

She claps her hands. Literally claps at the order and arranges herself, her knees on the couch cushion and her hands on the back before flipping her hair over her shoulder to look at me with a smile. I take myself in hand, giving my cock a few encouraging strokes, but I'm ready to go. Years of fantasizing about this are nothing compared to the reality of Penny.

Stepping up behind her, I tease my cock along her entrance, testing to see if she's still wet enough for me, and find her still soaked. "You liked sucking me off?"

She nods eagerly. "I told you, you're mine. That was like me claiming you, which is powerful as fuck."

I get it. It's not about being the one doing the moving—it's about being the one giving the pleasure. It's the same way I feel about her riding my face and my fingers. And my cock.

Thrusting in slowly, inch by inch, I fill her, soaking up every moment of the feeling of her wrapped around me. "God, you look good on my cock." I grip her hips, giving us both a few shallow strokes.

When she arches her back for more, I begin to thrust a bit faster, then harder and deeper until I'm roughly fucking her and we're both panting with need. I spit on my fingertips and reach around her hip to find her clit.

She whines, and I think it's something like, "Again?"

"You can take it. Take it all. It's yours," I grit out. "I'm yours."

"Griffin!" she cries out at the same time I feel her pussy clamp down on me. The quivering flutters of her walls are too much for me to withstand, and my head falls back, my eyes close, and I shatter into a million pieces. Sparkles of light dance behind my lids and the world disappears as a dull roar fills my ears. It feels like forever, or maybe a moment, and I think that's what life with Penny will be like—an eternity in a second and a lifetime gone by in the blink of an eye. I can't wait.

As my awareness comes back to here and now, I realize I'm panting hard and Penny is resting her head on the back of the couch, looking over her shoulder at me. Surely I'll get a *wow* this time, because whatever the hell that was, it sure as fuck wasn't sex. Or at least not any that I've ever had. Unless maybe I've been doing it wrong my whole life? But no, it's probably just because it's finally Penny. Surely she's as rocked as I am.

"Where'd you say those Thin Mints were? After that, I'm absolutely starving. And don't say you've got something for me to eat." She holds up a warning finger, glaring at me.

I wasn't even thinking that. I don't think I'm thinking anything yet. My brain's going *dooooooo* like it does after a bad scuffle, like ear-ringing static, but in a good way. But if Penny wants cookies, Penny gets cookies.

"Hang on. I'll get 'em."

"Good boy," she teases, her brow arched high.

Death of me and Penelope Lee—same thing, and I love it.

Chapter 28

Penny

Where do I sit? Things are so different now that I'm not sure. Do I take my usual seat at our usual table at our usual pregame dinner place, Pro-Bowl, where Dom will be at my side and Griffin would be across from me? Is that part of their superstitions, which preclude any change for the duration of the playoffs that begin tomorrow? Or do they switch places now that Griffin and I are together so that we're the ones sitting side by side? Or should I sit in the chair next to Griffin?

I instantly dismiss that last option because I like being able to see the whole restaurant from the booth side of the table. So I sit where I always do, deciding the guys can figure out their spots themselves.

Apparently, they have none of the worries I did, easily falling into their seats. Except this time, Griffin's foot is touching mine beneath the table. I glance at him to find him grinning at me wolfishly. "You could sit in my lap if you'd rather?"

"Abso-fucking-lutely not. What we're not gonna do is . . . *that*," Dominic declares, pointing his fork at Griffin even while I continue to mull over the fun of the possibility. "I think we need to set some ground rules here about acceptable ways to behave if you don't want me to blow an aneurysm, which I think we can all agree is for the best. First, no sex talk. I do not want to hear how you rawdog railed my sister, ever. Nor do I want to hear how you pegged my best friend's prostate and made him shoot like a fountain." He wiggles his finger in the air, which I'm guessing is supposed to be a prostate massage. An overly dramatic shiver runs through him as he makes a gagging noise.

"That's what I sounded like this morning," I tease under my breath, repeating his gag with a much different insinuation.

At the same time, Griffin sputters, "Dude, what the fuck. I don't tell you that kinda shit anyway." Then he looks at me. "Do you talk to him about stuff like that?"

I shake my head. But Dominic's declaration has had the opposite of the intended effect. Now I want to share too-intimate details just to irritate him, because that's how siblings show their love. Or at least, it's how we do. "So you're saying you don't want to hear about Griffin's magic dick? That's totally the best I've ever had. And *biiiig.* He let me measure it against a hockey stick, and guess who won?" I blink innocently before answering, "I'll just say I'm the winner-winner, chicken dinner. Ding, ding, ring-a-dingaling, *dong.*"

Griffin chuckles. Dominic's face goes slack in horror, and he slams his hands over his ears, singing, "La la la la. I can't hear youuuuuu."

Torturing my brother is so fun, and the best part is, I'm telling the truth. Griffin did let me do a comparison, one hand on his stick and the other on his *stick.* And yeah, I'm definitely the winner here, with Griffin.

When Dominic releases his ears, he mutters, "Now I'm scared to say rule two." At our expectant looks, he sighs. "I'm not your mediator. Fight or don't, but leave me out of it. Though, if you hurt her, I'll break every last bone in your body in multiple places, maximizing your pain as much as possible." That last part is directed at Griffin, and I can't help but be touched by my brother's caring. His "rough around the edges" continues clear down to his core, but he does truly care about me, and his protectiveness is how he shows it.

Griffin dips his chin, agreeing. "Deal. What else?"

"We still get bro days without Penny-Nickel-Dime invading and wanting us to go shopping or get our nails done or some shit like that."

I scoff, holding up my short, bare nails in protest of his stereotyping. I rarely wear polish, because my work would ruin it, and on the occasion that I do, I have Talia help me. I'm not the type to sit in a salon for the whole day, getting pampered and primped.

"Dom, in my whole life, the only time I've gotten a pedicure was with you," Griffin announces.

"What?" I screech, turning on my brother. "You got a pedicure? Did they do a rose-petal soak of your little piggies, and scrub between your janky toes, and paint your nails Bubble Bath? Or was it Funny Bunny?" Grinning at my obvious win in our never-ending battle of one-upmanship, I shove a bite of my chicken-rice bowl into my mouth.

But Dominic isn't the least bit embarrassed. "The fact that you know those colors says I'm right to worry you're going to girlify my bro here."

"The fact that you know they're popular colors says maybe I need to be the one worried?"

"I know because I date," he explains. "Telling a girl her new Bubble Bath manicure looks good is a surefire way to get her to wrap those fingers around my dick."

That actually makes sense. And also, *ew*!

"You're disgusting," I scold my brother.

"To clarify, all the Hawks went for pedicures as some sort of team sponsorship deal from the salon," Griffin informs me, interjecting into our sibling back-and-forth. "You should've seen Jacofovich. He jumped every time they touched his feet. So ticklish."

"She should've seen Brody and Pretty Boy arguing over who had the better feet and demanding we hold a blind competition where we all voted on whose were prettiest. As if it's not obviously Brody, but we would never tell him that because he'd be even more insufferable than he already is."

The guys are grinning and laughing like friends again, not an angry glance between them, and I'm glad. I certainly didn't expect to fall for Griffin, but even though I have—completely, totally, and wildly—I wouldn't want to come between the two of them. Especially because I know how important the friendship is to Griffin.

"Oh! Before I forget, last rule," Dominic says, reminding us where our conversation began. "I get to tell Mom and Dad about this new development." He swings a finger from me to Griffin, looking gleeful. I don't know why he wants to do that. Mom and Dad will be happy for me, and they love Griffin. But the devilish light sparkling in my brother's eyes makes me question his underlying motives.

"You're already Mom's Least Favorite, so go ahead and steal my thunder and tell her that I've finally found a great guy and have fallen in love. I'm sure she'll *love* that," I say sarcastically.

That brings him up short. But it's Griffin's response that draws my attention.

"A great guy? Fallen in love?" He looks shocked. "Me?"

"Duh. Yeah, you. We've got to work on your confidence here, Gruffy." He frowns sharply, and I twist my lips, nodding in agreement. "Yeah, that's not the one. I'll keep workshopping it."

I'm trying to find a good pet name for him since he doesn't want me to call him Honey like the Hawks do, and Griffin seems a bit formal when we're being lovey and playful. Side note, I'm teaching him to be playful, and he absolutely is ticklish despite his statements to the contrary. But so far, he's vetoed Babe, Griffaroni, Stud Muffin, Boo Bear, and Cookie Monster, which has nothing to do with Thin Mints and everything to do with how much he likes to eat my . . . *cookie*. But back to his lack of confidence, I tell him fiercely, "You're all 'mine' when it's bang-a-rang time, but when things are just normie-normal, you're all 'who, me?' like you don't know how awesome—and hot—you are."

"Ahhh! No!" Dominic screams, a bit too loud to be polite, but thankfully the restaurant is nearly empty tonight, and reminds us of rule one. "No sex talk."

Oh yeah, he did say that. "Sorry," I say, not actually sorry at all. "But also, you're not telling Mom and Dad. I am."

Dominic frowns, his bottom lip pouting out like a child, but he's fighting off a grin. Was he testing me? I think he might've been. Testing to see how serious I am about his friend, because he already knows Griffin is serious enough that he risked their friendship over me. I sigh happily at their cute bromance, and the way they look out for one another. My brother isn't only overly protective of me, he's apparently overly protective of his friend, too, which is basically the sweetest thing ever. And let's face it, now that we're at this point, that's going to make life better for all three of us.

"I'll tell them," Griffin offers. "That way, they can tell me firsthand that I'm not good enough for their daughter."

Dominic and I meet eyes, my own worry matching his. "See what you did?" I accuse, bumping him with my shoulder so hard that he rocks to the side. Reaching across the table, I take Griffin's hand. "We can tell them together, because they're going to be so happy for us. They love you. Honestly, probably more than they love me. And if they have any doubts, it'll be them checking if you're sure you want to take on *this.*" I gesture to myself, knowing that, of the two of us, I'm definitely getting the better deal here. Dominic nods, agreeing with me wholeheartedly.

Self-esteem off the ice is definitely something Griffin needs to develop. The good thing is, I'm a skilled cheerleader, and now, knowing the issue, I can help. It might take some creative cheers, but I'm good like that. My latest from this morning included some real gems such as "bring that fine ass over here" and "if you're happy and you know it, say yeehaw." Okay, so those two kinda rolled into one when Griffin had carried me naked, piggyback style, while I fake rodeoed, to the kitchen, where I learned that although he hates coffee, he surprisingly has a coffee maker, sugar-free vanilla syrup, and milk. He blushingly told me that he got it all for me, and offered to get an actual espresso maker if I want to make official skinny vanilla lattes at his place.

I'd stared at him, gobsmacked, as though he was speaking another language. I've heard the expression "if he wanted to, he would" and laughed because I don't think I've ever met a guy who wanted to. Until Griffin. In his mind, he's still making up for all those years of bullying, but I've already forgiven him, and he's just getting extra brownie points with me for his sweetness.

Griffin starts to smile, and I watch as his boyish, hopeful expression turns wolfish. "I definitely want to take on this—" He lets his eyes drip over me, and though he can't see below the table, I feel very *seen*. "Anytime, anywhere, any way you want, Penelope."

I love it when he uses my full name. No one else really does. Of course, I also love it when he groans out "Pen" like the two syllables of "Penny" are simply too much for him at that moment. Hell, he could call me anything he wanted to then, and I'd respond to him.

"Ugh! You two have ruined my appetite." Dominic huffs, pushing his bowl away as though he can't finish it. The only problem is, he's already eaten the whole thing and the bowl is empty. "Fine, you tell Mom and Dad."

"They'll be here in the morning, right?" I ask, grinning. Our parents are coming to town to watch the first-round playoff game, ready to cheer both Dominic and me on inside the Hawks arena.

"Yeah, they said they'd see us at the game because they know we have routines to maintain. Speaking of, I'm gonna break my own rule here, just this once—" He cuts his eyes left and right, pinning both Griffin and me. "No sex during playoffs. It's bad luck and bad for endurance."

Griffin laughs. "If you think I'm not fucking Penny as soon as we get back to my place tonight, you've lost your damn mind." My brother opens his mouth to argue, but Griffin cuts him off. "You brought it up, so no whining now. But don't worry, I'll be good for the game."

"Are you sure? Maybe a little sexual frustration would be good for you?" I suggest. "It's worked all these years, and it is just one night. We could abstain, and I could *not* take one for the team so to speak."

"Nope." And like that, Griffin's declaration tells me that it's time to go.

❧

"You're supposed to be sleeping," I tell the reflection of Griffin in my mirror. He's sprawled out in my bed, his feet hanging off the bottom edge and his arms folded behind his head, which makes his biceps look enormous. He's watching me put on my makeup, and not resting the way he should before such an important game.

We stayed at his place last night after dinner with Dominic, and when he got up early to go into the arena for morning skate with the team, I came home, figuring I'd see him after the game because I didn't want to interfere with his routine. Instead, he'd come knocking on my door by noon, asking why I'd left. We'd ended up in my bed for a while, just talking and cuddling, but it takes me a lot longer to get ready than it does him, so I snuck off to shower an hour ago. He's been watching me ever since I came back in—with my face bare, my hair wet, and wearing nothing but my favorite silky floral robe.

And yet he doesn't care. He sees me at my rawest, and the look in his eyes is just as hot as if I were dressed my sexiest. If that doesn't help the ol' ego, nothing will . . . but I'm still worried about him and his routine.

"Afraid if I go to sleep, I'll wake up and this will have all been a dream," he confesses.

"You mispronounced *nightmare*," I quip, setting down my makeup primer and turning around to face him. But he's serious. I think this is bigger than us, or the upcoming conversation with my parents. This is about hockey. "Are you nervous about tonight's game?"

He sighs heavily, heaving himself up to a sitting position with his elbows resting on his knees and his head hanging low. "I've wanted to win the Stanley Cup for my entire life. It's been the one constant north driving me, even when life was so fucking bad that I wanted to quit everything. And now that we have a shot, I'm terrified I'm going to crash out in the first round."

"One, I don't think that's going to happen. And two, what if it does?" I challenge.

He tilts his head to side eye me, deadpanning, "Your pep talks suck."

I go over and sit down beside him on the bed. "You've already won, Griffin. Think back to when you first picked up a hockey stick. What did you want?"

"Stanley Cup," he quickly answers.

"Okay, fair. But I know what Dom was like, and so I bet you wanted to go pro. You are. You wanted to play against the best of the best, and you are. You wanted to earn that cup, and you will. I have no doubt that a younger version of you will get every single one of his wishes. If it's this season, awesome. If it's next season, that's okay too. You've wanted it, you've worked for it, and it'll be yours. When it is, I'll be screaming louder than anyone in that arena, because I am already so proud of you."

"Still sucks."

But he heard me. The Hawks have a real shot this season, better than any other in their recent history, largely in thanks to the great team they've built together. And I hope they win the Cup, truly I do. But tonight is game one of the playoffs, four grueling series to the end, and if Griffin puts too much pressure on himself from the jump, he will crash out. Mentally, if not physically.

And hockey is more mental than one would think, even for the team enforcer.

"Thanks. I think I'm gonna head out before you get dressed. I hate that skirt and don't want to get pissed off before the game." He stands, grabbing his wallet and keys from the nightstand.

But I stop him. "You hate my uniform?"

He looks darkly at said uniform, which is hanging off my chair, then at my legs. "It's too damn short. That thing has taunted me for years, Penny."

I press my lips together, fighting to hide my smile. "Hold on one second. Don't leave yet." I grab my uniform and disappear into the bathroom for one minute, pulling it on the way I have countless times before.

When I strut back into my bedroom, Griffin has his arms crossed over his chest, his jaw set. "Hate that thing," he spits out.

"Because you think my ass is hanging out or I'm gonna have a lip slip?" I guess, and he dips his chin, now staring at the skirt like it's personally offended him. "Look," I say, lifting the skirt up to reveal the tiny shorts underneath. "And my legs are covered in tights."

That grabs his attention, and he zeroes in on my legs, looking doubtful.

Laughing, I stick my hand down my skirt to my thigh, showing him that the leg portion that sticks out beneath the skirt isn't opaque. It's flesh-toned leggings that definitely don't show my ass. "If our legs were bare, we'd freeze in the arena. It's not pond hockey, for sure, but it's still a fuck ton of ice sucking up all the heat in the building."

He touches the fabric. "I have studied—and I do mean *studied*—you in this skirt, and never once realized it wasn't your bare legs. It's like sorcery."

"The magic of women's hosiery," I say, spreading my hands through the air like a rainbow. "The more you know."

And just like that, Grump-a-potomas Griffin smiles.

"See, I am a good pep talker," I preen, poking his cheek. "Now, get out there and defend that goal, beat some guys up—preferably not a teammate—and make the Oil Riggers your bitch like the monster you are, Honey." I purposefully use his hockey nickname, getting him into the right mental headspace for tonight. He's going to do great, though. I have no doubt.

He nods.

"Would it help at all if I promise a victory blow job, with me wearing the skirt that's apparently always driven you crazy?"

I can't help but giggle a little at that. How did I never know? I'm not sure, but I truly had no idea. For years, I was completely oblivious. But now? It's as obvious as the sun in the sky—big, blinding, and hotter than fire. That's Griffin's love for me, and mine for him.

"Are you fucking with me?" he asks.

"Not yet," I tease. "Now, go get 'em, Honey."

The look in his eye almost makes me feel bad for the Riggers.

Almost.

Chapter 29

Griffin

The Oil Riggers are an easy five games, and it's on to the Aces, a tougher six-game punch-up that gets nasty in game six when they decide if they can't win, they can at least make us remember them. The conference final is a close one, the Wolverines take us all the way to seven games, but we come out on top, with only one more hurdle to go, the Blizzard. The winningest team this season, with the highest-scoring offense. And the fuckers have home ice advantage.

But we attack hard, taking the first two on the Bliz home ice. Sure, we drop one back home, but now we're on the cusp. One last game, three periods, against the Blizzard, and the cup will be ours.

We're doing it. We actually might win this whole damn thing.

Hawks, Stanley Cup champions. Griffin Mahoney, Stanley Cup champion.

"Rawrrr! Let's do this!" Brody roars, flexing his arms and posing.

"Put your jock on," Howe tells him, covering his eyes like he hasn't seen Brody's dick dozens of times before.

Brody, being Brody, puts his hands behind his head and swirls his hips around, helicoptering his dick instead. "You know you like it," he taunts.

Even Howe can't resist laughing outright at Brody's awful moves. "Careful, bro-man, or Dom's sister's gonna have you cheering with the dancers up there. Oh wait, maybe I should call her *Griffin's girl* now instead."

That stops all dick talk and dancing instantly as all eyes turn to Dominic and me, waiting for our reaction. It's been just over six weeks since everything blew up during the second game against the Torches. Things are technically still new between me and Penny, but honestly, it feels like I'm finally home. The invisible weight I've carried on my shoulders for years has fallen away, and I can be lighter, happier, even sillier, and those are three words that have never once been used to describe me. But now, with Penny's influence, I'm growing and doing better. All thanks to her.

Well, not forcing down my feelings probably has a lot to do with it too. Now that everyone knows and has accepted it with less fanfare than I expected, the anger inside me has lessened measurably. At least off the ice. So far, I'm still hitting harder than a Mack truck on the ice.

"Guess we'll have to see what sweater she's wearing tonight, won't we?" I quip, arching a brow and flashing a cocky smirk. Of course I already know what she's wearing, because I saw her pack her suitcase for the trip to tonight's game, and there wasn't a single Lee jersey in sight. More importantly, she wore a Mahoney jersey last night while we had a double round of intense sex that was more than fucking, but a whole lot less tender than "making love." In other words, just the way she likes it.

Seeing my name on her while she took my cock deep inside her did strange things to my brain, primal things I don't want to examine too closely, but suffice it to say, it was sexy as hell, and I can't wait to repeat that experience with a custom Stanley Cup champion jersey on her. And nothing else. Except maybe those knee-high socks? Those are hot as hell too.

Just the thought of it has my cock responding, and I have to adjust myself, which is no easy feat through the layers of gear I'm already wearing.

"Quit thinking about my sister," Dominic orders, popping my cup with the tip of his stick.

It doesn't hurt through the thick plastic, but it does send blood flow elsewhere. Namely, to my face, where I can feel a flush heating my cheeks. I'm not embarrassed by my thoughts of Penny, but ten minutes before the most important game of my life isn't the best time to be fantasizing about your girlfriend.

Girlfriend? Yeah, Penny and I are moving fast. Hell, I already asked her to move into my condo, but she wants to finish out her lease with Talia, which means six more months of back-and-forth between her too-small bed and my king-size one. I'm also paying extra attention to the ring she's designing for Miles Conniver. She's making it specific to his fiancée's taste, but I'm learning a lot about what Penny herself would want in a ring.

"Oooh, they're fighting again!" Brody singsongs.

Coach pops his head out of the office. "Lee, Mahoney, do we need to have a chat?"

"No, sir," I bark.

"If it's about Brody getting traded to the Beavers next year, yes," Dominic answers with a grin. Brody mimes stabbing himself in the heart, and Dom responds by drawing a tear falling down his cheek.

"Get ready, you bunch of assholes," Coach calls out. The stress of tonight's game is hitting him, and he's done with our bullshit.

Penny keeps telling me that she believes in me, that this is the Hawks' season to win the whole thing, while tempering it with reminders that I'm not retiring after this season and I'll have another chance to win again, or win for the first time if tonight doesn't go the way we hope. But for Coach? He's nearing the end of his career, and this might be the last chance he gets to drink champagne out of the most special cup in hockey.

"Let's do this for Coach," I shout.

A chorus of "for Coach!" rings out through the locker room, and all conversation about me and Penny and Dominic is forgotten.

As soon as we take to the ice for warm-ups, I skate the wall in front of the section where Penny's supposed to be sitting, looking for her. She's a spectator tonight since the Blizzard's cheerleaders are performing and the Hawkettes are scattered around the arena, supporting but not performing. As family, Penny and the Lees have prime seats only a few rows behind the bench. Dominic and I both made sure of that.

I quickly find Mr. and Mrs. Lee, a.k.a. Mom and Dad, as they've repeatedly insisted I call them. And truthfully, they're more parental than my own parents, so though I've resisted for so long, I'm happy to surrender and use the honor-filled names and be truly included in their family. Or as Dominic likes to call it, indoctrinated.

True to Penny's expectation, they were thrilled when we told them that we're dating. Mom hugged me tight and whispered in my ear that she was glad I finally figured it out. I was shocked, but she simply gave me a knowing wink. I guess I wasn't as good at hiding my feelings for Penny as I thought I was, but Mom had kept my secret until I was ready. Or fate intervened, as the case may be.

"Where is she?" I shout, making sure they can hear me over the excited fans around them who are cheering.

Mom rolls her eyes, her smile bright as she answers, "Spilled her nachos all over her lap. She went to clean up." She points up the stairs to the upper level where the restrooms, concessions, and thousands of people are currently wandering.

"Alone?" I bark, about to come over the wall and go hunt Penny down in the bowels of the arena behind the seats. She's safe from the Mob, but there's no telling what mess she could get into or what damage she might cause. Admittedly, I've picked up the baton on Dominic's overprotectiveness where Penny is concerned, but we are in an away city, in a less familiar arena, with a high-stress game on the line, and she's walking around in a signed Mahoney jersey. Any number of things could happen to her, or because of her.

"Talia went with her. She's fine."

Oh.

I check their block of four seats, belatedly realizing that both women are missing. I knew Talia was coming—Dom and I bought her seat, too—but I only have eyes for Penny. I tell myself that Penny will be fine with Talia, who can go into the actual restroom, too, unlike me, who'd have to wait in the hall and would likely end up mobbed by fans. In short, my presence would cause more problems than potentially help.

I grin sheepishly at Mom and Dad, knowing I almost grossly overreacted. But they're smiling kindly. Honestly, I think they like knowing that I'll always take care of Penny, and also aren't nearly as worried about me now that Penny's taking care of me. We take care of each other. It's a dynamic I never thought I'd have, with a woman I never thought I'd be worthy of. But somehow, through whatever magic she possesses, it's working.

Dominic bangs his stick to the ice beside me. "Check up!"

He lifts his chin, greeting his parents, and then together we skate away to finish warming up. While we run through our usual drills and routine, I keep one eye turned toward Penny's empty seat. When she returns, she waves both arms in the air with a big smile to grab my attention, totally oblivious that her absence might've distracted me. I grin back around my mouth guard.

"God, you're such a pussy." Dom laughs.

"For her? Fuck yeah, I am. Wouldn't have it any other way," I reply, pushing at him playfully, getting us both ready for the upcoming battles we'll face down tonight.

Minutes later, we're in position for the opening puck drop, all banter falling away as we get serious. This game is the culmination of years of work, blood, sweat, and tears.

I can't hear Jack Off and the Blizzard's center, McKinnon, but they must have words, because the instant the puck hits the ice, they drop their sticks to go at each other. The crowd goes wild, loving the aggressive action right off the jump. It's messy and more of an ugly hug than actual fighting, though they act like they're throwing power punches here and there. It ends with McKinnon getting two minutes, the refs not wanting to hand out five in the playoffs unless there's actual contact or blood, and being escorted to the box.

My gut tells me the Blizzard's goal was to get Jack Off taken out for a full five-minute, and now that they've failed, he'll be the number-one target. Pretty Boy and Castaway are good, though, and they'll work together to keep Jacofovich clear. The three of them quickly run a slick power play, pitting their offense against the down-a-man Blizzard and slipping around the backside of the crease to score an early goal.

The crowd explodes, and to be honest, the boos of the Blizzard faithful are music to my ears.

Play continues like that, with endless back-and-forth battles across the ice, but when the horn sounds at the end of the first period, it's still *Hawks 1, Blizzard 0.* As we hit the locker room for the first intermission, Coach checks in with everyone, telling us to stay alert and be aggressive before disappearing into his office. No specific guidance means we're doing well, but I think we already knew that. We can feel it in the air surrounding us, the energy flowing through us, and we're ready for more.

In the blink of an eye, we're hitting the ice again.

It's immediately obvious that the Blizzard are changing their strategy from period one's Take Out the Offensive Line plan. Now they're coming after defense. I guess they figure if they can't keep us from scoring, they need to make sure they can score too. It'd be a solid plan except for one ginormous problem.

Me.

Every time they cross the blue line, I'm there to do a meet and greet . . . with my hip, my shoulder, and a couple of times, with my forearm. *Elbows up, motherfuckers.* Somehow I manage to only get in the box once, and though the Blizzard do score, so do we.

By the end of period two, the score is *Hawks 3, Blizzard 1.*

The locker room this time has a different vibe. We're not prematurely celebrating, but it definitely feels like the Cup is close, barely out of our reach. Even if we don't score again, the cushion we've gained makes our victory feel like a near sure thing.

I sip a Red Bull and steadily chew through a bag of sour apple gummy bears, getting the caffeine and sugar into my bloodstream for what promises to be the longest twenty-minute period of my life.

"Ready?" I grunt at Dominic, who's sitting next to me, wiping his face with a cold towel.

"Fuck yeah. You?"

"Absolutely." As we line back up to take to the ice one more time, he holds his fist out, and I pound it with my own. "You and me, two against the world."

"Always, brother. Hey, maybe one day you'll actually be my brother."

"That's the plan," I tell him, totally serious.

He's not mad. In fact, he looks excited about us truly being related. But he still punches me in the shoulder. "You'd better tell me before you do it. You owe me that. It's literally the least you can do."

"All right. That's fair," I agree easily. I wouldn't have it any other way. I'm basically an open book at this point, with every thought that passes through my head falling out of my mouth, which is a new experience for me. Both to express myself that way, but also to have someone—or *someones*, if I include Dom, which I do—who want to hear it all.

The small break is just the mental refresher I need, and when we hit the ice again, I'm ready to finish this game the way I've always dreamed . . . as a winner. As a Stanley Cup champion.

We fight hard. We play harder. And when the final horn sounds out, I can't believe we've actually done it. We're not on home ice, but it doesn't matter. Helmets and sticks scatter across the ice, confetti and streamers fall, and the Hawks fans' cheers are a loud roar as the whole team mobs Howe, making a dogpile of Hawks players, all celebrating.

I feel the sting of tears as my heart bursts in my chest with joy. Even feeling the truth of it, I double-check the scoreboard on the jumbotron, needing to see it spelled out for me. *Hawks 4, Blizzard*

2. And then the whole screen goes black before it flashes *Stanley Cup Champions—Hawks.*

We did it. I did it.

And though it was a team effort and I love my guys, I search for Penny in the crowd once more. She's crying openly, a wide smile stretched across her face, and her hands clutched over her chest. Making a heart with her hands, she mouths, *I love you.* Or maybe she screams it, I can't be sure in the chaotic cacophony surrounding me.

I don't think this day could get any better.

I got the girl. I got the trophy. I kept the best friend. And I found myself along the way.

"I love you too!" I yell across the ice. She can't hear me, either, but I know she reads my lips all the same, because she throws her arms in the air, shaking her fists like she's cheering with invisible poms.

That's my Penny. The best cheerleader I've ever had.

Chapter 30

Griffin

"Do you think he's going to like it?" Penny asks me for the tenth time.

She's staring at the engagement ring she custom-designed for Miles Conniver like it might've somehow cracked in half since she popped open the box to peek at it "one more time" five minutes ago.

"No," I deadpan from my sprawl on her couch, the best part of the offseason, in my opinion. This thing is so comfortable. The only thing that'd make it better is if Penny came over here and relaxed with me, but she's too wound up. Understandably so. Working on this design has consumed her for the last few weeks. While I watched scouting videos, preparing for every round of the playoffs, she sketched, made mock-ups on her computer, and even created a 3D printed sample. And that was all before she started melting down the rose gold to actually make the band.

She huffs, a pouty frown marring her face when she tears her eyes away from the ring to glare at me.

"He's gonna love it," I finish.

I watch her expression brighten, then soften. "I think so too. I hope Georgina will want me to design her wedding band."

"Of course she will. How could she not want the most talented jewelry designer—and the sexiest—to make her ring?" I pause, tilting my head. "Though she is marrying a Mob boss, so good decisions might not be her strong suit."

Penny laughs. "Fair point. But you should hear the way he talks about her. He loves her so much. It's not the norm, but what's normal? I mean, look at us." She waves a hand between us, and though I hate to admit it, she's right. Nothing about the two of us should match.

She's sunshine, I'm an asshole (though I'm working on it). She's never met a stranger, people are just friends she hasn't made yet, while if I never had to talk to anyone but her and Dom for the rest of my life, I'd be fine. Probably better than fine. She's short and soft with curves in all the right places, and I'm tall and built like a brick shithouse, and planning on getting brickier soon with offseason lifting.

And her softness extends into her soul, the same way my hardness does . . . right down to my core. Though I am learning to trust, to be vulnerable, to feel things and share them, secure enough with Penny to believe that any ugly thoughts or fears I express won't be the thing that finally sends her running.

In return, I'm doing my damnedest to love Penny the best I can. I want her to *want* to be with me, not just because I'm a work in progress but because I make her life better, her days happier, her brilliant soul buzz with joy. Yeah, I'm always going to be overprotective, and chances are, there are going to be sprained ankles here, sketchy choices there, and of course her new bestie, the Mob boss, to contend with. But more than protecting her, I want to be the solid foundation she can return to after she flies off on whatever tangential whim strikes her. Never caging her, just being her safe place, the same way she's mine.

"What'dya mean? We're totally normal!" I counter, not even remotely sounding like I believe that. "Normal people have lunch plans with the most powerful and scariest man in the city at his private table in the impossible-to-get-a-reservation restaurant he owns. And I'm sure everyone drinks champagne from a giant silver cup after a good day at the office. Or creates art out of thousands of dollars' worth of diamonds. Everyone definitely comes home to someone they love more than life itself, that makes them glad to have had another day on this earth just to spend those twenty-four hours with them."

Penny's initial laughter at my list of normal chokes off. "Aww, you're the sweetest," she says, setting the ring box down and crossing the room to sit half on me, half on the couch. "I am glad to have today with you."

I grin wolfishly. "I meant that I'm the lucky bastard who gets to spend time with you, but thanks." I gather her into my arms, burying my nose in her neck and simply inhaling her. I truly could sit here with her like this all day, or longer—like forever.

There's just one problem with that plan. Miles Conniver is not the sort of man one is fashionably late to lunch with.

Penny

Every table in Aqua Est Vita is full, and as the hostess escorts us to the very back, eyes turn to follow us. Well, to follow Griffin. He sticks out like a sore thumb in the fancy restaurant, and despite his slacks and oddly suave sports coat, he might as well be wearing a jersey with his name emblazoned on it. Everyone knows who he is, even if they're not hockey fans. How could they not, when the Hawks have been plastered on every news show, billboard, and ad across the city?

I wouldn't normally have my boyfriend go with me to a business lunch. But Griffin is no ordinary boyfriend, Miles Conniver is no ordinary customer, and this is no ordinary meeting. This is going to open an entirely new door for me. It already has.

I've been creating content out of my work on this ring for the last few weeks, and those videos and images have led to several messages from potential clients who want pieces that are more amazing than any other I've had the opportunity to work on.

Well, other than Mr. Conniver's, of course. This commission from him isn't in another world, but, rather, another stratosphere. But the new-client requests are not only for redone heritage pieces. They're for from-scratch-anything-I-want designs from people who simply want to own my art.

My art.

I've been successful for a while, but PLDesigns is on an entirely different trajectory, to a new plane of achievement now. And I owe it all to a little mishap with a very special ring, not to mention a very special man.

I glance over my shoulder at my man, and somehow manage to catch the toe of my business pump on a chair leg. I cry out, feeling the world go wonky-donkey as I start to fall, but strong hands firmly grip my waist, righting me.

"I gotcha. You're good," Griffin rumbles in my ear.

"Miss Lee?" Mr. Conniver says in concern, an arm outstretched like he intends to help as well. But when he sees Griffin's expression of *touch her and die*, he lets it drop with a nod of understanding, though he looks like he's fighting off a smirk.

Once I'm securely on my feet, Griffin pulls out a chair, and I lower myself into it slowly, as if it might evaporate into thin air from beneath me. The two men shake hands and take their seats.

A nearby waitress immediately rushes over to pour two additional glasses of water for Griffin and me before disappearing once again.

I should look at the menu. I should make polite small talk with Mr. Conniver. I should take a sip of water. I do none of those things. Instead, I blurt out, "Do you want to see it?" with huge eyes and an even huger grin.

Mr. Conniver smiles graciously. "I would love to."

I reach into my bag and pull out the engraved wooden box I special-ordered to house the ring. Holding it tightly, I say, "This is my most favorite piece I've ever designed, but if there's anything at all that you or Georgina want to change, I'm happy to do so."

I'm nearly bouncing out of my seat—truthfully, out of my skin!—with excitement. I've put myself through hell, all in an attempt to create something that honors the original stones from Mr. Conniver's mother's ring while designing an updated piece that his fiancée-to-be will treasure for her lifetime and be proud to pass down. A generational heritage ring that's not only beautiful and amazing but also absolute wearable perfection.

But for all my hyperactive buzzing, Mr. Conniver is as bland as can be, as though I'm simply giving him a boring business card, not the most special thing I've ever created. Not the symbolic representation of his undying, never-ending affection for his bride-to-be.

"I'm sure it's beautiful," he says kindly.

I glance quickly at Griffin, silently asking, *Are you hearing this bullshit?* He gives the smallest shrug of agreement that Mr. Conniver's reaction is underwhelming, to say the least.

I pull the ring box back into my chest, holding it hostage. "I need you to get a little happier about this. Excited or eager or something. It's the engagement ring you're going to hold up to Georgina when you get down on one knee and ask her to spend forever with you," I emphasize heavily.

Admittedly, telling a client how to behave is a business faux pas. Telling a Mob boss? Downright stupid. But I can't help myself. It's an engagement ring!

"Miss Lee," he intones warningly, "I assure you, I am excited to see what you've come up with." I tilt my head doubtfully. "And to give it to Georgina."

He holds his hand out expectantly, and I begrudgingly set the ring box in his palm. I watch his face as he opens the box, wanting to memorize and analyze his reaction to later obsess over and dissect with Griffin.

His face is typically fairly flat, expression-wise, never giving away too much of the heavy thoughts in his mind. But when he sees what I've created, his jaw softens, his lips part as if he's whispering something to himself, and the beginnings of crow's-feet crinkle beside his eyes. I swear I even see a hint of shine in his eyes, something I doubt anyone's seen in a long, long time.

He loves it. And I instantly forgive him for the lack of anticipatory giddiness, considering I had more than enough for the both of us.

Now that we're on the same page about the awesomeness of the ring, I rush to explain my design. "You said that Georgina appears to be delicate, almost dainty, so I wanted to give it a very feminine look with the rose gold and the garden vine–like band. The vines twist in and around each other, the way the two of you are merging your lives together. And they're rooted together on the underside, solid and strong—like she is, and like your love is. The center stone is from your mother's ring, and the smaller leaflike accent diamonds are new. I saved the baguettes from the original source for Georgina's wedding band, which I have ideas for too."

His eyes roam over the ring as I describe it to him, taking it all in. He closes the box, the clack of the wood almost sharp in the air, giving me a serene look with zero hints as to his actual thoughts. "It's better than I could've hoped. Thank you." He clears his throat roughly, and I belatedly realize it's not that he doesn't like the ring or isn't excited about it. It's that he doesn't like showing emotion with everyone watching, and people in the restaurant are definitely side-eyeing us. This time, I don't even think it's the unexpected appearance of a local sports hero. They're eyeing Mr. Conniver, curious about what he's doing, how he's reacting, and what's in the jewelry box. I'm sure the city's grapevine will be buzzing in moments, if it's not already.

He passes the box to the nearby security guard, who places it in his jacket pocket without a word.

"I'm so glad," I gush. "I've agonized over it, and if you didn't like it, I was gonna be so pissed." I laugh, being honest, but also aware that's not something I should say to him. If I hadn't seen that quick glimpse of the man behind the stoic facade, I would've snatched the box back and made a run for it. Okay, maybe not, but I would've played the scene out in my mind a hundred times—complete with me slapping Mr. Conniver and hauling ass out of this place with a yell over my shoulder that I'd sell the ring to someone who appreciated it. Considering it's his ring in the first place, and he's paid me twice over for the work I've done, I'm pleased that little possibility didn't happen.

"Well, I'm glad to have not angered you, then," he replies evenly, quietly amused underneath his blasé exterior. Pretty sure that line usually goes the other way. He's most definitely the one you don't want to piss off.

"For the band, I'm thinking channel inlaid baguettes. Something a little harder-edged to represent you in the relationship, the way the engagement ring represents Georgina, and that together make a perfectly balanced set."

Mr. Conniver smiles thinly as though calling him hard is a compliment. "Please go ahead with that design. I'm happy to leave it to your creativity, and I'm sure Georgina will feel the same once she sees your work. How soon can you have it completed?"

"Is there a date you have in mind?" I'm mentally already clearing my calendar for my best and most favorite client.

"Next weekend?"

My eyes bug out like one of those cartoon characters. *Ah-ooo-ga!* "What?"

"Friday, to be precise," he answers, not making things any better. "We've waited long enough, and I'm ready to make her mine officially."

With effort, I pull myself together. If Mr. Conniver wants a wedding band in six days, then yep, I'm your girl. Yessiree, I can make that happen. "Make it Thursday night," I quip, shimmying my shoulders, "because why the hell not?"

He laughs lightly. "Sounds good. I'll send someone by to collect it, if that's acceptable? I'm afraid I'll be otherwise indisposed."

"Not Thomas or Mark," Griffin, who's been silent this whole time, now interjects.

So maybe the two guys weren't necessarily hunting me down to cause me harm, but I have to agree with Griffin that I'd rather not deal with them for Mr. Conniver's order, especially at my home. "That. What he said," I agree, pointing at Griffin and nodding vehemently.

"Of course. I'll send Junior." He gestures to the security guard standing tableside, who is no less intimidating than Thomas and Mark but has none of the bad history they do. And when Junior dips his chin, agreeing, he even flashes me a kind smile and pats his shirt pocket like he vows to keep my work safe and secure.

"Sounds like you and me have a date Thursday night, Mr. Junior." His smile vanishes and Griffin grunts. I chuckle, adding, "Not like *that*. I mean, to pick up the ring. Ugh, you guys are such Neanderthals. Grumble, grumble, grumble." I actually grumble the word, not just make the sound to demonstrate, which applies to all of them, it seems.

"It's part of our charm," Mr. Conniver declares flatly. "Speaking of, it appears as though congratulations are in order," he says, lifting his water glass in a toast as he glances from me to Griffin. Given the interested glint in his eyes, even Mob bosses who run the city and strike fear into the hearts of most enjoy a bit of drama.

"To you and Georgina too," I say, tapping my glass to his. If he's not spilling all his dirty details, neither am I. Fair's fair.

After a quick sip, he says, "On that note, I'm afraid I do have other business to attend to. Please stay and have lunch as my guests." Mr. Conniver stands, gives us a polite tilt of his head, and walks away, Junior by his side. There's equal chance he's off to intimidate someone into selling their soul or a ribbon-cutting ceremony with the mayor. Hell, maybe both, simultaneously.

It's silent for a long stretch where I'm simply staring off in the direction Mr. Conniver disappeared. My eyes jump to Griffin. "I think he liked it," I whisper-shout, attempting to be mindful of the other diners in the restaurant but mostly failing.

Griffin chuckles. "I think he loved it. How could he not? It's your best work."

Awww. I swear, he's making up for all the cutting things he's said over the years with copious compliments now. The best part is, he actually means the compliments, and he never really meant the insults.

"My best work *yet*," I correct. "You haven't seen what I have in mind for the wedding band."

"Honestly, I think I'm your best work in progress," he jokes, laughing at the self-deprecation.

But I'm serious when I say, "You're not broken. You don't need to be fixed. You're perfect just like you are, and I wouldn't change a thing about you or our story. It happened the way it did because that's the way it had to happen to get us here." It's circular thinking, but the loop-de-loop of it makes perfect sense to me. I think it does to Griffin too.

"I fell in love with you the moment I saw you, and I would go through the hell of the last five years a thousand times over if it meant that we would end up here, together every time. I love you, Penny."

"I love you, too, Honey Bunches of Oats." He frowns. "Get it? Like the cereal." He frowns harder. "No? I'll keep trying. I'll find the perfect name. Just you wait . . . Sugar Smacks."

His left eyebrow shoots up like he's Mr. Spock. Maybe that's the one?

Epilogue

GRIFFIN

Six Months Later

"Are you taking me shopping? Like, you're going to wander the aisles with me and hold my stuff like the sweetest boyfriend ever?" Penny asks, excitement sparkling in her eyes.

I understand why. We're downtown, near Yesteryear Antiques, so, of course, her brain is on jewelry. This time, mine is, too, but we're not going to see Carolynn.

I turn the corner, heading the opposite way of the antique store, and Penny pulls on my arm where she's hooked her gloved hand into the crook of my elbow. "That way," she informs me, jerking her head in the opposite direction.

As if I've forgotten where Yesteryear is. I pull her along, leading her toward our true destination. "This way."

A few more steps, and she figures it out. "Ice cream in the dead of winter should be eaten in the comfort of one's home, while wearing your rattiest of sweatpants and holiest of socks, cuddled under a blanket, with the fireplace going."

I'm well aware of Penny's ice cream preferences. And her cookie preferences, her favorite shops, and her coffee order—both seasonal and regular. I can read her expressions, her mind, and predict with near certainty when she gets tangled up in drama. It's like there's a shift in the universe's energy that only I can sense. Or so she thinks.

"Trust me. I have a surprise for you." I know that word is going to send her flying high, and I can't wait to see it and hear it.

"A surprise!" she shouts, drawing the attention of the few other people shuffling down the street despite the chill in the winter air. Surprises are rarer now that the season's kicked off again, and we're both back into the swing of professional hockey life. So that makes this one even more special to her. "Let's go!"

She nearly drags me the rest of the way to Kitty's Creamery, but she stops at the door, peering inside as she sees that things aren't quite normal. Her eyes are wide, her mouth open, and her feet are tippy-tappy dancing. "Oh my God! Griffin!"

I reach for the door handle that's shaped like a kitten's paw with pink-painted claw nails and pull it open. Felicity is already coming around the counter, a huge pink bowl of Chocolate Orgasm ice cream in her hands. "Hi, guys!" The greeting is quick, and after she sets the ice cream on a table, she basically peels out, disappearing through the swinging door to the back.

"What did you do?" Penny asks, looking around.

Kitty's Creamery is always a cat-themed pink-and-turquoise monstrosity. Today it has a few new touches that Talia and Dominic helped with, like the table covered in a white tablecloth, with a centerpiece of wildflowers I custom-ordered for Penny and a heavy sprinkling of multicolored confetti, and the Hawks jersey embroidered with "MRS. MAHONEY" laying over one of the chairs.

Taking her hand, I guide her to the table. Tears are already starting to fall down her cheeks, but she's smiling happily. She knows what's coming, but it doesn't matter. It's not about the surprise, but the process.

Once she's seated, I pull a box from my pocket but leave it closed as I drop to one knee. "Penelope Nicole Lee, meeting you was and is the best thing that's ever happened to me. I fell in love with you in that moment, before speaking to you, before touching you, before I really even knew you. I was drawn to the light inside you that glows so brightly that it can't be denied. I am the moth to your flame, the yin to your yang, the hard to your soft."

She giggles nervously. "You said *hard*."

She's not usually one for twelve-year-old-boy humor despite the overabundance of time she spends with hockey players, but she's excited, and it's making her wiggle nonstop and say silly things. I love that about her, but I've got a whole speech memorized here, and I've lost my place. "Penny—"

"I already know what you're gonna say." She holds up her finger, stopping my speech, and using the deep voice that's supposed to be an imitation of me, she says, "I can't believe this girl is funny, fine, and thicker than a Snickers. Like, damn, I'm a lucky man." She brightens even more. "Am I right?"

The whole thing I had planned to say is gone, simply evaporated into the ether of my mind. Shaking my head, I can't help but laugh. "Completely right. There's more, though."

She presses her lips together, fighting to stay silent for what she acts like is an eternity, and not a quick few seconds for me to ask her the most important question of our lives. "How much I loved you then is nothing compared to how much I love you now. And I can only imagine that what I feel today will continue to grow deeper, wider, stronger. I can't wait to find out, with you. So, Penny, will you marry me?"

"Yes! Of course! I love you too!" Every answer is shouted in my ear because she's thrown herself into my arms, knocking me over and leaving me sprawled on the floor with her lying on top of me. Thankfully, I'm doing pretty good so far this season, and nothing hurts. Her lips find mine, sealing our new engagement with a kiss, followed by approximately one dozen more kisses when she begins smacking my face all over while I laugh at her infectious happiness. Maybe I shouldn't be, but I'm surprised at how excited she is about being my wife and me becoming her husband.

"Did we just get engaged at a kitty-themed ice cream shop?" she whispers, looking around.

I look around, too, remembering all the times I snuck into Kitty's Creamery to inhale ice cream alone, and then to the one time I brought someone here. Well, the *first* time I brought someone. Penny and I have become Felicity's most regular of regulars.

"I fell in love with you in your parents' kitchen. But this is where I think you started to fall in love with me," I explain. "It was the first time I wasn't the asshole you always thought I was, and though you gave me so much shit about it, I could tell you liked that I wasn't as bad as you thought."

She smiles, her eyes pointedly not meeting mine. She's not agreeing, but I already know I'm right. That day might've ended with an explosion of a disaster, but I wouldn't even change that now. Mostly because it brought Penny and me together, but it also nearly tripled her business in the span of a few months. After Georgina posted a photo of her engagement and wedding ring set with the caption *Custom PLDesigns rings, Pieces of my heart*, online custom orders started coming in so frequently that she sometimes has to turn them down.

Hell, if that catastrophe hadn't happened, I don't think the Hawks would've won the Stanley Cup, and Penny and I definitely wouldn't have somehow gotten an invitation to a Mob boss's very private wedding ceremony.

"Wait! Did you get me a ring? I wanna see what you think I'll like," she sputters, reaching to where the ring box fell when she tackled me.

She heaves herself up, propping her elbows on my chest. I don't dare flinch or show a single sign of discomfort from her pokey elbows in my solar plexus, wanting to see her face when she opens the box I bought from the same place she ordered Georgina's engagement ring box.

Except there's not a ring in this box. There's five of them.

"Whoa," she says as the rings tumble to my chest. "What's all this?"

I can feel the heat of a flush rushing to my cheeks as I explain. "I listen to you talk about stones and rings, and knew you'd want to custom-design your own. But I wanted to give you the raw materials to do it with. This one is a marquis-cut three-karat diamond I think would be a perfect center stone." Using my nose, I point to another. "That one has a bunch of smaller marquis cuts that would be good accent stones." And another. "That one has a bunch of tiny round cuts for a halo setting, and the other two bands are eighteen-karat gold you can melt down."

Her eyes are teary again; I've definitely hit her deep in the feels with my spiel. But in a good way, I'm certain. "You listen to me talk about jewelry?"

I blink, surprised that she's surprised. "Pen, I listen to you talk about everything. And I will always listen to you talk, even when you don't know what you're talking about."

"I do that sometimes, don't I?" She laughs through her tears.

She does. But I wouldn't have it any other way.

"When do you want to get married?" she asks. "After the season ends, I guess."

"I was thinking as soon as possible. But I can wait if you want to do the whole big shebang." I wave my hands like I have any idea what weddings entail beyond Penny and me exchanging vows.

She lowers her voice, confiding, "I don't really want all that fuss and muss. I always pictured something simple—a white dress, some flowers, a very special guy." She wiggles her brows, making it clear that I'm that guy.

Instantly, I'm 100 percent on board with that plan. "I could call Conniver and see if we could reserve the restaurant tonight? Or maybe tomorrow? Or I bet Felicity would let us do it here? Or the courthouse? I don't care. As long as you're there, it'll be perfect." I nod, having semi-decided on the where and now mentally flipping to the when. "Monday, at the latest; we're flying to Vancouver on Tuesday. I'm sure we can get you a dress and flowers, and I'll put all five of those rings on your finger so that whatever you create with them, they'll have been the ones we said vows over."

She laughs like I'm not serious, but I absolutely am. I've waited my whole life for Penny. For the woman who makes me feel like I'm enough, like I'm worth something—no, like I'm *priceless* to her. And I'm ready to stand up and vow to love her with my whole heart for the rest of my life and beyond.

I just hope she's ready for me.

"Let's see if Mr. Conniver can do tomorrow," she squeals, throwing her arms around me. "That way Mom and Dad have time to fly in."

Her parents are already here, safely tucked away in Dominic's guest room, because I hoped we'd be celebrating our engagement with them. But celebrating our wedding will be even better.

"Tomorrow it is. That's the day we become husband and wife. Forever."

"And then you can't get rid of me!" she threatens.

As if I would ever want to.

I gather her back into my arms, still lying on the ice cream–shop floor. "I love you, Pen."

"I love you, too, Griffin."

And this time, when she says my name, it's perfect.

ABOUT THE AUTHOR

Lauren Landish is a *Wall Street Journal* and *USA Today* bestselling author who captivates readers with irresistibly steamy contemporary romance. Her stories feature alpha heroes who meet their match in bold, unforgettable heroines, delivering all the swoon-worthy tension romance readers crave. Whether crafting tales of grumpy billionaires, protective bad boys, or dominant athletes with a secret soft side, Lauren's stories always promise heat, heart, and a satisfying happily ever after.

Her sexy contemporary romances have garnered a legion of devoted readers who know that when they pick up a Lauren Landish book, they're in for a wild, wickedly fun ride. When she's not writing steamy scenes or dreaming up new book boyfriends, Lauren can be found enjoying oversized mugs of coffee and plotting fresh ways to make readers blush.

For updates on upcoming books, visit www.LaurenLandish.com or follow her on TikTok (@laurenlandish), Instagram (@Lauren_Landish), and Facebook (@Lauren.Landish).